Born in 1952 in Leicester, Spencer Coleman spent his early years near Portsmouth. He has been a successful artist in oils for over 30 years, working with Harrods and Danbury Mint to name just a few companies. He is a member of the CWA, and has had published two novels and two short stories. This is his third suspense book. His print, *Bottoms Up*, was a big seller around the world. He likes snow-skiing and tennis. He has one son who now runs the family gallery in Lincoln. In 2015, Spencer suffered a stroke but he is recovering well.

fossilhan
0800 363 459
MSIBN681S3130
JCNT

I would like to dedicate this to Jordan and Molly, Ann and Paula, Sara and Hilda and anyone else who knows me, who have all helped me in my long journey. Also to Kate Carty, a brilliant writer.

Spencer Coleman

THE DISTANCE BETWEEN US

To Hannah

Best wishes

Martin

AUSTIN MACAULEY PUBLISHERS™

LONDON ★ CAMBRIDGE ★ NEW YORK ★ SHARJAH

A CIP catalogue record for this title is available from the British Library.

ISBN 9781528995665 (Paperback)
ISBN 9781528995672 (ePub e-book)

www.austinmacauley.com

First Published (2021)
Austin Macauley Publishers Ltd
25 Canada Square
Canary Wharf
London
E14 5LQ

I would like to acknowledge Austin Macauley Publishers for believing in me when others did not. Thanks to the American writer, Pat Conroy, a brilliant author, now sadly deceased, who inspired me to tell stories.

"The killer always remembers the scene of the crime because it's where he became a victim too."
— Jorge Aguilar-Agon, B. Agri., AEA, AAPB, FRSA.

1973

I wear the white-painted mask.

    Alchemy and wizardry, the girl is spellbound...

    Clowns at the funfair can do this sort of thing: engage a child's playful instincts. I can mimic sadness, gaiety or plain tomfoolery. I am no funny man though, but I learn real well just how to draw in the comforting needs of this pretty little thing that stands so invitingly before me.

    Now that I have her approval, I edge closer in.

    I'm aroused by her and know this is a bad thing.

    But since when did that concern me? She just does it for me, and that's a good a reason as any.

    The old stirrings reawaken within me: My groin pulsates, my mouth is salivating.

    She catches my eye as she plays with her two friends beside the giant helter-skelter. It's a stiflingly hot afternoon, and I notice her mother is momentarily distracted at the ice cream stand.

    Perfect circumstance: I pull a funny face behind my grotesque smile and, as if by magic (Hey Presto!), the connection is made, enticing her further in.

    Her corn-coloured tousled hair shines so appealingly in the summer sunlight. I'm transfixed by her sparkling button blue eyes; and the matching powder blue cotton dress she wears with lace edgings around the neckline, which is utterly charming.

    The voice in my head tells me she is mine.

    Let no man be mistaken: tonight I'm going to write tomorrow's harrowing headlines.

    A rush of blood, a fearsome pumping of the heart...

    I move in for the kill.

Chapter 1

2013

Let me drop it on you from the start.

I have buried my daughter. She was only fifteen at the time. Apart from the death of an elderly member of a family, no one should ever have to attend the funeral of their own flesh and blood prematurely, especially that of a mere child: *my* precious child. Believe me, it gets to you. It eats out your soul…and twice this has happened to me (the actual funeral was heart-breaking enough), the first of the two being the occasion when I had to undertake the gruesome task of identification. Seeing her lying there on a mortuary slab…colourless, cold, butchered by an unknown maniac, well, take it from me that a certain belief in the kindness of humanity goes straight out the window. The legs buckle, to begin with, and then the *blankness* takes hold. I am still in that suspended state of numbness: it's called grieving.

I also have history. Not necessarily the type that you immediately conjure up…be it a violent one, a past life of sexual deviation, perhaps drunkenness or even a prison stretch. No, mine is rather more a kind of dependency. I know what you are thinking: drugs, right? Not that simple. I've dabbled for sure, mainly in my youth but I'm older and wiser now. I can't afford it either. I can barely afford the rent on my little flat.

We'll begin here, most people do, with a small resume to bring you up to speed and get you started. I was born in 1967 which makes me forty-six(ish). My name is Will Farmer, and I am currently separated from my wife, Isabel. I doubt we will get back together, but I'm going to try. Something horrible stands between us, pulling us apart. Not necessarily the death of our daughter. I'll explain later if you stick with me! Some couples cope with tragedy and manage to bind together like glue; we, on the other hand, bicker and fight and blame each other for our sorrow. Isabel is ten years younger than me, but she was always the mature one in our relationship. We had been together for nineteen years before the bad thing happened. Until then, our perfect world centred on the little home we owned called Eggshell Cottage, which we shared with our only child named Daisy. Life was idyllic at Langstone harbour, which is nestled (like the holiday brochures describe so alluringly) at the mouth of a small hamlet between the naval city of Portsmouth and Hayling Island on the south coast of Hampshire. Not many of you would have heard of this place. But we loved it. We felt safe in the boating community. It is a great sanctuary for wildlife too, which attracted us in the first place. We settled easily. My wife is a policewoman, following in her father's assured footsteps in the area. So we knew everyone. At weekends, we went sailing or crab hunting on the shoreline like lots of other young families. I loved the taste of salt air on the lips, the wind off the Solent blowing through my hair, watching the blood orange sun dipping below the flat horizon as the swans took flight over the marshland and beyond. We were happy then. This was our little piece of heaven.

Then the bad person came and plundered our lives. He or she forcibly took our daughter from us. Daisy often cycled home alone from school in the summer months, across the perfumed meadows that lay just off the English Channel between Nore Barn woods and Warblington village. One day she never came home. A couple walking their dog found her lying partially naked in a ditch. She was a vibrant carefree kid, undeserving of this seemingly unprovoked vicious attack. As a father, I blamed myself for not protecting her from harm's way.

You can see where this is going, *my history*. What happened to our precious daughter shaped the destiny of not just Isabel and me but caused a rift between the local inhabitants. They felt threatened, I suppose. Everyone in the community became a suspect. A divide of sorts occurred, as people took sides and fingers were pointed and whispers started. Townsfolk came under suspicion. Strangers were suddenly frowned upon. It was not long after that I felt like a suspect. The police interviewed me time and time again. It's weird how rumour spreads. Normal rational neighbours start to talk, call in debts. They like to think they are owed. They like to think that they can sit on a higher moral standpoint and cast judgment of those below. They know nothing of course. I call them narrow-minded, sanctimonious interfering bastards. Ever since the brutal killing of my daughter, I have lived with the fear of prying eyes boring down upon me as if I was a piece of shit. I label these people (the ones who stir up trouble for no reason) the disbelievers. Why? Because I am viewed in these parts as an outcast: one of the strangers. I wasn't born here, like Isabel, and that goes against me.

I originally came from Saltburn-on-sea, which makes me a northerner I guess. It takes time to gain acceptance in a new region. I imagined I had, but I was either misguided or just plain stupid. Anyway, we were a normal family, nailed down good jobs and mixed well. Thought I was liked. But the narrowing of eyes told me differently after the murder. I decided, through sheer cussedness, that I wouldn't run or hide from these people. I had nothing to reproach myself for. I am an innocent man. I want you to know this right from the start. This is why I need to tell you my story (no one is entirely innocent); in spite of the pity or loathing you might have for me by the end. You see, I am needy, perceived as being a weak man by some (including my estranged wife sadly). I am accused of having no backbone. You can judge for yourself.

My history then is obsession. My star sign is Aries and with this comes a certain inflexibility and stubbornness. Not to be confused with strength, according to Isabel. My past and my future are therefore based on this tricky combination that some learned people have termed obsessive compulsion. It consumes me, drives me to the edge of insanity. Not an obsession to find my daughter's killer but an overwhelming need – desire I suppose – to please the wishes of other good people. It is as if I must have approval from them. Perhaps it is the inadequacy I feel from letting down Daisy and failing my wife when she needed my support the most. A murder on our doorstep is a vile thing. It would enrage anyone. But this was our daughter's murder, and the senselessness eats away at my heart. Our world was utterly destroyed in a blink of an eye: a young girl's precious life extinguished in a second. Faith in hope and decency crushed beyond repair.

In grief, we can't seem to save our marriage. It is too hard, the mourning. And yet *somehow* we survived these long lost days by tiptoeing on eggshells, afraid of our own shadows, skirting around the bigger issues like love and death and the shaping of our fractured lives. Pathetic, I know. I can see the irony…the apt name we gave to our home, which my wife still lives in with her disjointed memories of family life. *Blame* is a hateful word.

I, like my elder brother, became a teacher when I left college. David went on to better things and is now Head at a grammar school in Dorking. We came south as a family after our dad got work at the docks in the city of Portsmouth. I met Isabel in a pub, you know how it works. We settled into a routine. Eventually, I became burnt-out as a teacher and retrained as a social worker which is what I still do today. I assist other needy people. So here we are…me and you and a whole host of unsavoury characters I want to introduce to you over time. The only person who is beyond reproach is Isabel, so give her plenty of slack when you cast your critical eye over her. I make no apologies but I'm still in love with her. I know I'm being unreasonable in my request, but you'll have enough on your plate just making judgement on my downtrodden existence (and my inability to cope with the stresses of the modern world). Don't snigger at my job either. I know what you are thinking: Christ, a do-gooder, a preacher without a compass. I hold my hands up…yes, I see those who are weak and rudderless and I want to help, because beyond their pleading eyes I see myself, for I too am in need of guidance. So don't mock me. I lost a daughter.

God forbid if you ever have to witness your child being lowered into the damp blackened worm-infested ground. I did. It leaves a mark, believe me. It isn't something you ever forget, not even in nightmares. The image stays ingrained forever in the subconscious mind. I am so fucking angry to tell you the truth, with everyone. Not so spineless, eh?

Therefore, I'd prefer it if you would watch over me and learn about me and judge me later. I see madness in my obsession, but I don't want your compassion or forgiveness. I just want clarity. I want to make sense of my life, find an anchor. And do you know what? For the first time in ages, well, since Daisy's death actually, I believe I may have found that safe harbour I so long for. How has this happened…? This miracle? Well, just recently, I have a new caseload on my desk and one of them unsettles me. Rather, it intrigues me and I want to get involved. It stands out like a beacon of hope in all the shit that I encounter in my job. I am drawn inexplicably toward this person's predicament and I want to share her story with you as well as mine, but I ask patience before I reveal her name. It will be worth the wait, I promise, for I see light where there is no light when I think of her. This person gives me hope because we share a common

13

experience so I want to help her. She is calm when I am irate. She sees goodness and I see evil. I'm also cursed in that I have a vision, a premonition, call it whatever you like, that a bad thing is going to happen again right here on my doorstep. I can smell it, almost touch it, but no one else wants to listen to my ranting except this dear old lady who feels it too. We have a deep-seated connection borne from the buried bones of our daughters. There I go, already revealing more than I should at this stage. I get overexcited and need to slow down in my desire to get you into the loop as quickly as possible. I'll count to three and breathe in more slowly.

One: Isabel thinks I need professional help. She could be right, of course. But I have an overriding fixation to stop *it* happening again. Two: Why is no one aware of such benevolence in the air? We have all suffered for far too long. I don't like injustice: for anyone. Three: The dead require a voice to speak up for them, for they are silent in their coffin. I won't be side-tracked in my quest, in spite of it hurting the one I truly love. Isabel must see that the truth cannot kill, even if the heart remains broken forever by it.

OK, take another breather. We'll move it forward one small step at a time.

*

My Rav4 gets me about. It is adequate for my needs but requires new tyres, which I cannot afford. I live in a rented two-bed apartment overlooking the creek at Emsworth, a small village near Chichester. It is damp (which describes me) and cramped (which my wife would definitely say describes me). Being on my own, I often crawl up the walls just like the dampness. But it does me, for now at least. I am not a materialistic person. I even have a deckchair to sit on to watch the TV. How decadent is that? I spend my time reading my books (historical) or listening to music, mainly American rock. Everything in the flat is chaotic. I don't need precision, neatness. Most of my possessions still remain at the cottage, which is my decision. I can't bear to disrupt what we had together. So I make do with small comforts. Besides, I want to get back with my wife. Time will tell.

My life can be looked at in four stages. The first was my upbringing, the second my relationship with Isabel, the third my daughter's birth and the fourth *after* the *happening:* Daisy's death. I emphasis the word *after* because I cannot bring myself to talk about the bad day, but of course, I will eventually. It is too sorrowful to share everything with you immediately, particularly the intimate moments. Bear with me: you're still trying to get to know me and I need a little space to slowly recover in. Everything is still so raw. Whenever I think of Daisy or Isabel, I die inside. I seem to shrivel up like a rose without water.

But this story cannot be told without me telling you something about Daisy. I'll stop when it gets too much. So here goes. She was a talented artist, just like me. I had over the years exhibited a few oil paintings in local exhibitions. Daisy excelled in watercolour and pastels and we often took our paints and brushes and camera on walking expeditions to find things to capture on paper. We lived in the ideal environment for this, with wildflowers in abundance which she was drawn to in particular. Our house was filled with her work. She also loved dance and thankfully inherited her mother's natural movement and beauty rather than my ungainliness to express such fluidity and grace on the floor. I dance like a donkey. She could do anything, this girl of mine. We called her Daisy because at the time of her birth the fields were covered by them. In truth, our daughter kept our marriage going at times. It was not perfect, having come from different backgrounds. My dad worked on the docks. Isabel's father was a high ranking police officer and hugely motivated and disciplined. She followed in his footsteps. I'm pretty sure he didn't approve of her choice in hooking up with me...a drifter and a dreamer would probably sum up his description of my character. But his daughter and I connected and settled down and Daisy was the icing on the cake.

Now she was gone. I'll move on if you don't mind.

So I'll focus on the present day, eighteen months after *the happening,* because a file on my desk has brought me into contact with a remarkable woman, a woman so inspirational to me that I have to record her name lest no one forgets what she too has suffered in her lifetime. You need to know about her because you will take her name with you long after this story has been told. I'll jump the gun and reveal it now, even though I wanted to hold back awhile. Her name is Meg Faulkner. She is sixty-eight and a widower. She is dying from bowel cancer. She has been served a court order to evict her from her home where she has lived for the past thirty-nine years. I am the liaison officer, the go-between brought in to relocate her and her assorted cats. She lives in the last of a row of empty Victorian townhouses due for demolition to make way for a new bypass. Meg refuses to leave. I am the compassionate arm of the law. I talk to her. I offer support. I listen. I want to help. But in nine days' time, the bulldozers will arrive and make her homeless.

I've met her three times so far. Each time I look into her melancholy eyes I see hopelessness...but also spirit and dignity, which puts my penchant for moaning to shame. She will probably die in a hospital eventually, as the cancer is aggressive and she is very poorly. She may even die in this house. It is immaculate downstairs and I can tell she is a proud woman. I feel compassion for her plight. Meg has her hair done every Friday and always wears an elegant dress and pearls around her neck. Good ones too. Having got to know her and gain her trust, I have discovered that she has a secret that we now share. Upstairs, which is just as immaculate by the way, a bedroom at the rear remains untouched, a shrine to a distant memory. Beyond the locked door, it is perfectly decorated in delicate pink and lace. A candle remains lit. Meg sits in here most days alone, except for a cat on her lap for company and prays for a lost soul: that of Miriam, her dead daughter.

It took a while for Meg to tell me her story, even longer to show me the room, but I am a patient man. I think she knew of my torment from the newspaper coverage after Daisy's death and felt she could talk to me. We had common ground. You see, Meg's daughter was brutally murdered at the hands of an unknown killer in 1973. I learned of this in detail from the library archives after our first meeting. I didn't want to intrude on her loss as she spoke, so I did my own research later. Then I told her of my own tragedy, assuming naively she was not aware of it. But of course, she was. She listened without interruption. I could see the kindness in her misty eyes which allowed me to unburden myself to a virtual stranger, as I had done for her in her hour of need. We were two of a kind.

At the end of my monologue, Meg took my hand, squeezed gently and spoke with deliberation: 'The history of our children shall be forever linked, and the stars will re-align and bring them together full circle, like an unbreakable chain, and make their combined life force one to be reckoned with. Then justice will prevail. You just have to believe in this, trust in this and seek guidance and you shall be rewarded.'

Those words have helped to forge my thinking from that day on.

After that, we got along just fine over a pot of Earl Grey tea, which we shared regularly. Meg had class. She explained succinctly her reasoning as to why she couldn't leave her home, for fear of disrupting her daughter's room, which was her last refuge. I understood although time was running out with the bulldozers parked outside! I listened tolerantly too. Then on my fourth visit, without any pushing from me, she showed me the bedroom at last and it all made sense. I wept with her.

Around these parts, she has become a bit of a celebrity, the local newspaper championing her cause against the intrusion of heavy-handed bullying from the local council. The journalists argued that she should remain in her home and support grew through their readership. A proposal was put forward to move the new road. It was denied by the bureaucrats. A petition to save her house was signed by over six hundred and fifty people. No one high-up listened. Vast money was at stake of course, which was a powerful motivator to keep any protests to a minimum. However, her supporters persisted and she was even interviewed on local television. The bigwigs on the Council hated this but, through gritted teeth, spoke of co-operation but did nothing except put pressure on me to relocate her as quickly as possible. Every delay was costly. I was caught in the middle but I made all the right noises and spoke up for her as best I could in difficult circumstances. I had empathy for her predicament.

She was an eccentric old bird, with a waspish tongue and a generous heart, taking in any stray animal or talking to a wayward person in need of spiritual support. I felt like one of these waifs and strays. We bonded instantly and I cared for her. It was rumoured locally that Meg could speak to the dead: connect with the hereafter. Naturally, in some quarters she was ridiculed; called an old witch. She would have been burnt at the stake in medieval times. One day a brick was thrown against her window. A youth departed shouting: 'We don't need your sort 'round here, *Mystic Meg!*'

From this moment on, she was forever known as this.

During one of our conversations, I was baffled to discover that my Isabel, so taunting of me, had, in fact, visited her many months ago to find comfort from a kindred spirit. Hearing this made me feel alienated for failing to offer such support myself. Agitated, I wanted to know more about my wife's behaviour before it was too late. Meg was weak from the cancer treatment. I felt she had very little time left. I wanted to understand why Isabel sought her guidance. I wanted to find my own space in which to find solace. Why did Isabel show such strength in public and yet sought comfort from a stranger? It made me feel worthless. Did I learn anything at all about my wife's mental siege? The answer is *no,* as she never returned to this house. Or perhaps Meg was just being tactful in not wanting to hurt me still further.

As I explained, Meg was dying before my eyes so time was at a premium if I was to accomplish my goal, which was two-fold: help her which in turn would help me. Medication was failing her. I didn't want to fail her. I wanted to obtain either a postponement from the planners and let Meg see out her last days in her cherished home or find her a decent place to live nearby. I also wanted to talk, to understand, to see how she coped with the loss of someone so dear. I guessed she had endured forty years of hell. We shared a universal pain: bereavement. It was a sense of being deprived, deprived of that special person and the answers to the million questions we wanted to ask. It was called *closure.* I wanted this more than anything and meeting Meg, I felt that somehow she held the power to do this.

Here's something else to drop on you. You see, her daughter looked exactly like my Daisy, although there was an age gap of six years between them. And they were taken from us in the same neighbourhood. Forty years apart. The killer or killers never found. Meg knows something! I can feel it. I vowed that I would speak with her and unravel the truth. It would bring trouble; that was for sure. I had less than nine days left before the bulldozers did their business: days before Miriam's bedroom secrets would be lost forever under a pile of rubble. I had befriended Mystic Meg. Would she now unburden herself to a stranger in her midst? I had to make her believe that I, like many others, wanted to bring an end to this terrible mess; that I was there to bring support, to find order. But I wasn't referring to the court repossession…or her intestinal prognosis. I wanted justice for my silent daughter: the girl who couldn't speak from beyond the grave.

Or could she?

Meg made me believe this was possible (sneer if you wish). I, in turn, convinced Meg that we could repel the contractors from tearing down her home. So Meg bought into my story that it was her moment in the spotlight – that we could expose the uncaring nature of the petty, overbearing business interests that threatened her existence whilst she still had the chance. I showed her the signed petition. It pleased her. I eluded that it was the will of the people that was keeping her alive, and she would prevail against the odds. Defy the court order. Dig in. What could the *suits* do? The story was beginning to attract national interest. The tide of public sympathy would surely win through. For my part, I wanted her sad story, to see if there was a connection with the death of my daughter and that of Miriam, which she so tantalisingly hinted at earlier. Because Meg is such an extraordinary woman, the seed has been planted in my head. Solve one murder, we solve the other and I am now selfish to this end. I'm using her. I'm beginning to realise that she is perhaps using me.

I'll live with that. What have I got to lose? She has no real chance to avoid the eviction. The odds are heavily stacked against her. But I wanted desperately to beat the demons in my head and I believed that maybe Meg held the key to unlock them and set me free from such torture. *Believe,* she said. So I toed the line for my bosses, gained favour and quietly championed Meg's cause to the press. I needed time, which was, as you know, fast running out. If she indeed had mystic powers, now was the time to unleash them. I was clinging on to this notion.

I didn't believe in such nonsense ordinarily, but for one small thing. Across her rear yard lawn a carpet of daisies sprang to life on the day I visited Meg Faulkner for the first time. No one came to cut the grass, so they stayed for every moment I was there, spreading even further as the sun kissed them into life. Meg smiled knowingly over her cup of tea as if it meant something. It did to me. It was a sign that Daisy was reaching out to me.

So hear my version of events, and learn about the ghosts that inhabit my world from yesteryear. As I've mentioned, I'll fill you in as we go along if that's all right with you. We have much to share, good and bad. Gradually, I'm finding out stuff that frankly is beginning to scare the shit out of me.

I don't understand the half of it.

So we'll go slowly.

Chapter 2

What defines the meaning of life? A big concept, I know, but it is often the little things that bring real fulfilment, that make the difference. Here is one such example.

When she was twelve, Daisy bought me a silver chain with the pocket money earned from her newspaper round. It's a beautiful thing and I wear it every day. It is a symbol of devotion and I cherish it. She said *I love* you when she gave it to me. My wife said the same thing when I bought her a wedding ring and she now no longer wears it. I still wear mine. I believe in the sacred marriage vows "for better, for worse..."

I throw in this little aside so that you have something to think about when you take time to consider our relationship. I need to express my love and therefore wear the symbols with gratitude and pride. It still means something. Isabel has moved on apparently. It hurts. Perhaps she is the one still hurting.

Let's not digress. I phone her. We have a terse conversation and I explain I want to pick up a few things from the cottage. I no longer have a key. She changed the locks anyway. We arrange a time for me to call later in the day.

So here I am, standing outside the front door with its peeling white paint. I notice too that the wooden gate is off its hinges. Her car is unwashed. She opens the door and the sun catches her face. She is still beautiful, a little drawn by tiredness and work but her eyes meet mine and I melt inwardly. I cherish her but I keep this to myself. She smiles thinly and for a second I catch sight of what Daisy might have looked like had she lived to this age.

'You'd better pop in,' she says coldly.

'Thanks,' I nod, pleased that I'm even allowed in alone.

The house smells of coffee and laundry and cat pee. We have two cats called smudge and nudge. They stare at me with disdain.

Coffee isn't on offer.

'Do you know what you are looking for?' Isabel asks impatiently. 'You see, I boxed up all of your bits and pieces and put them in the spare bedroom. You might need to rummage.' Then she adds, 'Sorry.'

I stand awkwardly and wait, a bit like a child at school waiting for instruction from a teacher.

She gestures with a flick of her head, 'You know where to go...'

I go. I'm back in the kitchen in seconds holding a shoebox.

'Oh,' she mutters. 'Is that it?'

I nod again.

'I could do with it all going, to be honest,' she says hurriedly.

'I'll sort it. Just give me a few weeks…'

'You've said that before, Will.'

She said my name. I feel human once more.

This time she stands nervously, aware that I am not moving toward the door. She grabs her car keys and bag which is a big hint. 'I must get back to the station…got a lot on.'

I need to say what's on my mind. That was the reason for my visit. Sod the box, which was just an excuse to get to see her.

'Isabel, one of my clients is Meg Faulkner…'

'Mystic Meg?'

'The very same.'

'I've seen her on the news. What has she got to do with me?'

'It's just that…well, she told me, in a roundabout way that you had been to see her.'

She pulls back from me. 'So?'

'It's just that having lost a daughter herself, she understood why you wanted to see her.'

'And that would be *what*, Will?'

'To talk about Daisy, of course…'

'That was a private conversation, actually.'

'I know, I know.'

'Has she been talking to you behind my back?'

'No.'

'I consider my conversation with Meg to be confidential.'

'I was just concerned as to why you felt she could help you…and I couldn't.'

'You have no right to meddle in my affairs.'

'Being your husband I thought I was the one to offer support.'

That does it. Her eyes burn into me.

'Do you know what, Will? You have no idea about my needs or my search for answers. I craved comfort. So let's not go there, OK?'

I flinch.

She moves to the door and opens it pronto.

'Look, if you'd prefer to talk about it later when you're not so angry,' I reply, instantly aware that I'm going to be shot down following my comment.

'You know,' she spits, 'what I really want is for you to fuck off.'

Patience and understanding aren't her strong points.

*

Later, in my flat, I realise I had no right to barge in and confront her like that. She had moved on from me. There was a rumour that she was with another copper from a neighbouring town. No business of mine. I am still pissed though. So I drink some whisky to console myself. Then clean my teeth and gargle a mint mouth wash. Eventually, I get to the office, sit at my desk, immerse myself in paperwork and try to clear my head…but her anger still rips into me, making me lose concentration. Her caustic words cut me in half. She knows how to assert control even when we live apart. I fill in forms and make a damning report on one of my other cases: child abuse, a hateful subject. I always have to wash my hands afterwards.

I phone my brother, David, for a brief chat. He is busy too and unusually sharp with me. What is going on with everyone?

The day moves on. I phone Meg. She asks me over for tea. I stop on the journey and treat us to fish and chips. We sit eating them out of the folded paper on the back patio, the last of the sun caressing our faces as we fill our mouths as if it is our last meal. I have ginger beer, she sips Earl Grey.

'You seem troubled,' she says. Pain emits from behind her pale grey eyes. Her voice is frail, her breathing short. She wears a lovely emerald and blue dress and white woollen cardigan. The pearls sit serenely, a beaded circle of soft light glowing from around her thin neck. Her skin is translucent, the blue veins in her forehead prominent. Still a handsome woman, though. A real beauty in her youth, I would guess.

'One of those days,' I reply, swigging my drink straight from the bottle.

'I haven't much longer to live,' she suddenly announces. 'I could do with many of *those* days.'

'I'm sorry, I shouldn't be so morbid.'

'Live for the future…'

'…And not in the past.'

'Exactly.'

I have to ask at this point. 'Why the memorial room, Meg? You can hardly call that the future…'

She looks at me in puzzlement. 'Although your wife probably cleared most things away, Will, I bet you carry a vivid image of your daughter's bedroom in your head still. I had the opportunity to preserve Miriam's memory and chose to. My husband, bless him, never interfered with my wishes. If I smell her clothes, I am still with her. I can talk with her. But the past holds everyone back, I have learnt to my cost. So don't you make the same mistake. I regret nothing but you are young enough to find a new beginning, find new love…dare I say it, have another child.'

The words hit home. A lump fills in my throat. How can I contemplate such an idea? It's unworthy. I still love Isabel. Was Meg's suggestion bliss or purgatory? Is it even possible? Do I have a future? Do I deserve such happiness? See, this is me! Always questioning myself. I'll kill myself before I'm done with all this self-doubt.

Meg reads my thoughts. 'You deserve to find someone. Stop beating yourself up, Will.'

'I'm still married.'

Meg tosses a hand out and grunts.

I get the message.

'In my day, you stayed together,' she says. 'Today, you can do as you please. My husband died and I chose to remain married to him. I had opportunities but I was set in my ways.'

'I bet they were queuing around the corner.'

'Some hope, but there were a few.'

'What did your husband die of?'

'Asbestos poisoning.'

'How long have you lived alone?'

'Fifteen years.'

'How did your husband cope with the loss of Miriam?'

'He didn't. He turned to drink to nullify the pain.'

'Did he approve of the room?'

'No, but I didn't give him any choice in the matter. Miriam is still here with me today…bringing me comfort. I don't think of Stan in the same way.'

I finger my chain and know exactly how she feels. It brings me closer to Daisy. And then she says something astonishing and right out of the blue.

'Your beautiful daughter is here too.'

*

I so *want* to believe her. All that night I sleep badly, just thinking about those words. That somehow my daughter is with me, right here. I want to reach out and touch her. But I realise that this is not possible in the true physical sense…what Meg really meant was that our girls were with us in spiritual terms only. I can't look beyond that notion for fear of going insane.

But it is a comfort. And her words were emphatic. It was a statement. Tears form in my eyes. I ache. *Are you there, Daisy?*

Eventually, I sleep, but not before padding around the flat, drinking wine and coffee and making the situation worse. I suppose exhaustion finally takes over. My last thoughts are centred on Isabel. *She can be such a callous bitch.* That's a statement as well. I'm not going to retract it.

Dawn breaks. I awaken and feel the throbbing in my head. I look at the empty wine bottle and curse aloud. A deep red stain from the upturned glass forms an ugly circle on the carpet. It reminds me of the dried blood on my daughter's body when I first saw her in the ditch. The throbbing intensifies.

I've slept in my clothes but I don't care. I decide not to shave or change. I simply clean my teeth and depart my sterile abode, ready for the day. I feel deflated. So is the rear tyre on my car.

Chapter 3

The shoe box contains personal things belonging to Daisy like silly scribbled notes, madcap photos, poems and little cartoon drawings.

Daisy wrote to me, and only me. It was our little game. A secret world for two. I can't remember when this started. Isabel was not aware of these little asides. She had a demanding job and Daisy found it difficult to confide in her. Besides, I was at home quite a bit and often cooked supper. Daisy and I were incredibly close. Sometimes, I think my wife was jealous of our secure bond. The jottings were often daft things really, like one which read "What are you getting me for Christmas?" Another pleaded: "I need a puppy!" I smile when I reread a classic: "Parents are crap!"

She wrote tons of them. She knew I was the soft touch, her mum intolerant. So she wrote the notes to me hoping to find favour. Generally, I was a pushover. I wrote back of course, often with caustic wit, but I never found my replies in her belongings, thank goodness, when Isabel and I had to go through her bedroom at the request of the police. Isabel would not have approved of our private little world. I kept all of her serious paintings in another box, which I intend to frame and display one day. She was a talented artist, as I have said. Some smaller ones are contained in this box and I am blown away with them. She loved nature and captured flowers beautifully in crayon. She was very observant with her studies. I get side-tracked quite easily and so put the pictures to one side and read a couple more observations. They make me laugh and cry in equal measure. One said, "Mum is mean". What was that supposed to signify? I laugh.

Another catches my eye: "I don't like him". I don't laugh.

I don't like him. This spooks me. She had a couple of boyfriends but nothing serious. She would have confided in me, I'm sure. But this troubles me.

I put the box under my bed and decide to read all of them over time. Make a scrapbook of her crazy sayings and requests. I'll probably discount the one to Mum though. I know my place.

*

You might find this odd, but I love flowers too. Although I dabble in art, over time my passion has become photography. So often Daisy and I would go out at the weekend or on camping holidays and collect, snap or paint wild meadow flora. Now, I rarely use the camera and the only flowers I treasure are those I take to the cemetery. Daisy's favourite colour was white so that is what I take every week, a new bunch, so they stay fresh by her graveside. It is the least I can do.

I go on a Sunday usually. Sit and chat to her. Another man is often there, grieving for his teenage son killed in a car accident the year before. I read of it in the local paper. We never talk. Anger is a solitary business.

I always end up in the pub afterwards and drown my sorrows. Most people ignore me but the landlord, John, is kind and decent and doesn't judge. We converse on trivial subjects and the rivalry between the local soccer giants. I support Pompey, he follows Southampton. But we get along.

Later, I read my case notes and prepare for the week ahead. But it is Meg that concerns me. I need to get her to leave her home before she is forcibly removed. I have secured temporary accommodation but she won't look at it.

Whenever I have insisted that she face the reality of the situation, that she is required by law to vacate within the week, I get the proverbial reply: "Over my dead body!" She means it too.

Dinner in the evening is often a microwave dish from M & S. I vow to buy fresh produce but sometimes can't be bothered. I know my daughter would be incensed by this basic neglect.

On this Sunday, the phone rings. This is rare. I awake from my TV slumber.

'It's David.'

'Oh, hi.'

'Sorry about the other day…the shit hit the fan. A visit from the dreaded Gestapo at Ofsted.'

'Shit,' I echo.

'Exactly. Then we had a suspected case of measles with one of the pupils, so we had to send a whole class home. How are you?'

'OK.'

'Just OK?'

'Fair to middling.'

'Did you want me for anything, Will?'

'No, just a chat…'

'Why don't you drive over some time?'

'Can do, but I'm busy at the moment as well. Can you come down to me?'

'I'll see what I can do.'

'You haven't been over since the funeral,' I say by way of a slight dig.

I could hear him sigh. We went quiet and then spoke as if in stereo.

'How's Isabel/How's Margo?'

I start. 'Like a ship at sea…hard to turn.'

'Are you likely to get together again?'

'No idea. She seems to blame me.'

'For *what*?'

'Everything, I guess. At the end of the day, we're doing a bollocks job of coping with the loss of Daisy.' I'll explain the real reason later…if I dare!

There's that sigh again, then silence.

I break the ice: 'I asked how Margo is.'

'Can I get back to you, Will? Another call coming in…'

'Fine.'

I click off and grab a lager from the fridge. David was never one to lend an ear. He and Isabel never really got on, in spite of a few shared trips to France with Daisy on tow. He was too high brow for my wife, always looking down his nose at our lack of ambition. She'd always be a constable in his eyes, but in fact, she was a police sergeant who did a regular shift down at District Headquarters, which was demanding enough with a daughter to support. He lived in a big house at Dorking with his invalid wife, Margo. She has been confined to a wheelchair for the past fourteen years, and they employ a day care nurse to look after her needs. They have a loveless marriage and I reckon they probably sleep in separate bedrooms. David is straight-laced, a neatness fanatic and generally too serious for his own good and the complete opposite to me. I am goofy and rebellious, he studious and a control freak.

As children, growing up on the East Yorkshire coast, we had an idyllic childhood though and we were very close, even though there was a thirteen-year age gap between us. I am the youngest. Without going into detail, I believe our mother miscarried three times in between our conceptions, hence the big difference in our age. I reckon that I'm lucky to be here, grateful for my parents' persistence! Anyway, we both eventually went into teaching, following in the footprints of our mum, but I became restless and eventually burnt out from the red tape. David thrived on the responsibility. He still does. Margo, who suffered from a degenerated spinal problem, always played second fiddle to his ambitions as he climbed the career path. Now, he is a bigwig in the educational world and revels in his standing in the community. He morphed into Mr Respectability. On the other hand, I am a lowly social worker beneath his radar of understanding. He thinks I'm a loser, which is probably a fair assessment. Isabel would concur.

So there we are, the family history laid out on a plate, a small one at that.

Out of nowhere, Daisy begins to talk to me. *I don't like him.*

I fall asleep with these words ringing in my ear.

*

The alarm goes off at five. I stir. I've slept badly again.

Slowly, I rise, take a pee and pad down to the kitchen. Out of the window, the silvery dawn lifts the brooding landscape. This is always the best time of the day for me, a certain ethereal stillness prevails. I marvel at a line of geese arcing across the broad sky. From my position, I can just see the outline of the old Mill in the distance which sits on the edge of the tidal creek further down the coast. The lights from the occasional car crossing the bridge shine into my eyes. I can smell the sea from afar. Love it here; the world wrapped in the cathedral quietness of early morning.

I brew a mug of tea and stand on the tiny balcony, overlooking the rooftops to my right. I am still troubled from insomnia, lack of sex and the message from beyond the grave. I'm generally frustrated, lethargic. *Something* nags at my subconscious.

I am reminded of Meg's assertion that Daisy was with us on the patio that day. The sense of comfort, this nearness brought relief to me, although at the time I so wanted to weep but was embarrassed in her company. I haven't done this properly since the funeral service. Sure I had a tear at Meg's place, but not a full-on bawl. Now I can feel a trickle of salty moisture running down my cheek. Fuck. I manage to hold myself in check again. A small boat pushes off from the jetty to my left. I long for the solitude, the peace…the calmness that the oarsman must be experiencing right now.

At the end of the day, I know I am torturing myself but to what end? I have a rage against everyone but I hide it. It is my way to rationalise things and compartmentalise the difficulties I encounter. It's my method of coping, but it is a bad way as I never find contentment or solace. Perhaps I never will. The sharp focus of grief is never far below the surface of controlled fear and loathing. I shower, dress, eat a slice of toast and slide out of the flat silently and without disturbance. I don't want to break waves if I can avoid it, just like the little boat gliding serenely from the harbour mouth earlier. It is calm at present but a heavy swell is forecast for later as gathering clouds on the horizon sweep in and threaten a storm. I can feel it. Trouble is out there. I worry for the boatman. I worry for me.

Inexplicably, after starting the car engine I then switch off and return to my home. I retrieve my daughter's box and shuffle through the contents until I find a group of photos from a holiday we had as a family in Narbonne, France. Daisy was then eleven. As I recall, it was a lovely time exploring the countryside from our campsite in the hills overlooking the Med. There was a stunning picture of Daisy, freckles on her face, cuddled up to Isabel on one of our visits beside the Canal du Midi. I must have taken the picture, because David, who joined us for the second week, hovered in the background with his own camera. I remember it as such a joyous time. There were several more snaps. I smile at each one and then couldn't quite fathom why I wanted to suddenly look at them. I see nothing but youthful exuberance and family togetherness. Great days…so why am I perturbed by these pictures? I go to work, briefcase in hand, anxious with the world. So what was new? I am forever in this state, at odds and searching…searching for a reason to live.

*

Isabel calls me on the phone late afternoon.
'I had no right to turn on you, Will.'
'I had no business to interfere.'
'What's happening to Meg? Will she be OK?'
'I'm trying to relocate her, but she's a stubborn old mule.'
She laughs. Can't remember that sound from her. It made me think of the good times.

'I'm…I'm thinking of going away. Can you look after the cats?' She asks.

'*Thinking?*'

'Just for a few days.' She adds.

'Oh.'

We go into a five-second silence (that's a long time on a phone).

I stand by the window and idly watch as workmen dig the foundations of a new garage extension across the road.

'Can you, Will?'

I'm miles away. 'Can I *What?*'

'Take in the cats.'

'I suppose so. When?'

'Next week.'

'A bit sudden…'

She becomes terse once more. 'If it's a problem…'

'No, no.' My brain is on overload. 'Where are you going?'

'Away, find some space.'

I instantly regret asking again: 'Where?'

'You're doing it again, Will.'

'Oh, sorry.'

Then she spurts it out as if unburdening her guilt. 'Paris,' she says.

Can silence intensify? It sure feels like it. The seconds tick by. I can hardly breathe. *Paris?* For fuck's sake…this was the place for lovers. I want to kill her, tell her to piss off, remind her that she still has a husband…

'OK,' I mutter feebly. 'Let me know which day.'

Then I hang up. The rumours of the copper down the road had just been reinforced by her sudden request. I feel like she has punched me in the gut. I watch the concrete being poured into a giant hole and feel like jumping in to finish everything. I want to drown my sorrows. I have to get used to the idea that the sun is setting on my marriage dashing any hopes I have of saving it.

I am being used, sat upon, but I am too tired to fight her. Instead, I'll get my own back. The cats will suffer for my jealousy.

*

For tea, I have egg on toast, pass on the alcohol. It is still early evening so I take a stroll beside the harbour front and out along the towpath, following the last of the sun. The lights are coming on inside the pretty weather-boarded cottages as I pass the last of them and hit open country. The fields are golden, the trees whispering in the light breeze. From somewhere, a heron swoops and glides over the backwater. This enchanting landscape still mesmerizes me after all these years. I never tire of its beguiling beauty. It's a good thirty minute walk from Emsworth to Langstone, but I always love the anticipation. I can still recall my dad telling me about the Hayling Island Billy train puffing its way over the old wooden bridge before it fell into disrepair in the sixties. What a sight that must have been. Same as the mill house on the harbour front, black and defiant

27

against the crimson night. I try to imagine how it must have looked in the old days with its regal giant white sails (now sadly removed) turning in the breeze. I cast my eye to the right. A ribbon of car lights snake across the bridge, dimming as they slowly disappear around the headland. Beyond, the island shimmers over the rising water.

I carry on, using a torch for assistance. It is at times like this that I should have a dog. I promised Daisy one but Isabel was against the idea. Now she has the damn cats. I pass a neighbour who is walking her two poodles. We nod and exchange pleasantries. It's now getting too dark. I slowly return, my head still spinning, conjuring up romantic images of Paris. I call into *The Anchorage* and down a pint of beer. I have another and exchange small talk with Doug, the landlord. Someone I know orders from the bar, sees me, stiffens and provokes me with his first comment.

'Hi, Will. I guess you're pissed by the criticism on the news tonight…'

'Oh, yeah?'

'Social services held to account again.'

'What's new,' I counter, not wanting to rise to the bait.

'Apparently, a little boy has been abused over at Bedhampton…the social workers failed to pick up on the public complaints that the drug-fuelled parents were neglecting him.' He shook his head in disgust. 'I reckon your type need a kick up the backside…'

I could tell he had been drinking heavily. He was with a gang in the back room, their raucous laughter carrying through.

'There'll be an investigation, John. Not everything you read or hear is as simple as it appears.'

He scoffs. 'Pathetic do-gooders…the bunch of you! It makes my blood boil, to be frank.'

'I don't know enough of the case to comment,' I counter, 'and besides it would not be appropriate to discuss such matters in a public place.'

'Oh, *appropriate, eh*! A good word to hide behind, I'd say. Politicians use that word all the time.'

I raise my glass. 'Just having a quiet pint, John.'

He huffs, lifts his tray of drinks, disappears and then returns.

'Are you moving back in with the missus?'

Christ.

'Why would that be your business, John?'

'It's just that I've seen her around…with a fella from out of town. I guess that answers my question.'

'I guess it does.'

'He's one of them.'

'*Them*?'

'A DS from Worthing. Cosy, eh?'

I turn to face him. 'How's that then?'

'Well, he has a reputation: a real ladies man. Apparently, he's shagged every female in the force all along the south coast as far as Bournemouth.'

'Isn't your wife a cleaner down at the station?'

'Yeah…part-time…Why?' He says guardedly, as if her lowly paid job somehow reflected on his inadequacies.

I finish my drink, button my jacket. 'I reckon he'll be shagging her as well, John. Why else would she be working there earning peanuts and cleaning out the loos?'

I leave him standing there open-mouthed with nothing to say. It seems *appropriate* to my mind.

*

It's typical that people can be so small-minded and malicious. I'd had a run-in with John Knowles before. He's a local mechanic who had serviced our car prior to the *happening.* We'd had a dispute over a bill. I'd basically accused him of cheating on the work done and the amount he wanted to charge. We settled in the end but the resentment between us remains. His wife did, in fact, do some odd jobs around the area, including the police contract. I try to avoid them both but sometimes our paths cross. I regret my remark but he was pushing me. Let him stew.

I have another shower and finish some case notes. I throw a sandwich together and make coffee. Later, I hear a commotion outside. I open the front door and find a puddle on my doorstep. It isn't raining. Down the cobbled street, I can see John Knowles staggering home, yelling profanities to anyone in earshot who would listen. It's just before midnight. No one was listening, except me. I look at the puddle again. He hadn't forgotten my insult, *clearly.*

I climb into bed, coffee in hand. I lay awake for quite some time thinking of Isabel with *the copper* and what my life was like back then…

We were happy, after a fashion. Isabel was very pretty with auburn hair and sparkling ice blue eyes. She was as thin as a stick but as tough as they came. She could argue her way out of any situation and had the ability to move her way through the ranks quickly after she joined the police force, but settled in the role of a PS which suited our lifestyle I suppose with the regular shifts on offer. I moved just as slowly professionally. It suited me equally. I wasn't ambitious, supplementing my income with photographic commissions and the occasional sale of one of my landscape paintings in the local church exhibition. I also wanted to be a writer, but I wasn't disciplined enough…the many half-finished manuscripts discarded under the bed lay testament to that.

But we soldiered on and eventually managed to get a mortgage for our dream home: Eggshell cottage. This was our happiest times. As a result of this, Daisy was born. I took to fatherhood easily but Isabel struggled, trying to combine her demanding duties with the idealism of motherhood. It was bloody hard and caused the usual friction that young parents encounter. But we survived. I suppose, looking back, that we stopped giving to each other and channelled our efforts into our daughter. We gave up on *our* time. But I always adored Isabel. Still do (I'll repeat it again, no doubt).

Daisy attended Warblington Secondary school; eventually, where I taught. She thrived and as a family, we seemed to thrive as well. More money came in, Isabel gained a promotion and…well, I just drifted on. I suppose I was satisfied with my lot. A good day for me was teaching my daughter the basics of decency and helping her find the creative side of her brain which she so obviously possessed. Her mother was practical but Daisy was a powerhouse of talent. She was a great athlete at school, excelled at dance class and was a very good artist. We had a lot in common. So after wandering the fields around our home in search of inspiration for subject matter, we often then settled in for the night…me doing the cooking, happy with a glass of red wine and listening to the rhythmic sounds of Santana on the record player, Daisy finishing her homework or painting a masterpiece in watercolour. We loved the dance beat of South American music, which came from my time in Peru as a child. My father was a structural engineer out there for a year, but that's another story. So that was that really. I'm easily pleased as you can gather. From what I have described, well, that constituted a good day for me. I looked no further.

Holidays were easy too. Being on the south coast, we simply clambered on board the ferry and headed for France in our beaten up Vauxhall Viva. We toured all over, always camping in the early years to keep the costs down.

At first, my brother and his wife, before she became really ill, joined us. David and I shared the driving and the financial outlay. Sometimes, we pushed the boat out and hired a caravan. One year, we even took on a small apartment near Perpignan: heady days indeed. The sun always shone. We lived in shorts and T-shirts and ran like idiots through the Iris fields, explored medieval ruins, visited old churches. Drank the local wine, feasted on rustic French cuisine…was there a better time in our lives?

A thousand memories flood in from these trips, the first being when our daughter was a tiny baby. I stop for a second. Fifteen years, gone in a flash. Christ, I could die just thinking about it.

My heart is heavy.

I finally drift off to sleep, with one such recollection stuck in my head: the imaginary aroma of freshly baked bread (collected from a French market on a glorious summer's day) seeping into my subconscious mind as Daisy, just ten, giggled and ate ravenously from the loaf she pinched from my backpack.

She would be dead within five years.

Chapter 4

I have an appointment with Meg about a vacant property. I want to show her alternative accommodation close to where she lives now, but I know as soon as I arrive it is going to be a losing battle by the grimace on her face.

She makes me a coffee as I describe the one-bedroom maisonette near Fratton Park, which I have to dress up to keep her attention.

'It's on the ground floor, Meg, so there'll be no stairs to worry about. It has gas central heating and double glazing,' I say in my best salesman's voice.

She hands me the cup. 'Any garden?'

'A small communal one.'

'I'll hate the noise from above.'

'These things are unavoidable sometimes…'

'Is there traffic outside?'

'Well, yes.'

'The cats will get run over…or me for that matter.'

'It's temporary accommodation, Meg. We can get you settled and then search around for something quieter. Nothing's perfect in this world.'

She tosses her hand around. 'This place is perfect, Will, but nobody wants to listen to me.'

'Things change, Meg.'

'Aye, and not for the better, I can tell you. Would you like a biscuit?'

'I'm fine.'

'I'm not.'

'I know how difficult this is, Meg.'

'You don't know anything, young man.'

'Will you at least come and view the property?'

'It's raining…I don't want to spoil my hair.'

'I have an umbrella,' I mutter, knowing that nothing will persuade her.

'What about somewhere nice overlooking the sea?'

'You mean Southsea?'

'I might think about that…'

'Property out there tends to be more expensive and difficult to find.'

'Well, you can finish your coffee and start looking today.'

This time I grimace and throw a line at her: 'Easier said than done, Meg.'

'I fancy one of those top floor places with a view. What do you call them?'

I have to smile, and enlighten her. 'A penthouse.'

'That'll do, one with a lift.'

'I wish...' Then I trail off, unable to support false promises. I look idly around her lounge (filled with porcelain knick-knacks and dried flower arrangements), wondering how to engage her, win her over and force her to confront her dilemma. Then I notice something curious which is missing from the overcrowded room.

'Meg, I can't see a photo of Miriam.'

'I beg your pardon?'

'There's a picture of your husband, one of you with the cats...but not one of your daughter.'

She sighs. 'I keep them in her bedroom.'

'Oh.'

'Although I think of her every day, I don't necessarily want to be reminded of my sorrow whichever way I turn.'

'I get that.'

She stands by the window, the pale light filtering through the net curtains. I guess she's deep in thought and I feel like an intruder with my questions. Then she slowly turns and speaks the words that make my heart jump into my mouth. I truly wasn't expecting this.

'Will, would you like to visit her room and say a little prayer with me.'

*

I feel most odd really, entering such a private intimate domain. The curtains are pulled tight and Meg switches on the light. I smell the musty aroma, although the room itself appears clean and polished. There is lace on the tiny dressing table and a pretty lace bedspread over pink sheets on the single bed. Behind the fluffy pillows is a cushioned white leatherette headboard. I have an overwhelming sadness as she beckons me in and invites me to sit on the only chair in the room. Meg shuffles around, opening drawers and peering inside. She gently touches an ornate gold-framed photograph of Miriam which takes pride of place on the wall opposite the window. As I look around, I see several more pictures of her and on one wall, above the bed, a line of certificates high-light her school achievements. Meg perches on the corner of the small bed and quietly speaks a few words which I can't make out. I close my eyes and think of Daisy and for a second feel guilty at my betrayal. It's an honour to be invited into this sanctuary and my thoughts should be centred solely on Meg's grief.

I cup my hands together and say a prayer. The air seems to suck from my chest and I begin to cough from the oppression.

'Do you need to leave for that?' Meg asks, seeing my discomfort.

'No, I'm fine, just a little tickle at the back of the throat.'

'I'll get you a glass of water.'

'Not necessary,' I say, but she persists and edges down the stairs. I stand up and meander about, straightening the bed where Meg had sat. There is a cut glass vase containing a single white rose: Daisy's colour. It is wilting from the lack of light. Just like me. I slide back a drawer and remove what looks like a photo album, the type with a cheap plastic cover. I open it and smile at the images of children playing on the beach. I assume one of them is Miriam. Other snaps were taken on a school sports day. There is a lovely picture of a birthday party with a group of giggly girls around a table with a big candlelit cake in the middle. My smile widens. Another page reveals a fairground scene: a bunch of happy-go-lucky girls licking ice cream. In the background, people milling around, some in shorts. The day was a scorcher obviously. The helter-skelter dominated the skyline. I thought I could recognise a youthful Meg standing beside the girls, slender with long hair across her strapless shoulders. I guessed her husband, Stan, took the photo…

'Here you are.' Meg says, holding out a glass.

I'd clean forgotten about the water, absorbed in Miriam's idyllic world.

'I didn't mean to pry,' I say feebly.

'I'm happy for you to look. She was a precocious child, so full of fun and mischief.'

I close the album and return it to its place of solitude. I sip the water gratefully. 'What will you do with all this stuff, Meg?'

'When I die?'

I ignore her sombre tone, and suggest, 'When you move.'

'I don't intend to leave this house. There'll have to drag me away screaming.'

'That day is close, I'm afraid. Help me to help you, Meg. I'll find a place where we can resurrect Miriam's room exactly as it is now.'

'That's not possible and you know it, Will.' She sits in the chair heavily, defeat etched over her face. 'When I'm gone, will you gather everything up in this room and keep it safe…'

'I can't…'

'Promise me, Will. Make an old woman happy. Just say *yes.* '

I hate myself for lying. 'Of course, Meg.'

'Promise?'

'I promise.'

Later, back at my apartment I linger under a blistering hot shower and find myself crying uncontrollably. I think I'm mourning the loss of optimism, the slow decline into the inevitable acceptance of futility. The life cycle: you come into this world alone, and you go out of this world alone.

*

It is Sunday. Always a difficult time if you live on your own. I eat a little cereal and gulp down a strong Columbian coffee. I dress in a white T-shirt and black jeans and drive to the corner shop five minutes away. There I buy the papers and, on this occasion, white lilies. Then I carry on to the cemetery. I sit there, in the car, and scan the sports pages and quietly prepare myself as best I can. It never gets any easier. Occasionally, I'd come with Isabel but that stopped when it became too much for us to endure as a couple.

I vacate the car and take my first step. The rest come with practice. The sun is shining, the ground dry…so I sit cross-legged beside the grave. I remove the old flowers and discard them in a bin bag I brought with me. Then I place the fresh flowers in a neat pile against the headstone and breathe in the scented air. It is beautifully quiet. A soft breeze cools my skin.

'Hello, Daisy,' I say. That is enough. She knows I am here.

For the next thirty minutes I ramble on about everything and nothing; shed a few tears and drink water from a plastic bottle I had purchased earlier. I tell her about Meg and Miriam. I don't tell her about Mum's new relationship. I fall silent as a young couple pass behind me holding hands, which reminds me of how Isabel and I use to be. I instantly regret thinking negative thoughts of her. Something is on my mind, so I say it aloud when I am alone again.

'Daisy, I have a handwritten note from you, and it baffles me. It reads *I don't like him.* Who are you referring to? It beats me because you were always secretive about your friends. Were you being bullied at school? Did someone have a grudge against you? I can't imagine you having enemies.' I stop, drink water again. I remember Meg's words, "Daisy is here." I find comfort and discomfort from this. It makes me feel joyous and then misplaced, vulnerable, scared of the unknown…

'Mum will come over this afternoon,' I add. 'She's off to…Paris (Aaaargh, shit, why did I just say that?).' What a jerk I am. I ponder my cock-up, I'll struggle to explain this statement, other than blurt it out, *Oh, by the way, Mummy has a new boyfriend...* which I can hardly bring myself to do. Daisy would be confused by this pronouncement anyway. I can hear her saying… *What did Dad just say?* As usual, I speak without thinking and get into trouble. On this occasion I manage to deflect the conversation as best I can.

'I'm thinking of exhibiting at the Royal Academy next summer. Well, submitting something anyway. No doubt it will be rejected. Or perhaps it will be third time lucky.'

Have I got away with it?

I leave the question hanging in the air like the thin sycamore branches which twirl about my head.

'I'm confused, Daisy. Your message scares me. I'm going to piece together all of our photos and your mad notes and see if I can discover who wants to harm you. I think you have left a message for me to untangle. That's what it looks like. Meg and I have a lot in common and she wants to help me find answers to our loss. She too has lost a daughter. I don't want to finish up like her. She is tormented, but her serenity and purity of thought puts me to shame. I reckon she would forgive Miriam's killer, fool her, I say! I would want to slowly torture the bastard who hurt you until their eyes bleed…so I'll keep on searching if that's all right with you. Help me, Daisy. Find a way to help me…but don't tell Mum, OK?'

I chat for another twenty minutes. Then I kiss her headstone and meander back to the car. I feel strangely relieved, focused even, and far stronger than when I arrived. The wind suddenly whips up and makes me look skyward. I'm captivated in an instant as the billowing purple clouds break apart to reveal a majestic sweep of cobalt blue and emerald green hues as far as the eye can see. It could have been one of Daisy's paintings. She's reached out to me. I can sense it.

*

I have no idea where to begin in my search for further clues as to the identity of Daisy's tormentor, but I need to gain access to Daisy's room once again. That has to be my starting point. So I phone Isabel and she agrees to leave the key to Eggshell cottage under the mat whilst she visits the cemetery.

'It would be great if you weren't there when I get back,' she says. *Cutting comment, just not needed.* Then she tries to correct herself. 'I mean, I'll be in no fit state to talk with you, if you understand…'

'I do.'

I arrive at the designated time and find the key under the doormat. I don't want to linger unnecessarily so I check Daisy's room first, removing another shoebox or two. I then add a couple of storage bags from the spare room and place everything into the boot of my Rav. I feel like a looter. The house still smells of cats, and sure enough, they doze in the kitchen, each one with an eye on me as I move around on tiptoes. On the table is a holiday brochure entitled: *City Breaks, Paris.* Great! That cheers me up. In the sink, the dirty dishes remain stacked up. There are two wine glasses. More cheer, eh? I'm feeling better by the minute. A man's leather jacket lays discarded over the sofa. For a split-second, I contemplate burning the fucking place down. But I keep control…*just.*

Back home, I grab a chilled Bud from the fridge and kill it in one. Snatch another, same result. I am furious, seriously pissed. It seems I have no right to feel I once belonged in *that* house. I correct myself: *our* house. But there is no sign of me, no recognition that I ever existed. Isabel has moved on, her memory short and self-selecting. In the great scheme of things, I am a goner, yesterday's leftover, tossed into the bin.

The two shitty cats warrant more status than me.

That sums up how far I have fallen. I wouldn't go back now, not to the cottage, or to her (who am I kidding?). It is too heart-breaking. I need to move on as well. I have what I had gone for. Isabel could have her shiny new life with her shiny new fella. She just had to be careful what she wished for in this brave new world of hers. I vow *not* to pick up the pieces if it all goes hideously wrong. Then I stop my bad-mouthing antics. I don't want to lower myself to her dubious standards.

Back home, I empty the contents from the bags onto the floor and survey the scene. *Christ.* This is a big job. I'm faced with hundreds of photos. It will take forever but I sit down and make a start, fully aware that my social diary is conspicuously empty of invitations.

*

Daisy was about seven when she first noticed boys. At eight, she brought Robin home for tea, then Simon. For a short time after, she hated all boys. On her ninth birthday, we travelled to France on our annual pilgrimage and stayed at a campsite near Narbonne where she met Romain Petit for the first time, a local farmer's son. It was on their land that we pitched our tent. He soon became part of our gang and we returned the following year on Daisy's insistence. Hmm, I wonder why?

Sitting here, I marvel at the photos of all of us messing about. These were carefree days, sunny days and inspiring days. We were totally in love with this region of France. The gang usually consisted of the three of us, my brother David (without his wife, Margo, who was visiting her brother in East Yorkshire) and the Petit clan, including their youngest, Romain. We have a *lot* of photos. I try to catalogue them in date order as I recall certain events and cherished personal memories, but it's confusing to my muddled brain.

One person I didn't like was Romain's oldest brother, Frederic, who occasionally hooked up with us. He was withdrawn, surly and hovered too closely around Daisy whenever he could, which I didn't approve of. If I'm honest, I'd say he was a bit backward. David warned him away on two occasions as he playfully tried to wrestle with her. I have the pictures to prove it. One time, now that I think back, Daisy had a strop with him for pestering her. There is a photo of us sitting at the dining table al fresco, with Daisy at one end and Romain sulking at the other end. In between the two of them sat Frederic, grinning wildly, happy that he had separated them. He was a pest. Fortunately, he wasn't around that often.

I don't like him. I find the note again and try to find a sequence. At the end of the day, it's just one of many crazy jottings that Daisy wrote down. It didn't seem to fit into a pattern of communication, or maybe I'm not astute enough to spot it. I spend the next hour fiddling between boxes, examining everything with no particular direction as to what I am after. It is upsetting. It's as if Daisy is in the room with me telling stories of our past. I wish she could fill in the gaps. I find a tiny furry rabbit and for a fleeting magical second, I can smell my daughter's fragrance as I press it to my nose. I feel bereft. In a tin box, I uncover more photos. She was an avid snapper and collector. Some of these I can't remember being taken. Some I had never seen before.

Then my breath is punched from me. One of them depicts Daisy in a bikini top. That was not the problem. It was her awkward stance that catches my attention. She was clearly embarrassed and trying to turn away, her hand waving in protest at the intruder taking the picture. *Now* that's one I would have remembered. It was certainly not taken by me. In the background, I can make out the fuzzy outline of Isabel, which discounts her. I reckon it was taken when we upgraded to the holiday suite the following summer. The newly built annexe was part of the farmhouse. I can make out a table with plates and glasses on it which indicated a gathering at a BBQ perhaps. *Who* took the picture which so offended Daisy? It knocks me for sixth just looking at it.

I pop down to the supermarket and bizarrely spot Isabel in the aisle. It's the day after Sunday. At first, I keep my distance but eventually, our paths cross.

'Hi,' she says.

'Did you manage to go to the cemetery yesterday?'

'You know I did.'

'Sorry.'

'You seemed to take a lot of Daisy's stuff from the cottage but left most of your belongings…'

'I'll get them another day or chuck them out if I'm cluttering up the place.'

'It's for you to go through them, Will.'

'I know…'

'You seem agitated. What are you looking for amongst her things that you haven't found already?'

I gaze around to make sure we are not overheard. 'Remember the boy named Romain Petit?'

'Of course, I do.'

'He had a thing for Daisy…'

'He was a bit clingy, I'll grant you…but that was a long time ago.'

'I was searching through the holiday snaps and couldn't help noticing her odd behaviour towards him. One minute she was mad about him, the next mad with him.'

'That's teenagers for you.'

'They obviously had a crush on each other.'

'Relationships at that age blow hot and cold. Been there, done that…'

'I found a note from her that possibly referred to him or his brother.'

'Frederic? Now he *was* seriously weird…' She fumed.

'I'm trying to piece together those years before…well, you know.'

'Before she was murdered.'

This is typical of Isabel. Her job meant she was hardened to these things, but I am still taken aback by her bluntness. I don't mention the offending photo at this stage. I'm still trying to get my head around it, to be honest with you.

'I was wondering if there is a connection,' I say.

'Look, Frederic was a troublemaker, granted. But you can't go round accusing all and sundry. Besides, we have no idea of his whereabouts since losing contact with his family when we stopped going to France.'

'Perhaps that's something we should be following up.'

'I'll look into it if it makes you happy.'

'No one should be discounted. The note could have easily referred to him…'

'What did it say?'

I tell her.

'I think you're reading far too much into this, Will.'

'What about Romain?'

'What about him? Are you suggesting that he followed her to England?'

'It's a possibility.'

She ponders; impatience in her glare.

'It's highly unlikely as they were still kids, and Romain doesn't fit the profile of the killer. Anyway, he has been interviewed.'

'And that would be…?'

'The investigation so far has largely centred on local people. Whoever did it had to have a good knowledge of the area. He probably watched her for several days, monitoring her movements. We think it was planned, and not a random act of violence.'

'You mean the killer knew her, picked her out.'

'Yes, she was no doubt targeted.'

'Romain knew her.'

'Agreed, but is he a calculating hardened criminal capable of such brutality? I'm not sure, Will…as I'm not sure about Frederic's involvement either. They were eliminated from the enquires after checking the alibies.'

'Have we discounted women?'

'A male fits the profile of a murderer and is more likely.'

'But it still needs checking, right?'

She sighs. 'What did the note say again?'

I repeat myself and wait patiently for an answer.

'That doesn't implicate either of them, Will.'

'It doesn't eliminate them either.'

She shrugs. 'I'll look into it as I said earlier. Satisfied?'

'That would be good.' I know Isabel is simply humouring me but I also know she is a good cop and will investigate my concerns.

She nods. 'Give me a week, OK?'

'OK.'

'Still all right with taking in the cats?'

'Yeah, I suppose,' I said dejectedly.

'You promised. By the way, I'd like Daisy's things back when you're finished.'

'Absolutely.'

'We can, of course, divide everything if you feel up to it.'

'Later, perhaps…'

She smiles thinly, hesitates and moves on, leaving me stranded. I long for her to come back, take my hand and squeeze it. Just not going to happen, I'm afraid. I turn and trundle to the bargain section and check the sell-by-date on a pack of pork chops. I noticed she had fillet steak for two in her basket.

Some days just have that feel to them: downright crappy.

Chapter 5

I get a call from the hospital. Meg had been taken ill during the night. I race over and sit with her as a doctor describes her symptoms of short breath, sweatiness and shaking. She appears OK at this point after undergoing precautionary tests, but I worry.

The indication from her nurse is that she will be kept in for another night of observation. I relay this information and Meg is confused, thinking her enforced stay is permanent. I reassure her that it isn't and agree to go back to her house and collect a clean nightgown and some pyjamas for her. She makes a list of assorted bits she wants from the bathroom and tells me where to find them. I have to feed the cats too. That will get me into training I guess.

Back at the house, I do the best I can, filling a holdall with her belongings.

The cats gather, circle my feet and stare at me with aloof expressions. I know what they want and carry out my duties. It is strange being here alone, kind of eerie. I elect to leave as fast as possible but then instinctively take the stairs to Miriam's room. It's unlocked. I can't help myself and enter quietly and just stand there, wondering how Meg copes with all that is going on around her. Then, inexplicably, I search the wardrobe and the clothes cupboard and peer under the bed, for what I just don't know. I find a plastic bag. Inside is a powder blue summer dress (with lace trimmings around the neckline), neatly folded. It is, as expected, child size. It breaks my heart to touch it.

My behaviour is inexcusable but I keep going. Eventually, I find the photo album and scan through it again. The pictures of the fairground intrigue me the most. They are at the back of the book. These must have been some of the last pictures taken of Miriam. I had done my research on her murder. The dress I revealed appears to be the one she was found in on waste ground, not far from where Daisy was discovered. Forty-odd years separate the killings. I ask the question again; could there be a connection? Everyone keeps telling me, because of the time frame, that this is highly unlikely. My mind wanders…*suppose though*…

Similarities between the girl's profiles are uncanny. Both were school children. Both died within the same locality. Both died from head wounds. Both had been sexually molested or interfered with although no semen was found. OK, a gap of forty years was a long time to try and pin a double crime on the same person. I know it doesn't add up. Anyone capable of such brutality would not be able to resist repeating it during the intervening period. It would be like a drug to him, surely, the urge to kill building and building. So…

Just suppose…and according to the police, it was most likely a man.

I do a wicked thing. I know you'll think the worst of me. I take the photo of the group of girls with their ice creams and put it in my pocket. Somehow, it means something to me. I'll return it later. I depart the room as immaculately as I had found it, closing the door behind me. One of the cats hovers on the top step and stares me down as I pass it. Luckily for me, the witness with the superior glare won't be able to give my secret away. I bribe her with more food just in case.

When she is better able to talk, I'm determined to ask Meg what really happened to her daughter. No research can compare to the words of a mother. I can gather the cold facts but I need to pick up on the mood of the times. Meg can provide that. In the meantime, a nagging feeling prevails. Two murders separated by four decades. Is it two random killers or one local madman patiently biding his time in search of another victim? I favour the latter option (mainly because of Meg's prophetic words), but I don't buy into the fallow period between the assaults. There had to be other victims…but just not necessarily on this patch. Could the killer be hiding his crimes by simply wandering the countryside in order to remain undetected? Back in the seventies, police procedure didn't link counties or even countries as they do so effectively today with the aid of computer databases. The modern era brings with it many advantages, certainly this greater level of sophistication in hunting down a target. But that doesn't mean the system is infallible. Being an Aries, I'm adamant; I'm right on this latter prognosis, but I have no evidence to back it up…yet. All I have is a hunch, but usually, my hunches are spot on.

*

I start my research at the local library, reading up on the newspaper archives which reported Miriam's initial disappearance. It was on a Sunday in July 1973 and she was nine. Within two days of the alarm being raised, her body was found by a man walking his dog. She was the only child of Meg and Stan Faulkner, who were Hampshire born and bred. Their daughter had been battered and sexually assaulted. A massive manhunt ensued but to no avail. No one was arrested for the murder. DNA was a tool of the future back then. Her killer remains at large until this day. He could even be dead. He could be in prison. He could be living abroad. Or he could be living right here, on everyone's doorstep. Very much alive. I read on. Miriam came from a loving maternal background and no members of the family were considered under suspicion. Police were baffled by her senseless slaughter. The area where they lived was deemed a safe environment and neighbours expressed universal horror at this atrocity. It left a mark on everyone, according to the local press. One reporter went so far as to heavily criticise the police at the time for their bungling approach. Clues were obviously missed.

Digesting this brought it all back to my ordeal, although personally, I had no complaints against the police, who handled everything with Daisy's death with great sensitivity in the beginning. I was grateful for that. It was what happened after which hit me the hardest. The finger of suspicion was pointed at me. People I didn't know began to talk. Rumours persisted, and, as you are aware, mud sticks if enough is thrown. I was the outsider. Apparently, I had a temper. Apparently, I was the oddball coming down from the north. Apparently, I was seen as too possessive toward my daughter, unnaturally so. I know now that you can't stop gossip but my protestations at the time were seen as a little too loud. Hell, I was in a bad place and just wanted to grieve in my own way. Yes, I hit out at the unfounded speculation but I was portrayed as this ugly vile beast…a man with a stain against his character. I was a good teacher, a great father…the last thing I needed was for ignorant oafs to pour slander in my direction. The police calmed things down and eventually put out a statement that I was not part of the ongoing investigation. But do you know what? I still feel guilty, that *somehow* I was responsible for some fuck-faced mental case bastard to come on the scene and destroy my daughter's very existence. Even Isabel looked at me differently. Always will, I reckon. Read on.

I'd just like to get her on my side, see things from my perspective. Raking up the past, discovering new evidence is what she does best. But in the case of Daisy, well, Isabel shuts down, finding the very notion of her murder just too unbearable to contemplate. Yes, she maintains a hard exterior and can be flippant to the extreme when dealing with me but she has to face the facts: our beloved daughter is dead. She pretends to cope, but I know differently. Grief divides us, pushing us in a different direction. How do I get her to reason with me? I'm not to blame. Whenever I approach the subject, I generally get a backlash. She is angry. I feel punished for a second time. I can't handle the rejection. But I have to somehow nibble away and prick her conscience and face the shit that comes my way. I have to find justice for Daisy, peace of mind for Isabel. Doubtful, but you need to see the bigger picture. Slowly, I am getting to it…so persevere. I am a coward. My confession to you will explain her anger!

That's what drives Meg on (the truth), in spite of her terrible illness and the fast-approaching eviction. She won't give up. Neither will I in spite of my deed. I have to come clean sometime. You might not believe in me then.

I make notes of Miriam's murder and add a list of comparisons with my daughter's initial disappearance. Only their ages differ. In both instances, thousands of able young men have been interviewed but none arrested. It was frustrating then and it is frustrating now (still is) but here's the thing: if my hunch is correct, then we shouldn't be searching for this type of man at all today…rather we should concentrate on a man in his sixties, assuming he first killed when he was in his early twenties. This sounds far-fetched I know, but my idea can't be discounted entirely. Apart from Meg, am I the only person willing to follow this line of enquiry? It appears so, but I'm driven by hunger to see the man behind bars. That would bring a lot of satisfaction, banish some of the heartache. My family has been destroyed forever; he can rot in prison forever.

Some hope, eh? Whichever way I turn; I have to consider the central role of the police. I don't have the confidence in their dynamism. I don't believe Meg and her husband were taken seriously in their quest for justice. I don't believe (my idea) I am either. I've thought about this. If there is a connection between us then there had to be something, a line of sorts, which has not been so far uncovered. I can go over old ground, but will the police? They seem reluctant to do so. I suppose too many years have passed. This pisses me off. With modern forensics, coupled with police nationwide computer link-ups, then surely this would mean the database of comparison crimes could be established more easily. The technology is there, so why the resistance?

I'm convinced Isabel is the key to knocking it down, but I'm losing patience. I can trust her, and her alone; she needs to up her game. I need Isabel to look into it further and pressurise her colleagues to put the hours in. This means harassing her boss, DI Jimson, but he's hard work. Thinks I'm an idiot. He has always maintained this was a random isolated murder. The police, therefore, have not looked back at past similar cases. I am aware of their lack of manpower so I ask: Is this a financial decision or is there another motive which over-rides my concerns? I ask because I am largely ignored, particularly by this officer. I do not share his static narrow view regarding my daughter's death. To reinforce this, I need hard facts and a plausible line of enquiry. At present, I possess neither. But I do have a point of view and I want it heard.

*

Isabel describes my way of dealing with difficult things as *the blankness:* that I possess an emotional void. I call her way of dealing with this same issue as plain fucking stupid. She has the problem, not I. So I skip around her (I told you I'm losing patience) and contact her boss, DI Carl Jimson, to explain my concerns. I'm expecting to hit a brick wall. I'll clear this up right now, so not to confuse you. I don't like this guy. Do I have to have a reason? OK, his eyes are too small. He has crooked teeth. So here I am in his office.

'This is highly irregular, Mr Farmer. Are you sure you don't want Isabel to join us?'

'No. I want you to hear me out in private. I don't want someone being judgmental sitting in on our conversation.'

'And that's the reason for omitting her?'

'Yes.'

'You'd better start at the beginning then.'

So, for the next ten minutes I blurt out my feelings, fears and theories whilst he stares at me with *those* eyes. I note that he remains detached and somewhat puzzled by my monologue. At one point he even checks his watch, which throws me. I don't necessarily think my ramblings impress him. We drink tea from mugs and he says nothing. Eventually, I stop and take another sip.

'Interesting,' is the initial response from him.

I feel foolish, despondent.

'Assuming the killer of Miriam was in his mid-twenties then we have him at around sixty-five now,' Jimson says flatly. 'So, we have an arthritic pensioner as a cold-blooded killer, yes?'

I hate his mocking tone.

He continues. 'Plausible, of course, but in that case why the forty-year gap between the murders? Initially, we discounted a connection for that very reason alone but we did, of course, look into the possibility, as you have suggested, that maybe he was detained elsewhere and therefore prevented from striking again. Our problem is that we haven't found anyone with a criminal record who could fit this profile. We even checked with the armed forces…zilch.'

Right. 'Right.'

'So, our line of enquiry leads us to suggest that they are separate incidents and that the killer of Daisy is younger than your estimate and is also unknown to us, in this area at least. We are widening the net, of course, with the help of our colleagues in other counties. Perhaps this was his first attack. As you are aware, we have interviewed hundreds of men, but mainly in the vicinity, as we initially believed him to be a local man. He would have to have knowledge of those bridleways in the woods and have a plan of escape. We also think he knew Daisy, perhaps walked with her. The attack was swift. Daisy had no chance to defend herself. She hadn't been running either, trying to escape. I think there was a confrontation, which suggests familiarity. That's why you were under suspicion initially. I believe Daisy knew her killer.'

I bridle at this last inference.

He just had to get that in, the bastard.

'But, of course, you know all this, so I'm trying to keep everything low key so as not to cause further anxiety. You and Isabel have been through enough.'

I won't rise to the bait. 'Have you made any further progress in identifying him?'

He breathed in heavily. 'To be perfectly frank, Mr Farmer, we have not…'

'How can someone simply vanish into thin air?'

'How can someone simply arrive from thin air?'

I'm stumped.

'I cannot go into the details, but we are actively carrying out several strands of the investigation which as you can imagine are sensitive to the integrity of the case and therefore confidential at present.'

'Is Isabel part of that investigation team?'

'No, Mr Farmer. She could compromise our position.'

I slump in my chair.

He leans forward and whispers, 'He will *make* a mistake. He will probably try again. We will get him. I've noted your concerns. You're exhausted, so go home and leave us to do our job, OK?'

We shake hands and he escorts me to my car. What he says makes absolute sense, but I still don't like him. There is nothing else to add except he has big ears as well.

*

I get home in the late afternoon. The phone rings and I know who it is. I check the time, lift the handset and wait for the blast.

'What the hell do you think you're doing, Will?'

'Hi, Isabel.'

'I have enough on my plate without being hauled in front of my boss and told that my husband is conducting his own investigation into my daughter's death.'

'*Our* daughter…'

'Fuck, Will, what are you playing at?'

'I didn't infer to Jimson that I was doing anything other than what any father would do in the circumstances. I'm an outsider looking in, Isabel.'

'You're interfering in a police investigation and you're not qualified to do this. Keep out of things, Will. You could do more harm than good…'

'Have I made things awkward for you?'

I can hear her inhale breath between her teeth like sucking nails.

'Isabel?'

She exhales. 'Let's just leave it, Will. Do me a favour and don't make a fool of me in front of my colleagues.'

'That was never the intention. I just feel so frustrated.'

'We both have to live with this shit, Will. It's not *just* you, OK?'

I desperately want to connect with her, express my feelings, but I know the timing isn't good, so I shut my mouth and say, 'OK.'

Then the phone goes down on me. I think she is largely hacked off with me.

*

Later, I get on the road, pick up a burger from a drive-in and visit Meg with her things.

'Bless you, Will.'

She looks better. I finger the stolen photo in my pocket and feel guilty.

'Have you eaten?' I ask.

'A little, but it's difficult to swallow. You look tired, Will.'

'A tough day,' but then I reflect on her predicament and instantly regret saying it.

'Had a row with Isabel?'

'How did you guess?'

'Call it a woman's intuition.'

'Why did she come to see you, Meg?'

She pulls herself up in bed, and suggests, 'For spiritual comfort, perhaps? I'm known in these parts as the loony…'

'…Yes, Mystic Meg.'

We both laugh.

Then she gets serious. 'I can reach beyond the living, see things, touch things…make contact, and that helps people with their sorrow.'

44

I frown. 'Can you reach out to Daisy?'

'There are moments when I can sense her presence, but I can see this upsets you.'

Jimson is right; I am utterly exhausted and have difficulty believing such a weird concept. I deal in the practical side of life. So I ask the obvious question: 'Do you see or still feel Miriam?'

She reflects, and then whispers, 'No.'

'Then how can you trade in such things to other people? It seems unfair…offering false hope.' Truthfully, I was a bit hard on her but I am carrying a heavy degree of anger locked inside of me. It's sheer frustration, I suppose.

'I use to see Miriam, and the connection was strong, but over the years it has slowly disappeared. But I do have her room. It is enough.'

Again, I regret my crass remarks. Who am I to deny people a degree of comfort? 'Tell me what you told Isabel…'

'I explained that her daughter was in a good place and that she was in the safest place possible now…contained within her mother's sacred heart. She could no longer be hurt there. We talked about the need to go on living, how the pain just keeps on intensifying and how lost love can be so fragile, so breakable.'

'Is that how she feels. Broken?'

'I would think so. It takes a long time, Will.'

'That's how I feel. Smashed to fucking smithereens.' I glance around me. 'Sorry for the language…'

'My husband would have concurred with that.'

'Who do you think killed Miriam?'

My comment takes her unaware.

'Gosh.'

'I'm sorry, Meg, but I'm just trying to put a picture together that will perhaps shed light on whether our daughter's deaths were somehow linked. I haven't forgotten your words to me.'

Her eyes moisten. 'You suddenly think the worse of everyone, looking at behaviour that you wouldn't normally look at. For instance, a cousin of Miriam's suddenly left the area which naturally came under the radar of the police. But his motive was innocent and totally plausible. A friend of my husband stopped calling around and I began to wonder why. Was he guilty? I even suspected the window cleaner whom I saw chatting to Miriam in the garden one day. Everything gets magnified when a crime has been committed. The torture, the mistrust, never leaves you, Will.'

'Was anyone arrested?'

'A fairground worker was questioned but later released.'

I remind myself of the photo again.

'Tell me about it.'

'It was a young lad that took a shine to her. The fair arrived from another county and stayed for two weeks and Miriam and her friends often went as it was naturally exciting to them.'

'Did you go with her?'

'Not always. But one of the parents accompanied them to keep them away from mischief.'

'But this boy got an attachment to her?'

'Well, yes, but I'm sure it was only innocent fun. She never left the protection of her girlfriends though.'

I nearly corrected her, but thought otherwise. How else was she found alone and dead in a ditch?

'When was she found?'

'Two days after the fair left town.'

My heart misses a beat.

'Did Miriam seem upset when the fair packed up?'

'All the kids were; it was the focal point of their lives.'

'Did you notice anything different in her behaviour that day?'

'You're asking me to go back forty years, Will. Nothing untoward struck me…'

I could sense the cogs in her head moving around. I push, '*Although*?'

'Well, thinking about it I overheard her say something to Lizzie, her best friend…but it didn't mean much at the time.'

'What did she say?'

'Something like *I don't like him.*'

My gut twists.

'And that wouldn't concern you, Meg?'

'It was just girls gossiping. They were always talking about boys. And besides, she was alive and well then. I didn't expect anything to happen to her. I didn't expect…' Her voice trails off.

'Did you tell the police?'

'I'm sure I would have.'

'Did they find the boy from the fairground?'

'No, he was never identified, even when the fair returned the following year. The man questioned and the boy were not the same person.'

I am no Inspector Morse, but I felt I had my first breakthrough, my first clue. *Those words again.* I keep cool and change the subject so as not to alert her then make my departure soon after Meg dozes in her bed.

Outside in the hospital car park, I light a fag and inhale deeply. I'd arrived an hour earlier feeling crestfallen, beaten up, now I have a spring in my step. I drive away elated. Isabel told me not to interfere, but that goes against my nature. Well, nothing will stop me now. I'm on a quest, not just for Daisy but for Miriam and her deserving mother, Mystic Meg. We all want this thing called closure.

I also want revenge.

Chapter 6

It's the morning after, and I'm feeling pretty sorry for myself. Yesterday was a big-hitting day and the bravado I experienced then is now somewhat diminished.

Jimson has no faith in me. Meg has too much faith in me. My wife sits somewhere in between, but I need her support more than ever. Yes, I want revenge, but I can't do it on my own.

Rather than confront Isabel face-to-face with my demons (and receive a barrage of abuse in return), I decide to email her directly and spell out my frustrations in the hope that she will reason with me, rather than against me. I have become the fall-guy and I'm not prepared to be one from now on. She can like it or lump it.

I type something which I'm not going to bore you with because you've got the gist of my argument so far. Besides, it's a long-winded rant that I'm not particularly proud of. There you go; I'm not clever with words like Stephen Fry.

I mull it over, correct it, press SEND and have a brandy (or two). Then wait. My heart thumps and I try to keep busy. I tackle some files but I'm not concentrating properly and therefore I'm failing my clients. It's no good. I go for a jog along the harbour front, the gulls scattering at my approach. There are a couple of small boats moving on the estuary, their gleaming hulls reflected in the calm green waters as they chug along under diesel power. One tries to raise a sail but to no avail. I can smell crab meat and oysters which makes me hungry.

I eventually run for six miles and stagger home, feeling worse than before. I obviously check the emails before anything else: nothing. I drink a bottle of water. If she's out and about then I won't get a response until this evening. Besides, there is a lot to take in. She might even threaten to divorce me or call in a psychiatrist. Sometimes I do think I'm over the edge, so I wouldn't blame her if she flips too. I'm pushing her to the limits.

I reread the outgoing email and realise that I have overworked it. I sound like a raving lunatic. Too late now: the damage is done! I grill sausages and microwave a jacket potato. Treat myself to a Bud and carelessly drop it, beer everywhere. I'm all over the place. As I eat, I read the local paper and catch up with the latest catastrophe concerning Pompey, my beloved team. They, like me, are in the shit. They lurch from one crisis to another. Need I say more? I'm not expecting any sympathy from you, just an understanding of what I'm trying to do. I might be treading on toes but it is a necessary duty. I don't believe that any of you would do it differently. I know I'm not flavour of the month and I know I'm talking in clichés but they sum up the situation perfectly. I'm not a learned man, so I express myself simply in the hope you'll be on my side. God, I need someone on my side.

I'm a lost dad. There are plenty of us out there but we remain under the radar, unable to shout out our frustrations. We'll never meet, of course. But I'll tell you my version of this shit life and perhaps one day you'll tell me yours. We just want a voice.

I have another beer. Switch on the TV: watch *Pointless,* the title of which seems appropriate to my situation. Then the phone rings. This is it. My mouth goes dry. I answer feebly, 'Hello?'

'It's me, Isabel.'

This time her voice is soft. I haven't heard that for a very long time.

'Hi.'

'I got your email.'

Silence, as if I'm supposed to second guess her.

'And?' I mutter.

Silence again, then: 'I've been unfair on you, Will. Your email brought me to tears. I've misjudged you. I realise now that you are as fucked-up as me. Only I show it differently. I cope by putting a wall up. You're desolate, I know, and just want answers.'

'Just like you,' I say, in response to the last bit.

'I've been in denial, but yes, just like me.' I sense she is sipping from a glass of wine. Then she continues, 'I must say you scared me. There is a lot to consider and not all of it I agree with.'

'Which bits?'

'Not now, Will. I can't analyse it in this state of mind. I just want to let you know that I'm on your side and we can work something out. I can do some research and check out the facts. It'll take time so I need your patience, OK?'

I don't have patience, and ask, ' How much time?'

'Don't push me into a corner, Will. It took a lot for me to phone you. You can't just accuse people of wrongdoing just because you have a hunch.'

'It's a conviction, Isabel.'

'Maybe so, but we need to do the research. I can do that.'

'What do I do in the meantime?'

'Stay calm…'

'I'm struggling with that concept.'

'If it's any help, I think what you say in the email makes a lot of sense. I'm not on the case for obvious reasons, but I can approach my superiors and put your theories forward. Let them do the rest, OK?'

'Will they take my accusations seriously?'

'Absolutely.'

'Jimson doesn't.'

'I will go above him if necessary.'

'Thanks, Isabel.'

I love saying her name, especially when said so tenderly. I pick up on her reaction as she sighs heavily. It takes an age before she responds.

'You're not alone with this, Will.'

'Sometimes I think I am.'

'Sometimes you have to trust others.'

'I don't trust Jimson.'

'Try.'

'I feel like it is the end of things.'

I hear myself gasp, tears welling up in my eyes.

'Have you eaten?' she asks.

'Yeah…'

'Get an early night, Will.'

'Are you alone?'

'Yes, I'm alone, Will.'

I can sense the indignation in her voice.

'Can I come over?'

'Not tonight, I'm tired.'

Not tonight. My heart leaps into my mouth. This implies I can go over another time. It lifts my spirits.

'Goodnight, Will.'

Then the phone clicks silent.

I retreat to my bed, drunk on emotion. I cry like a baby and pull the duvet over my head shutting out the harsh world that invades my brain. But at least I have one thing going for me. Isabel and I have started those first important steps toward each other once again. I sleep.

*

In my dream, I see faces, people who have shaped my destiny down the years and in particular, my brother looms large. David has been a huge influence, steady and focused, whilst I drifted and searched as a youngster for some kind of meaning as to how fate conspires against us as individuals. Whereas I see negativity, David was always the positive one. You know, the glass always half-full/half-empty thingy. He pulled me round though, I guess. Saw that I was meandering and got me into teaching and somehow I flourished. I was good with kids. For a long time, I loved my work, but I was a stick in the mud. David, on the other hand, was ambitious and became deputy Head and then Head. He had the respect, status and income to match his ego. I wasn't envious of him, because I never wanted the trappings of success. He had a big house and a prestige car. I had a tiny cottage and an old banger. But it suited me. Whenever I got caught short, he was the one who always coughed up with the readies. He bailed me out several times, and naturally, I feel indebted. Then his dutiful wife fell ill, and they had a tough time. Eventually, her illness forced her into a wheelchair. I noted that David became distant from her as the years slipped by. He could help me with cash, but he wasn't a carer to her in the true sense. He employed nurses; as if all problems could be solved with money. That was his way. In spite of everything, he stood by her though but I couldn't help feeling that this was to do

49

with how people saw his standing in the community: steadfast and loyal, a beacon of nobility.

In later years, David took to coming on holiday with us, mainly camping around France. It was his escape, I think. They were good times and we were close. Sometimes Isabel resented his presence and wished for our time to be just the three of us, especially when Daisy started to grow up. We kept some holidays apart from him but I couldn't push him aside altogether: he's my brother. But we managed it, insisted upon by Isabel. Our last trip which included him was to Carcassonne, as I have already told you. David is a serious wine buff and this area, known as the Languedoc-Roussillon region, was rich and fertile for the cultivation of red grapevines. He was in his element and became very knowledgeable in both wine growing and the local dialect. I, of course, was crap at speaking French so as usual felt inadequate. Isabel and Daisy could get by. But they were terrific times and I remember each vacation with immense fondness. Isabel and I agreed on our final return home that, because of Daisy's age and growing independence, we would call a halt to this type of holiday. Daisy was restless and a little distant anyway, as girls tend to be at this impressionable age. Basically, she was starting to outgrow us.

My dream was full of good memories, dry hot summers and plenty of laughter (and alcohol). I thought of Isabel and realised I had not put enough into our marriage. She had a demanding job and was trying to live from under the shadow of her father in the force, who was a top man. It was tough. For the first few years after Daisy was born, I undertook the task of raising her. It made sense. I left my teaching post and became a house husband. Later, I took on the job of being a part-time counsellor. It was a good choice that we made: Isabel was the dedicated one, the professional. I took the slow road. I regretted not making my mark, but I never resented my role of bringing up our daughter in her early years. It was the best thing I did. Perhaps Isabel resented me for it because Daisy and I became so very close. We shared everything.

Then the *bad* thing happened. I awaken with a start, soaking wet in my own sweat. My head thumps and I feel nauseous. I stagger to the bathroom and drink water and I am feeling dizzy. *Christ.* For a fleeting moment, I had escaped my torment and floated on cherished memories...memories without shadows cast over them. But my happiness is short-lived. It is dawn. The alarm shrills. I shower and drag on jeans and a white T-shirt and make tea and crumpets. Then I think of young Romain and his obsession with Daisy. My stomach ties in knots. He niggles me, even though he doesn't fit in with my plans. I hope when Isabel wakes this morning she'll still take my claims seriously. Then he invades my space again. He could so easily have followed our daughter over here to England, tracked her down. He knew of our whereabouts from his parents' address book. Perhaps he hitchhiked to Calais, took the ferry over the channel. He would then have been on our doorstep. My imagination goes into overdrive: He watches her and then approaches her. My girl rebuffs him. Then he turns nasty...

I'm torn between my heart; it responds to Meg's cosmic enlightenment (the conviction that a link exists between the two murders), and my head which follows most strongly towards the culpability of this young man. I'm tempted to phone Isabel but think better of it.

Instead, I shave and catch sight of my gaunt features in the bathroom mirror. My deep set eyes have a lifeless look about them, like distant uninhabited dying moons. Grey flecks my hair, which needs cutting. My cheeks are hollow, my skin pale and flat. I splash water on my face and inspect my teeth, which are probably my best feature: white (in spite of fagging) and neat. My smile used to be my best asset but I have forgotten what to do with my lips. Come on, what is there to rejoice about?

It looks cold outside so I grab a zip-up jacket and make for the car. Another day: another shit-hole experience awaits me.

*

My boss, Ms Bottomley (a staid woman, also incapable of smiling) calls me into the office and gives me a kind of dressing down. It concerns my comment to the local newspaper about the insensitivity of trying to relocate Meg during a time of hardship, highlighting her cancer as a reason for the big bullying business to leave her alone. Someone with influence at the council has obviously come down on her hard and now I'm getting the backlash.

Basically, "zip it," I'm told; do my job, leave the politics to others. I nod compliantly. I hate these faceless corporations and the way they trample roughshod over everyone in the name of progress. I'm dismissed for now, given an official warning by my boss, who almost smiles (at last) at this rebuke. I know she feeds on the power.

Come lunchtime I buy a revolting plastic tasting sandwich from the local supermarket and digest it with a Zero Coke. I have a sneaky fag on the street and try to uncoil from the meeting. A car goes past, window down, and the driver who obviously recognises me, shouts "wanker" and then speeds off. Charming. A woman passes on a bike, stops and expresses her support for what I'm trying to do to help Meg's cause. I didn't realise I was such a local celeb! It still baffles me, the way people are divided. It seems you can't please everyone with your endeavours.

Sadly, it won't be long before Meg passes away, I surmise. There's no getting away from it. Then they can do what they like with the fucking road. In essence, they'll just cement over her life as if she never existed; gone in a flash. Until then, I think she deserves better.

My mobile rings its familiar tone.

'Will Farmer,' I drone.

'This is Portsmouth general hospital. We are sending Meg Faulkner home today by ambulance but she has asked me to contact you in the hope you will be able to come and fetch her. Is that possible?'

'What time?'

'Within the hour would be good.'

I check my million-dollar Timex. 'I'll be there.'

We disconnect. I chuck my fag in the gutter and make for the car park. Sometimes, I feel totally disconnected with the real world. It seems too hard for me.

*

'Bless you,' Meg says.

I help her to the car in a borrowed wheelchair and slowly position her so that she is comfortable beside me and then I get going through heavy traffic. She looks drawn and fragile as if disappearing before my eyes. I hold back the tears.

'I'll make a lovely cup of Earl Grey when we get in,' I announce cheerfully.

'Perfect. Have you been feeding the cats, Will?'

'Yes, and I've watered the plants.'

'You're a saint.'

'Hardly.'

'Will you have the cats when I've gone?'

I glance over. 'Definitely not!'

'You're a bad man, Will Farmer.'

There you go again: contrary folk.

We get in, I turn the heating up. The cats look at me with that bored look they reserve especially for me. I feed them first (under instruction from madam) then make a pot of tea and put some biscuits on a plate.

We huddle by the gas fire, Meg wrapped in an extra blanket I've brought her. She feels the cold even though it's still summer.

'Tell me about Daisy,' she says.

'I thought I had.'

'Tell me more.'

So I tell her. I rabbit on for what seems like an hour, uninterrupted. I feel guilty that she has only just come out of the hospital but not once does she nod off or take her eyes off of me. She has beautiful sensitive eyes. In her youth she must have been quite a catch. I've remarked on her beauty before.

At the end, it's me who is exhausted. My tea has gone stone cold.

'Feel better?' She asks.

I raise my eyebrows. 'I guess so.'

'It's good to unburden yourself, Will. It's cleansing.'

I nod, feeling the tension unravel from my shoulders.

Then she floors me.

'Now be quiet whilst I tell you about Daisy.'

How is it possible for a relative stranger to gauge the character of someone who is deceased, and grasp how that person felt about things? It is impossible in my book. But Meg has empathy. Perhaps being a mother herself gives her this unique view…who knows? What surprised me was the bond they seemed to share, as if Meg actually knew her. I sit gape-mouthed as this lovely kind lady paints a picture of my daughter as if she is sitting between us right now, as she describes her weird humour to her deepest fears. Meg explains that Daisy is

52

"here" in essence and that I should take comfort from the pride I have in her. Meg talks about Daisy's love of art and dance and photography, and her ambitions to be an actress, which I confess I wasn't aware of. I always thought she would be an artist or writer, or both. I do take enormous consolation from her words and yes, my eyes do mist over. Then the mood changes…

According to Meg, my daughter was also troubled but, frustratingly, she cannot get to the bottom of it at this precise moment. The vibes apparently are not ideal.

I'm sceptical but hooked. *Wouldn't you be?*

Meg says, 'Daisy is holding back from me…'

'Why?' I ask. I was feeling vulnerable; a little scared of grabbing at thin air as if my life depended upon it. I *so want* Daisy to be in my presence. Equally, suppose Meg is duping me. I'm perplexed. However, what motivation was there for her to do this though? I hate being used. Was I?

'She sees trouble…'

I jump in: 'What trouble?'

'*Someone* is giving her grief, and she doesn't know how to handle it.'

'Who is giving her grief?'

'She is frightened.'

'Frightened of whom?'

Meg goes quiet, and then she stares at me in an odd way.

'You…' she ventures.

'Me?'

I am flabbergasted, my throat tightening.

'*Me?*' I repeat.

'She wants to warn you…to make you aware…'

'Of what?'

'That someone is hurting her.'

I'm in a rage.

'Stop it, Meg! Stop it right now!' Now I do sense trickery.

I bounce up off my chair and circle the room, almost spitting blood at this intrusion. Just moments ago, I embraced Meg's words…now I'm scared stiff of her candid revelations. This is altogether different: something sinister from the dark side. How dare Meg suddenly change the mood? I was excited, now I am utterly overwhelmed with guilt.

I return to my seat, but remain standing and confront Meg. 'I don't need this…you're doing my head in. What are you playing at with this hokum-pokum nonsense?'

She remains calm, serene even. 'Will, sit down. I tell it as it is.'

I do as she commands. 'This is hurtful, Meg. I don't know of any other way to react…help me understand, please…'

'Daisy is reaching out, but she is still afraid.'

'Of what?'

'…Of letting you down.'

'Tell her she couldn't possibly do that!'

'I'm losing her, Will!'

'Keep her with us…I beg you!'

'There is a dark object, something you have to find…'

'Christ, what dark object?'

'She shivers, Will, and speaks a name but I can't pick it up…she's disappearing I'm afraid.'

I watch horrified as Meg slowly slumps back into her armchair, and closes her eyes with extreme tiredness. I feel helpless and leave her alone, refreshing the tea to keep myself occupied. She sleeps for an hour but I don't dare disturb her. Instead, a million agonising thoughts run through my head. I hardly dare believe our absurd conversation…it is just impossible to digest. I crash onto the sofa, totally wrecked.

Eventually, Meg stirs and I can see immediately the compassion in her eyes. She is as upset as I am. It takes ages for either of us to say anything.

'Will you help me to my bedroom, Will?'

'Of course.' It takes a big effort as she is weak and unsteady on her feet, but we get there in the end.

'Can you manage some toast, Meg?'

She nods.

I fumbled around in the kitchen and bring a tray up.

'Do you want me to stay tonight?' I ask. 'I can kip down on the sofa.'

She smiles. 'No, Will, get home to your own bed.'

'Will you be OK?'

She nods again. 'You know, don't think badly of Daisy, Will. She came to us voluntarily, after all. What's done is done. Like Miriam, she is in a suspended place and it disturbs her as well to see me reach out like that and not make the connection. It's a big effort, I can tell you. I have a gift of sorts but I'm no miracle worker. Whatever needs to be communicated is all that I can do, be it good or bad. I cannot manipulate the words of the dead, and that is the truth of the matter.'

I haven't a clue what she is talking about, so I simply say: 'I need to know the truth, however bad it is.'

Her words in response are calming to my ears. 'Then she will return, Will…just give it time. She trusts me to tell the truth.'

I leave her to sleep peacefully and return home in a daze. Is Mystic Meg a crackpot, a lonely recluse? Somehow I doubt she is a crackpot. And if I can defer disbelief and trust implicitly in Meg's words then…my heart skips a beat…surely Daisy would come back to us, as Meg promises.

I sleep deeply but have no idea how. I just feel the protective shield of an angel floating above me, guiding me home.

*

My mobile rings. I awake startled and check my watch. I have slept in late and my mouth feels all furred up. It takes a moment to get my jaw working.

'Hello,' I mutter.

'It's Isabel. Have I disturbed you?'

My brain clears in an instant. I sit up in bed, locate a glass of water and guzzle madly.

'Are you all right?' she asks.

'Yeah, what's doing?'

'A bit of information, I said I'd get back to you.'

'I'm anxious to know anything…'

'The French gendarme has investigated the whereabouts of Romain Petit and so far have come up with a blank.'

That's not information. 'He's disappeared?'

'Not necessarily. Apparently, after we left in July he continued to work locally, mainly at the winery in the village, doing odd-jobs. He lived at home for two months and then, after an argument with his folks, decided to up sticks.'

'And?'

'And…so far he hasn't been seen since in the region.'

'So he has vanished?'

There is a moment of hesitation. 'More likely keeping his head down,' she says.

'Jesus, Isabel.'

'A friend of his suggested he found work in a restaurant in Paris which has been confirmed. He was there for about a week, probably to earn some money. He was staying in a hostel which cost pennies, and so we assume he managed to save some of his wages. Anyway, that's where we draw a blank.'

'So he wasn't far from Calais?'

'Just as you imagined. Remember he has already been interviewed.'

'Are the police checking the ferry passengers again?'

'Of course, but this will take time. There is more than one port.'

'We haven't *got* time, Isabel.'

'Everyone leaves a track to follow, Will, especially a farmer's boy. He can't be that smart.'

'Smart enough to…'

'Don't say it, Will.' She hesitates. 'We don't know enough about him yet to start accusing him of things. Just remember that this all comes from your initial suspicions. He could be an innocent boy caught up in misguided love.'

I'm not persuaded by her reservations. I just want to beat the shit out of him, but then I check myself for fear of jumping the gun. The boy remains a long-shot. I am clutching at anything to justify my wayward conviction as to who killed Daisy.

Someone is giving her grief,

Meg had said. So it has to be him. There were too many instances of friction between them for this assumption to be ignored. They were always having words. On one occasion we even cut short our stay and moved up the coast nearer to Marseille. Did he have a plan to follow her to England? I'm more than convinced he did. I wanted to blame anyone, in spite of Meg's view. How desperate was I?

'Isabel,' I say after a long pause, 'keep with this. If he had money from the restaurant then he could afford the ferry over to England. We need to find him.'

'I know, I know.'

She seems preoccupied.

'Are you losing faith with this idea of mine?'

'No, Will, it's just…'

'Just what?'

'I said I had some information. We have another suspect.'

*

I sit in an office, opposite DI Jimson. We are alone.

'Well?' I ask nervously.

He brings up a folder from the desk drawer, opens it and begins to talk, not looking up from the file. 'We have formally detained a man late last night. He is not local but visits the area each month on business. He stays at the Best Western. On this occasion, we arrested him for molesting one of the waitresses in the car park just as she was going home and he was out there having a ciggy. It turns out that he has done it before, in another town.'

'What…having a ciggy?'

I instantly regret my crass comment. It was simply a panic reaction.

He ignores me. 'He's a dangerous guy. We suspect he is a predator of young girls, but he's clever too or just damn lucky. So far no one has come forward to bring charges against him, including this unfortunate girl. This is where we hit a dead end. Although she was clearly manhandled he blames his behaviour on excessive drink and the fact that she egged him on, which is his defence: his word against hers.'

'Is he here now?'

'Yes.'

'Why is he a suspect in regard to Daisy?'

'Because, on looking into it further, we discovered he was staying in this area at the time of her…murder.'

I pick up on the hesitation. Jimson had been to a party at our house a couple of years back and I reckon he is embarrassed to use such a blunt word in these circumstances. It is not an easy word to say when you are familiar with the father's anguish.

'We are checking DNA comparisons,' he adds before I get a chance to jump in with the same request myself.

I ask, 'Is the girl OK?'

'A bit battered, but he was verbally abusive as well…and threatened to kill her.'

'And that's why you are treating him as a serious suspect.'

'He fits the profile, young, strong and sexual in his intent.'

Meg reaches out to me, and I am guided by her.

'When are you interviewing him again?'

'Today.'

'Is he married?'

'Yes.'

'Kids?'

Jimson's eyes scan down the file pages. 'Two,' he concludes.

Intuition is a powerful weapon…

'How old is he?'

'Thirty-nine.'

I must believe in this, follow this route…I sense our daughters are calling us, showing us the way. None of it makes sense…but I'm not about to turn my back on them.

I lift myself from my chair, Jimson follows suit. We shake hands.

'I will, of course, keep you informed, Mr Farmer.'

I note the formal tone again.

'Not necessary,' I say and make for the door.

He hesitates. 'Pardon?'

I turn and speak slowly. 'He isn't the one.'

'How can you say that?'

'I just know.'

'OK Smartass, how do you know?'

Not so formal now.

I watch him gather his papers in a huff.

The first murder was in 1973.

This guy wasn't even born then. Besides, I back the police on one thing: Daisy knew her killer. She never ran. Unless we get a full confession from someone like this, which I doubt; or from young Romain for that matter, then I'm starting to stick with Meg's crazy assertions until I hear otherwise or they cart me off screaming to the loony bin. Then I might have to reconsider my viewpoint. Misguided or not, she knows something that I can't explain even to myself. But I have faith.

I have no faith in Jimson.

'What about our investigation into Romain Petit then?' He asked. 'Because of his age, can we drop this costly line of enquiry as well?'

He made sense but my bitterness spilled over.

'Mark my words; I just know the suspect you have conveniently found isn't the one,' I say. I am full of contradictions. I am convinced he is not the one. Me and me alone believe it. Am I getting sicker by the moment?

Chapter 7

Isabel is still annoyed with me for being so dismissive with Jimson. In her opinion, they now have a legitimate lead and Romain Petit suddenly fits neatly in behind this new and persuasive line of enquiry. I don't go along with it, as you are aware. I have my reasons, although my reasoning is becoming suspect.

We are on the phone again, which I don't like. I'd prefer to be face to face.

'Don't be arrogant in your assumptions, Will.'

'I'm not.'

'Romain can only be considered as the killer if we can prove he came to Britain to do just that.'

'I know that...but there are other options to be explored.'

'What other options?'

I fall silent.

'You are so contrary, Will. One minute you want me to do this, the next minute you want me to follow that...What planet are you on, eh?'

'Meg says...'

She ignores me. 'Cut the claptrap and see sense, *please*. This new development is a stronger link.'

'In your book, yes, but I believe that there is a stronger link between Daisy's murder and that of Miriam Faulkner back in 1973.'

'On what assumption?'

'There are too many similarities to be ignored.'

'You're off again on the merry-go-round, Will. That is based on conjecture. Next, you'll be blurting on about the forty-year gap...'

'This man is only thirty-nine.'

'Romain is in his early twenties, so you're not making sense if you want to make an issue with regard to age being a barrier to a double killing.'

'There is a line, Isabel, a connection...but we haven't found it yet. It doesn't exist with this oddball you have in custody.'

'Sometimes you can be so pig-headed.'

'I believe in Meg's prophecy...it has substance.'

'Meg, Meg, fucking Meg! How about giving us a little slack, eh? We're not complete morons down here. How could Romain have a connection with Miriam's slaying, have you thought about that? You're way off track...'

'It's in the line.'

'What fucking line? Forget Romain for a minute, and consider this: there wouldn't be a forty-year gap between the slaying of two girls and nothing in between if there was a link...it simply doesn't make sense.'

'Who said there was a gap?'

That stops her momentarily. 'We've been over this before.'

'I'm fed up with all this talking on the phone. *Please* can we meet up and discuss things properly?'

Silence.

'*Please, Isabel.*'

Silence like a tomb.

'I'm still your bloody husband…'

'OK, OK!'

I am ecstatic and push my luck. 'Tonight?'

I still feel like a leper.

'I suppose that will be fine.'

'I'll bring a bottle.' I instantly regret saying this…*too cosy by half.*

'Don't think this is going to be a regular thing, Will.'

'I don't.'

'Come round at seven.'

'At the cottage?'

'Yes…'

I was surprised, expecting her to suggest neutral territory.

'I'll make supper, she adds.'

Jesus fucking Christ. I'm stunned by her generosity which renders me speechless. Ten seconds elapse with me still holding my breath.

'*Will?*'

'Yes, I'm still here. I'll see you later.''

After I switch off, my legs begin to shake.

I shower and shave and do some body pampering. I'll repeat that: I shower and shave, and dab Ted Baker on my face and apply skin softener to my lips (I know, I know). I even comb my hair. To top off I pull out a white linen shirt (which I know she likes) and polish my shoes. I look half decent in the mirror.

On the way over I buy a bottle of Malbec from the supermarket. I am nervous and dry-mouthed and drive haphazardly all over my side of the road. I'm just not safe. I arrive five minutes early, clean my teeth with my tongue, grab the wine off the seat and walk up the cobbled path. I feel like a gawky teenager, all fingers and thumbs.

She opens the door and I fall in love again.

'You look lovely,' I announce far too eagerly.

She wears baggy linen trousers, tied at the waist and a pastel pink top, sleeveless, which shows her toned arms. Her brown/blond glossy hair is tied in a ponytail, which is kind of cute to my doting eyes. She's wearing no jewellery and no lipstick. The effort is minimal but I'm still captivated by her high cheekbones and wide expressive eyes. These eyes meet mine but she doesn't reciprocate the compliment. Instead, she hesitates and then moves back to let me in. I feel even more nervous.

I hand over the bottle of wine and she sets in on the sideboard and sips from her coffee. It is awkward at first but Isabel then turns to the kitchen and stirs a pan on the gas hob.

'Lasagne OK?' she says, not looking up.

'Great.'

The wooden table is laid prettily and I notice a glass vase with little yellow flowers sitting neatly in the middle. A touch of softness, thank God.

'Shall I open the wine?' I volunteer.

'Not sure I'll have any,' she says.

I fumble in the drawers for a corkscrew and she laughs, unexpectedly.

'*What…?*'

Isabel points with her eyes. 'It's a screw top.'

'Numbskull!' I bounce a hand off my forehead in mock stupidity but at least the icy atmosphere is broken.

'Make yourself useful and do the salad,' I hear her instruct me.

I do it willingly because I want to be relaxed and I feel useless just standing there. I want things to be how they were. I wanted to kiss her at the door but I knew it would be the wrong move, so I didn't.

Without thinking, I pour her a glass of wine but I notice she grabs it quickly enough and takes a swig. She's nervous too.

'If this isn't working, I'll just go,' I say, washing my hands.

'What needs to work, Will? You're here to talk about the email you sent and we then discuss it. End of story. But let's get this settled first: Carl thinks you're a complete prat.'

Christian name, I notice: 'Jimson?'

She's on a roll. 'What were you playing at, dismissing a genuine suspect in that manner? As if we are a bunch of amateurish twats…'

'I was out of order, yes.'

'You don't have an edge over the police, Will, just a crackpot idea about a romantic crush going badly wrong between a simple French country boy and an English girl. Is that all you have? The rest is…well, just plain crazy.'

'But you'll go along with it for now…maybe?'

'I must be crazy! For now, until we discover a hole in your theory.'

'We won't. Romain has been over here, I'm convinced.'

'We'll need more than that, Sherlock.'

'It gives him proximity and chance.'

'We'll see.' Then she mocks me, 'and did he also have proximity and chance forty-odd years ago, hmm?'

I see the stupidity in my reasoning, but I'm bullish. 'There is a correlation between the deaths.'

'Oh, yes, I forgot: Meg has decreed!' She laughs.

Isabel tosses the salad and plates up the lasagne, which is delicious, certainly better than my pre-packed stuff from the supermarket.

At least the wine goes down well, if not the conversation. Foolishly, I had drunk two lagers before leaving my flat (Dutch courage required) and I was now feeling the effects of the alcohol consumption. I'm exhausted actually. Shot through. I know too that I will be over the limit if I drive.

'Had you been drinking earlier, Will?'

Oh, hell. She's like a witch.

'Couple of beers…'

'How do you plan to get home?'

I'm suddenly bullish. 'Perhaps I can sleep on the couch.'

'Get a taxi.'

'Can't afford one.'

'I'll pay.'

I bite my lip, anger rising, 'Isabel, how about giving me a little slack, hmm? After all, I'm your bloody…'

'…Yeah, yeah…husband. I know, you have a habit of reminding me.'

I take another gulp of wine, emptying my glass. The bottle on the table is empty as well. Isabel sees my aggravation, leaves the table and miraculously returns with another bottle, already opened and half full. My anger intensifies. I immediately think that her boyfriend had been drinking from this bottle. I have to be careful how I react and I need to keep calm. She pours into my glass and I'm grateful though. The booze kills the pain but I'm currently hurting, big time. Confusion and alcohol are not good bedfellows.

She then slaps a tenner down beside me. 'You owe me that, but I can tell you need to say things so drink and talk, and I'll listen but don't expect a way back into my life. I'll call a taxi for ten o'clock sharp.'

I check my watch, one hour. Then I talk and talk and talk. And, unbelievably, she listens. I unburden myself. I bring up every issue that bothers me, tortures me, fucks with my head. Above all, I want to fuck my wife, right now. I'm in a dangerous place. She is cold, distant. I have to be careful not to make a fool of myself. Can she not recognise my desires… My natural physical needs? It dawns on me that she is sexually closed-off from me as I sit in the same room as her. I've done that to her. I'm shell-shocked. A thought enters my head: I bet she fucks her boyfriend in *our* bed.

I'll kill the bastard if I get the chance.

My resentment is getting out of hand.

'Can I stay over?'

'No, Will.'

'Is *he* coming over?'

'Let's not go there, OK.'

'This is my home, you're my wife.'

'I want a divorce, Will.'

I now know what it feels like to be shot by firing squad.

I echo those famous words: 'You cannot be serious.'

'I've thought about it for a long time, Will. I've tried to forgive; I've tried to forget.'

The past rears its ugly head again. Our secret, my utter shame…

I'm scared suddenly knowing full well where this is going. I've done this to her. Now she wants revenge of sorts.

'OK,' I say, deeply deflated. I know she isn't talking about Daisy. She's talking about me, us, our little secret and the secret I've tried to keep from you…

I knew this judgment would come to pass. It isn't going to blow over.

Her anger has boiled up and it's heading straight for me.

Our horrible secret kills us and I know there is no way back from this. I told you to keep reading if you dare. Isabel wants to move on, that is perfectly clear, and wants to put the past behind her, discard me from her life. Erase me. I've brought this on myself. I was hoping, praying, wishing for some kind of reversal of fortune, a way back in, some kind of compassion from her…but…but…I stop the torture for a second and reflect.

I need to calm down. Take a breather. You see, I've done this terrible deed and I want to drag myself away from the intensity of her accusing eyes.

I want to turn and run but my legs won't carry me.

Do me a favour and turn away at this point, would you? This is between Isabel and me and at this exact moment I cannot invite you in to share in her revulsion and my disgust. We'll finish here and I'll explain myself later when I'm more composed (and sober). I've done a shocking thing to her. It's a big deal and I'm not right in the head at this precise moment to explain things at this juncture. I'm well aware that some of you would call this cowardice, but back off just for a second. Give us space.

There are *some things* in life which should remain buried in a trench so deep and wide that nothing can bridge them. This is one of those things. And the timing isn't great either but she's not going to let me off the hook; so best to leave it where it is. I live with my shame as I listen to her cutting words as she lets rip. I feel dead as she puts another nail in the coffin with her venomous words. You don't really want to hear this so I'm not allowing you in… I'm happy at least that I have spared you this indignity and humiliation (for now anyway).

I created this situation; I now take the flack on my own.

Her seismic rant lasts a full ten minutes, face on. I can feel the spit from her mouth on my skin.

There, it's done. She's finished. You can come back in now. I find myself alone. I hadn't noticed that Isabel had left the table. When she comes back she says: 'The taxi is waiting. You can collect your car tomorrow if you like as I'll be at work early.'

I stagger up from the table and try to hug her but she politely pulls away and guides me to the door.

'I'm so sorry,' I mutter.

'So am I.'

'No, I'm really sorry, for what it's worth.'

'I know you are, Will, but some things aren't easily forgivable…and this is one. If anything, this evening has helped me decide on my future, so I'll speak to a solicitor later in the week to start the divorce proceedings.'

'You won't get any trouble from me.'

'Fine, we can make this as straightforward as you wish. I suggest unreasonable behaviour, and if you agree to this there is no need to contest the divorce…this way nothing needs to come out, OK?'

I'm grateful and relieved. Isabel could make so much trouble for me if she wished.

'Go home, Will. Rest up and tomorrow is another day. That's how I'll deal with it. One day at a time.'

'Can I at least still speak to you?'

She twitches. 'Of course, after all, we had a beautiful daughter between us. We have history…'

I cry in the taxi and I believe Isabel will cry too over the last of the wine. I feel the trench is at least a little narrower now, but still not enough for me to jump over. The fall would be the finish of me. I get home and now that we are alone I'll explain what happened earlier tonight. I know you are wondering: What the heck was that all about? Now I'll tell you. However, you might want to consider giving up on me after my confession, but I hope not. This is brutal, so I pour a good measure of whisky. I feel sick.

I lay awake on my bed in the darkness, cold and sweating.

Her words haunt me, kill me.

Why did this suddenly come up tonight?

OK.

Give me a second to compose myself: I will confess.

Hold fire. Deep breath…

Count to three.

This is the first time I have admitted this, even to myself.

My statement:

Six months after we buried Daisy, in a moment of drunken madness, I raped my wife.

Chapter 8

It was a combination of things, I suppose, which brought me to this hideously low point. Immediately after the funeral, I became impotent. It proved to be a temporary thing but in those awful months which followed, Isabel and I could not recover the spiritual or physical bond that we had before. We became like those insects hovering over a stagnant pond, avoiding contact but whizzing around all the same. We backed away from the big issues like, where was our marriage heading?

We should have been close; we should have drawn together as one. Instead, we withdrew into our own castles and pulled up the draw bridges to repel outsiders and nullify our raw emotions. If you like, each of us was besieged in our own fortress of guilt and sorrow.

I felt starved of affection but bottled any kind of confrontation. I suppose the tension built. For me it became intolerable. Eventually, I recovered my manhood and naturally wanted to have a physical release from my pain. I needed Isabel desperately but the more I pushed for action the more she shoved me away. I felt rejected and for a while managed to keep my distance. I suppose Isabel wanted hugs, I wanted sex. For me, it was the same thing.

Looking back, retracing my footsteps, I figure that sex to Isabel meant the prelude to the birth of Daisy…and it was just too damn hard to go down that route again so soon. She felt vulnerable, scared, betrayed, let down, pissed upon…who knows? But I was always the one who took the brunt of her anger. Because I was in the firing line no doubt. God, I screamed at her as well when things got too unbearable. I take my share of the blame. We were angry with each other for our loss. My needs, I'm ashamed to say, came first.

We lived with murder. Can you grasp that notion?

We survived but in a vacuum of emotional stress which we suppressed to the detriment of our relationship. We were sinking fast. One night, I suppose I snapped. I had been drinking all day and Isabel was angry with me and the whole fucking world out there. I'm not sure how it happened, but we started fighting, verbally at first. We managed to call a truce but later started again, over something trivial no doubt. This time I let fly with a few home-truths and she slapped me. I was stunned.

This time I didn't retreat but grabbed her wrists and tore at her clothes. We didn't even make it to the bedroom. I remember pulling her down in the lounge and at first, she responded. But then something happened, I have no idea what but she wanted to stop. I was hot for her and persisted, thinking it would be all right. She fought me but I overwhelmed her, pinning her down and then she began to cry. I was just too damn mad at this stage and cursed her name, blaming her for all and sundry.

She gave in and we had sex. I forced myself on her, not once but twice, about an hour later. That was my worst crime…the second time because I had the opportunity to consider what I had inflicted upon her and I was selfish to the extreme. She said nothing, but I could tell she was *gone* but at the time I had my rights, yeah?

Well, obviously not. I had done a bad thing, and she didn't talk to me for three days, taking refuge in her bed. After that, we slept in separate rooms and I have never touched her since that horrible day. She had her rights as well. Now the worst case scenario: divorce.

I am gutted. There is no way back for me. I have destroyed our marriage and must live with the consequences of my actions. Isabel could so easily have reported me and sent me to jail. But she didn't. I am a free man but I still feel imprisoned. I will never escape the torment of my brutality, especially upon someone I loved. I'll immediately correct that: someone I love. That will never go away. But the two most important girls in my life have done exactly that…gone away.

I am left with my dreams, which turn out to be mirages. All is lost. I drink and I smoke and I live. That is it. Just try to do some good, repair my conscience, knowing that at least I was a good father but perhaps a rotten husband…well, especially at the end. I got what I deserved. Isabel has found a new bloke and will move on. I hope she sells the cottage. I couldn't bear going past and imagining someone else in my bed, next to where my daughter slept.

I raped Isabel and in return, she allowed for me to carry on without punishment, although no doubt her delayed revenge is the termination of our marriage. I won't contest it and she knows I won't. I'll walk away and realise my good fortune. She could have nailed me, full stop. The ultimate control now lies with her, and she has decided to use it as I used her.

I send an email which reads simply: *OK. I will comply with whatever you wish. Let's make it easy and fast and without hassle. Will.*

It's done. I can draw a line. My past is finished. Now I need to look to the future but my next thought is David. He lent us the deposit on the cottage. I think it was five thousand pounds. We never repaid him and so that will need to come into the equation. I'll ring him tomorrow and explain things as best I can. I know he'll be deeply shocked. He hates any kind of mess and will view this as another failure of mine which of course it is. He is stoic and stiff-backed and the eternal organiser. I'm the loser, weak-limbed and wallowing in self-pity. He'll offer sympathy and support but I know under his breath he'll give a sideways glance to Margo and whisper "loser" in reference to me.

I'll handle his derision like I handle most things. I'll pretend I'm in another dimension. I'll block out all the shit and try to regroup, to find purpose in my life. Before the *bad thing,* I had a family, a marriage, a future imperfect but a future all the same. Now I exist within a vacuum and it's a horrible place to be in. I have to find the killer of my daughter. It consumes me. That is my only purpose left which has any meaning. Everything else, except helping Meg I feel, is pointless. She deserves my attention. Daisy deserves my attention. I might be a useless bastard but I can at least fight their corner. So that is what I'll do. You can either come for the ride or butt out. I want people on my side, not those who see things through jaundiced eyes. I have enough of that with the idiots who surround me. I'm on a mission now.

No more self-pity.

Are you coming with me?

Chapter 9

Isabel phones and I am surprised to hear from her so quickly. We don't mention the night before. It's too awkward. Instead, she lifts my spirits with her words:

'Will, I've just had confirmation that Romain caught a ferry to Portsmouth two weeks before Daisy was killed.'

Fuck. Perhaps my theory has substance. I remain silent, in shock.

'Will?'

'I'm here.'

'Did you get what I just said?'

'Every word. He was in the country as I suspected. Can we track his movements?' I say.

'We're onto it. It depends if he had money with him or he needed to earn his way.'

'Probably getting cash in bars or restaurants…'

'That's what we're looking into.'

'Hostels as well?'

'That too but he could have slept rough. At some point he would have wanted to approach Daisy. It's hard to imagine him coming over and not doing that…'

'He was obsessed, Isabel. He was hunting her down.'

'We don't know that, Will. She may have known or even encouraged him to come over.'

I dismiss this last remark. I am hardly thinking straight. 'But it is a good lead, yeah?'

'Thanks to you.'

'Are the police taking this seriously?'

'They are now…'

On the one hand, I am elated; on the other, I feel sick in the stomach. This is coming home to roost. I dismiss Meg's theory. I just want to clutch onto anything to find the culprit.

'What next?' I ask.

She states the obvious. 'We need to find him.'

'Do you think he is back in France?'

'That's the likely scenario. Again…'

'…You're doing the checks. And you have a good suspect already.'

'Correct. This is time-consuming, Will. We have the break-through but it has to be a patient and thorough search in order to find him.'

'I know.'

'It's not like in the movies. We want to be adamant this time…'

'I know…'

She adds, 'We'll get him.'

I like her confidence.

'I'll be back to you as soon as I have something to tell, OK?'

'Thanks, Isabel.'

'And Will…?'

'Yes?'

'Whatever happens, you and I will always be Daisy's parents, remember that. That will never change.'

I'm choked and mumble something but she doesn't respond. Then she clicks off.

Alone in the kitchen, I make coffee and begin to shake, thinking of this new development. It is a huge turn up and vindicates my suspicions. I'm overwhelmed and start to cry. I'm doing a lot of that lately. I can see an end to this nightmare. This boy just has to be found. But I don't feel triumphant, strangely. Instead, a new apprehension begins to creep over me.

If Romain is responsible for Daisy's murder, then my rant to Jimson had no substance. We are all being made to look like fools. *Who can I really trust?*

I gulp my coffee and feel uneasy, unsure. Pointing a finger at someone is simple. Proving them guilty is something else entirely.

*

I try to put these things to the back of my mind. I attend a meeting at work and on the agenda is a new property which I'm to show Meg. It seems this is the last chance saloon for her. So far she has rejected several homes, but I'm hopeful of this one. It's situated close to her existing house and she can use the same shops. It's also a ground floor flat with a garden, so she can accommodate her cats. Time is running out and I make an appointment with her. She seems receptive, the stubbornness in her evaporating. This is good news at last, but I remind myself that we have been here before.

The meeting concludes and I tidy up some of my files in my office, which is a cramped space at the back of the building without a window. I try to spend as little time here as possible. It sums up my life: lacking light.

I grab a bite to eat: one of those chicken & pasta containers from Tesco. It does the job, washed down with a cold Fanta. The drink bloats me. I read a text on my mobile from a friend, suggesting a get-together with the girls at the pub tonight. Seems like a good idea, but I'll be the only one without a partner. Still, they're a decent bunch and it will take my mind off matters.

Part of me wants to rejoice at Isabel's revelation on the phone. It's lifted a cloak of depression from my shoulders. Getting justice is a momentous thing when it centres on a member of your own family. Any kind of wrongdoing eats away at the flesh like a cancer. It slowly kills you. People say bereavement is slow torture and I now know what they mean. Basically, you suffer every day until you reach the grave. I want to stop this agony. I want to stop Isabel divorcing me but I'm asking for the impossible to happen here. *Hang on in there,* I say silently but my head is ready to bust.

I collect Meg in my car and she seems upbeat about the viewing, with a renewed energy about her. Whatever she's on, I want some. I feel like shit but I maintain my optimism for her sake.

Miracles do happen. She actually likes the flat. We spend time going around, trying to fit in the imaginary furniture. She even likes the neighbourhood and the nearness to the hospital. This could be the one. Actually, it has to be the one and I emphasis the point. I think she gets the message.

I take her home, get her comfy and make tea. She's tired and a little overwhelmed with such a big decision to make. I agree to help her move in and things look positive. We also agree that she can sleep on the decision and make an announcement tomorrow. We're cutting things a bit short but it is manageable. Luckily the vacant property is clean, with new carpets and fitted kitchen which the Council undertook. It's a no brainer, decision wise but you can never be sure with Meg. Deep down, I think she wants to simply go to sleep tonight and never wake up. I can't let her do that. I still need answers.

I'm feeling *mean*, and try to trick Meg.

'What's the name of Daisy's puppy?'

Without hesitation, she says, 'I'm not aware of any dog.'

Of course, we didn't have a dog, and I feel meaner.

'How do you reach her?' I ask.

'I don't…she comes to me when she is ready.'

'Why doesn't Miriam come to you?'

'She did at one time, but not anymore. The signal gets weaker somehow as the years go by. Maybe I'm just too weary to wire into these things from yesteryear.'

'How can I believe in what you say?'

Meg smiles and cradles her cup in her lap. 'You can't, Will. I'm no magician, nor am I a miracle worker or psychic. I've told you this. I'm simply a vessel of communication. Daisy is either here or she isn't.'

'And now?'

'She isn't.'

I make bread and jam, more tea and leave Meg alone. Tomorrow will be a difficult day for her. The decision has to be hers. There will be no going back. But it would be a truthful decision. I believe that she always speaks the truth. I believe every word she utters, especially after she mentions that Daisy had a pet hamster called Jasper.

I had never revealed this to her, and I doubt whether Isabel had either.

Chapter 10

I'd known my mate Philip for about five years. He's a good lad and normally fun to be around. He and his wife, Erica, had been there for me after Daisy's murder. We met at the local Badminton club some years ago. Philip is an electrician and he did some work for me. We struck up a good friendship. His circle of friends is pretty good too and slowly we formed a pub group which attended the Friday quiz night at the Dog & Bone. I carried on the tradition after Isabel chucked me out, finding comfort from the antics of this odd bunch. We have fun, full stop. They don't judge me.

Tonight, for the first time, I notice something weird as I sit with my friends. I'm a good people watcher. Grouped around a table I am aware that Erica sits away from Philip, and they seem distant from one another. Plenty of beers are consumed, the laughter raucous as usual and the banter wicked and close to the knuckle, but here is the thing: they remain uncommunicative, their eyes not meeting over a crowded room. Am I the only one noticing this?

In the toilet, I have my chance, standing with him at the urinals.

'Everything OK, Phil?'

'Just dandy, mate.'

'Erica OK?'

He glances at me. 'Smashing. Why?'

'No reason.'

We return to the table and the stand-off continues, I notice. At the end of the evening, we bade our farewells and go separate ways, but again there is a space between them as they stroll down the street without talking. I am none the wiser and decide to forget it. But it bothers me.

*

It's late. The phone disturbs me and I'm surprised to hear from David.

'I got a message…'

I'd clean forgot I wanted to speak to him but now wasn't the right time. I'm slightly pissed and don't want to say anything I'll instantly regret.

'Sorry, David,' I mumble. 'It can wait.'

'You sure?'

'Positive.'

'Well, I'm away for a few days. We can talk then.'

'Anywhere nice or is it business as usual?'

'Both.'

'On your own?'

'Yes, Margo is well catered for.'

Our conversations were always sharp and to the point. We didn't really *do* trivia. He had no time for it, too fucking busy for other people's problems: *Mr important goody-two-shoes.* His reference to Margo was code for *I'm getting out of here.* I don't even ask where he is going. Couldn't care less really.

Looking back, our trips to France with him in tow was hassle thinking about it. Isabel was right to put her foot down. As brothers, we have less in common as we get older. We have a bond but not deep love. Somehow that got lost, probably as he climbed the social ladder and I slipped off it. He was at the top looking down on me. He occupied the superior position and he knew it, often reminding me of my responsibilities and lack of success.

If I'm honest, I think I endured him, which is a terrible thing to say. I felt a duty to support him after his dear wife succumbed to her illness. I know he saw what befell her as a stain on his character. He hated weakness and saw her as a liability, but he remained loyal. His chance to escape with us to another world was my way of helping him overcome this blot on his landscape. At first, he was good fun. Later, Isabel felt the strain, Daisy too as David became demanding and controlling. He wanted to plan the whole itinerary; we just wanted to go with the flow. And so in time, we got him off the holiday agenda. He's been peculiar with me ever since.

'I'll give you a call in a few days,' I say.

'Sounds like a plan.'

Then he is gone in a flash. Mulling it over, I reckon he will be delighted with the news that Isabel and I are to divorce. He was beginning to find fault with her character recently and always managed to criticise her behaviour whenever I spoke of our ongoing troubles. *Better off without her,* was his last gem when we spoke a month ago. He was becoming nasty, not like the old David, who always found time for her when we were much younger. I reckon he was even smitten with her, but that was just me being consumed by jealousy. These days I suppose he is simply sick of me bleating on about my issues when, if the truth was told, he had more to cope with: the pressures of work and Margo confined to a wheelchair. Well, that was probably true until what happened to our Daisy. Then anything else paled into insignificance. Even David struggled with this and his way of dealing with it was to withdraw into himself, in denial.

Actually, he was intolerable for a while and kept his distance after the funeral just when I needed him the most. Maybe I didn't help. I went crazy and rejected his initial guidance, thinking I could handle things as this proverbial all-conquering tough guy, you know, me against the world.

I decide I'll go over next week and talk him through what was happening. I'd stay at his house if invited. Then we could start rebuilding bridges. I so wanted that even though he was a pompous asshole. Our childhood was fantastic, in spite of there being an age difference between us. David always included me in activities like fishing and took me under his wing. When he was around twenty-two though, he mixed with a different group of friends, became sullen and later a loner of sorts. He changed.

Our parents were wonderful and decent people. We were never rich but never wanted for anything. I was heartbroken when David joined the army, but it didn't last beyond three years. He then studied at Newcastle University and gained his first degree honours in English. His career was set and he took to teaching like a duck to water. I followed reluctantly; mainly because he pushed me into finding a position on Tyneside once he had his feet under the table. If it wasn't for him, I would have just drifted. Go on, laugh if you have to!

In our teens, we holidayed at Butlin's on the east coast and then our dad purchased a caravan on the Yorkshire moors which were truly great days. Our parents are now dead but I often wondered what happened to our caravan. It wasn't big but perfectly formed with a sun canopy that extended over the little makeshift garden at the front. A white picket fence completed our little piece of paradise. Funny how you hanker after the good old days of endless summers, whipped ice cream, strawberries in a punnet, funfairs, donkey rides, ghost trains, toffee apples, candyfloss and fish and chips wrapped in greasy newspaper: heaven to a kid like me who lived in the shadow of a hard city like Middlesbrough.

Days remembered. Days cherished. Days never to be repeated…

I can only recall one bad moment from my childhood and it involved David. Mum and Dad were summoned to the school. I think David was sixteen. It was something to do with a playground fight that carried on after school hours. Apparently, David had beaten this boy badly, even after being separated by his mates. He kept fighting and a small blade was used to cut the other boy's hand. The so-called knife was never found, David was disciplined and my parents shamed. It took a long time to live it down but I remember other boys being wary of David, who now had a fearsome reputation. He was tall, athletic and not to be messed with. For me, this was brilliant because I was never bullied at school because of big brother. Of course, I knew him as a softie, a boy who studied diligently and was generally very quiet. What happened with the fight I'll never know but it took a lot to rile David. He was a commanding type but would always employ words before fists to win an argument. That's why I found it odd when he joined the army. He didn't look like the adventurous type. The library seemed more appropriate. He loved his football too, and I remember him playing in a team with fancy shirts. He looked like a real Nancy boy, and I always got a clip round the ear for mocking him and his teammates, especially when they were beaten, which was often.

I try to sleep, but ghosts invade my space. It's like having worms crawling around my head. What is better: staying awake and being fearful of what lies ahead or nodding off and succumbing to nightmarish images reminiscent of Borsch's famous painting depicting Hell on Earth?

I decide on an alternative option and grab the brandy bottle and drink myself into oblivion.

The pattern is set, the decline terminal. Maybe that's what I wanted.

Chapter 11

Saturday: my weekend off. It's hot so I take the Rav to the carwash and head for the beach on Hayling Island. I park up and walk the endless shingle beach and gather my thoughts and try to banish the hangover from the night before. The surf crashes in, the gulls encircle a dead fish washed up amongst the seaweed. It is here that I'm at my happiest; where those damn ghosts cannot get to me. Sometimes I wish I had a dog and I'm envious of the young couples walking their trusted companions. I also miss companionship and the closeness of skin, holding hands and whispering intimate sweet-nothings. I miss Isabel dreadfully but try to shut the thought away.

I torture myself: Is she with *him* right now?

A big Alsatian dog muscles past me and dives headlong into the glistening surf; followed by shrieks of laughter from his owners. The dog is on a mission and swims strongly against the tide, ignoring the command of his master to return. I laugh too, then meander on and think of Meg. She has asked for the weekend to think things through, although I have made my position clear: it's now or never. I elect to give her space but reflect on her recent comforting words. She never pushes with regard to Daisy. I always have to ask. That gives me reassurance, the idea that I'm not being manipulated. I want answers, for sure, and I'm desperate to pursue any thread of communication but I like her easiness. She doesn't give me anything that I cannot believe in…even my horrible trick regarding Daisy's fictitious pet was handled with aplomb. Meg wasn't guarded or thrown by this…she merely answered my question without fanfare or mistrust. And she never asked for money for her trouble.

I feel much attachment to Meg. I genuinely want to help her find peace and fulfilment whilst she is still alive. She needs to know what happened to her daughter. The police bungled, I reckon.

Some mysteries stubbornly remain and hurt like an open wound. How had Meg endured this eternal pain for the past forty years? Obviously, her dear husband could not and died a sick and tortured man. He too must have had to withstand the suspicion that fell his way from outsiders. In the eyes of some, those closest to the victim were always deemed the guiltiest. It came with the territory. I have a huge amount of sympathy for his forgotten plight. I've been there. Got the T-shirt. Even today there is probably a few folks still alive who whisper his name with a pointed finger.

Look at me: I've been spat at, manhandled and had shit pushed through my letterbox. The police have verified my innocence publicly on several occasions in the past but there is always someone wanting to start an argument. I have to ignore it but sometimes it is impossible…and to fight my corner just brings the heartache to the fore again and in turn warrants bad press and intrusion. I don't want my name in lights. I want to be left alone to find my own path to redemption.

Mind you, I could start a fight with one particular person very easily, and damn the consequences: Daisy's killer. I just have to find him first.

My head is beginning to clear. The bracing sea air is doing the trick. I've perhaps walked two miles and decide to head back, this time with the sun in my face. I feel the warmth trickling through my veins and it feels good. I'm hungry and can almost smell the aroma of deep-fried battered fish and chips enticing me in at the headland café in the distance so I march on in anticipation.

The beach is getting crowded. I unbutton my shirt and remove it, tying it around my waist. I don't remove my trainers because the shingle makes walking barefoot difficult. As a boy, I cut my foot on this beach from a broken bottle and so I am forever wary. I don't take chances. A strange thought invades my head as my shirt sleeves flap around my legs: Whatever happened to Daisy's school jumper?

This sudden thought won't go away.

I remembered so clearly the police taking me to see my daughter lying stricken on the ground. She looked like a broken doll. Her school blazer was removed from her body and discarded over a fence. She was wearing a buttoned-up short-sleeved white shirt, so her arms were bare. Her skirt had been torn at the front. But her jumper was not accounted for. I assumed she had not worn it that day and Isabel has still got it. The thing is Daisy often took it to school but folded it up in her satchel bag. But, if my memory serves me well, she normally put it on for the return journey home and carried her blazer over her arm. I cannot recall anyone mentioning this or bringing it up during the investigation. Of course, it wouldn't matter if it was still in her bedroom but what if…

…it was missing? I've only just thought about it because my own bare arms are on show, just like hers. This has obviously triggered my subconscious memory. Had we overlooked something vital to the crime? I try to dismiss it because there is bound to be an innocent explanation and I will look like an idiot, a real plonker when it is found in her wardrobe. But it nags away at me like a bad toothache.

I get home and phone Isabel but she doesn't answer which makes me feel anxious. I vow to keep away from Meg and allow her to rest but phone her anyway. She answers eventually, a bit groggy, and I guess she is sleeping in her armchair.

'Hello, Will. Are you enjoying the sunshine?'

'Been on the beach and got a suntan.'

'Well, you be careful…it can get a bit fearsome at this time of the year.'

'Are you OK?'

'Just taking a nap.'

I hesitate, thinking my words through before speaking. 'Meg, something is bothering me and it concerns Daisy. Actually, it concerns Miriam as well…'

'Oh?'

Tread carefully.

'I'm sorry to burden you with this but…well, can you think back to the time of your daughter's death and try to answer a question that's playing on my mind.'

'I'll try, but I wouldn't bank on my memory being reliable.'

'Well, it's a long shot but do your best. When they found Miriam, was anything missing from the scene?'

'Do you mean from her body?'

'Well, yes…'

She took an age.

'Nothing was recorded at the time of the discovery.'

…*At the time?* My heart pumps.

'I'm picking up that there is a "*but*" coming next…'

'It was year's later in fact. Miriam had a favourite hair clip that she always wore because her hair was so unruly. Anyway, it wasn't on her at the time of her death. No one particularly thought about this, not even me. It didn't seem important. But going through her photos, that is, the one's that her friends took of her at the fair, it was clear she was wearing it. It had gone missing when they discovered her body.'

'Did you tell the police?'

'Yes. They searched the area in the woods again but it wasn't found.'

'Perhaps she lost it…'

'Perhaps, but Miriam was a tidy soul.'

'Or…'

'Say what's on your mind, Will.'

'It was taken as a keepsake by the killer.'

She drew breath, loud enough for me to hear. 'Like a trophy?' she asks.

We are silent.

'Will?'

'Yeah…?'

'*What* was missing from Daisy's body?'

Chapter 12

The weekend is over, nothing achieved. Sometimes I think I spend my whole miserable existence as someone else sitting in the wings. I wait and watch, the passive observer. It takes a lot for me to get involved and it is a fault of my nature that I hate the most.

A friend once remarked that the hardest part of making a decision was thinking about making a decision.

Just make the decision, act upon it and then things take care of themselves.

In other words, there is an order to life. I want to ask Isabel the question of the jumper but dread it all the same. But I ring and get her before she's left for work. This is considered bad timing because she is always tetchy in the mornings, especially when it's a Monday.

'I have a meeting in half an hour, Will.'

'I'll be quick.'

'Something you should know first. The suspect held in custody on assault charges has been released.'

'Oh, I thought Jimson was confident he had his man.'

'There was no DNA match linking him with Daisy.'

'I wasn't convinced by him.'

'Well, he's one lucky son-of-a-bitch as the waitress didn't press charges so he's a free man, but we'll watch out for him…he's a nasty piece of work.'

I was anxious to move on.

'I know you need to get on duty but hear me out. Do you recall what Daisy was wearing on the morning of her death?'

I can hear the long drawn out sigh.

'Where is this going, Will?'

I can also hear car keys jangling in her hand.

I begin with a starter for ten. 'Well, I know she was wearing her school uniform.'

'Spot on.'

'But I don't recall seeing her blue jumper when we got her possessions back from forensics.'

'She wouldn't have taken it.'

'I thought…'

'It was summer, Will. She wouldn't need a jumper when she is already wearing a blazer.'

'I know that, but sometimes she carried it with her and wore it home, taking off the jacket which always made her skin itch. She hated the birthmark on her arm and often tried to hide it which was not possible when wearing a short-sleeved shirt.'

'Correct, she carried the jumper, but not always.'

'I know, but more often than not…'

So why are you asking me this?'

'Is the jumper in her room?'

'Yes.'

'Have you checked?'

Silent reflection.

'I was never asked to check, so I suppose the answer has to be *No.*'

'It wasn't an issue at the time because it wasn't picked up by either of us.'

'Why are you asking now?'

'Because it's important.'

'You want me to look now?'

I speak from the corner of my mouth, 'If I can trouble you.'

'I'm sure it's there…oh, very well, hang on.'

I'm not going anywhere. I wait calmly and fully expect to be shot down at any moment. I can tell Isabel is fed up to the back teeth with my endless list of conspiracy theories.

'Will.'

'Yes?'

'It's not there.'

'Could it be anywhere else?'

'There are a couple of bin bags in the wardrobe. I'll look tonight. What are you thinking, Will? You've got me spooked.'

'Probably nothing.'

'Tell me.'

'Perhaps the murderer took it.'

'As a souvenir…?'

I blurt out my thoughts, mention Miriam's hair clip and hear Isabel gasp.

'Perhaps they still have it,' I conclude.

*

I spend the rest of the morning reading up on the murder of Miriam Faulkner. Between 1973 and now there had only been two recorded murders in the region featuring young pubescent girls, the other being Daisy. This clearly suggests no obvious link (as I had considered) and the long time span between the crimes also indicates this could not be the work of a serial killer.

This is the official view, rubber-stamped by Jimson.

However, the age of the girls, their similar appearance, the month they were killed, the dumping of the bodies in woodland near the coast and the manner of their deaths did point to a connection.

This is the unofficial view, rubber-stamped by me.

It requires a huge leap of faith to think that a young man (if we are to believe this) could molest and kill, sit quiet for all that time and then coolly repeat the same type of violent crime again. The very idea appears preposterous. Assuming the killer of Miriam was perhaps in his middle twenties in 1973 then, of course, he was now in his middle sixties, and still a free man. A dangerous man as well.

Statement: The police have not connected the crimes. Similarities do not make certainties and the evidence was and is scant in both cases. Hundreds of men were/have been interviewed and no one arrested. Back then there was no DNA profiling but so far it hasn't helped in the case of my Daisy, as yet. You need a match for this to work, and the killer in our case is cunning. He refuses to be found. At least my suggestion of tracking down the whereabouts of Romain Petit is being taken seriously. Or is it? I'm not sure of Jimson's commitment. He's been keener on the guy under investigation, now released. That says a lot about Jimson. I think the French boy is a strong lead now and he has to be found quickly. In my opinion, he is the prime suspect (at the very least he has to be eliminated from the enquiry).

But if that proves to be the case, then it also shoots down my theory that the two killings are somehow connected. It also means that I am fighting against my own argument, balanced on one hand by Meg's words of prophecy and on the other hand my fear of Romain's involvement as a lone killer. I would make a useless cop! Am I missing something from the equation? Statement: Romain was born in the nineties, eliminating him most emphatically from the first enquiry. So how come I have this deep, deep feeling that we are looking for one killer. Are the two girls not able to reach beyond my natural limitations as a mere mortal and give me a better grasp of the situation? Even Meg is struggling with this concept and she's the mystic queen. I need help. *Think, think.* Is there a second killer from the same family bloodline going back into history? It begs the question: Could this be a replica killing?

My brain is playing havoc at this stage, spinning around with absurd madcap scenarios that don't make sense…or do they? I snatch a sheet of paper and scribble furiously, determined to question the police about checking infantile crimes in France over the same period of time. I know that Romain's father, Remy, had a brother who had been in trouble with the police and was estranged from the family. He was considered a drop-out, a waster and unwelcome into the family fold. I learnt this during one of our stays at the farm but at the time it wasn't remotely important to us. It was just idle conversation. It was important now. Funny how these things suddenly lurch up from the subconscious mind when you least expect it. I'm clinging to any notion that keeps me focused. For instance, I was born in the early sixties and travelling funfairs were part of our childhood, made up of gypsy workers from all around Europe. Why not from France?

I make a note: Get Isabel to check the Petit family history tree.

I know that I'm all over the place with this, but you try filling my shoes. I'm desperate, rudderless and alone, abandoned by my wife and feel about as rudderless as the current predicament of my beloved football team since winning the FA Cup in 2008. Then, we were top of the pile. Now? We scrape the bottom of the barrel, deemed of no lasting value. A bit like the Euro as well: almost worthless. That's how I feel…of no lasting value.

I want above all else my dignity back. Although it appears that I've lost everything, I still wish to climb up from the floor and gain some begrudging respect from all those doubters that look down on me. You can laugh at me, ridicule me, even kick me when I'm on the canvas but don't be surprised if I suddenly kick you back, but harder still. I'm feeling sore, angry and wanting to fight with the devil. He just has to show his face.

Then we'll settle matters once and for all.

Do you want to bet against it?

Chapter 13

I do the weekly food shopping at the supermarket and a funny thing happens. I see Erica ahead of me and briefly, she chats to another man. Nothing weird in that, of course, but they appear close and dare I say it, intimate. Then they part and go their separate ways. Later, at the check-out desk, she sees me and waves but I sense she is embarrassed, a little awkward. The man is no longer visible and she soon departs ahead of me and out of sight.

Idly waiting in the queue, I think about her and this little liaison. The pair of them seemed cosy, close, almost breathing into each other's ears as they engaged banter. That's not how she would react to me for instance if I had suddenly engaged her in conversation down the aisle. No, this was something different. Something up close and personal.

I settle my bill and suddenly see this same man dash out from the manager's office. He takes an assistant aside, whispers a few words and leaves the premises in a hurry. I load up my Rav and find myself behind him at the traffic lights. He turns left and I need to turn right.

I turn left and follow him. I know, I know, I can hear your derision but I'm curious. I keep my distance for about two miles and watch as he pulls into the car park of the Admiral Nelson pub. I don't need to stop. I can see Erica's blue Mini already there. I drive on, perplexed.

So there it is. No wonder there was a distance between her and Phil the other night. What the fuck do I do now?

I have the world on my shoulders. I vow to keep silent, for the time being.

*

Meg looks me straight in the eye. I hold my breath.

'Time to move on,' she says matter-of-factly.

I want to hug her but refrain.

'Hallelujah!' I shout. Then I look out of the window and see a couple of reporters camped on the doorstep. At least they'll disappear now that they have nothing to report on. At last, the ballyhoo will die down.

'On one condition,' she announces.

My heart begins to sink.

'And that would be?'

'You help me pack up Miriam's room. I don't want total strangers going in there and disturbing her things…'

I smile. 'Of course I will, it will be a privilege.'

'I'd hoped you say that.'

'Shall we have some tea to celebrate?'

Megs nods gleefully and whispers, 'I have a bottle of sherry.'

'You little rascal,' I say, and follow her directions to the cabinet in the hallway.

'When do we move?' she asks.

'We have two days, Meg, but I can extend the time frame once the authorities know you have given them assurances of your departure.'

'Can you organise everything?'

'I'll do the lot. Leave it to me. I'll even help you settle into the flat.'

We drink a toast and sit quietly.

'Thank you, Will.'

'No need for thanks.'

'There is because I couldn't possibly do this without you. I thought I would never leave this house. I thought I would die here.'

'It holds a lot of memories, Meg.'

'Time to let go.'

'Time to let go…'

'I won't have a separate room big enough for Miriam's things when I move.'

'We can set it up as best we can in the circumstances. I'm sure we'll manage to squeeze everything in.'

'No, Will. Her time is gone. I need to move on from this place. We'll just box everything up and I know you'll help me do a good job. Some items we can discard.'

I'm surprised by this. 'Really? In that case, we'll do it together and as slowly as you want. Shall we start tomorrow and I'll come early. That way I can go back to the office and sort everything out today. There'll be paperwork to do and a removal van to book. It'll also give you a chance to prepare yourself this afternoon and decide what you are taking and what you can let go. Are you happy with that?'

'Happy with that.'

I know her words are hollow (she is actually devastated I reckon) but it is the right move for Meg. Her situation was getting desperate and the last thing I wanted was for her to be confronted by a forced removal with the media looking on. That would be a terrible ordeal for anyone. The shit would really have hit the fan at that stage. Crisis avoided, but only in the nick of time.

Now all I have to do is prepare myself for the job that I'm dreading: the emptying of Miriam's room. This will be a hard task and I wonder if Meg is really up to it. After all, her health is fragile and I worry if she has really thought this through. I am fearful that dismantling her daughter's shrine will impact on her well-being and cause further stress. I feel sick just thinking about it. And how will she cope with closing the front door behind her for the last time?

I'll be with her but I can't save her.

She reads my mind. 'I'll manage OK, Will.'

I have to believe it.

*

If I have a choice, I'll usually bite my lip in any situation to avoid confrontation. Most of us do. I sit on the side-lines and only fight my cause when I'm pushed in a corner. I now feel pushed in a corner. I've just had word that DI Jimson has called me in to discuss the investigation into finding Daisy's murderer. I get word of this from a text message on my mobile from Isabel. I'm to attend a meeting at 4 pm this afternoon. Perhaps something has materialised. My hopes are raised and I return Isabel's call.

My brief excitement is dashed by her manner: she informs me it is a routine briefing in order to keep me in the loop. There has not been a breakthrough. I'm feeling despondent.

I ask about the jumper and I get short shift. She'll apparently look in the bin bags tonight. This annoys me too. She should have done this by now. Then she tells me that she will be at the meeting with Jimson as well. This is when I start to feel jittery.

I make the big mistake of blurting out my latest theory involving Remy's wayward brother and suggest there could be a copycat killing to investigate. There is a long silence from Isabel.

'Are you still there?' I ask.

'Yes, Will. Is this something you intend to bring up at the meeting?'

'It has merit…'

Jesus, I hear her whisper.

'It needs…'

'Stop right there, Will. I can tolerate so much but this is going too fucking far. The only thing that needs investigating is your head.'

'I'm just trying to make sense…'

'Stop trying to do anything, Will, and leave it to us. Sometimes…'

'What?'

'Sometimes I think…I despair, look, just get a life, OK?'

'Oh, like you have done?'

'Back off!'

'Is that how it works?'

'Don't *ever* try to tell me how to live my life.'

'It seems too easy for you to move on.'

'Too fucking easy, is that how you see it? Do you think for one moment that you're the only one who still suffers from all this shit? I love my daughter and I miss her every single second that I breathe so don't try to lecture me on how to run my life, is that understood?'

I close my eyes.

'Is that understood?' she shouts.

I moan aloud and mutter: 'Yes, I'm sorry.'

She wasn't letting go.

'You need your head testing.'

Then the phone disconnects.

*

The meeting gets underway and I'm on my best behaviour. I am less bullish (as you can imagine after being berated by Isabel) and sit in a room with Jimson, another officer and Isabel, who occupies the seat next to me but away from me if you get my meaning. This, coupled with her uniform, emphasises the authority she holds over me in the office. I'm suitably humbled.

Jimson does most of the talking, and I feel that I am slightly spoken down to like I was an intruder in the conversation. Perhaps it's just the mood I am in. The damning news is that Romain had travelled to Portsmouth and found work in a bar as a bottle-washer and later in the kitchen of a downbeat restaurant. According to Jimson, it was difficult to follow his precise tracks but he knew our address and therefore it would have been easy to catch a bus to our neighbourhood. I'm sure he was over here to contact Daisy. What other motivation did he have for coming to the south coast specifically?

We were, of course, aware of his obsession with her during our vacations in France. At first, it was kind of cute that they went for long walks beside the river. My mind wanders back as Jimson drones on. One summer the French boy asked to take her to a village dance. We were comfortable with his protective arm around her and if the truth be known, Daisy was getting to the stage where she wanted her freedom from us. She developed that rebellious streak that all teenagers aspire to. She wanted to get a piece of the local action and as he was older it was easy for him to introduce her to a more fun way of life…more than we could offer, being boring old farts who saw a BBQ as the highlight of the evening. Yes, she was still the wonderful and dutiful daughter but she was changing, which was the natural order of things. He wasn't exactly *Mr Sophistication* but his tearaway attitude appealed to her…and he had a moped as well, which meant added excitement to her. Bluntly speaking, we had to give her the wings to fly. She did, and we became the immediate afterthought.

Where did it start to go wrong between them? Difficult to say, but Daisy did confide to Mum that Romain had tried to kiss her one day. No big deal but even I noticed he was beginning to get possessive, always trying to either tickle her or put his arms around her which she often brushed off. I think he began to swamp her. We tried to remain cool but it became difficult. They were kids testing out the sexual boundaries. One day she was lovey-dovey with him, another time gave him a verbal earful. Once, she stayed alone in our Gite and refused to join in at dinner and so he sulked as well and disappeared for two days. Basically, she was too young and innocent and he was brash, immature and high on hormones. She was an attractive girl and he was ready to push through the barriers. She wasn't.

Thinking back, Daisy was showing signs of withdrawing from our gang and began to distance herself from us. Something bothered her but she refused to discuss it with either Isabel or me. I thought she was just being moody and seeing us for what we were: staid, boring and middle-aged. Who could blame her? Even David got the brunt of her tongue on a couple of occasions and knew well enough to keep out of the way. Isabel laughingly labelled her as a *stuck-up proper little madam.*

We coped at the time with the tantrums but secretly Isabel and I had had enough. We no longer wanted the hassle. In future, Daisy could help decide our next destination, which would also exclude my brother. When we put this to her, she was gleeful and excited, and on our return home the brochures for Ibiza soon began to clutter up the lounge. We had been warned!

Sadly, what we didn't know was that our decision to let her spread her wings actually took away the future. Within a few months, our family was destroyed beyond repair. In truth, the future killed all of us.

'Do you want some water?' Jimson asks, aware that I was drifting off into my own little world.

I couldn't stay at their intellectual level: it was as if Daisy was an "object" to be discussed; an enquiry to be solved in order for the casebook to be ticked off and closed. This opinion was totally unfair on Isabel but it was tricky to see her as a mother of my child wearing such sober formal clothing and talking *officially* in a sterile environment to two men who wore the look of resignation and defeat on their faces.

We stop for refreshment. The room is hot and sticky, poorly serviced by the desktop fan. Jimson opens a window but it doesn't help.

'You're keeping quiet,' Isabel says, refilling my glass.

I raise my eyebrows in mock surrender. The last time I opened my mouth to her over the phone I got a broadside. So this time I elect to listen and learn. I'm not learning much. It's hugely disappointing to hear of so little progress being made.

We carry on, and I note Jimson checks his watch. He has a habit of doing that. It doesn't give me confidence in their endeavours.

'Is there anything you need to ask us, Mr Farmer?' he asks politely.

'Are you done with the guy held in custody?'

'We are for the moment but I'm sure our paths will cross again.'

I wasn't surprised by his release.

We muddle on. Most things have been covered but the general lack of urgency frustrates me. I'm well aware of under-funding and lack of manpower but statistics and league tables don't interest me. A crime needs to be solved. We need to move faster and be more decisive.

I spell it out. 'We need to move faster and be more decisive. I'm even more convinced that Romain (my only creditable link) is implicated now that we know his movements were centred in this area. He needs to be questioned again and soon.'

'He will, when we find him,' Jimson replies.

'Where has he vanished to?'

'He returned on the ferry to Calais on the 23rd of July. From this point, we have lost track of him. We are in daily contact with the French authorities and they are conducting a country-wide search for him. If he's still in France we will get him eventually.'

'Have you spoken to his parents?'

'Yes, but we are keeping it low key for fear of spooking them. We haven't suggested that their son is connected to Daisy's killing. Instead, we have asked for their cooperation with related minor offences which they can deal with. He's been in trouble before so this won't necessarily alarm them. A murder enquiry is a completely different ball game.'

'You mean they may protect him or help to hide him?'

'It's a possibility. If he surfaces and pleads for their help, they will obviously do so, as most parents would. But they may also be willing to contact us if they feel the crime is trivial and he needs reprimanding. So far, the news of your daughter's death has not reached over there extensively and so the regional TV programmes have not picked on it. That's the way we want to keep it.'

'The family know of Daisy's death…'

'Of course, but we don't want them thinking that our concerns relate to this matter. Let the French do their job and flush him out.'

'Have you looked into a pattern of similar crimes in his area? Perhaps Romain was a persistent sex pest and had a police record…'

The other officer, a short weedy man, intervened. He wiped his thinning scalp with a handkerchief as the sweat trickled down his face. 'We're on to that and currently the authorities there are comparing database files over the last ten-year period. It's a big area they are covering and extends from the Pyrenees to the Mediterranean. We should have that information in the next couple of days…'

'I assume then that Romain has a police record.'

The man shrugged. 'Mostly petty crime: car theft, breaking and entering, recreational drugs.'

'Assault?' I ask.

Isabel looks at me.

'Nothing serious,' he replies. 'He was once detained for carrying a knife and got caught up in a couple of local gang fights.'

I'm on a roll. 'Has he a police record for attacking women?'

'No.'

'What's his employment record like?'

'He trained as a chef and had various jobs, mainly drifting around the tourist spots but he didn't stay long at any particular bar or restaurant. He also worked for his dad on and off and also took jobs during the grape harvest.'

'Did he always live at home?'

'It appears so, although sometimes he got lodgings at a hotel if he was employed in the kitchens there.'

Isabel cuts in. 'We should check his employment records to see if he had any disciplinarian issues…'

It was a good point and the other officer jotted down notes.

'Anything else?' Jimson asks, rechecking his shiny watch, which I notice for the first time is very expensive. A Tag Heuer, I believe. I glance at my battered old thing, handed down by my father. It did the job just as well.

Jimson starts to rise from his chair.

'Romain's father, Remy, has a wayward brother,' I say.

Isabel shoots me a cutting glance.

'His name is Robert and if still alive today, would be in his late sixties by now.'

'So?' Jimson said, electing to remain standing.

'He had a history of violence and at some point worked in England.'

'What is the connection…?'

'I want you to investigate his whereabouts in 1973.'

'Oh, for fuck's sake…' Jimson rolls his eyes. 'You're going back to the Faulkner case, aren't you?'

'He could have been a funfair worker.'

'This is fantasy world. Are you suggesting that a family line of murderers exists which connects Miriam's murder with that of Daisy's?'

'It needs looking into.'

'I don't have the resources to do that, Mr Farmer. There is a forty-year gap between the crimes. It is unthinkable to suggest…'

I cut in. 'At least look into it. There is a clear indication that the murders were virtually copycat in design. Look at the facts: sexual, but no penetration. The girls were partially stripped down and items of clothing taken…'

'That's enough, Will,' Isabel replies sharply. 'We don't know that Daisy's jumper was taken.'

'Jumper?' Jimson asks, his eye darting between us.

I have his attention. 'Both girls were strangled. Both girls were similar in looks and build. Same colour hair. Both were school kids, both from the same area. Both crimes are as yet unsolved. The killer removed a hairpin or clip from Miriam as a keepsake. I'll lay a wager that the jumper is not found at our cottage.'

Jimson, annoyed, turns to his colleague: 'Check the records for any mention of a missing jumper, and look back into the alleged missing hair clip.'

I then startle myself. 'Why did the killer in both cases partly strip the victim and not have sex with them?'

The room falls silent.

'Because,' I add, 'they couldn't, for some reason, finish off the job they started. They had the power, the inclination but maybe not the ability to get an erection… Is that something we should be considering?'

Isabel gasps at my crudity.

'Because I reckon the bastard or bastards who did these vile disgusting things was or is impotent. That should help narrow the search down a bit, gentlemen…'

I depart the room fast, leaving the door wide open behind me. I hear Isabel shout my name but I don't stop. Outside, next to the car, I throw up unexpectedly.

I want people to start taking me seriously but it's like banging my head against a brick wall. I shocked myself in there with my sudden rant. It then dawns on me that Romain wouldn't be impotent at his age, which rather rules him out of this supposition of mine. I'm too eager in my confusion to place blame without thinking it through.

I throw up again.

Can you at least see my point of view through the contradictions or am I truly going mad, as Isabel suggested earlier?

Don't answer that.

Chapter 14

I'm still aggravated half an hour later and go for a drive. I need fuel and put twenty quid of petrol in the car and spot Phil ahead of me in the queue to pay. We chat and he reminds me of another quiz tonight and wants me there. I'm unsure but he persuades me that I need to let my hair down. I resolve to get smashed but then I think of the trauma ahead of me tomorrow with Meg and know this is a poor choice. I need a clear head as it promises to be a long day with the packing up of Miriam's belongings. In the meantime, Phil looks drawn and preoccupied, as if something is bothering him. I think of Erica in the car park and decide to speak to him when the time is right. I don't like to see a mate pissed upon.

I go to the office and organise for two helpers to accompany me to Meg's in the morning. It'll be a big job. I then book a removal firm to come over in the afternoon. The new place is having a final clean at the same time and I want things to progress fast and smooth in order for Meg to think ahead in a positive manner. If I can, I want to avoid tantrums. I don't want her changing her mind at the last moment.

The phone rings and its Isabel.

'I'm sorry,' she says. 'That was a horrible meeting.'

'Forget it.'

'I'm sorry for doubting you. I went home immediately and checked the bags in Daisy's room and there is no sign of the jumper.'

'So it is missing.'

'Seems so…'

'Could it be anywhere else?'

'I searched around, nothing. So you could be right.'

'She may have left it at school.'

'I checked the records and nothing had been handed in at the time.'

'Months have been lost on this, Isabel.'

'I know. But no one thought about it until you suddenly brought the subject up. The only explanation is that the killer has kept it.'

'I hope so; then we can use it as evidence to nail the bastard.'

We take a moment to catch our breath.

'Good news,' Isabel says. 'We're narrowing down the search for Romain. Apparently, he has been spotted working at a winery near the Pyrenees. We should get a progress report in the next twenty-four hours.'

'Great…'

'Jimson's a good one, Will.'

'You reckon.'

'Have faith, OK?'

'It's not easy.'

'We'll catch up tomorrow.'

I detect a softening in her voice which surprises me. From where I sit there are hard edges to everything, including the upholstery nail that is sticking in my arse from the rickety old chair I sit in.

*

I change chairs and get a splinter in my finger from the replacement. When it rains it pours… I have a stack of work to do and try to plough through it but my brain is all over the place. Frazzled is the best way to describe how I feel.

I get home at six and have a bowl of soup and a mug of tea. *I know how to live the high life.*

I shower and put on The Script CD to lighten my mood as I dress in navy cord trousers and a black cotton T-shirt. I decide not to shave and simply ruffle my wiry hair and splash Armani (the last dregs) on my stubble chin. I look in the mirror; not bad, I suppose. With any luck, I reckon I could pull a blind girl in a deaf school tonight and the good thing, in this case, is it wouldn't matter if the charm offensive wasn't up to speed.

I glance at the time and decide to walk to the pub. That way I can indulge myself tonight and not worry about being over the limit. Besides, the walk will do me good and it's still warm and muggy. Maybe a storm's on the way, as the weatherman on the TV had predicted, but I'll risk it.

Firstly, to get in the swing of things I grab a quick beer and clear up the dishes; then I'm on my way. The quiz is challenging (our group achieve second place), the crack even better. As you would expect on a hot night, the pub is packed and sweaty. I'm on my fourth pint, take a pee and get some air, have a fag and return to my table. Phil is beside me but I notice that once again Erica has found a seating space even further away from him this time compared to the last occasion I was with them. I observe the body language and at no time do they make eye contact. You would think there was an invisible wall keeping them apart. And then it strikes me like a hammer to the head.

The photos… Sometimes you don't always see the things that have been staring you in the face all along.

Like a madman, I make my excuses and race home, my heart pounding uncontrollably from what I think I've uncovered. It was *there* all the time. I get in, collect the box of holiday photographs from the wardrobe and spread them across the bed, my eyes frantically scanning the images. I discount many and those that remain I try to put into date order. There are probably forty snaps that grab my attention.

Fuck. The evidence has been there all along. I only pick those pictures that feature Daisy in the company of other people, notably our gang and concentrate on these group images in particular. I can't guarantee that I have them in perfect sequence but it is good enough to clarify my thoughts.

It seems clear but I look again for confirmation. Starting from the top line of photos, assuming these were from an earlier dateline, Daisy appeared comfortable sitting next to Romain but as the summers rolled by it was evident that they began to sit apart from each other. And as with Phil and Erica, the eye contact and general body language also illustrated tension between them as I progress down to the lower row. In fact, when I examine the most recent ones, I notice what I'd missed before: Romain either pointedly has his back to Daisy or stares, unsmiling, into the distance even when it was obvious that whoever was taking the picture (usually me or Isabel) was making the effort to include everyone. He wasn't playing ball and didn't care who knew it. This, to me, was evidence that their friendship was strained and difficult at times, just as Isabel had told me. I reckon that Daisy had given him the cold shoulder on numerous occasions and his mannerism, here in front of me, suggested a sulky kid making his frustrations all too obvious, to her at least. Who am I to talk?

I'm now more than ever convinced of his compliance in Daisy's death. Perhaps Meg is wrong. There is no connection between the murders. His sexual advances were obviously rebuffed by her and he probably felt aggrieved enough to confront her in England and vent his anger and resentment. Christ, maybe he forced himself on her during our last visit to France? Something happened between them to create a void as such. The photos point to this. I shudder. Was that motivation enough to kill her if she rejected him again?

It has to be a compelling argument. A picture tells a thousand words. I am reminded of the inescapable truth, written in her handwriting: *I don't like him.*

I'm shaking, and guzzle neat vodka in a tall glass to calm my nerves.

I'm also euphoric, satisfied with what I have found. *Thank you, Erica!*

Then caution takes hold. Photos never lie, or do they? I try to get a grip on the situation. I have to restrain myself from phoning Isabel and think better of it. The time is gone midnight. I can't settle and the buzz gets to me. I pace the room, the heat of the night prickling my skin. I go for a walk along the harbour front and breathe in the damp salty air. The estuary is still, the moon reflecting intermittently in the shiny deep water as the shifting black clouds roll in from the southwest. I am as mixed-up as the turbulent weather front which is promised during the coming hours by the TV weatherman.

I walk to the end of the promenade. There is trouble on the horizon, borne out by the first rumblings of thunder I can hear far out to sea. This echoes my situation: I can't see the storm as yet, but it is coming and the more I think about things the more I realise that this noise is just a prelude to the bigger thunderclaps that gathers behind it. In the same sense, I haven't quite grasped the enormity of what I'm seeing and feeling right now: the significance of the photos begins to truly scare me. A flash of lightning comes in behind the latest rumble, compounding my worst fears. I find myself backing off from the impending attack, searching for shelter, but I still feel threatened by an unknown force of nature. I'm reminded of The Doors song:

The killer awoke before dawn and put his boots on…

Someone killed my Daisy.
Who are you? Where are you hiding?
I run for home to beat the rain.
Once inside, I try to relax but it proves impossible.

I can't put a finger on my continuing unease. I allow all connections of Daisy's murder to influence me. Perhaps it is fact that I am her father and I want the whole damn thing settled! And soon…no stone left unturned?

I'm frightened.
What have I missed?

Chapter 15

I sleep fitfully, the storm fierce, and when the alarm goes off at six-thirty I am drenched in sweat. I shower quickly but cannot shake off this feeling of foreboding. I have a massive day in front of me and I'm already struggling to cope with the expectations. Meg deserves better and I need to clear away the crap in my head. I somehow have to put my problems on the back burner and devote myself to her. After all, she has her own misgivings of what lies ahead and it's a massive day for her as well.

And so to battle, I spoon down a bowl of muesli, make toast and black coffee and prepare a peanut butter sandwich for later. I manage to banish my nerves, drive across town and pick up my two volunteers, Kate and Molly, who I know will be sympathetic to an old lady's plight. We'll make a great team and on the journey discuss how we will undertake the task in hand. I am aware, of course, what my job will entail and I'll try to keep the upheaval as low key as possible. I'm sure there will be tears.

I phone in and notify my boss of our movements, and she tells me the empty cardboard boxes have been delivered already, stacked up by the front door under the porch.

We arrive at eight-thirty and Meg is up and brewing tea. Last night, the heavy rainfall washed everything down leaving the air clearer and cleaner and less oppressive, thankfully. This would enable us to work faster.

Meg gets on with my colleagues admirably and, after detailing the work rota, each girl knew what to pack and what to discard. We have a skip on the drive that, secretly, I hope to fill thus reducing the load for Meg to contend with at her new abode: her new beginning. I feel good (and anxious) in my heart.

I drag some boxes up into Miriam's bedroom and we began the slow and agonising process of deciding what to keep and what to throw out. The latter items were to go on the bed. After an hour there wasn't much on the bed.

Patience is the key in situations like this. Meg slowly goes through each item of clothing, a pile of shoes, school kit, books and toys and caresses each thing lovingly before handing them over to me to carefully pack away. I can tell this is painful and I don't rush her…instead, I listen and let her tell a little story to illustrate each memory of Miriam. Eventually, I go downstairs to make more tea and check on the girls, who are a marvel at this sort of thing. Most of Meg's possessions and furniture are already loaded on the van. Slowly, slowly, the house is being vacated. I never thought I'd see this day, expecting Meg to cling on and rebuff all intruders. Ugh, what a disaster that would've been!

When I return upstairs, Meg is sifting through some photos and smiling to herself. I have to remind her that time is slipping by and that she can go through the collection at the new house. I need to be firm. She nods compliantly and stops for tea and biscuits thus increasing my frustration. I eat my sandwich, I empty another drawer and come across a pile of old postcards. One catches my eye. It depicts a fantastic red and white helter-skelter featuring kids gleefully bombing down the wooden chute on the outside. Against an impossible blue sky, a slogan reads, "Have fun will travel!"

Somehow, this jolts my memory.

'Where was this taken, Meg?'

She looks over and says, 'The fair at Havant.'

I turn it over and see for myself. Then the horror of my lack of thoughtfulness strikes home. *Idiot, idiot!* I can't stop myself: 'Is this…?'

'Yes,' Meg simply replies, a tear forming in her eye.

I try to deflect my embarrassment by stacking some comics into plastic bags but I know the damage is done.

'People came from miles around,' Meg adds wistfully.

'I was there too,' I conclude. 'I reckon we travelled down to the south coast as a family for our summer holiday. Seeing this postcard brings it all back.'

'How old were you?'

'Eight or nine I guess. I recall being car sick on the journey.'

'Around Miriam's age…'

I'm digging a bigger hole for myself…

'Where did you stay?' She asked.

I was relieved that she thought to move on swiftly. It was difficult enough without further morbid thoughts. I had to think about her question. 'We had an auntie living not far from here actually. I suppose visiting her enabled us to take advantage of a cheap break.'

'Money was always tight in those days.'

Then I say: 'I've seen this postcard before *somewhere…*'

'There were thousands printed. Miriam collected them as you can see.'

Silence suddenly suffocates the room. I sift through the collection and put them neatly in a box and try to shift my guilt, fully aware that this was *the* fateful fair, judging by the postmark on the reverse of the postcard: the summer of 1973, the year Miriam went missing I feel like a complete prat.

I also experience an abiding twist in my gut. The postcard bothers me. Where had I seen it before? Why did it conjure up a bad feeling in my head? It was just a relic from the past but it disturbs me. My knuckles have gone white and I suddenly realise I am gripping the bedpost with unnecessary force. I'm sweating and feel giddy. I gasp for fresh air.

'Are you all right, Will?'

'Yeah, I just need a breather…'

'Be a dear and open a window.'

I do, but it is still stuffy. I take a break and steal a fag from Kate in the garden which was now in the shade, and a cooler place to unwind. Kate and I chat for a while. I can't get the image of the helter-skelter out of my brain. I can remember as a child the thrill of the funfair, for sure…the smells, the music, the gaiety but just seeing this innocuous postcard reacquainted me with something else…but I'm damned if I can think what it was. It's like a sinister tumour eating away at me. I chastise myself for thinking only of myself when Meg had a lot more to contend with. My irrational fears can be put aside for the moment, but I'm still haunted by the past.

I apologise to Meg for my crass remarks and she takes it in good spirits. We soldier on and by tea-time have the bedroom clear. The removal men dismantle the bed and carry it in parts to the van, the girls finishing off by taking down and folding the curtains. There was still plenty to do but I wanted to get Meg on the move. Surprisingly, I get her out of the house without fuss or histrionics, mainly with the promise of fish and chips at the local café. This we do, aided and abetted by a glass of fizzy shandy to wash down the dust in our throats. It's the least I can do. I can tell Meg is feeling vulnerable.

It's been a long and demanding day. Meg is shattered and I drive her to her new home. Although she seems a little lost, the girls have made the flat look homely in the circumstances; which helps her settle. Molly elects to stay the night which makes me feel good knowing I'm able to leave Meg in safe hands. It's a tearful farewell but I promise to call back in the morning. I get home, strip off and adorn a comfy tracksuit, open a beer or two which allows me to unwind. Overall, the day has gone well, without hiccups. I check the time: ten o'clock. I watch the news headlines on the TV and fall asleep quickly in one of the deckchairs.

Startled, I'm awoken by the phone.

'It's me, Isabel.'

It's late so I know something is up.

'Can you talk?' she asks impatiently.

I check the room for the bevvy of half-naked girls dancing around a pole and then realise it was a dream. 'Of course, what is it?' I ask in trepidation.

'Romain has been arrested.'

I don't know whether to laugh or cry.

Chapter 16

I awake early, having tossed and turned all night. I go over what Isabel told me on the phone: Romain had been tracked down to a campsite near Toulouse and arrested after a brief chase by the gendarme. He was now held in custody. According to Isabel, Jimson was organising a team to fly over to France to interview him again, and liaising with Interpol to set everything up. I am shell-shocked. I expected a development but not this soon. I nibble on an apple but I'm anxious for more news. I talk again to Isabel but she asks me to remain calm and she'll keep me updated. What else can I do? I feel helpless.

I check on Meg. Thankfully, she is in good spirits.

'You seem a little edgy,' she says.

'Just tired…'

'And?'

My voice has betrayed me. I try to be clever but it doesn't suit me and I regret my reply. 'You tell me.'

Meg laughs kindly in my favour. 'Well, it was a difficult day yesterday and you were very sweet to me. I couldn't have done what I did without you. I feel that you deserve some good news. I sense something has happened…have you had good news?'

'Maybe, the young man who befriended Daisy in France has been arrested.'

She raises her eyebrows, 'The one who you suspected of travelling to England?'

'Yes, he was over here when she was attacked. The police have confirmed it. He is a strong suspect, Meg.' I hated saying this for obvious reasons.

'It must be a relief for you, Will.'

'Sort of… It's a bittersweet moment so I'm not sure how I'm feeling right now.' I didn't want to betray her views with my excitement.

'Will he be brought to England?'

'Probably. I don't know how these things work. The investigation will begin over there in order to substantiate his involvement if any. Maybe he'll confess, perhaps they'll find evidence. He might just deny everything. We just don't know at this stage.'

'It's a breakthrough,' Meg says. 'At least something is happening. Are you going over?'

'No,' I shrug. 'I'd just get in the way and become a nuisance but I'm tempted of course.'

'I sense you have a strong feeling about this, Will.'

I grit my teeth and swallow hard, imagining my rage if I could get my hands on Romain, just for a few seconds. 'I do,' I say coldly. Then I open my big mouth again. 'I could kill him if I had a chance.' What made me say that?

She bamboozles me.

'I feel Daisy is restless, Will. Be careful for what you wish for.'

*

I feel restless as well and cannot settle just padding around the flat. Isabel's message has thrown me and Meg's cracker of a comment has pushed me over the edge. If Romain is responsible for Daisy's murder then the sooner we know the better. However, I suspect that nothing goes smoothly in this sort of situation. A quick confession from him would certainly bury a few demons but in the same breath it would rake it all up again. The guilt, that is.

Every parent wants to protect their children and the thought that Isabel and I had somehow failed in our duty destroys me inside. It's like slow torture and the deep sorrow never diminishes with time. The heart is shattered and remains that way. It cannot be repaired. It's like walking around with a black heart, black eyes and black soul, glaring down a black tunnel. The thoughts in your head are black as well, distant, dead. Is there a future in technicolour? Forget it. The imprint of blackness blankets everything: like being confined alive, nailed down inside a coffin.

What do I do now?

I promised Meg I'd call over but I'm shot through. I make coffee and await news from Isabel but I know it will be some time before she calls again. Finding Romain is one thing, getting to him is another. There will be a protocol to abide by and the French police will be protective to one of their own and sensitive to the letter of the law. That's where Interpol come into the equation, Isabel had explained earlier. Me? I only wish for swift justice.

I scan the holiday photos again and try to rearrange them on the unmade bed, getting dates mixed up. I'm in a bad place right now. I've got to make sense of these two kids' fractured relationship. Since Romain's arrest, I don't feel the same level of anxiety with regard to the images set before me now. It's as if the whole situation has been taken out of my hands, which I suppose it has. I feel like a spare part again. But still, I ponder…

I blink and blink again. My eyes suddenly linger over one particular photo. It shows both Daisy and her mum embracing at the edge of the swimming pool, half-submerged in the glistening water. They radiate happiness and well-being. It is a glorious shot with the sun bearing down on their suntanned shoulders. I know I took the snap because in the far background I recognise Romain and David together under the shadow of a tree in the garden.

I look closer and realise that they are face to face, almost eyeball to eyeball. It is the first time I've spotted this. It appears that they are embroiled in a heated argument. Is this a trick of the light? I wrack my brain and cannot recall a confrontation like this between them. They had so little in common and generally avoided each other. I try to dismiss the idea. After all, we were on holiday, having fun. Why would anyone want to provoke a fight?

Then it dawns on me that this specific photo wasn't taken by me. It was Isabel's birthday and the designer sunglasses she wore were a gift from Daisy and they were posing like starlets on a film set, pouting their lips. In fact, we were all playful and slightly tipsy from the Cava we had with lunch and I sat by the pool (out of shot) making a nuisance of myself. I reckon Romain's mother, Nicole, took the image because I was busy playing with a new toy; I was filming them on a portable hand-held movie camera. I was the director *par excellence*, not quite Cecil de Mille, more like Woody Allen.

My brain somersaults. Somewhere, hidden away in storage, I must have this episode recorded, which means I also had the lead-up and follow on as to what happened in the background, assuming I kept filming continuously. I reckon I did. That day is still fresh in my head. It was only a few years ago. So, the question is: Where is the videotape?

I don't have it. It seems logical that Isabel does. I undertake to get it and take a peep. I phone Isabel and leave a message that I want to call over tonight to collect some bits of mine. I suggest around seven and leave it at that.

Somehow, I put a level of importance to this strange episode that no doubt will prove to be inconsequential. I have a habit of making mountains out of molehills. Although I am intrigued, it is probably nothing to be alarmed about. Then again, I have always trusted my instincts.

I'm in a big hurry to see Isabel but she will be busy and so I don't want to pressurise her. She'll simply push me away.

To fill in time, I go over to Meg's and do a few odd jobs around the place. I hang pictures and curtains and move the heavier furniture into place. It's beginning to take shape and resemble a home that Meg can be proud of. I'm mightily relieved that the relocation went without a hitch. I was half-expecting her to have a paddy and renege on her promise to move quietly and without fuss. She was as good as her word, as you know. We celebrate with tea and chocolate biscuits.

Molly has done great too and intends to work on for a few more hours and organise Miriam's bedroom as best she can. Meg smiles and I leave them to it.

I get back to the office and fiddle around for a couple of hours but I'm hyper-active under my cool exterior. I might look placid but nothing could be further from the truth.

I leave early, pop in to another client who has also been relocated and then head home, via a burger bar for a take-out. I fill in file notes for an hour but keep checking the bloody time. It ticks slowly. I ring the police station and they inform me PS Farmer is not there. I take a chance and drive over early, hoping to catch her at the cottage.

Bingo! Her car is in the drive. My heart races, my hands clammy. For the first time in ages, Isabel hugs me tightly as if in recognition of what is to come. The ordeal of interrogation, the waiting, gathering evidence, the waiting, the trial date, the bloody waiting and then the verdict. Is he guilty or not? This is all new to me but Isabel is hardened to it and the hug reassures me that I'm not alone. It means a lot to me.

Over coffee, she goes over what is happening and what is likely to happen during the coming days, weeks, months. I pick up from her that we need to be cool under pressure and trust Jimson and his team. I nod incessantly but inside I'm like a cat on a hot tin roof. I'm a bag of nerves. I need a brandy but I keep quiet and nod again as she outlines the case against Romain. He apparently did a runner when he was spotted, which indicates a measure of suspicion against his reaction and character. So far, under arrest, he is showing signs of breaking down and his story appears to be full of holes. Isabel is confident, but there is no elation. Why should there be? Daisy still remains dead.

I show Isabel the photo of her and Daisy pouting in the pool. She gasps and trembles at the memory of treasured days.

'Am I right in thinking we have this on video?' I ask nervously. I so want her to say *yes.*

'It was my birthday…right?'

'Yes.'

'Why do you want it?'

I point out the blur in the background of the two figures under a tree. At first, she shrugs indifferently and then I explain further. Isabel puts the photo on the kitchen table and fumbles through the clutter in the TV cabinet. No joy. Frustration creeps in. She then searches the pine sideboard. Nothing. She comes back from the bedroom (it seems ages) and holds up the cartridge in mock triumph. She inserts it into the TV.

We watch as she skims on FAST PLAY until we find the segment. We remain silent and open-mouthed trying in vain to stop it at the exact moment.

'There!' I shout. 'Now rewind.'

'Where do I stop?'

'There!' I jump up and down. 'Stop there!'

'OK, OK…'

'Can you zoom in?'

'It's not that easy, the technology isn't good.'

'Look,' I pronounce excitedly, jabbing madly with my finger.

We catch our first sight of the two protagonists: Romain and David facing each other, virtually nose to nose. As I thought they appear agitated, which is surprising because it was a fun day and I couldn't recall any intolerance. Perhaps too much wine had been consumed.

As we move on frame by frame, Romain holds his hands up to David's chest as if restraining him. Then David clearly pushes him back. They seem to be arguing, but not playfully. Another shove, *this time from Romain.* It's hard to tell who is more aggressive. Certainly, no one in the foreground is aware of what is happening. Then the two of them separate with Romain backing off first and shrugging his shoulders. Then he's out of the frame. David looks at him, shouts, waves a finger and then looks sheepishly towards us at the pool edge.

'What do you suppose that was about?' Isabel asks.

'Fuck knows.' The word just slips out, so I apologise.

'I've heard a lot worse down at the station,' she laughs.

I feel dejected. I haven't heard her laugh like that for a very long time. I feel the weight of sadness and my legs start to buckle, but I stop myself from making a fool of myself. We are standing close.

I desperately want to kiss her.

'I can get this magnified,' Isabel says.

I come back to earth. I can smell the perfume on her bare neck and it makes me dizzy.

'It just seems odd to me,' I say calmly, hiding my intoxication.

'What? *That* they argued? Romain could pick a fight with anyone when he was in the mood. Add in the alcohol…'

'Was he drunk, do you reckon? He seemed to be angrier…'

'Pissed, actually.'

'You can actually remember the moment?'

'Of course. I reckon we got through about ten bottles of Cava that afternoon…everyone was in high spirits.'

'David doesn't usually do *confrontation*,' I protest.

'Well, he does now.'

'Do you think he's being provoked by Romain?'

'Can't tell, but your brother has a viper's tongue, and can give as good as he gets. He wouldn't take any crap from a boy, now would he? Maybe Romain was goading him. Anyway, why don't you ask him?'

'I will, and hopefully, Jimson can do the same with Romain.'

'I'll get the message through to him.'

'Thanks.' I'm thoughtful, and add, 'I'm surprised we hadn't spotted this incident before…'

'It was in the background, Will. No big deal.' She stands back and says coldly, 'And now you need to go.'

I get the message. The alluring perfume isn't for me. That's why she came back early, to get ready for *him.* Her skin also smells of soap.

I linger, but she gets me to the door and watches as I reach the gate.

'Will?'

'Yes?'

'Don't let what's on the tape get your knickers in a twist, OK? It'll be nothing of any consequence…'

'You're probably right.'

'I'll call you if anything happens, I promise.'

But not tonight, eh?

Someone else will no doubt be getting her knickers in a twist when I am truly out of the picture. Was he out there hiding on the street, watching and waiting for me to go?

I look but see nobody. I depart with a heavy heart but on the journey home I can still smell her scent as if she is sitting right next to me in the semi-dark. I breathe her in.

Isabel, Isabel, I whisper but no one answers.

Chapter 17

I knock back a brandy and then take another, savouring this one. It's not late so I phone Margo out of the blue knowing David won't be there. I'm fishing but I don't know what for. I've lost touch with Margo so we'll see how it goes, although we've never been that close and I could easily get the brush-off. It's a fact that Isabel and I have always considered them a "distant" couple, jealously guarding their privacy to the exclusion of all others. In that respect, Isabel never took to them having come from a large outgoing family. Me? I just went with the flow. Who was I to judge how people lived their lives?

The double brandy bolsters my confidence.

'Hello, Margo.'

Delayed reaction. Is she composing herself?

'Will, good gosh… Is that really you?'

'A blast from the past,' I joke.

'How-er- lovely… I do miss seeing you, Will.'

Yeah, sure.

I give off the right noises. 'It's been too long, Margo, and I apologise. I'll make the effort and come over in the next few days, I promise.'

'You've had a lot to contend with, so you don't have to say sorry. David isn't here, I'm afraid…'

'I've spoken to him. When will he be back?'

'The weekend: ready for school on the Monday.'

'I'll pop over next week then.'

'Please stay over; we have so much to catch up on.'

'I know, I know.'

'How is Isabel?'

'Oh, fine…'

'I'd love for the two of you to get back together again.'

I was struggling now. A lump forms in my throat. Typical Margo: always so thoughtful in putting other folks' problems ahead of her own. I shouldn't judge her so harshly. I try to redress the balance.

'And how are you managing?' I ask.

'So-so. I'm even losing the use of my hands now which is dreadful. I'm always dropping things, which drives David mad. I'm so grateful that I have Claire to help me.'

I'm aware that Claire is her full-time nurse. Margo is now confined to a wheelchair permanently and her illness is slowly killing her. David hates weakness or failure but sticks by her mainly out of duty I fathom. Claire takes responsibility which allows him to pursue a life away from school and marriage. Both are demanding and her vital role gives him his much-needed release. It begs the question, where does Margo get her release from?

'Is David fishing?' I ask.

'Who knows… He's gone to the caravan. What he gets up to is anyone's guess.'

I'm thrown. 'What caravan?'

'The one at Whitby.'

'You have a caravan at Whitby?'

'Yes, we've had it for over twenty years.'

'He's never mentioned it.'

'Of course, he has!'

I laugh. 'No, Margo, I would remember if he had told me.'

'I haven't been up there for ten years or more, ever since my legs gave up on me. So he goes alone, usually twice a year. It used to be in Skipton.'

'What used to be in Skipton?'

'The caravan, but he moved it over to the east coast.'

'When?'

'When? What is this, twenty questions!'

'I'm sorry, Margo. I'm just curious…'

'In the last ten years, I guess.'

'I just can't see David owning a caravan, especially one that I didn't know about.'

'You did, I'm sure.'

I didn't, I'm sure.

'Tell David I called. I'll get him at the weekend and arrange something, OK?'

'You're a darling, Will. Don't let me down now.'

'No chance, Margo.'

I wait for her to click off, and then I attack the brandy bottle again. I'm baffled by the existence of the caravan. Why was my brother so secretive? Perhaps Margo is right, and my memory has malfunctioned. It's no big deal. There are no bragging rights to owning a caravan. Perhaps it was his personal *thing*. Like a man furtively wearing ladies underwear. Then I start to giggle. I'm losing the plot. The brandy is taking hold and my imagination is running riot. David and a caravan: the last of the big spenders. I wonder how opulent it is. Gold taps? Plasma screen TV? I bet it has a well-stocked supply of chilled German Liebfraumilch in the fridge. Then I really giggle and need a piss. I picture him, arms folded; surveying his pride and joy like the elusive billionaire Howard Hughes did with his gleaming aeroplane, the *Stratoliner*. I can't contain myself any longer.

I piss in my pants in one of life's best moments. My big brother, David, Mr Tycoon *Extraordinaire*, a man of means. Who would have believed it?

*

102

I'm fast asleep when the phone goes. I grab it and mumble something.

'Will, its Molly.'

I sit bolt upright and check the time: 2 am.

'What is it, Molly?'

'Sorry to ring at this hour. It's Meg…she's frantic.'

'What's wrong?'

'She's incoherent.'

'Should you call an ambulance?'

'Not that frantic.'

I'm still dozy and wet! 'Then why the call, Molly?'

'She's tearful and wants to see you.'

'Now?'

'Well, I'm struggling to keep her calm…'

'Molly, I've been drinking.'

'OK, got you.'

'Make her some tea.'

'Done that,' she says.

'Has she had a nightmare or been sleepwalking?'

'Possibly… I found her on the landing, waving her arms about and shouting.'

'Where is she now?'

'I got her back into her bedroom.'

'Well done. Listen, cool her forehead with a cold flannel and get her to drink more tea or water. Soothe her, she'll be fine. It would be crazy for me to risk coming over.'

'Agreed.'

'You did the right thing phoning me.'

'I wasn't sure but it freaked me out.'

'You've handled it brilliantly. Get some rest, OK? I'll set the alarm and get over first thing.'

'Thanks, Will. I just wanted reassurance. We'll be fine I'm sure.'

'And Molly?'

'Yes…?'

'Could you make out what she was shouting about?'

'It wasn't absolutely clear…something about a helter-skelter and a man in black.'

Can blood freeze in the veins?

It seems that way. I stand like a marble statue, unable to react immediately. Then I begin to thaw, but not before Molly calls my name several times in desperation at my silent response.

'I'll get a taxi,' I say and change my pants.

Chapter 18

Now be honest with me, have you ever experienced irrational fear?

I feel it now. I have no reason for it, other than those words relayed by Molly strike a chord deep in my heart. I keep composed in the back of the taxi but my head spins and my chest heaves violently. Meg has seen a vision and I desperately need to see it too from her perspective. Only we know what this really signifies and I'm positive that her sub-consciousness has lifted a lid onto the past. Showing her the postcard of the helter-skelter has unlocked a key moment – a passageway – which has taken her straight back to the horrible events from forty years ago. It was enough to reawaken the ghosts of yesteryear and cause untold panic. What had she seen? Who was the man in black?

I couldn't get there fast enough but I was soon disappointed. Meg was fast asleep, soothed by Molly's expert hand.

I'm shattered anyway and settle down on the sofa with one of the bloody cats for company. We do a staring competition and I lose. I nod off, wake up, nod again and then fall under the cat's intense spell. Just as well, because the little fucker is still staring at me in the morning, only this time I have a crick in my neck. I can still taste the after kick of brandy on my breath and to top it all off I receive the first big boot to the head from a looming headache ready to pounce at any moment. I thought I had that problem with the stupid cat.

I manage to stagger to the kitchen and take aspirin with a glass of water but I know I'm in for a hard time.

Molly's a gem and makes a round of bacon sandwiches, which miraculously conjures up a circle of hungry cats around her feet. I make myself busy by brewing up a cuppa and tidying away my makeshift bed sheets. Then I take Meg her breakfast. She is very fragile and tearful, especially as she has awoken in a strange room. I'm actually dead pleased I'm here for her and she smiles her appreciation.

'Thank you for coming, Will.'

'Wouldn't have missed it for the world,' I reply joyfully.

'Have I been a bad girl?'

'You had a nightmare and woke the whole neighbourhood up.'

'Oh, dear…'

'But apparently, the Vera Lynn rendition went down well with the over eighties. Those slightly younger were not amused. Perhaps in the future you should entertain them before the midnight hour…some people don't like to be disturbed in the early hours of the morning.'

'Oh, dear,' she repeats.

'And charge a ticket price if you intend to repeat the entertainment.'

That gets a welcome laugh.

But my laugh is cut short.

'I saw him, Will.'

The hair on the nape of my neck rises.

'Who?' I whisper, sitting closer on the edge of the bed, dabbing her forehead with my handkerchief.

'The man in black.'

'Did you see his face?'

'He had his back to me.'

'What was he doing?'

'Watching the children come down the helter-skelter.'

'Was Miriam there?'

She hesitates, and then whimpers, 'Yes.'

'What did he do, this man?'

'He stood and watched them.'

'Have you seen him before?'

'Yes, thinking about it...'

I was starting to sweat. 'At the fair?'

'Yes.'

'How many times did you take Miriam to the fair, Meg?'

'On three occasions, I think.'

'And you saw him each time?'

'Yes.'

'How did you know it was the same man if you didn't see his face?'

She was silent, her head tilted back against the pillow.

I repeat the question.

'Because,' she said slowly, 'he was an oddball sort of character. I noticed that even in the heat of summer he wore the same dark suit. Everyone else was in shirt sleeves. He had it buttoned up at the front. It struck me that it didn't look right...'

'Why have you remembered this now, Meg, all these years later?'

'It was seeing the postcard, I assume.'

'Was he following Miriam?'

'I can't say he was for sure, but he spooked me at the time.'

'Did you tell the police of your concerns?'

'I'm sure I would have, but it's so long ago. I'd forgotten about him until you reminded me of the helter-skelter.'

'What else do you remember about him, Meg?'

She fell silent for a second, a haunted look in her eyes.

'It frightened me, so god knows what other folk thought...'

'*He* frightened you?'

The silence prevailed. '*It*...frightened me.'

Fuck. I tried again.

'You're talking in riddles, Meg. What is…*it*?'
'The white mask he painted over his face.'

Chapter 19

Meg was by now agitated, clammy to the touch and I didn't dare pursue further questioning at this stage. What would you do? Frankly, I didn't want a heart attack on my hands. You can imagine what the tabloids would make of that.

I try to settle her down and changed the pillowcase which by now was damp from her perspiration. I'm scared, bewildered by her revelations concerning the mysterious man. Where had this suddenly come from?

Meg certainly wasn't in one of her trances during our conversation. She looked me straight in the eye and I believed her story.

There was a man and he took Miriam.

I think Meg knows more than she is willing to share, so I vow to slowly get to the heart of the matter without putting her under more duress. This was real enough and Meg too was only just coming to terms with it. Had she in fact been hiding this information down the years in order to suppress her own guilt at losing her only daughter?

I can't press it. Instead, I'd let her speak her mind when she was good and ready. She is in poor health and digging up the past will surely exploit those problems. But this episode just highlights my own anxiety. So much is happening but I don't seem to have any control over events as they unfold. I feel like an onlooker, a spectator at a football match. I can shout and scream and demand answers but I am powerless to act, to change things, speed up the play. I am frustrated and it does my head in. Then I think of the mask. What the hell is that all about?

I decide to have the rest of the day off, after helping Meg select her daily pill intake: there are eleven in total. She gets confused but now she is calm and Molly agrees to stay until after lunchtime. I go home, skip a shower, clean the car (I do a half job) and generally try to sober up. The best way to do this is to go for a run. The day is overcast, but the sun promises to break through. I jog along the harbour wall route, down onto the tidal path and out towards St. Thomas A Becket church. I stop on the journey to lay a small posy of wildflowers beside Daisy's grave that I had hand-picked on the way.

The sun peppers through the grey gloom and I read this to be a good sign. The tide is coming in so I venture a detour through Nore Barn woods until I reach, by way of the cycle path, the equestrian farm and stop for a breather. Shit, I never needed a break in the past. I'm getting old and can feel my bones creaking and my muscles aching. I carry on, past the windmill and watermill at Langstone harbour (the place of the Long Stone). I settle on a bench outside The Crown pub and take a swig from my water bottle. The view across the estuary always inspires me, corny as that sounds. The tiny boats glisten and bob against the incoming current as a line of Brent Geese swoop low over the horizon. A black-tailed Godwit sits at my feet, pecking at the ground. A shaft of sunlight suddenly breaks through the clouds over Northney Marina on the other side of the bay, illuminating the gloomy sky. In spite of everything, it was good to be alive sometimes.

From here I could see Eggshell cottage with its blue shutters and clapperboard facade. My mood somewhat changes to melancholy as I see a man leave the cottage, with Isabel in tow. They hug and kiss. Then he is gone. All my hopes are dashed in a second. I'm the past, a forgotten relic: consigned to the trash can. If I was feeling old earlier, I now feel a whole lot worse. The Godwit looks at me with comical curiosity. I know I'm a joke, forever wishing for the impossible to happen. I watch as the bird takes flight, circles once and is then gone. Just like Isabel.

I haven't the heart to go on, past my former home. It would crush me. As always, my timing is crap. Even the pub is closed. I slunk off in the direction I came but this time I walk. All my energy spent.

*

As a child, I recall our family annual holiday on the east coast at Whitby or Scarborough. They were the glory days and David and I had an idyllic time with our parents. My father was strict but fair and was an engineer by trade, so we lived decently in those days when the country slowly recovered from the terrible effects of the Second World War.

I remember our later trips to the south coast, where we stayed with an auntie because we couldn't afford hotels. We'd spend the whole day on Hayling Island beach and play hide and seek in the sand dunes and around the beach huts. Our mum made sandwiches and cakes which we laid out on a blanket, which we thought was right proper. But we were northerners and things seemed so different and so refined in the south. Our auntie was considered rather posh and David did a brilliant mimic of her speech and mannerisms. As we got into our teens, dark days appeared. Dad was made redundant in Middlesbrough as the work dried up in the industrial wastelands. Eventually, he sought employment on Portsmouth docks as a welder, which was our saviour I suppose. He came down first and we followed after his income seemed more secure. And so over time, we became familiar in the ways of the southern folk which was probably no bad thing. We didn't necessarily prosper, but we had a bit of money and a roof over our heads.

David and I went to Warblington School, near Havant, and I, in particular, had a love of sport but it was David who was the academician and excelled in science and maths. He was always going to succeed and looking back he really benefited from the transition. He grasped the nettle whilst I sat on the sidelines with my studies, which failed to excite me. It was a case of big brother forging ahead and I so admired him. He moved on to grammar school, then university and then teacher training. A stint in the army didn't last long. He met Margo quite early on but they never had children. I would say they had a contented marriage in the beginning, and judging by the trappings of success, an affluent one as well.

I, on the other hand, had no serious ambitions. I was a dreamer who needed a kick up the backside and it was David who provided that large boot by getting me into the teaching profession. I at least made something of my life. I wasn't brilliantly happy but I wasn't unfulfilled either. Isabel was the making of me, the birth of Daisy the icing on the cake.

Now, as I sit by my daughter's graveside still smarting at seeing Isabel with *him*, I think of her cruel death and the waste of her many talents. And I cry unashamedly. This is a beautiful spot, surrounded by wildflowers and the glimpse on the Solent through the hedgerows. The trees sway gently and the silence is welcoming: the silence of the dead. I so wish Daisy could talk to me. God, I know, looks down upon her but I am a tortured soul at this moment and the screams echoing inside my head seem to intensify. I so want to ask her about Romain and what he did to her. Did she know he was stalking her? Had he been in touch and she was afraid to mention it to me? What hold did he have over her? Did she know that she was going to die…?

Fuck, fuck, fuck. I whimper like a dog and check that no one is staring at me with pity in their eyes. I would hate that. And then I almost jump out of my skin as I look up and find Isabel standing there, swaying on unsteady legs. She sees my utter anguish and falls to her knees and holds me so tight I think I'm going to suffocate. She cradles me and we sob together and I realise the howling above the wind is our lament. The crows settle around us and the black clouds loom high as the first heavy spots of rain crash down. We cannot bear to look at each other, terrified by the ghosts of our past, but we reach out anyway in gratitude and compassion and claw at our souls in the hope that we can be saved. I hear a distant crack of thunder. The rain cascades down now and soaks our skin but we remain, fused and huddled, in this position.

Our family will not be divided, I hear myself bellow above the din.

Chapter 20

'Hi, Will. I gather you wanted me?' My brother asks.

It's late and I still feel the chill in my bones from the thunderstorm. I decided on a long hot bath when I got back to my humble abode and hoped this would do the trick to warm me through. I sense a fever coming on. The brandy bottle is empty so I have to make do with a whisky, a cheap one at that. The call interrupts a bland film featuring Nicole Kidman. I can never remember any of the titles in which she appeared in but this one passes the time effectively, allowing for the emotional upheaval with Isabel to gently subside.

I could do without this call. I'm wiped out.

'Hi, David, nothing vital,' I answer quietly.

'Margo said you'd had a good chat.'

'Yeah…' I turn the sound down on the remote.

'It did her the power of good.'

'She mentioned a caravan. I had to laugh.'

He's cagey. 'Oh, why?'

'Well, you kept that a secret over the years…'

'I'm sure I told you.'

'Not so. I wouldn't have been so surprised if I'd known about it.'

'I thought you knew… It's no big deal.'

'Where do you keep it?'

'At a site overlooking Whitby harbour… I'll take you up there when you've got the time.' He laughs, and adds, 'A boy's adventure, yes?'

'Sounds like a plan. Is this your secret bolthole ?'

'Well, let's put it this way, it gets me out of Margo's hair. Sometimes we both need a little release from each other.'

'What do you do when you're up there?'

'Oh, usual things: a spot of walking, golf, fishing and drinking. The local ale is damn good. Get this; I'm even into dominoes having joined a pub league. How sad is that?'

'Very sad, I might skip on that bit. But I'll remind you of your offer.'

'Anytime, Will.'

'It'll take me back to my childhood. Speaking of which, do you still have your collection of seaside postcards.'

'Bloody hell, they'd be stored in the attic probably. Why do you ask?'

'I'm just intrigued by one I've recently come across. It featured a red and white helter-skelter on the front and I seem to think you have a copy.'

'Quite possible.' He laughed again. 'Is it worth a bob or two?'

'Hardly.'

'Then why is it so special?'

'It isn't. It just seemed to resonate with me.'

'Do you want me to search for it?'

'No, no, no.'

'Are you coming over next week? I'll cook something snazzy…'

'Sounds great, and I did promise Margo…'

'How about Wednesday? My tennis night is cancelled and I'm free.'

'Done.'

'Are you coming alone?'

He knew the answer to that.

'Yes,' I reply.

'I saw something on the local news tonight about an arrest in France in connection with Daisy. Is it serious this time?'

'It appears so.'

'Would it be that lad Romain the police want to interview?'

'I can't talk on the phone, David.'

'I never felt comfortable with that prat,' he snapped.

'We'll talk next week, OK?'

'It's him, mark my words.'

I'm getting fraught. 'I'll know more in a few days, I can't speculate beyond that…'

'Remember what I said, Will.'

We click off and I finish my drink. He always has to get the last word in. Perhaps going over next week isn't a good idea after all. But a promise is a promise.

*

Whether it was the alcohol doing the talking or the sheer weight of pent-up emotion pouring out of me at the cemetery, I don't know, but I immediately phone Meg.

'You OK?' I ask.

'Snug as a bug,' she says.

'Can you talk?'

'I'll try but the cats need feeding.'

I breathe in slowly and get straight to the point.

'Meg, you mentioned a mask. What kind of mask?'

'You know like they have at the circus…a funny face.'

'A clown's mask?'

'Well yes, it could have been the same type of heavy white make-up.'

'Did he have a red nose and all that?'

'I suppose he did. He wore a bowler hat and kept play acting to entertain the children.'

'That's what clowns do, Meg.'

'I know, I know, but this man was different somehow…'

'How was he different?'

'I don't know but I'm wracking my brain, Will.'

'Keep trying.'

'I won't be beaten by it.'

'Do you think he is connected to Miriam's disappearance?'

'I can't point a finger for sure, but it disturbs me enough to dream about him. That can't be right.'

'Ring me any time, night or day…'

'I hate to lean on you, Will. You've done enough for me already.'

'Permission granted and that's the end of it.'

'That's told me!'

I emphasis the point: 'If you think of anything…'

'…I have to ring you.'

Then we disconnect.

Weirdly, the phone buzzes in again.

'I forgot to say goodnight, Will.'

'Goodnight, Meg,' I say, with a comforting smile she can't see.

Chapter 21

Isabel describes my obsessive nature in regard to my daughter as *blankness*. I understand what she is implying. I blank out what is going on around me, compartmentalise the issues which confound me, bury my emotions and generally "get through each day at a time".

Meg has taught me to see things differently, and through her dignity, I have found renewed hope. If she, through adversity, can find a way through the mire then I can follow her path. Life is a brutal playground and Daisy would not want me to carry on like this. I have to make sense of her loss to me personally and move on. It is a delicate balancing act but I owe her to succeed, to honour her name and not besmirch it. Daisy lives on through me, not in spite of me. Anything else is selling her memory short.

Since Romain's arrest, Isabel has softened somewhat and I am touched deeply by her reaching out to me at the graveside. Considering our history, this was a big deal. Whether it was pity on her part I will not know without asking, but I have no intention of doing this. I was simply overwhelmed at the cemetery and had reached crisis point…and Isabel was there for me, like an angel of calling. I will never forget this thoughtfulness, which is the way I prefer to describe it: *An act of kindness.*

You may see it differently, but frankly, I don't give a fuck. She saved me and I am stronger for it today.

She texts and instructs me to call in to the station for an update and I reply that I'll be there within the hour. No chance though: I open the front door to be met by a half dozen news reporters all jostling for an angle on the breaking news concerning Romain's impending arrest. The story has clearly gained momentum. I'm shocked, not anticipating this level of media coverage. I push my way past, grim-faced, and shield the barrage of questions with the obligatory "No comment" response.

There is more press waiting at the police district headquarters. A girl in uniform escorts me into a small anteroom with chairs and a desk and a man who I don't know takes me through the events so far. Isabel comes in and sits quietly and listens too, but she is primed I can tell. We glance at each other occasionally.

I interrupt him.

'Has he confessed?' I ask.

'No,' the man says.

'Is there anything that links him directly to the killing of our daughter?'

'At present, there is no evidence, only conjecture.'

My voice is sharp. 'What have we got then?'

'Romain has confirmed his longstanding friendship with your daughter. He confirms his journey to England at the time of her death but he is adamant that he came to protect her and not harm her.'

'Protect her against *what?*'

'This is what we are trying to establish...'

'She grew to dislike him,' I say.

'That's not entirely true, Will,' Isabel replies, taking up the reins. 'At one stage they were close...you must remember when they held hands down by the river. But something happened and there is evidence from the holiday snaps that a distance grew between them, but dislike is probably too strong a word.'

I was a bit surprised at this defence of the boy.

'Do you think he is innocent?' I ask incredulously.

'I haven't said that. They emailed each other frequently. I think he was a bit pushy and she wasn't ready for that.'

'You mean they were having a sexual relationship?'

'Don't get angry, Will. At fifteen she was bound to experiment with her feelings...but I repeat, I think she probably rebuffed his advances and his inflated ego probably got the better of him.'

The man cuts in, 'And that doesn't necessarily make him a murderer, Mr Farmer.'

'You two sound like a support group,' I snort.

'We are searching for hard evidence,' he continues. 'We need a breakdown in his alibi or an incriminating comment which will prove his guilt. He's not handling it well and for what my opinion is worth I think it is only time before he cocks-up under pressure and we'll have him on a platter.'

I climb down off my high horse. 'That's reassuring to hear,' I mutter.

Isabel stares at me. 'Jimson starts his interrogation tomorrow, Will, so let's wait and see.'

'We need to ask him about the altercation at the poolside,' I say, 'find out what happened...'

'We will,' Isabel confirms. 'Everything has an order and Jimson knows what he is doing.'

'And then there's the note.'

'What note?' The man asks me.

'The one she wrote to me. It said *I don't like him.*'

'We need to have that,' Isabel says.

I nod.

'Listen, it could refer to anyone, Will, so don't rely on this as evidence.'

'I know...' I rub my head.

'How many notes are there?' The man asks me.

'A lot, but most of them refer to me.'

He pushes me further. 'Is Romain's name mentioned anywhere in these notes?'

I'm deflated and answer, 'No.'

Then I perk up. 'Have they searched the room where he was staying? Have they turned over his parent's farm to find the missing jumper? Has he got a lock-up security box somewhere or a trunk hidden in a disused garage where he could hide things?'

The man rises from his chair.

'We're onto all of those possibilities, Mr Farmer, but thank you for pointing them out.'

I notice Isabel raises her eyebrows and looks away.

The man adds, 'Let's talk again in say, twenty-four hours. Does that suit you?'

I look for any crumb of comfort. 'Unless there is a breakthrough in the meantime…'

'Of course, we'll naturally keep you informed of any developments.'

I shake his hand and nod to Isabel, who walks me to my car at the rear of the building, avoiding the attentions of the media.

'Who's he?' I ask.

'Morris. He's in charge whilst Jimson's in France.'

'I can't help opening my mouth.'

'I know, but you must learn to trust us.'

I shrug.

'Anyway, thanks,' I say.

'For what?'

'For reaching out to me at the graveside. It meant a lot.'

'If you'd been a dog, I'd have had you put down.'

The joke can't deflect from her sincerity, and I'm secretly touched. It's her way of dealing with the awkwardness of what she might term my neediness. I call it raw exposure. I feel I'm being shot at from all angles.

'It's difficult for me too, Will. But working in this environment I just see the shit more often and I'm immune to it, especially with this bunch of cynical morons around me.'

I manage a laugh.

Then she backs away, but not before I see a flicker behind her eyes; a flicker of recognition that perhaps I'm not the bad bastard after all. Or am I just kidding myself with this delusion? I see what I want to see. I know that I'm easily fooled.

I'm surprised when she suddenly turns.

'I've put the divorce on hold. It's only right in the circumstances…'

I nod my appreciation: something less to think about.

Later, I buy a Big Mac and coke and sit in the park to unwind and soon realise that this was where Daisy and I used to sit, watching people and their quirky mannerisms. She would sit and sketch and giggle while I snapped away with my camera at anything that took my fancy.

But today I am alone, without Daisy or my camera. And there is nothing to grin about. I eat but it is just fuel. I think of Meg and her uplifting spirit and try to pull myself together. How many times have I tried this and failed?

The camera…

115

My head swirls.

I snapped away at anything that took my fancy.

Christ.

The man in black…

I chuck the food away and head over to Meg's place as fast as I can legally drive.

Chapter 22

'What are you so excited about?' Meg asks as I force my way in and pace the room like a crazy man.

'Photos, I need to see the photos,' I say speedily.

'You're not making sense, Will.'

'When we packed up Miriam's room, there were hundreds of photos in boxes under the bed. Who took the photos?'

'Well, Miriam did. She had one of those Instamatics and just clicked away at her heart's content. She'd snap anything that moved.'

'And that would include the fair, right?'

'Of course. What are you trying to get at?'

Then the penny drops and her eyes widen.

I make the suggestion, 'Let's get them out and have a closer look, shall we?'

'I feel like Miss Marple,' she beams, and adds, 'Wait a moment.'

I put the kettle on and then lose patience, following Meg into another room. Together we lug several boxes into the lounge. We sift through the pictures, discounting everything that didn't have a big top in the background. Most of the photos, all black and white, were as amateurish as you would expect from the hands of a child, but some were fantastically clear and precise which surprised me. She was good at capturing the moment. She had talent. There must have been over fifty photos of the fair spread over the three days she attended with her friends, and most were silly portraits of girls pulling funny faces and eating candyfloss and toffee apples and generally mucking about.

I pour the tea and search the sea of faces. It was almost impossible to identify anyone amongst the big crowds. I was also resigned to viewing several midriff shots as you would expect from the eye of someone so short. This aspect would normally bring a comical touch to the proceedings but I'm not in the mood for humour.

My enthusiasm wanes somewhat.

Where was the man in black?

'Do you reckon this strange man was employed there?' I ask.

Meg creases her forehead. 'Thinking back, he appeared to be on his own. That's what caught my eye, I suppose. The other clowns were in a group larking about. He just seemed to stare at the children. It freaked me. I eventually confided to a policeman nearby but the mystery man had vanished when we looked for him.'

'And you reported this fact after Miriam's disappearance?'

'Yes, of course, but nothing came of it. The police at the time interviewed all the staff but no one knew of his existence…'

'So you had every reason to be suspicious.'

'Looking back, yes…but it doesn't help now.'

I feel downtrodden. It's a false dawn.

'Hang on a minute!' Meg's eyes light up. 'I have a scrapbook that all the pupils were supposed to complete for a school project.'

My spirits lift again. I follow as Meg goes into the bedroom again and fumbles around in the last of the unopened boxes which contained Miriam's precious belongings. Meg curses as the search goes on relentlessly from one box to another.

'Got it!' She shouts gleefully, holding the book aloft.

We sit on the bed and open the pages and see him immediately. He features in four photos, mainly in the background, with no detail to attract our attention.

'I nearly forgot about this album,' Meg says quietly. 'If the truth was known, I'd put it to the back of my mind because of what it meant. It hurts to look at these pictures.'

'I know how devastating this must be for you,' I say. There was one startling picture of Miriam herself in a very pretty summer dress, smiling nervously for the camera. It was the dress she was wearing when she was found murdered; the one in the plastic folder which I took out and handled. A friend of hers or one of the mothers must have taken the snap. She looked so innocent and wide-eyed. 'I'm so sorry, Meg.'

Meg put a hand to her mouth. 'Look at her tiny shiny shoes, Will, and the curls in her hair…'

In the background, three teenage girls stood in a group with four women chatting to the side of them.

'Did you take this picture?' I enquire.

'No, that's me on the right, in the poker-dot dress.'

'Four girls, four mums…'

I let her study the image, waiting for a reaction.

It's slow coming.

'Is this the usual suspects?' I ask.

'Yes, it was always the same bunch, Will. We glued together as we all lived on the same street.'

'So who took the picture?'

I could see the change in her expression as the horror grips her.

'Oh, gosh, Will…what are you saying?'

'Whoever took this portrait was a stranger. Look carefully…'

'What am I supposedly looking at?'

'Miriam's smile,' I instruct.

'She's…almost nervous.'

'Bashful,' I counter, 'And look at the half-turn in her body which is sub-consciously leaning toward you, her protector.'

'I hadn't noticed…'

'I'm a photographer, so it's easier for me to spot these things. Her body language suggests she was uncomfortable in the pose.'

'So you're suggesting the man in black took this?'

'There's a good chance, Meg. I'm sorry to say this, but he was stalking her and slowly befriending her.'

Meg reaches out and takes my arm, speaking softly, 'And gaining her trust.'

'Exactly, we call it grooming today.' I close the cover. 'He even used her camera, so he must have been on speaking terms with her by then.'

Her face is ashen.

Keeping hold of the scrapbook, I ask, 'Can I keep this for a few days?'

'Of course.'

'I promise to look after it.'

'I know you will. Do you mind if I lay down on my bed? I think I need to rest up.'

I guide her to the bedroom, settle her in, tidy up the lounge and make fresh tea. I sit for another hour until she drifts off. I am gutted for her. The past never disappears entirely. It always comes back to haunt you. I should know.

*

At home that night, I suddenly have a compulsion to email Romain's parents and express my sorrow as to what is happening to their son. We had become very close over the years but we have drifted apart since Daisy's death. Not surprising really. What can I say to them? They will be suffering too. I compose a message but alter it several times. Whatever I say will be of no consolation. There are no winners here, only victims. Eventually, I settle on a few words of comfort and press SEND. I've no doubt this will backfire on me. I seem to get everything wrong these days. I don't want to be the grim reaper!

I slap cheddar cheese on bread and pour a glass of cold milk. I need to cut down on the booze. I go in search of the note from Daisy which I promised to give to Isabel as part of the investigation. Not being involved with this does my head in. I'm so pissed off that I hatch a mad plan to travel down to France and start asking my own questions. Then I remember Isabel commanding me not to interfere. She'd probably have me arrested for obstructing the police in the line of duty.

I phone Meg to make sure she is comfortable after her ordeal and then watch a bit of TV, but I'm not able to concentrate. I stick a CD on of The Beatles *Revolver* to help lighten my mood. I turn up the sound to irritate my neighbours. Somehow, I possess the devilment in me tonight. After a short walk along the harbour front, I get back in and my resistance fails me: I have a beer. No complaint about the loud music from the neighbours thankfully!

Then I brace myself and open the photo album. I can feel Miriam in the room with me. It's heartbreaking. I turn each page carefully so as not to soil her memory. *Help me, Miriam,* I plead. Meg was right: she was a mini David Bailey and snapped away happily at everyone and everything. The camera had automatic focus and so the images were good overall. You just pointed and clicked: child's play.

And that's what she was…a little child. And I cried, for her and Daisy and every other child who had the misfortune to come across the wrong sort during their short lives. Lives extinguished, gone forever. What remains is the wreckage, and *what* wreckage to contend with for people like me and Meg and Isabel. I too felt gone, done. I had a beating heart but that was all. Sure, I found solace in other lost souls (mainly in Meg, bless her), and a degree of acceptance in the weakness of humankind, but basically I was a crash scene, written off and ready for the scrapheap. Fuck, the beer did this to my head. I need to learn about survival, not wallow in the misery of self-pitying analysis.

I try to move on, clear my head. I turn over the last page and there he is, as bold as brass, staring back at me.

I shudder at the image. The man in black.

Meg and I had closed the album halfway through when we looked earlier… no doubt nauseated by what we had found. Now I had my reward by searching all the pages. On this occasion, Miriam had the courage to face her demon and snapped back, catching him by surprise. He held his hand up to protect his face, which was half-hidden, rendering him unidentifiable. He wore thick white makeup, the obligatory plastic nose (which I assumed was red, we're talking black and white photos here as well) and inked-on tears down his right cheek. He wore an ill-fitting dark suit (reminiscent of an undertaker) and adorned a bowler hat. I'm spooked out, so God knows what Miriam felt. The man had a balloon in one hand and a – well, what appeared to be – toy rabbit in the other. This was weird. Was it a toy rabbit or a real one? Had he enticed Miriam to engage with him with this offer of a gift?

He didn't appear happy at being photographed, that was evident by his reaction. Her sure-footedness momentarily threw him off balance because he wasn't expecting it. Did Miriam unknowingly take a photo of her killer? I'm beginning to think this is a possibility. The police bungled the investigation and he was allowed to get away undetected. I bet the police at the time had never set eyes on what I'm staring at now: incrimination photos. I ask the question: was he a local man? I ask the question: if so, was he one of the hundreds of men interviewed by the police? This to me seems a logical conclusion. Again, if this was the case, then his identity is known and recorded on a file somewhere; but not as a clown. Clearly, away from the fair he would have forsaken this persona. I follow this up in my mind: is his true identity therefore still hidden away among the thousands of related documents now held, gathering dust, in some storage basement? He's there, I'm sure of it.

I try to imagine his type: shrewd, manipulative, a hunter of prey and deadly in his pursuit. He hid behind the mask and got away with it because he could…Why would anyone, joyful at the fair, suspect the motives of a clown? In other words, little girls like Miriam were seduced into his creepy world and *softly* befriended. After that, the victim was callously dispensed with. I look again at his eyes. This *had* to be him. And if he could get away with it once, he would get away with it again and again. It was his compulsion. His fix.

I've got you marked, I say to his cold soulless eyes.

And I make this promise to myself: If you are still alive, then I will find you. And if I discover that you harmed my Daisy as well then I will kill you with my own bare hands and rejoice in my deed. An eye for an eye, that's the way I see it.

I'm torn nonetheless, as you will gather from my mounting hatred for this man, because although unmistakably at the scene of a crime, he is not committing a crime. I, therefore, see two perpetrators, one from the past and one from the present. They cannot be linked but I blindly follow my conviction that there is a line of destruction, directly from Miriam to Daisy (and God knows how many other girls in between), and the police should be listening to me. But the police don't want to buy into my oddball theory. And I have to ask: Why should they? They consider that I am a crackpot and a nuisance. According to them, they have a credible suspect, whom I encouraged them to find in the first place. Anything I say or do now will only add weight to the theory that they shouldn't even be giving me the time of day, let alone the opportunity to discredit them still further.

The police have their man and until this moment I too thought they had their suspect.

But they haven't. I repeat: it's to do with the line. I'm convinced it exists but the edges are blurred, making it difficult to pursue the shadowy figures lurking here. I'm frustrated. There is so much more I need to understand. Romain surely didn't wish Daisy harm (protesting his innocence to Jimson after his arrest): he was a mere pawn, a young punk, an accidental bystander. Why do I now feel so strong in defence of his denial? Because he loved Daisy, he adored her. I listened to Isabel's words earlier and rejected them, calling her his *support group.* I was wrong to overreact, blinded by prejudice. He is a red-blooded young man: Why wouldn't he lust after Daisy? Why wouldn't he make a play for her? She was a real looker; a stunner who turned heads. But his volcanic desire didn't make him a heartless bastard, one capable of murder in an English field.

He came to England to warn her. *To protect her,* he indicated to the police.

It was becoming apparent that it was someone else who wanted to harm her. A man on a mission: a man with a black heart under a black suit.

I just have to find him, assuming he is still alive today and still active in his lust for cruelty. I just need to find the line, before he strikes again and makes a ruination of another family's hopes and dreams on this earth.

This evil predator has to be stopped.

I check the time and take a chance.

'Sorry to ring so late, Meg.'

'What's the matter, Will?'

'Did Miriam have a pet rabbit?'

'No.' Then, she adds, 'But she always wanted one…but my husband wouldn't entertain the idea.'

'Thanks, Meg.'

'Is that it?'

'Yes.'

'And you don't think I'm going to worry about this?'

'There's nothing to worry about.'

I click off and sit back in my luxurious designer budget-priced deckchair and close my eyes and try to visualise the wicked bastard I'm hunting down.

Yes, he is clever, and it scares me just thinking about it.

He'd done his homework.

He knew about the rabbit.

He knew the Faulkner family.

Chapter 23

The phone goes at eight in the morning and my world is thrown into turmoil once more.

Isabel says: 'We've got him.'

'Got *who*?' I'm half-asleep.

'Romain has confessed.'

I sit up abruptly and clear my head in a second. *'What are you saying?'*

'We have a full confession.'

I'm confounded. 'He *admits* to killing Daisy?'

'Yes, this is what we were hoping for, Will.'

I could tell she was mightily relieved but I feel hollow inside, dumbstruck to be honest with you. Where did that put my latest hypothesis, which had spun around in my brain all night long? This is quietly destroying me.

'At last we can find some kind of closure,' I hear Isabel whisper.

I think of the email I had sent last night to France. I knew it was a big mistake: another cock-up.

'Will?'

'Yes…'

'You seem preoccupied.'

'No, just shell-shocked.'

Let's just get this straight for a moment. This French boy has done a complete u-turn from protesting his innocence to an admission of guilt in a matter of hours…

'It's what you wanted.'

…Something isn't right.

I search for a bottle of water on the bedside table and gulp the contents. Then I ask, 'What will happen now?'

'Well, hopefully, he will be extradited without appeal from France and his trial will commence over here.'

'What did Jimson say?'

'Only that it went much smoother than he dared hope. His exact wording was "Tell your husband we have the little shit". The boy contradicted himself and got backed into a corner. Carl is very good at cross-examination. The boy was a wreck by the end of it, apparently. I think there has been drug abuse in his past and he had no resistance left. I get the impression that he was relieved to unburden himself with the truth.'

I'm suddenly apprehensive. 'We'll hear things at the trial that we won't want to hear.'

'I know, but hell is hell and we've been there once already.'

I concur.

'The papers will get hold of this now big time, so be prepared to be hijacked.'

I nearly laugh but refrain from doing so. I'd been there once already as well. 'They'll be camping out on our doorsteps hungry for a story,' I reply.

'Will?'

'Yes?'

'It's over.'

I could sense the lump in her throat and I desperately wanted to hug her.

Then I thought, what does she really mean by those words?

*

'I'm really pleased for you, Will, I really am.'

I had agreed to accompany Meg to hospital for her latest treatment and we sat in the waiting room.

'It's a surprise,' I announce.

'You seem a little subdued.'

'Oh, just the pessimistic side coming to the fore, Meg.'

'You're not convinced, are you?'

'It's just a little too convenient or clean-cut for my taste.'

'Be grateful, Will.'

'Really?'

'Just think, you can finally draw a line under it.'

'There's still Miriam to think about…'

'Get real, Will. I bless your concerns but you can't take on the whole world, you need to concentrate on the future now. The trial will be an ordeal.'

'I can't just walk away without helping you do the same. We've got the future to think of.'

'A future!' She laughs, and people stare. 'What future?'

I raise my eyebrows in mock surrender.

She jokes, 'At my age?'

I share the humour.

The consultant calls her name and I sit for over an hour, drinking tepid coffee and reading an old auto magazine. I look around and it is a depressing view; a room full of old folk either coughing and snorting or dribbling at the mouth. I promise to shoot myself if I ever get in this position. My job is to assist people in need but the inclination was fast receding to do this anymore. I am simply *beaten* if that is the best word to use. I have nothing else to offer, I'm running on empty. After seeing this through with Meg I decide that I'm getting out of here for good. My job stinks. I'd rather wash cars for a living. My life is a mess, a total fuck-up. It's reached meltdown.

Then Meg comes into view and her broad smile wins me over again and for a fleeting moment, I am renewed. She always seems to rise above adversity, whereas I sink with it.

'Well?' I say.

'I continue to breathe,' she replies.

*

I'm anaesthetised by Isabel's last words: *It's over.*

It's never over. The wounds heal but they are a constant reminder of the infliction endured. So there is no escape for any of us. We are touched by evil and this marks us down for a lamentable future of regret and remorse. We are cursed.

I don't believe that her words were directed at our faltering relationship, but I am picking up on any little thing that questions the hope I still carry in my heart.

For me, it will never be over between us. I love Isabel. She can put the distance between us if she likes but my feelings will never diminish. She knows this, and she knows she will never be loved more by another man. For we have had a child. And so any punishment she deems worthy (to fit my crimes against her) I will take on the chin. Thankfully, for now at least, the threat of divorce has been put on the back burner. But she too must live with the consequences of her actions. If she chooses to push me aside then eventually I will stay away. Sometimes she acts like a martyr to the cause, but I would remind her that she is the architect of her own path in life, and sometimes we don't always make those right decisions.

Anger causes destruction.

Destruction is wilful.

Wilfulness is the end of things.

Chapter 24

I catch up with Philip at The Ship Inn for a couple of pints. I can tell he has the world on his shoulders. So have I.

'Let's have it,' I venture, sinking the second beer.

'Erica's walked out on me.'

'Shit.'

'The cold-hearted bitch,' he snarls.

'I'm sorry, Phil…'

'Don't be.'

'What's happened?'

'I don't give a fuck…she's gone.'

'Where to?'

'Her mother's, no doubt…and good riddance,' he says, his eyes like lasers.

I have my suspicions on the cause of this separation, recalling her liaison with the man from the supermarket, but I hold my tongue for fear of a backlash.

'Is it over for good?' I ask.

'If I'm lucky.'

I could tell this is the start of an all-night bender. Phil has already caught the eye of a couple of girls at a nearby table. He then winks at me. Trouble is brewing.

I brace myself and order two fresh beers. 'Are we in for the long haul, mate?'

He then winks at me again and glances over his shoulder in their direction.

'If I'm luckier still,' he remarks, his anger subsiding.

*

I'm in a bad place, completely smashed.

It so happens we get turfed out from the pub for being over raucous after the girls ditch us for two businessmen who splash the cash on champagne in order to win them over. We are obviously cheapskates by comparison and carry the mantle of big time losers tonight. I'm actually relieved as I'm down to my last tenner. To be honest, I can't envisage pulling either of them with the exotic promise of a tonic water on ice, can you? Our chat-up lines let us down as well. At one point, Phil suggested that as a musician (he lies), his horn needed regular polishing. It went downhill from then on if I'm to be truthful. To be fair, it's no real loss: they were just the local slappers from the old town looking for a good night out. They found it by dumping us.

It's past midnight. Now I am suffering big time, and regret meeting up with Phil. My pal crashes at my place (more to the point, he actually collapses on the floor!), and sleeps in his own sick. In the morning I open the window and manage to get a bucket and mop from my neighbour and offer them to him in the hope he'll clear up. He hardly stirs.

'Clean up the mess and get a shower,' I bark. 'I'll make us a fry-up.'

He promptly throws up again.

After breakfast (I eat, he doesn't), I let him sleep it off on my bed while I try for a jog to clear my thumping head.

I get half-way along the tidal path and halt, gasping for air. When I look up, I see Isabel walking along the headway with another man. My sombre mood deepens.

Decision time: If we pass each other I just know I will say something I regret. I'll probably end up in a fight with lover boy.

Like a coward, I turn and slink off in the direction I came. Oh sod, I'm confronted instead by the reporters that have arrived outside my home. They spot me and give chase when I try to avoid them as well. No peace for the wicked.

*

Have you ever had that deep-rooted sickness in the gut when you know something is wrong?

I have that now, walking the wood instead of jogging, thinking out loud.

I was the first to suspect Romain, and I was the first to point a finger at him (ignoring Meg and her plight) but his confession is somehow too clean. That's the only way I can explain it. It troubles me. I rushed in, too eager to find a scapegoat. Typical of me! He's just a boy and the manner of Daisy's murder suggests the hand of a mature and highly skilled killer. If anything, I reckon this boy would have bodged it, left DNA, been caught in the act. It was a barbaric attack, and I try to imagine his terror if he was the assailant…he would have panicked, a foreigner in a strange land. It simply defies logic that he could then vanish into the background without attracting attention. No, I don't buy it. And If I do have to buy into it, then I have to consider the obvious motive: a crime of passion. Instinct tells me it was not.

Daisy was killed because she *needed* to be silenced. Her attacker wanted to exercise control and power, and the right to decide her fate: between living and dying. And he chose the latter, quickly, cleanly and effectively. He wanted her punished, to be made an example of. It seemed to me that his ruthlessness proved this wasn't his first time. He had killed before. He left no trace of himself. He disappeared effortlessly. He was a pro, on a mission.

Romain was a fucking amateur, a spotty runt of a lad with a brain the size of a pea. He wasn't capable of calculated murder. If he did do it then he got extremely lucky.

I don't believe in good fortune. Just look what happened to Phil and I when we tried our luck last night. We got found out. We were amateurs too.

And so a seed of doubt has been planted in my head. And as the cogs begin to slowly turn, I also begin to see a foggy image on the horizon as to the type of man who wouldn't ever allow himself to be found out. He was the type of man who could approach a girl on a country lane and not cause alarm. This suggests a man of integrity, perhaps a man whom the victim knew. He had familiarity, just like the clown in Miriam's situation. He could win over his victim. My mind wanders. I can see him, but I can't touch him. Yet.

Chapter 25

Phil has gone, and thankfully so has the press after they had collared me down the road and nailed me for a quote or two. Back from my walk, I clean up the flat, wash the floor, remove the bedding and curse my friend for the utter humiliation of the night before. I'm getting too old for chasing birds. I'll stick to the feathered kind in future. I doubt I'll follow my own advice though.

I call in to see Meg late in the afternoon.

She says, 'I dreamt about Daisy last night.'

I'm all ears.

'She came to me…'

'And?' I'm on the edge of my seat. I'd called over to put some lampshades up and fix a blind to the bathroom window. I didn't expect this development.

'She's troubled, Will.'

Meg had mentioned this before when we first got together.

'In what way, Meg?'

'She won't give in to me.'

'What is she hiding?'

Meg closes her eyes, exhausted. I fetch her some water.

'There is someone in the background…a man. She frequently turns to him…'

'Is she frightened of him?'

'No, if anything she is shielding him.'

I'm confused. Another fucking riddle…

'Will, there is something I should tell you, but I'm afraid to…'

'You can tell me.'

She takes a deep breath and exhales, her lips trembling. Her face is white and showing signs of distress, the blue veins on her forehead protruding under the thin skin.

'Well?' I prompt nervously.

'Don't get angry, Will…but as she draws closer and tries to talk to me or rather beckons to me with her outstretched arms I notice something very peculiar…'

I'm stressed now. 'Spit it out, Meg!'

She takes an eternity to speak as if the words refuse to come.

I can't be doing with this, so try a softer approach.

'Say what you need to say…and relax.'

This just makes her more agitated.

Then she rushes it out. 'They're both naked.'

Chapter 26

I'd be really interested to know how you would react to such a bold and totally bizarre declaration from Meg?

Me? I just freak out. For the first time, I lose my temper with Meg and suggest she is playing mind games with me. I'm fast losing my sanity. To cool down, I storm off and walk the block for half an hour. Christ, I'm spitting mad. What kind of crazy talk was this? Frankly, I had had enough of this mumbo-jumbo nonsense. I didn't need to conjure up images of my daughter naked. Fucking hell, the last time I saw her like that was in the morgue: lifeless.

Bollocks. I want to put my fist through a door; such is my dismay. Then I recall the fear in Meg's face as I ranted at her and I've come to my senses. I rush back and find her on the stairs, gasping for breath and sitting precariously on the edge of the top step.

'Meg, Meg, Meg…I'm so very sorry.'

I manage to lift her and discover she has urinated through her paisley nightie; such was her distress at being shouted at. I lay a thick towel over the mattress on her bed and slowly position her over it, supporting her head with an extra pillow until she is comfortable.

'How embarrassing,' she mutters.

'Forget it,' I say.

'I'm such an old doddery fool.'

'Hey, I piss myself all the time.'

'I couldn't help it; it just came in a rush.'

'Don't worry. Where do you keep a clean nightdress?'

She points to a cupboard.

I find a pretty lilac one plus fresh underwear and hand her another towel.

'If I leave the room and make tea, can you manage by yourself?'

'I'll call if I need assistance, Will.'

I scuttle off; greatly relieved (and praying) I'm not required still further.

*

To make amends, I buy fresh scones and jam from the corner shop and we munch away merrily, trying to avoid the topic of conversation which brought all the friction to the surface in the first place.

Eventually, she says, 'I'm sorry for what I said earlier.'

'It was a bad dream.'

'More than that, Will.'

'How come?'

'People seek me out for guidance, and I just point them on their way. These are lost souls, Will, so I don't need to embellish the message they convey.'

'Hmm…'

'I know you are sceptical, Will. I would be too, but I believe in the genuineness of their calling. And I always tell the truth to those that they wish to reach, even if the facts are sometimes upsetting.'

Her sincerity wins me over. I know now not to doubt her again. I was probably still steaming from my encounter with Isabel and her knight in shining armour down beside the bridle path. Poor Meg got both barrels, and I was foolish to the extreme with my ill-mannered response.

'What is the truth, Meg?'

'I'm reluctant to tell you…there's a whole lot more to the story.'

'I won't over-react this time.'

'Promise?'

'I promise.'

'I saw something else in the dream…'

'Go on, hit me with it.'

I'm trying desperately to remain cool at this stage, but I'm being pushed to the limits.

'Do you really want to know?'

I observe her eyes as they harden, her hands twitching, and her dry lips as she tries to rub her tongue around them.

I grasp her hand for reassurance, but I'm trembling with apprehension.

'Tell me what I need to know…' I plead, almost in a whisper.

I wait.

'Daisy was pregnant when she was murdered,' she says.

I watch as the tears of the dead cascade down her hollow cheeks.

Chapter 27

When she opens the door, I almost spit in her face as my words tumble out in a mad rush: 'Why the fucking hell didn't you tell me, you stupid cow!'

Isabel's startled eyes dart the length of the road. 'Keep your voice down, Will!'

I'm having none of that. I rant louder still and Isabel suddenly grabs me and hauls me into the cottage before the neighbours are alerted to the commotion on her doorstep.

I really don't care; I'm fuming and go on the attack once more.

'You *knew,* didn't you? You fucking knew, and you kept it from me.'

'We only discovered the pregnancy much later, during the autopsy. You were distraught enough and I'm sorry to say but, yes, I did hide the fact from you. What good would it have done, Will? I'm so very sorry…'

'It's unforgivable…this is like being trapped in a shitty living nightmare.'

'I had my reasons.'

'You had no justification!'

'I…'

'Christ, it makes me sick just thinking about how you came to that decision. You need to get down off your fucking high horse. This is your husband you're talking down to.'

'I foolishly tried to protect you…'

I slam my fist on the table so hard both cats shoot into another room.

'You were playing God!'

'I didn't think at the time that you could have handled the news…you were in a bad place. After all, she was your precious daughter. I was wrong, I'm truly sorry!'

I circle the room. 'Who else knows?'

'The pathologist, obviously…and Jimson,' she whimpers.

'Jesus fucking Christ, Isabel…my daughter WAS pregnant. Every parent has a right to know these things.'

'She was only fifteen, Will. She had underage sex. Get it? Would you have been truly happy with that knowledge, because I wasn't! I'd have killed her myself if I had known that information!'

'Not the best choice of phrase,' I remark, quietening down.

She comes toward me but I back off.

'Will, it serves no purpose for the world to know of this. What was done was done. Daisy was dead, and I didn't want her reputation sullied…so I took the decision to bury the pregnancy with her, OK?'

I cry.

'Oh, Will…'

I snap. 'She deserves better.'

'She deserved dignity.'

We continue to circle each other.

'How did you find out?' she asks of me.

I shrug, my words hesitant. 'From Meg.'

'Meg Faulkner?'

'Yes.'

'Why did she tell you that? I swore her to secrecy.'

'That's another person on the list then.' I was struggling big time, and retort, 'So you told Meg when you first made contact with her?'

'I was all over the place at the time and I needed some kind of support or spiritual guidance. I had heard about her daughter and the healing powers Meg possessed and, to be frank, Will, you had shut down on me and I desperately needed help. It all just spilled out. I felt I had no one to turn to.'

I was pissed with Meg now, knowing she had previously withheld this information from me. Who could I trust?

'Who else knows?'

'No one, I swear.'

'Your boyfriend?'

'That's sick, Will!'

I slump in a chair and watch as Isabel busied herself making coffee. I truly feel betrayed, my deflated ego bruised and battered. I have to ask myself: Who is this stranger in front of me, a woman who would lie to her husband?

Daisy was pregnant. This altered everything to my mind.

'Meg didn't mention you specifically,' I say eventually, cutting through the pinched silence. 'Rather, she told me after one of her dreams, so she didn't break the confidentiality between you.'

'A dream?' She hands me a steaming mug, which seems ironic to me!

'As you know, she experiences these weird mystic trances and people like Daisy come to her and connect through a portal of some kind. This was one such occasion.'

'How many times has this happened?'

'Two or three…'

'So you're telling me now, uh? It seems so fine for you to keep secrets.'

'Not quite the same. Your secrecy is based on deception.'

Eyes ablaze, she counters: 'I was wrong, wrong, wrong! I know that now…are you going to beat me up over this one error?'

The coffee tastes bitter, a bit like my mood.

One of the cats ventures back in. I give it the evil eye and it wisely retreats.

'Do you think the impregnator was Romain?' I ask.

'That's a horrible word, Will.'

'Well?'

'It had to be.'

'Do you think he is aware of what he had done to her?'

'I think Daisy kept it to herself, but maybe.'

'It could have been the reason for his trip over.'

She looks at me deeply, lost for words.

'Did you not suspect there was something up with her?' I add.

She takes a long time to answer.

'There were the mood swings, of course, but she dismissed my concern as that of a nagging interfering mum, so I didn't push it. She was a teenager, after all…and I assumed her obnoxious behaviour was just the hormones kicking in.'

'Looking back, she became distant towards me too.'

'She was frightened, Will, frightened to tell us I guess. God, I just wish…'

The tears flow from her, but I remain in my seat, steadfast. Even though I am seething I so want to hug her but I am fearful of the rebuttal. That's how far apart we are these days. We're dead people too.

'Could you tell how long the pregnancy was?'

'Just weeks…I never once detected a bump.'

'So she was sleeping with him on our last trip over.'

'Don't think unkindly of her, Will.'

I somehow finish my bitter coffee and then break the silence.

'I don't believe Romain killed her,' I say quietly. 'I think his confession was extracted under duress.'

'Why do you say that?'

'Because the killer is probably impotent and clearly Romain isn't…and, more importantly, I don't like Jimson and I think he wants to close the case.'

'That's outrageous, Will, and completely unfair.'

'Has Jimson mentioned the pregnancy to him during the interview?'

She shakes her head violently and wipes her eyes. 'No, of course not.'

'Have you managed to extract anything from that camera video?'

'Should hear in a couple of days, but I wouldn't bank on anything.'

'Can you do something for me, and it's pretty important?'

'Try me.'

'Can you trace the case notes from 1973 which relates to the murder of Miriam Faulkner?'

'Christ, Will, that's a big ask…'

I'm exhausted.

Everything in life was a big ask at the moment.

'I've got to go,' I say.

I stand up and make for the door, turning in my stride.

'Can you do this?'

'I'll need to seek permission.'

'From whom exactly?'

'Probably Carl…'

I smile ruefully and she catches my reaction.

'I know, you don't trust him.'

I cold-stare her with my proposition. 'Is there another way?'

'Jesus Christ, do you know what you're asking of me?'
I do, but I'm a desperate man and I'm not letting her off the hook.
I wave a finger in her direction.
'You owe me big time.' I say sternly.

Chapter 28

I take a couple of days off from work in lieu. I have to get away. My boss was not best pleased but there you go. I head up to London to get together with an old mate, Chris, who puts me up at his apartment in Brixton. I've been offered the sofa to sleep on but I've done worse so that's perfectly fine. Remember, I'm the guy that has deckchairs in the living room. Anyway, he's a good mate from college who's made a serious pile in the financial quarter of the city and he wants to splash the cash. So we hit the bright lights around Piccadilly and end up in a lap dancing club until three in the morning. And *that's* just the first night.

Now I know what you're going to lecture me on, but who said I was a fast learner? Give me some slack. I need to wind down so butt out.

Anyway, it's the next morning and Chris disturbs me at seven by clattering around the apartment. He's off to work, all bushy-tailed whilst I slumber on until lunchtime like a lightweight. His pad is slick, all polished steel, oak and glass with a Bang & Olufsen hi-fi system to boot. I look around: expensive art on the walls too. Am I envious? Too bloody right I am.

In spite of that, I clean up for him and then walk down to the Thames, order a latte from a café and sit in the sunshine and watch the short-skirted office girls go by. For a fleeting moment, I forget my troubles and contemplate an alternative existence. Chris reckons he can get me a job and I can kip down at his place for six months in order to set myself up. I'm sorely tempted.

What else is there for me in Emsworth? Heartache, for sure. There are too many sad memories down there which will ultimately suffocate me. At least here in London I can start afresh and remain anonymous in the big crowd. I'm not judged here, I feel. It's a vast metropolis of what, ten million people? I'd be like a grain of sugar in a bowl…unseen, one of the crowd; not under the glare of the spotlight. That would be bliss. There'd be no one to point a finger at me. Better still, Isabel would not be at the forefront of my thinking. Maybe I need to move on.

That night we go even crazier. My pal has hired a couple of escort girls and we head to the Burlesque club at Tower Bridge. I am nervous about the cost, but Chris spots this flaw in my character and tells me everything is on him. Apparently, its bonus time and he's feeling ultra flush. By the look of the girls, he'll need to be. As a way of thanks, I pay the taxi fare. Even that swallows up fifty quid. Perhaps London isn't such a good idea after all.

I feel so inadequate (I'm not used to this kind of life, OK?) that on our return to the apartment I can't even make it with one of the girls. I can already hear you sniggering. Don't get me wrong, she's great and a real stunner and comes on to me after Chris and his companion move to his bedroom which leaves us alone in the lounge. I know she has been paid and is playing her role, and playing it damn well. She almost convinces me that I turn her on but this is bullshit…it's just a job and she'll forget me within an hour of buggering off and counting the dosh stuffed down her bra. I can't do it. I'm basically pissed anyway, and coupled with the stress I'm under it is impossible for me to perform. Sex on a plate and what do I do? I make some lame excuse, embarrassed by my inability to rise to the occasion. At first, Leah (is that her real name?) dismisses my protestations with a winning striptease, tipsy as she is, but even she can see she's on a loser tonight. It's not long before she's irritated with my woeful response and the word "tosser" emits from her mouth. I can't argue with this assessment. She dresses quickly, swigs from the champagne bottle, and gathers her things and exits from the apartment with a last gesture towards me featuring a two-fingered salute. I am left standing there, sad and alone, my trousers bunched around my ankles while I listen to coarse laughter ringing in my ears from the room to my right. Chris is certainly getting his money's worth.

What did I say about keeping a low profile in London being good for me, low being the operative word? I am low on confidence, low on self-esteem and definitely low down on the list of expectations from a good-time girl who doesn't do rejection and wants being paid for her efforts. I've fluffed my lines basically. I feel I can't do anything right.

In the morning I lie to Chris with tales of wild abandonment with Leah, but I fear I will be found out if he rebooks them in the future. It cost Chris plenty. I express my gratitude. He is a good guy and was just trying to cheer a mate up. What a jerk I am.

I take the train back to Portsmouth, humiliated and chastised. I'm not ready for the high life that's for sure (yeah, yeah). Leah will be with another willing client tonight whilst I get home and settle for beans on toast and a *Die Hard* DVD. Sad or what?

Weirdly, I clean the windows to the flat later and feel better. Then I remember I need to be at David and Margo's for dinner. Fuck. Everything is falling apart, including my memory. I shower, shave, change into jeans and sweatshirt and grab an overnight wash bag just in case I stay over.

The journey takes forty-five minutes. I pull onto the crunchy gravel drive and see the lights on in the double-fronted Victorian pile. It's an ugly looking house, but worth a million I reckon. I think of my brother. *The boy made good.* I park next to a shiny Lexus hybrid and ring the doorbell.

David answers with a big hug (a bit over the top) and beckons me in, shoving a glass of wine in my hand.

'Gerard Bertrand,' he announces as if I should know what he means. He blinks, and says, 'The Clappe region…near Narbonne…remember? We went to his bloody vineyard at *Chateau L' Hospitalet*. Stunning red, yes?'

'Yeah, right,' I reply, taking a gulp.

'Sip it and savour, idiot! Taste the summer berry notes of…'

I thankfully spot Margo and brush past him. She pushes forward in her wheelchair and I bend down and kiss her warmly.

'Miss you,' she says.

'Sorry,' I whisper in her ear.

'I'll forgive you.'

David slaps my back. 'Let's eat!' He bellows.

To be honest, David is a fine cook and serves crab cakes and spinach salad, followed by sliced grilled chicken and roasted Mediterranean vegetables and noodles and poached pears at the end. I'm impressed. It beats my measly efforts any day of the week. However, he bores me rigid with a wine tasting lecture as he opens each bottle to accompany the three course meal. Even Margo rolls her eyes and winks at me. She looks tired but surprisingly robust. Perhaps it is just my presence. I seem to lift her spirits. Living with David can be warring, I bet.

Chat is surprisingly robust and I am at ease in their company as the wine loosens our tongues. We joke, reminisce and mock the world in general but...I notice we do not tackle anything closer to home. It's as if David has given his wife a list of no-goes. And so we amble on: football, school politics, films, my work, his work (again), their new conservatory, the merits of owning a hybrid (that's fifty grand, yes?) blah, blah, blah. But I'm having fun, probably more fun than my night with Leah. Actually, I feel sick just thinking about her! At least this experience is free, although I'm reminded of the saying: *There's no such thing as...*

You know the one. I've brought a bottle of plonk but notice David has consigned it to the larder. That'll end up as cooking wine no doubt. Ouch.

Then Margo cuts through the politeness.

'How are *you,* Will?' I see genuine compassion in her eyes.

'Not brilliant,' I confess.

David looks uncomfortable and starts to clear the plates away. Margo takes his arm and squeezes and he sits back down again.

'Tell us,' she says.

And so I do, all of it, the whole nine yards, the whole fucking mess. I pour out my heart and even I'm shocked that I am so candid with them. Margo sits quietly and listens intently; David, of course, sips his Burgundy, purses his lips and pretends to understand the depths of my depression. It's not his fault; he's just a cold-hearted wanker. He hates small talk and apparently this is it.

'Are you getting divorced?' He finally spurts out, yawning at the same time.

'David!' Margo shrieks.

'It's all right,' I mutter. 'That's probably what will happen.'

Margo turns to me. 'How is Isabel coping?'

The name *Daisy* is never mentioned of course.

'OK, I suppose. She's adjusting and throws herself into her job...'

'David tells me that a French boy has been arrested for the murder, Will.'

I see him nod in her direction. He *so* wants to get up from the table.

'Yes,' I say.

'What will happen next?'

'He'll probably be brought to trial in England.'

David cuts in. 'He was always after her. I warned him several times.'

(I have a flashback of the videotape, but avoid mentioning it, for now).

'Obviously, he didn't take much notice,' Margo mocks. 'I hope this brings comfort and closure for you and Isabel, Will.'

'It doesn't change the fact that my daughter will never come home,' I snap, but then I see the hurt on Margo's face. 'I'm sorry,' I add, 'but it's been a long day and the wine is swilling about in my head.'

'A brandy then,' David announces.

'Are you trying to finish me off?'

'Stay the night', Margo says.

'I'll have to now if you don't mind.' I've checked my watch: gone midnight.

'I had the bed made up, just in case,' Margo adds.

David pours the antique Hine (what else?) in Waterford fine cut glass (obviously) and suddenly places a musty smelling bundle in front of me.

I'm slow on the uptake. 'What's this?'

'The postcards.'

'The postcards...?'

'You asked if I had a postcard of the helter-skelter and so I dug it out and found my vintage collection in the process.'

I had clean forgotten, the alcohol numbing my brain.

Their contents are pristine, just like everything in David's life: everything had an order, logic, a history. Books were shelved in author preference, CDs in alphabetical sequence, the food in the fridge in date "sell-by" use. Even as a child he was compulsive in his search for things, be it postcards, marbles, stamps, bottle tops. I made Airfix models (badly), but he countered this by constructing a real remote-controlled aeroplane which he triumphantly flew from the local park. His obsessive nature meant that he always had to have the biggest and most important collection in the neighbourhood, even if it was chewing gum wrappers. Thinking back, our father was similar in that he listed train numbers. I couldn't see the fascination but each to their own I suppose.

I thumb through the pile.

'From Somerset to Carlisle,' David says proudly.

'We went to all of these?' I ask.

'You didn't, I did.'

'Did Mum and Dad take you?' I am feeling somewhat left out.

He laughs. 'Good god, no! I was old enough to travel by myself. I saved up and took the train on my own. They would have spoiled my fun...'

I pull out the one with the helter-skelter.

'Was I at this particular fair?'

'I accompanied you on the first day and you got hurt coming down the chute. Someone bundled into the back of you at the bottom. I accompanied you to first aid and after that, you had to rest, so Mum and Dad took you to the beach with Aunt Ivy. That day I got sunburnt on my face and decided to stay at the fair on my own. I spent several days there in fact. I wasn't one for sunbathing. I preferred to suss out the local talent.'

Margo raises her eyebrows and says, 'Typical.'

David ignores her and says, 'More brandy?'

I don't protest.

Margo backs away from the table. 'I'll make coffee whilst you two escape in your boyhood memories.'

'How often did the fair come to town?' I ask.

'Every summer I guess.'

'What happened when it moved on?'

'Well, it set up in another town or county.'

I shuffle the pack. 'When did you start collecting these?'

David scooped the pile up in his big hands. Strangely, they were like builder's hands, which was at odds with his job. He's strong. I recall that he built his own treehouse in the woods when he was sixteen. Then he ruthlessly charged his school friends a fee to go up in it.

'This was the first in 1968.' He flips it over. 'Bridlington.'

I take another. 'And this one?'

'Skipton. It rained every day.'

I hand another in his direction and his eyes light up.

'Oh, Woolacoombe 1978. Bloody fantastic beach…'

'Is there anywhere you haven't been to?'

'Wormwood Scrubs.'

'Ha-Ha! This one?'

'Can't remember…' He flipped it over. 'Frinton-on-sea. No pubs.'

'What?'

He sneers. 'The only town in England without a pub…very dreary!'

Margo returns with a cluttered tray on her lap. I take it from her and spread the cups.

'Good to see you two bonding again,' she remarks.

'I'm taking Will up to the caravan,' my brother remarks as if he's giving me a prize.

Margo laughs, and observes dryly, 'Drizzle and dominoes, Will.'

'Can't wait…'

'And a spot of fishing,' David adds.

I'm intrigued. 'Where is it exactly?'

'Above Whitby. The site's called Spring Ridge.'

'When did you buy it?'

The third brandy for David. I decline and sip my coffee.

'I didn't.'

'Then how…?'

He slurs his words. 'I inherited it from our parents when Mum died.'

'Christ, *that* caravan!'

'I felt no obligation to keep it, but I was feeling nostalgic.'

'It was falling to pieces,' I joke, shaking my head.

'After Dad died, Mum didn't have the heart for it anymore. And when she passed away, as you know, you got a little money and I kept on the caravan. Over the years I've spent a bit of cash doing it up.'

'Tarting it up,' Margo responds.

'Wasn't it originally parked up near York?'

'Skipton, but I moved it. Whitby was more convenient. I prefer to be by the coast. I get bored easily but I reckon I'll keep it where it is from now on.'

'It's not roadworthy,' Margo says with merriment.

'I'd forgotten about it,' I say.

'It'll bring back memories,' David responds.

'For sure...' Personally, as a child, I wasn't keen. I liked the adventure but never the travel. I always got car sick.

'Shall we go into the drawing room?' Margo suggests.

Margo and I sit and have a last chat before bed as she lists her ailments. David clears up in the kitchen. I notice that they don't have a great deal of time for each other but I know my brother is loyal...but only for the sake of appearance and status. He would hate the idea of being seen as a failure, or somehow diminished as a pillar of local society if he left her. And so he would just grin and bear it, show his support, maintain his status quo and get his kicks somewhere else. I was not remotely like David, nor do I envy him, but I did wish for some stability and comfort which he clearly gains with Margo. I feel like an outcast. In my imagination, I'm like a piece of driftwood washed up on the shore. Worse still, I remain there alone as passers-by ignore me. I'm not even worthy of being admired or even collected. I'm a reject.

I know, I know, I'm being morose again...

It's way past midnight and we do the hug thing. I stagger up the stairs and collapse on the bed. I'm done for, but I quietly reflect on the evening and it's been a success.

This is a big house for the two of them and upstairs it feels weird because I am alone and isolated. Since her confinement to a wheelchair, both Margo and David sleep downstairs in a specially converted room, or so I was led to believe. Then I hear a muffled argument from the direction of the kitchen and lo and behold movement outside on the landing. I peep through the gap in the open door and realise it is David creeping further down the corridor. I now know that they sleep in separate rooms. Worse still: on separate floors.

Another nail in the coffin I surmise.

Chapter 29

I open my eyes. For a split second, I have no idea where I am until the bedroom becomes familiar once more in the pallid light. I check my mobile: there's a text message from Isabel requiring me to contact her urgently.

I have a quick cup of tea with Margo (David has already left for school) and make a hasty retreat, but not before lots of hugs and kisses and promises of a return meal sooner rather than later. Actually, coming over here did me a power of good.

I phone Isabel.

'What's so urgent?'

'Jimson is back from France, and he wants us in his office.'

'Now?'

'Is that possible?'

I didn't have to check my diary.

'I can be there in just over an hour,' I say.

I can tell she is conferring with someone.

'That'll be good,' she replies.

*

Jimson stares at me, then Isabel, then me again.

'We have a full confession. We are not looking for anyone else in connection to the murder of your daughter.'

That's it. Clean and neatly packaged, as I had envisaged. I am stunned, unable to cry but Isabel suddenly makes do for the both of us. She sobs uncontrollably and leaves the room. I just feel numbness.

I manage to say something stupid. 'Are you sure?'

Jimson doesn't mock me. Instead, he pours me a glass of water and clears his throat, careful with his words.

'We apprehended Romain Petit at a small country pension where he was doing menial work for cash on the side. He had a grotty room provided in the staff annexe. Inside, we found numerous photos of Daisy stuck to a wall from the time you spent as a family in France. He had written hundreds of notes expressing his undying love for her. It was an obsession, unrequited we believe. When our French counterparts tracked him down, he escaped and ran but he didn't get far. He was obviously frightened and bewildered. I led the investigative team from Hampshire with the cooperation of Interpol. Under interrogation, he soon confessed to killing your daughter.'

'Do you have incriminating evidence?' I ask nervously.

He nods. 'Afterwards, we returned to his parent's farm and searched the place from top to bottom. In a barn we found a box belonging to him, which he had clearly hidden from prying eyes.'

I could hardly draw breath. 'And?'

'In the box we found…'

I buried my head in my hands, fearful.

What the fuck was he going to say next?

'In the box we found a pair of girl's knickers and some photos. We will require Isabel to try and identify the knickers, but that may not be necessary if we match the DNA samples we took from her body when she was in the morgue.'

I ignore the insensitivity with his last comment. 'What photos?'

Jimson looked to the ceiling then back at me. My hands fall limply to my lap.

It was his turn to draw breath. 'Naked photos of Daisy.'

I have to ask the worst kind of question:

'While she was alive or dead?'

He exhales. 'Thankfully, while she was alive. In one of them she is wearing the same knickers, we believe…'

How the hell were we going to tell Isabel *this*?

And then I look in his eyes again. There is more.

'What is it?' I ask in a whisper.

He stands, circles the room and perches on the edge of his desk, peering down at me like I am a specimen in a jar.

'The thing is, we believe, at this stage in the enquiry…'

'Spit it out, man!'

'…that Daisy purposely posed for these pictures.'

I stand and eye-ball him.

'You mean that my daughter willingly cooperated with him?'

Jimson, this time, doesn't hold back.

'That is exactly what I am saying.'

*

It is difficult to imagine any child doing this, but, when it is this close to home I find it impossible to take it all in. My own daughter engaging in sexual experimentation. But it happens, of course, and it is every parent's dread.

I think back to my own puberty and the first fumbling of desire behind the bike shed. But this was different. I knew Daisy was somewhat developed for her age and, with make-up on, she could easily pass for an eighteen-year-old. Isabel had often warned me that she was reaching that dangerous age when she would break our hearts. I just didn't want to know at the time and turned a blind eye.

Jimson goes in search of Isabel to explain things.

An hour later and sufficiently calmed, I walk Isabel to the park and try and digest Jimson's words. He had to tell us and tell us straight, but it hurt like hell.

143

I have to face facts: Daisy was a girl growing up fast and was sexually active with Romain (we are surmising now). So much so she got pregnant by him (we think). On returning to England, it doesn't take much imagination to realise she would be frantic by this development. By not confiding in us just worsened the situation for her, I believe. It would have been a terrifying place to be, alone and traumatised. What happened between them we will perhaps never know or fully understand. Only his confession will shed light on why Daisy is no longer with us.

I literally find my tongue unworkable. My brain whirls around insanely but no words come forth. Isabel, still in shock, stumbles and sits on a bench beside the white-lilied pond, her vacant expression highlighted by the glare from the lemon sun pushing through the clouds. What could we possibly say to each other? I hunch down beside her and take her hand in mine and thankfully she keeps it there. In the silence, we comprehend the suffering we share. Words are not needed. Any intrusion into our secret world would be like a dagger to the heart.

We are learning things about our wonderful precious daughter that we wish we didn't.

Chapter 30

I get back to my flat, microwave a baked potato and pull a finger ring on a can of lager from the fridge and hear the satisfying *hiss*. I dispense with a glass and drink greedily direct. I check my laptop. Almost immediately I'm almost thrown off my feet in total shock by an email from Romain's dad. In amongst all the shit that was coming my way, I had forgotten I had sent a message to him. I feel light-headed but take a breath and click on his reply:

My son is innocent and we will prove it.

I sit back and ponder. How could a father *not* try to protect his son? I would do the same in identical circumstances. Two young lives would now be wasted, and the aftershock would reach out and destroy us all. I am utterly confounded and bereft.

I have no answer for him, as I had no answer for my wife in the park. At the moment I can't even bake a spud. It's ruined, just like me and everything I touch. I get up and toss it in the sink and grab a packet of crisps instead and open a second can. I'm up for several, I'm afraid to admit. I can't possibly go into work and pluck up the courage to phone in and say that I'm poorly. I then try to think of a single word that sums up the insidious collapse of my existence, and *poisoned* comes to mind.

That would do. It just gave me perspective.

Somehow I sleep deeply. I awake to the sound of my mobile.

'Yeah?' I mumble.

'It's Isabel.'

I sit up, fully alert.

'I've got that information you wanted.'

'On Miriam…?'

'Yes.'

'That's quick. You must be shattered…'

'I am.'

'When can I see it?'

'Come over tonight, around seven. I'll cook supper.'

I click off and slump back on the bed, relieved. My heart is lighter, but I don't know why. There is no explanation, except that I feel…well, kind of useful once again and on track with what my gut reaction is telling me. At this moment in time, I'm not buying into Jimson's triumphant proclamation of Romain's guilt.

Yes, it appears cut and dried. A confession is indeed a damning verdict. But I want to find out more about the man in black. Stick with me on this.

*

You know, stranger things have happened but I detect a softening in Isabel's contempt of me. The realisation that our daughter was not perfect and had a secret side to her has, I feel, made my wife more tolerant to my failures and shortcomings. I know I did something bad. I can't even *say* the word. I know I have a *blankness* where my conscience should be, but equally, I have owned up to this crime against her and I don't want to be accountable forever and a day. If it's going to be thrown back in my face every time I want to share a certain closeness with her then we are doomed to eternity. I just want recognition that what is done is done; I was wrong and now let's move on. I'm not asking for forgiveness, nor do I expect any, but I do need a little less antagonism from her when we are drawn together in mutual unity.

And so we sit opposite each other at the kitchen table, as if this is an interrogation room. The central ceiling lamp just somehow intensifies the strained atmosphere as the harsh glow furrows our brows. What I really want is a beer. What I get is a glass of tap water.

Supper is good though: a salmon pasta dish with asparagus tips and crème fraiche mixed in. She's always been a dab hand in the kitchen.

'This,' she says, getting down to business, 'is a file containing the press cuttings from 1973, and this file contains the investigation itself and those suspected of the crime. It's a weighty set of documents. It is highly confidential material and I will be shot at dawn if it is discovered in your possession.'

'I've seen the press cuttings,' I reply and push the envelope back to her. I then open the other one and browse the contents. 'Have you read them?'

'Yes.'

'And?'

'If you're asking me if I see a connection between this murder and that of our daughter then...no. The gap between the two crimes is too long, Will.'

'I'm aware of that. But humour me, OK? Give me a logical reason as to why someone could effectively kill again after such a huge gap in between?'

'The person could have been in prison, I suppose, or had lived abroad and came home...'

'Yep, that's a good starting point. Christ, Isabel, any chance of a glass of wine or a beer?'

Startled, she nevertheless gets up and grabs a bottle of Chianti and two glasses.

'Happy, now?'

I pour and relish the first mouthful. She keeps to water.

I return us to the quiz. 'How about someone who travels the country?'

'Quite possible.'

Then I see her eyes light up. She's a bit dull to be a policewoman.

146

'Are you suggesting that there wasn't a gap between the murders?' she asks, and this time she did reach for the wine.

'Just suppose the killer roamed the country. How many missing girls are registered on the national database over the past four decades?'

'Hundreds…'

'Exactly. How many unsolved cases are there of girls found killed, just like Miriam and Daisy, which are still on file but no longer investigated?'

I top up our glasses. Isabel is no longer a reluctant participant.

'Many.'

'So perhaps there isn't a gap.'

'He's killed in other counties.'

We fall silent, digesting this hideous prospect.

'Back then,' I venture, 'information of this type wasn't shared between forces as it is today with the use of sophisticated computer links. But nothing is foolproof. It's fair to say that no one has put two and two together, even with the aid of this technology, and highlighted the connection of these two girls.'

'Except you, but I think you are way off course.'

'I'm not so sure, because the two murders are right on our doorstep. That is the link, Isabel, and the forty-year gap is viewed incorrectly as a reason of improbability, so no one wants to investigate it. Too costly, no doubt…and from the outset it doesn't make sense, so it is ignored.'

'And you've put two and two together, right?'

'Yep.'

'And those in our department haven't, right?' She carries on. 'Even though we have the superior manpower and technical and financial resources at our disposal, right?'

'Yep.'

'You arrogant bastard,' she snorts.

Chapter 31

Isabel stares at me as if I am stark raving bonkers before she carries berating me.

'Hold on, smartass, you can't just decide that this is to be the case and simply ignore the work Jimson has put in. He has a confession, which somewhat destroys your theory that we might have a pensioner still on the run and still finding victims to kill. It's too far-fetched.'

'Not if it's true.'

'We need a direct link; we need solid proof to back your judgment. No one is going to sanction such a sweeping investigation without compelling evidence. The costs would be prohibitive.'

'Then let's find it,' I say.

'Whoa, steady on!'

'Another bottle?'

'Did you not think to bring one?' she huffs indignantly. She again gets up and marches to the pantry and comes back armed and dangerous.

I raise my eyebrows and mutter, 'Rioja, Tesco's finest.'

'Are you complaining?'

'No…'

'Then pour.'

I do as I'm told, not wishing to push my luck any further.

'Why are you obsessed with this, Will?'

'What, the wine?'

'Sod off…you know what I mean. Are we just on a wild goose chase?'

'It was Meg who got me thinking.'

Isabel digresses, which irritates me. 'I hear she got settled into a new home…'

'In the nick of time,' I add.

'I'm pleased for the sweet old dear.'

'But here's the thing, Isabel. During my chats with her I've discovered that Meg is not so sweet and innocent…she is a canny old bird. Her capability to connect with the past and the non-living is pretty powerful.'

'You mean the dead?'

'Yeah.'

'Well, we all know that. What's new?'

'She told me things about Daisy which she wouldn't necessarily know about.' Then I catch Isabel's eye. 'Unless of course, you revealed the information when you saw her?'

'No, we arranged a second visit but I backed off…so I never got a chance to discuss Daisy in depth.'

'I'm convinced Meg is genuine and her insight into the *other* world is real enough. I can see the distress it causes her…' I pause and close my eyes.

'What else is there, Will?'

'It's just…'

'Don't hold back on me.'

'During the move, I helped to pack up her daughter's room, which was traumatic enough with Meg standing over my shoulder. Anyway, I found a bunch of photos which got me thinking…'

I relay the story of the clown.

'Gosh, and you think he could be the man who killed Miriam?'

'He appeared to be stalking her. Certainly, he is one suspect that the police apparently overlooked.'

'How do you know that for sure?'

'Because Meg alerted them to this odd character and nothing came of it.'

'OK, we can look into that. It will be in the report somewhere…leave it to me. So, you think that this man may still actually roam the country and, under this disguise of a jovial clown, attract little girls at the fairs, yes?'

'I think you're taking the Mick. It's a possibility, but he might have many disguises, the clown being the only one we can follow up on. But if we can substantiate a link between the time and place of the fairs and any murdered or missing girls at the same time and place then we have our man.'

'Not so easy! It still doesn't prove anything.'

'No, but it will be a compelling argument to reopen the case on Miriam Faulkner. Then we can follow through the line of victims to the present day…'

'To Daisy?'

I see a tear form in her eye and caress her hand like I did in the park. She squeezes back.

Nothing lasts. She removes her hand and blows her nose and then swigs her wine.

'I can't see an ageing killer clowning about in this area without looking a little conspicuous, Will.'

She's mocking me again.

'Take me seriously just for a minute. He would now be forty years older, possibly in his middle sixties and no longer involved in the travelling fairs. He's moved on to new pastures, that's the secret of his success, for want of a better word. His disguise could now be simply *Mr Anybody*. He hides in plain sight. Who would be suspicious of an older man just walking down a country lane in broad daylight?'

'Maybe he wasn't just any old *Mr Anybody*…'

'What do you mean?'

'In Daisy's case, perhaps she knew him.'

I think about this and elaborate, 'Perhaps because she passed him as she cycled home on the same route every day?'

'Yes. It could be that if he was preying on her then a quick hello or a gentle wave each early evening would be enough for her to stop and talk eventually…fuck, Will, we're making this guy a real possibility and I don't like it. It's conjecture and you're twisting my viewpoint as to what really happened to Daisy. It goes against everything I've learnt so far about Romain.'

'What do you make of Romain's confession?'

'Well, I haven't seen the transcript as yet but he was in the country at the time and he had a motive.'

'Which is?'

She takes a stab at it. 'Jealousy, rejection, obsession…who knows? We'll need to ask him.'

I get my jacket from the back of the sofa and extract a pile of holiday snaps from the inside pocket and I spread them out on the table.

At first, Isabel is confused, then shocked, and starts to cry again. Many of them feature Daisy and precious memories flood back for her. 'I haven't seen these for a while…' she says quietly.

I make a pot of coffee and slowly put the photos in order to show her the disinterest I've spotted between Daisy and Romain over the time span of our holidays in France.

At first, Isabel fails to see anything and stares at me in bafflement.

'What am I searching for?' she asks.

'Keep looking.'

She does and I'm disappointed with her lack of response.

'There's cake in the tin,' she says, gazing up.

I'm impatient and leave her to it and slice the chocolate gateau and momentarily stare out of the window and across the sunlit bay. It is a stirring sight as I catch sight of a heron swooping low over the muddy waters.

'Christ,' Isabel shrieks.

I turn delightedly as she looks up and smiles at me for the first time in a manner of sudden rejoicing, rather than the usual mocking smile that signifies accusation…yes, the one that I've had to get used to, much to my shame. A rapist is always a rapist.

Isabel says, 'They've sitting further and further apart.'

'It doesn't make him a natural born killer,' I add, 'which was my first inclination. But it does show how people can react to one another when stress is in the air.' And there was a lot of stress in the air.

I'm trying to get her to see things differently. I change my viewpoint as every new evidence comes in, good or bad. It alters things, but I still crave for the truth as to what happened to our daughter. Why do I include Miriam in this…maybe I think I have to solve her mother's problems as well. I obviously do! Wouldn't the conflict drive you mad with so many variables?

I bring the cake and sit down, pulling my chair closer to hers.

It feels good, the distance between us.

Chapter 32

The next day, Meg phones.

'Hello, stranger,' she moans.

'I'm so sorry, Meg, but things have been piling up…'

I curse under my breath for ignoring her.

'I've bought more scones and jam from the corner shop. Mr Levi is my new best friend.'

I laugh aloud. 'Are you inviting me over?'

'If I can tempt you.'

'You didn't mention any cream.'

'Mr Levi has got everything it seems.'

'Really. Does he do home delivery?'

'For me, anyday…'

'Seems like you have got him tied around your little finger, Meg,' I say.

'Well, he is a spinster like me and I think he enjoys coming around and making a fuss of a damsel in distress.'

'Hmm, sounds like he's the cat that's got the…'

'You're a bad boy, Will. It's nothing like that at all.'

'If you say so, Meg. Shall I pop over at midday?'

'Perfect.'

We click off. I smile. Perhaps I'll pop into the shop as well, buy some flowers for Meg and check out lover boy.

*

I wash some clothes in the sink, daydreaming of a holiday in the Algarve which I can't afford when the phone goes again. Surprisingly, it's Margo and I'm caught off-guard.

'Am I *that* underwhelming,' she states dryly.

'Sorry,' I say, preoccupied with lifting a pair of jeans from the soapy water with my spare hand. 'I just wasn't expecting a call, that's all, Margo.'

'I'll forgive you, thousands wouldn't.'

'I'm pleased about that. What's doing?'

'Just a big thank you for coming over the other night…'

'It was great.'

'It gave me a big lift.'

'I could tell.'

'David's not the easiest man to live with at times.'

'Didn't realise he drank so much…'

'It's got worse over the years…living with me I guess!' A ripple of laughter comes down the phone.

'He has a stressful job,' I say.

'He's at a meeting today. I think he has to announce a couple of redundancies and there's a shortfall in funding for the new sports hall.'

'It's never ending, I suppose.'

'It gets to him.'

'When does he retire?'

'The year after next, and then he'll have to put up with me all the time.'

On this occasion, I join in with the merriment, but I know there is a home truth lurking behind the sentiment.

Then she adds: 'I'm worried about him.'

'Oh, why?'

'He's sharp with me and less patient these days.'

'There must be more than that.'

'He's got a problem, Will, and he's not sharing it with anyone, and it's getting him very depressed.'

'A *problem*?'

Pause.

'I think you should know.' Longer pause. 'David has been to a consultant and been diagnosed with prostate cancer.'

I drop the phone in the hot water.

I can only think of one word: *Death.*

*

I can't just rush over to see him. Anyway, David is at work and if I bowl over tonight he's the sort who will brush it aside and dismiss my concerns. This is a massive blow. I would hope he would tell me but he is a very private man and would try and maintain his air of invincibility. I'll play it calmly. According to Margo, the cancer is small and slow-growing, and surgery is not necessary immediately. Instead, he is under observation. I still feel desperately sorry for him.

I take solace and visit Daisy's grave and lay fresh flowers and share a few words with her. I need her help, a sign, anything to dispel my fear that Romain is being stitched up. Everything points to his guilt, but I feel uneasy about it and have my own perspective of where the blame lies. At least now I have Isabel onboard, however reluctantly she shares my views.

I check my watch and rush over to Meg's. I'm not so keen to visit as I have my brother on my mind, but I elect to hide my worries from her.

I needn't have bothered.

'What's troubling you, Will?' she asks as I enter the front door.

'Is it that obvious?'

'I can see it in your haunted eyes…'

I've brought Meg a box of *Terry's All Gold* which she's thrilled with. The flat looks great and she's done wonders in such a short space of time. We hug, and I tell her about David whilst she brews the tea and prepares the scones. I'm looking forward to this treat.

'I'm so sorry,' Meg says.

'It's a real bummer,' I retort and carry the tray into the lounge.

'It doesn't mean you have to fear the worst, Will.'

'Well, it's not a good prognosis. I hate the word cancer.'

'Wait and see. A neighbour of mine had an operation to have the prostate removed and he lived to be eighty-six. It's not the end of the world…'

I was suddenly reminded of Meg's health problems and realise I have to be guarded with my histrionics. I pour the tea and spread the plates.

'Yummy,' she shouts and we dig in with extra dollops of cream.

'How's Mr Levi?' I ask with a twinkle in my eye.

'Naughty,' she rebuffs me.

I sit back and admire what she has done with her knick-knacks and pictures and things. It's real cosy and I say so.

'Bless you for helping me, Will. I would never have managed it on my own and Molly is a star too.'

'Our pleasure.'

'It seems a lifetime ago.'

'You faced up to the challenge with great dignity.'

'I'm not sure about that.'

'It was difficult for you, especially disturbing Miriam's room but we got there eventually. It took a big leap of faith for you to trust in me, Meg.'

'That reminds me, I found some more photos in one of the boxes. Perhaps you would like them to peruse through. You still have the others, haven't you?'

'Of course, Meg.'

She fumbled under her chair and passed me a bundle. 'Do let me have them all back sometime soon…'

'I'll call in next week then.'

'Is that a promise?'

We sit in silence, happy with our company. Time passes, the tea replenished.

'Have you anything new to tell me?' she asks quietly.

'Well, I've got the police file on Miriam's death and I am trying to piece together a pattern of events which I hope will somehow include our mysterious clown, but it's slow going.' I change the subject. 'To be honest, I was a little embarrassed after my outburst on my last visit because you completely threw me with what you said. Daisy was pregnant, but you knew that anyway, didn't you?'

'I'm sorry but I couldn't betray your wife's confidence, even though it hurt me to hide this fact from you. It was easier to unburden myself when I foretold the dream.'

'No more secrets?'

'No more secrets.'

'I shouldn't have raised my voice in the manner I did.'

'It was a shock but you reacted as any father would.'

I reflect. 'The horrible thing is not being able to understand your own child.'

'You can't be sure of anyone in this world.'

I think of Isabel and what we had been through and nod my agreement.

'Are you going to find some kind of peace at last if this young man is found to be the one?' Meg asks.

'Yeah, I guess so.'

She catches my eye, and says: 'And your wife?'

'That's difficult to answer.'

'Will you get back together?'

I squirm in my seat. 'That's not difficult to answer.'

'I take that as a *no* then.'

'There's too much friction between us, I'm afraid.'

'Keep trying. You're a good lad, Will.'

I could have cried in my teacup. 'Thanks,' I mumble.

'I won't be here *much* longer…'

Now I *do* start.

'Meg, don't say that!'

'It's true; the heart is giving up on me as well.'

I lament: 'But not yet, eh?'

'Months, I reckon.'

'Years,' I insist.

'Stop kidding with me,' she barks. Then she studies me intensely and says, 'Find who killed Miriam before I kick the bucket, that's all I ask.'

I go to the kitchen with the cluttered tray and look out of the window at the wondrous sky and swear to do just that. Strangely, a ray of light breaks through the clouds at that precise second. It's a positive sign.

'Shall I make some more tea?' I shout back.

'Yes, please.'

The words echo in my head. *Find who killed Miriam…*

It is more than a vow, actually. I consider it a mission.

I am mad, but you knew that already.

Chapter 33

At home, I do some research on prostate cancer upon the laptop and visit my GP to get a handle on things. It's a scary situation for David and I feel powerless to help, but a little understanding of his condition and the seriousness of it puts me to shame with my own problems. I have a word with Margo again to get further information in order to put a perspective on what I can do, which, in all fairness, is very little. I google "pioneering laser treatment for prostate cancer" and discover reams of stuff on the subject. What I don't know at this stage is how urgent radical action is required, because Margo too has been kept in the dark. I will have to ask David directly, man to man. I will need to choose my moment carefully though, as he has a habit of closing in and being evasive. It'll be a hard one to crack, if you'll forgive the pun. The prostate gland is often referred to as a walnut shape. Dark humour prevails. If you don't laugh then you'll certainly end up crying.

The doorbell rings. I never have a visitor so I panic when I realise I'm sitting around in my boxer shorts and grubby T-shirt. I peak out of the window and see Isabel in uniform and now I definitely freak out, pulling on tracksuit bottoms and a hoodie, at the same time clearing the dirty pots into the sink. Fuck, the place is a tip. I open a window to emit fresh air, push my hand through my hair and check my teeth in the mirror. The bell goes again.

This time I'm ready and resolve to play it calm.

This is so bloody unexpected though.

'Hi, Isabel.'

'Just got out of bed?'

I've been rumbled.

'Something like that.' I say.

'Can I come in or are you going to keep me on the doorstep?'

I see raindrops forming on her hunched shoulders. Why the hell couldn't she have warned me of her unexpected visit?

I open the door further. 'You'll have to excuse the mess…'

'I've probably seen worse.' She enters, removes her hat and follows me into the lounge and remarks, 'Er, maybe not.'

I'm gutted, and make amends by offering coffee.

'No thanks,' she says, eyeing the stained cups.

I can tell the niceties are over and ask, 'Why the visit?'

'Take a look at this,' she says and hands me a police DVD. 'It's an enhanced version of the one you gave me for analysis.'

I raise my eyebrows.

'The one featuring your brother and Romain, remember?'

I try to clear my bird-brain head and note that she prefers not to use the word *David*.

She mocks me. 'Are you awake yet?'

This is what a uniform does to people. I pour myself a glass of milk and hope she relaxes a little.

'Deckchair?' I offer with a smirk.

She declines again. The great thaw is *not* going to happen...

'Have a look,' she continues, 'and see what you think, then come down to the station and examine what we have on audio and freeze frame.'

'When?'

'Now would be good.'

'Do I have thirty minutes?'

'Jimson will be in attendance, so don't be late.'

Then she turns and is gone in a jiffy. Just *fabulous*. I've really made an impression on her, I can tell. I reckon our newly found coming together recently had just been blown out of the water. It was probably the tracksuit bottoms I'm wearing, real passion killers.

I insert the DVD and watch attentively as the background is brought into sharp focus. For the first time I can witness a full-blown argument, with David pushing Romain twice and then the young lad retaliating. At one point they are face to face, inches apart. What the hell was that all about?

I wash and change into clean check shirt and chinos and comb my hair, remove the DVD and head down to the police HQ in record time. Well, in forty-five minutes to be precise. *Someone* won't be best pleased. And my estranged wife will be pissed off as well.

I'm shown into a video room, offered tea and watch a technician setting up on a computer screen. I wait several minutes and suddenly Jimson and Isabel barge in, with him holding a bunch of thick files under his arm.

'Glad you could make it,' Jimson remarks, checking the wall clock.

I sip my tea and keep under the firing line.

An image comes up on the wall screen, and I recognise the characters, as we all do. There is a fine adjustment, and then Jimson nods to the man on the keypad. I'm nervous.

'Right there,' Jimson says. Then audio comes in but it isn't particularly clear.

'Try again.'

And we wait. I catch Isabel's eye but she blanks me.

'Freeze,' Jimson barks and looms over me and points to the screen. 'We've tried to analyses this footage and had a lip reader interpret the dialogue. Unfortunately, interference stops us listening to the actual words but at this point, we believe we have something meaningful.'

I'm all ears.

'The words are "She doesn't like you".'

It's now my turn to freeze.

'Does that signify anything to you, Mr Farmer?'

I'm stunned. This is almost the exact wording on my note from Daisy. Then it hits me, and I notice that Isabel is staring directly at me searching for my reaction. I'm slow on the uptake. It isn't the actual words that they are bringing to my attention…

I ask in as calm a manner as I can. '*Which* of them is saying this?'

'Look closely, Mr Farmer,' Jimson says, and whirls his finger in the air. The imagery moves on frame-by-frame so there is no mistake. 'The words are actually spoken by the French boy.'

Hell.

That's put the cat among the pigeons.

I hear Jimson's voice reverberate in my head: "The words are actually spoken by the French boy…"

I'm confused, unable to comprehend the meaning of this revelation. Then I see the disgust on Isabel's expression and my world is suddenly turned upside down. Again.

The camera doesn't lie.

Chapter 34

I won't be intimidated by Jimson, who still hovers over me.

'Ask Romain what he means by this,' I demand.

'We will,' Jimson says. 'We fly out tomorrow and will question him again in the afternoon. Depending on what we learn, we will then perhaps commence our investigation nearer to home.'

I know what he is implying.

'And,' he adds purposely, 'I do not want this conversation, and what we have seen on the screen, to leave this room under any circumstances. Do I make myself entirely understood?'

'Entirely,' I reply, numb from head to toe.

'Then we have an understanding.'

'Yes.'

'This line of enquiry could mean nothing, of course.'

'Just two guys having a stand-off,' I offer.

'Or it could open up a whole new can of worms. Is your brother in the habit of picking fights with people?'

'He's a Head of School, and knows how to control his temper.'

'Apparently not,' Jimson counters.

I couldn't argue with that one.

The DI continues. 'However, there is no need to alarm anyone else while our investigation is progressing well and words such as this do not imply any wrong-doing on the part of someone else at this stage. They are just words, but I need an explanation as to what they imply. Hopefully, we'll know tomorrow. Don't forget we have a confession.'

Isabel walks me to the car park in icy silence.

'Can we talk later?' I ask.

'Best if we leave it until tomorrow.'

Then I watch as she turns her back on me and marches off.

I feel like I have shit on my shoes.

*

For lunch, I treat myself to a pizza at a local restaurant on the little square in Emsworth. Gulls circle low outside and I think perhaps a storm is on the way. Certainly the leaden sky matches my forecast, or is it just the sombre mood I'm in. I get out the envelope Meg presented to me, empty the contents on the table and flick through the snaps taken by her daughter. They're the usual thing a kid would take. Nothing leaps out and I concentrate on the meal, which is great. A sad thing to say, but this is the highlight of the week. So much so, I even splash out on a second bottle of Corona. I'm the last of the big spenders.

This Italian restaurant is a favourite haunt of mine. Often I came here with Isabel and Daisy. It was our little treat, especially on Sunday lunchtime. Luigi, the owner, has been here a hundred years (or so it seems!) and always has a kind word to say to everyone. He strolls over, pats me on the back and we share a half carafe of Chianti and talk Italian football. He supports Juventus and so the subject of corruption in the game soon comes up. It's good banter and my jovial companion is a mine of information on local gossip to keep me amused for hours. The time flies by.

We finish with coffee and Limoncello and watch the pretty girls stroll by the window: sad gits that we are. Then he looks down at our table, points and shouts as only an Italian can, with much gusto: 'Ah, Juve, Juve!'

I follow his gaze as he prods one of the photos left lying around in front of him. I'm perplexed by his excitement.

'Juventus,' he repeats, and points to a man in the crowd wearing a football shirt and I suddenly get it.

'Ah, the classic black and white,' I say. I hadn't noticed…more to the point, I wasn't very interested. It was just one guy amongst many guys milling about at the fair getting drunk on a summer's day: a melee of hardcore rockers, some dandy mods, and one or two gypos working the crowds.

Then my mobile rings and I'm distracted.

'It's Isabel.'

'We can't keep meeting like this.'

'You'd better call in again.'

'To the station…?'

'Yeah, it's urgent.'

I watch as Luigi, with his big stupid grin, clears the plates. I put a twenty-pound note on the table and whisper to him, "Chow".

Out on the street, I say sharply: 'What's so urgent, Isabel?'

(I'm still smarting from the way I was treated earlier in the car park).

'Do you remember that man we questioned who had molested a waitress in a car park?'

'The one interviewed in connection to Daisy?'

'The very same,' she says. 'He was released without charge on that occasion, the waitress unwilling to press charges. Well, he's just been arrested for attempted rape on a schoolgirl at the digs where he is staying near Gun wharf Quay. Jimson is grilling him now. This is different, Will. He tried to strangle his victim this time.'

'Hell, that's frightening.'

'He travels to this area quite often and we know he was in the vicinity when Daisy was attacked by virtue of a petrol receipt found in his company car. Now we know what he is capable of. We think this guy is a predator, not just a chancer.'

'And Jimson has a feeling about him?'

'He does now…We can't ignore the violence.'

'This further complicates things.'

'It does, but we have to explore every avenue. This man fits the profile, Will. We just didn't have enough to nail him last time.'

'And Romain doesn't fit the profile, is that what you're saying?'

'If he's guilty then he fits the profile. And the boy is still under arrest, don't forget that.'

The pizza starts to repeat on me and suddenly I can't digest it properly.

I insist: 'And a boy can be made to confess to anything, right?'

'I'm not being drawn on that one…'

'But that could preclude him from murder?'

Too late: Isabel had cut me off with my question still hanging in the air.

Chapter 35

There is no plan for tomorrow.

I just take each day as it comes. Everything seems hopeless, and I've come to realise that I do *hopeless* rather better than most. I sit in the waiting room at police HQ and ponder, eager for news but downhearted about the outcome. What if this guy really did kill my daughter? Isabel has her stern face on as she brings me tea and I can see that this new development is a serious business. According to her, the man in custody is under pressure to confess to his crimes…and the list is growing. He is a serial rapist and brute to match. Even more disturbing, he is unremorseful for his sickening deeds. *The worst kind,* she emphasises.

And so I wait and wait. And think.

I make a mental list of oddities that need explaining:

Who, for instance, is the flash snapper being reprimanded by Daisy for taking a photo of her in the bikini top?

The inference: *I don't like him…* Who is this directed at*?*

Who is the mysteries man dressed as a clown at the fair?

Meg's startling revelations/ are they fact or fiction?

Why did my daughter allow intimate photos to be taken of her?

What was the gist of the argument between my brother and a simpleton boy?

I want to discover why the child called Miriam had such a fearful reaction to someone standing close by her at the fair/was she being groomed?

The forty-year gap between murders…What happened in between?

Why didn't Daisy tell us she was pregnant?

Where was Daisy's school jumper?

Why did I rape Isabel?

I stop and want to throw up.

Am I any better than the bastard banged up somewhere in this building? I feel shame and regret for my deplorable actions and realise that within Isabel's dark eyes is revulsion for what I have become. A lesser person, diminished in her estimation as a father and a husband. It doesn't get worse than that.

Shaking, I rush to the toilet and vomit in the sink. I catch my reflection in the cracked mirror above and shudder. I am yesterday's man, like yesterday's newspaper I notice flung on the floor…a thing of the past, to be discarded, kicked around. I wipe my mouth on my sleeve, gargle water from the tap and sit in the cubicle, my head in my hands. I forfeit any right to expect tolerance from the one I love. I've pissed on our parade, and the parade isn't coming back this way any time soon. I'm the fall guy, just like a clown. To be laughed at.

Then I think of the clown I'm searching for, but no one is laughing at him.

161

He's a predator, not a chancer…

These words have stuck with me.

I think of my random list, and re-examine the photos that Meg gave me. And then I remind myself of Luigi and turn up the image that caught his attention. A man in a black and white striped jersey. A man with a penchant for wearing a Juventus football shirt.

Cogs slowly turn in my head, but they turn nonetheless.

Chapter 36

I can't wait here forever. It's been over three hours without any kind of update. Frankly, it's been a waste of time and I'm fatigued and dirty and need a shower. I still have the crumpled *Sun* newspaper that I found in the loo (I'll stoop to anything if it's free) and so go home, grab a beer, strip off and jump into bed. The wash can wait until the morning. I browse the sports pages and half-complete the crossword until exhaustion takes hold. I sleep deeply, without interruption and dream of driving a convertible Porsche along the clifftop highway from Nice to Monte Carlo. With the music blaring and sun beating down on the azure sea I whip along the bending road: full throttle. This is paradise, a world without *blankness.* And what I really want is for this magical road to go on forever so that I may never look back and see the burnt-out and mangled wreckage I have caused on my journey so far.

But fantasy doesn't last forever. The roll of thunder and the crack of lightning rudely awaken me from my slumber. Beyond the blinds, a turbulent dawn noisily approaches. That's the least of my problems. I'm sodden from the beer bottle that overturned on the bed during the night, careless that I am. I strip down the sheets, ram them into the washing machine and stand naked under a steaming jet of water from the showerhead, which soothes my brain if not my soul.

Although my head feels like scrambled egg, I'm famished and cook just that, devouring it with buttered toast and baked beans. Eat your heart out, Jamie boy. I even find clean clothes (not ironed) but what the hell...who's going to be looking at me? After a bit more effort I resemble something half-human and find renewed energy for the day ahead. I feel like a proud soldier on the march...chin up, shoulders back, firm stride.

I get to work and I'm duly sacked.

Now that's what I call a haymaker, square on the chin.

Ms Bottomley is unimpressed with my lack of dedication and extended days off and wants me replaced forthwith. I'm technically suspended, and so I technically tell her to go screw herself and offer to show her how...which she politely declines. I follow that with an array of expletives and strangely our conversation is quickly terminated. Security is summoned. I calm down sufficiently and elect to walk the plank with dignity. I need to show a touch of class in this situation. I leave quietly enough and get to the lobby, then piss in the cactus plant as a parting gift. What else could I have done?

Security then escorts me forcibly from the building.

*

'You did *what?*' Meg asks incredulously.

I don't repeat my story of the *incident*, as the image is strong enough I reckon. Joining the ranks of the unemployed, I suddenly realise that Meg is no longer classified as a client of mine, but a dear friend she will remain I'm glad to say. It feels surprisingly good, but where is my next pay packet coming from? Meg senses this.

'How are you going to manage, Will?'

'No idea.'

'I have a little savings.'

'Meg, cut it out.' I check my pockets and count the loose change. 'I'm loaded…'

We sit in her lounge, facing each other. She looks frail and jaundiced, her grey wiry hair thinning slightly on top. I have seen the decline in her health during the short space of time we've known each other and it saddens me. In spite of her illness though, she looks a picture in twin set and pearls and I compliment her. I calculate that Miriam would be near fifty by now if she was alive, and I suddenly feel morose. Daisy would be seventeen this year. Meg and I share a damnation of sorts that we'll carry to our graves.

'I've got thirty quid stashed under the bed if that would help,' she says.

'I'll manage,' I whisper and top up our teacups.

*

'You did *whaaat?*' Isabel says angrily.

Again, I don't repeat myself.

'Have you absolutely no sense in that pig-head of yours?'

'Obviously not.'

'Don't be so fucking flippant, clever dick.'

I stand on the doorstep to Eggshell cottage and put on my best hound dog expression.

She weakens. 'You'd better come in.'

It works, as usual. I enter with my head bowed, overdoing it slightly.

She puts the kettle on but I'm sick of tea and sympathy.

'Any chance of a beer?' I ask.

'In the fridge, and get me one too.'

I duly oblige, and we sit for five minutes in silence, which if you care to try it that's a fucking long time just listening to slurping sounds.

Then she says: 'How will you survive?'

'Prostitute myself,' but I instantly regret the words uttered.

'You need to grow up and fast.'

'I'll sell some photographs at the local gallery.'

'And when did you last sell anything?'

'Oh, two years ago…so the omens are good.'

'Do you have to make a joke of everything?'

I berate myself and fall silent again. Isabel grabs another beer for me and vacates the room. When she returns, she pushes a tightly rolled bundle into my hand.

'Two hundred,' she says, then adds, 'but it's a loan, get it? I want every single penny back.'

I'm humbled, and feel guilty taking the cash, which reminds me of a promise I made…

'I thought you were going to Paris?'

'Let's not go there, Will.'

'Oh?'

'Drop it, OK?'

I'm more than curious, I'm ecstatic.

'But I was so looking forward to having the cats…'

She thrusts at me with her best dagger glare.

'Back off!'

I know when to retreat, but I can't hide my delight, much to her displeasure. She's like a wounded animal. Is lover boy off the scene, I wonder?

'Sort your own problems out,' Isabel snorts.

She's right, of course. I'm out of work. I suddenly feel the weight of responsibility on my shoulders. I've truly buggered this up, as I actually liked the job in a perverse way. I'm weird, and my clients weirder still; a perfect match. Now I'm jobless by my own making and any chance of a decent reference has vanished. I'm stuffed…and unemployable. Shit. I hear the sniggering from the back row, so cut it out. Has anyone got a single grain of sympathy for my plight right now? Don't answer that, but I put the question to Isabel anyway (hoping the cash will have swayed her judgment a little).

'Like hell…' she mocks.

That sounds very much like I'm a loser.

'Will Farmer, you're a loser of the first degree and I'm ashamed of you.'

I'm pleased she has my interests at heart. I'd hate for her to really let loose.

I try the hound dog again. 'Can I stay here for a while?'

'Not a chance.'

'Supper?'

'No.'

I grip the money in my hand and chance my luck. 'I can treat us to an Indian takeaway if you fancy it.'

'*Jesus,* Will. Will you ever learn? You need to shop at Lidl for the foreseeable future and seek out the bargain counter. There'll be no more handouts from me, OK?'

'Just trying to lighten the mood,' I venture.

'You can't lighten the mood. It's been a massively shitty day compounded by your idiotic antics.'

'Any news on the suspect?'

'He's playing hardball.'

'Let me know what happens. You sure I can't stay over?'

'Go home, before my patience runs thin and I demand my money back.'

'I'll get a job, even if it's bloody cleaning cars.'

'Who said you're even capable of that task?'

I get the message and know that I have reached rock bottom by the intensity of her withering glare as she slams the door in my face as I depart.

Chapter 37

I've now got two hundred quid in my pocket, about ten pounds worth of fuel in the Rav, tomato soup in the cupboard and stale bread on the kitchen table. Oh, and a couple of beers in the fridge. I'm laughing at such lavish abundance at my disposal, so why am I staring at a face in the mirror that resembles a car crash. I'll tell you why. In less than three weeks the rental on the flat is due, the vehicle insurance will need settling and I have a speeding fine of sixty quid to pay. On top of that, I have a dental invoice to pay as well and the second reminder for the electricity bill will be a red one, so that's another hundred smackers. So I'm stuffed. I check the internet for the nearest Lidl (ten miles away) and start planning how to eke out the extra miles from my meagre fuel tank reading, which is already touching reserve if my eyes aren't deceiving me.

I count my blessings which come to precisely...*one*! Thank god for Isabel's generosity. I've got to admit though, I'm in a bad place right now. I make a mental list of the negatives:

No wife (technically speaking).

No daughter.

No job.

No prospects.

No money (how am I going to pay back the loan?).

No future.

No car if I have to sell it (how am I going to run it?).

No flat if I have to give it up (how am I going to pay the rent?).

No sex (Leah doesn't count for obvious reasons).

I'll have to sign on and bite the bullet: claim financial assistance. Or (wait for it...) do what I always do and ask David for help? I'll rephrase that. Do I dare to ask him again for another hand-out?

I ponder my predicament for five seconds and decide to beg (if necessary) for his assistance. I'll hate grovelling and he's a tight-fisted bastard at the best of times but he won't turn his back on me. I'm his brother, I'm his blood. And Margo will be on my side if I appeal to his better nature with her in the room as my ally. It's all about strategy. So I ring Margo and arrange to go over tonight to discuss David's recent prognosis, which she is concerned about, but I don't mention my urgent need to recapitalise my finances at their expense. I thought I'd just slip that in later in the evening, after a glass or two of wine. In fact, I'll buy the wine as a gesture of goodwill and friendship. I'm thrilled to discover a Lidl handily placed on the journey over and plan my route accordingly. At least

Isabel will be impressed with my new found dedication to saving costs on essential items.

*

'Stop fussing,' David bellows.

Margo defends my overbearing concerns. 'Will is worried, like me.'

My brother is tetchy and strides up and down the dining room as if he doesn't want to be cornered by our questions. 'I have a top consultant looking after my welfare and I need to trust what he says, and that is my condition is not life-threatening…at the moment.'

'So it's not aggressive?' I ask.

'No. Well, not yet anyway.'

'What is your Gleason scale?'

He turns on me. 'Christ, when did you become a bloody expert in the field?'

I've impressed myself, having done the research.

'Well?'

'3.3, central to the gland.'

'OK,' I mutter, realising my inadequacy in the finer points of medical analysis. I let him do the talking.

'Basically,' he continues, 'whilst the cancer sits dormant and stays within the prostate then I can remain under supervision and carry on with a normal life. They will monitor the growth by way of an MRI scan. If and when it reaches the wall of the prostrate then I must undergo radical surgery.'

'Oh, David,' Margo mutters, visibly upset.

I've always hated that word *radical*. It gives me the creeps and conjures up all sorts of scary possibilities. I instantly decide to undergo a blood test and find out my own PSA reading. What is happening to David brings it home so sharply. It could run in the family. We are all vulnerable.

'We'll beat it,' I venture.

'Easy for you to say, brother.'

There is an uneasy silence.

'Coffee, anyone?' Margo asks.

I raise my hand whilst David leaves the room clearly agitated.

My problems seem minuscule at this precise moment and I'm not entirely sure David can be approached in this mood of foreboding. My strategy is not panning out as I had hoped.

We take coffee in the drawing room and David rejoins us, less hot under the collar. Margo hands out some chocolate mints and we catch the late TV News, bringing more despair to our little group of observers. You name it, the newsreader mentions it: war in Syria, global recession, the Euro collapse, increase in petrol duty, corruption in the city, the rape and murder of a young girl in Harrogate (of all places) and…you could almost laugh…the financial plight of Portsmouth football club, who are entering into administration again.

Basically, the club is about to collapse into oblivion at any second if the report is to be believed. A bit like me.

David is intolerant to the depressing catalogue of human frailties and yells with a clenched fist and switches off in a further rage against the TV screen.

I haven't seen him like this before, but his shortening temper is to be expected. This cancer is a horrible, horrible thing. It kills people. It could kill my brother.

I try and lighten the atmosphere.

'David, can you lend me five grand?'

Where the hell did that slip from? I know I moved my mouth but even I'm shocked at my audacity.

'Are you kidding?' he asks, his eyes narrowing in my direction.

'If I was kidding, I'd ask for one hundred thousand. As I'm not, I thought I'd go for small beer, but I can see you're not impressed.'

'Of course, we can,' Margo announces, darting her gaze between Shylock and I.

This time David attempts to stab me with his laser stare. 'What do you want that amount for?'

'I've lost my job...'

He laughs in a nasty mean way. 'What a surprise...'

'What a terrible thing to happen,' Margo says, trying to show support.

He wasn't letting go. 'Have you been sacked?'

'Something like that.'

'That's a *yes* then, you prat.'

The sympathy is overwhelming.

'I wouldn't normally ask, but...'

'You will anyway.'

'This isn't easy, David.'

'It isn't easy finding five grand either,' he bridles.

Margo refereed in the nick of time.

'Stop bickering, the pair of you!'

I could feel the tension rising in the room.

'Will's in need of our help,' Margo emphasises.

I actually think David is going to mumble *humbug* with the glare he shoots at me, as he drowns the contents of his glass.

Margo volunteers: 'I've got some savings...'

'That won't be necessary, Margo,' David retorts. 'I've got three grand in an ISA that's doing bugger all. That will have to do. Take it or leave it.'

I attempt to speak ("that'll do!") but Margo cuts in.

'Why are you being like this, David? Will is your only brother and when has he ever asked you for anything in the past?'

David snapped. 'When he wanted a deposit for the cottage.'

Didn't think he'd let that one go.

He's on a roll. 'When he was eighteen and met a girl and wanted a Johnny from my wallet, and I only had one…so I told him to sod off, but he stole it anyway.'

For a second we were all stunned, and then we simultaneously burst into laughter.

'Did you get to use it?' Margo asks in a fit of giggles.

'Did he hell!' David yells. 'I reckon he's still got it.'

Well, that broke the tension, thankfully. David pours brandy and we chink glasses. Margo kisses me goodnight and retreats to her bedroom, leaving David and me in a face-off. I wait for the lecture but it never comes. He simply says, 'There'll be no more, Will. You'd better sort yourself out and fast.'

I simply concur.

He downs the last dregs of brandy. 'I'll transfer the money to your account in the morning. Now I must get to sleep. Are you stopping over?'

I check the time. 'Nah, I'll be home by midnight.'

'Nonsense. Take the same room; I don't think the sheets have been changed since the last time. You OK with that?'

I try to calculate when I last changed the sheets on my bed at home, but decline to brag. David would just put another marker against my name. I feel bad enough already, having to come to him cap in hand.

'Thanks, David,' I reply meekly.

And that is that. I'm solvent again, for a while anyway. Three thousand was better than a smack in the mouth. I always thought I was pushing my luck with the larger amount. Besides, there is always Margo to fall back on. She could be relied upon to keep a little secret if I needed a top up.

When I hit the pillow, I'm quickly out for the count.

Something nags at me in the morning, and then I remember. I forgot to question David about the argument he had with Romain. I wanted to hear his side of the story, but on reflection, maybe the timing wasn't right and I'd be poorer still for my persistence in the matter. I am grateful for small mercies. Let's leave it at that for the time being. I'll choose the appropriate moment…after I've got the relevant dosh in my bank account.

It's all about strategy.

I doze off again.

Chapter 38

It's rare for me to sleep in. But then I don't have any pressing engagements, do I?

So I make myself useful and, after a late breakfast, I help Margo clear the leaves in the garden as a soft diluted sun bathes us in a yellow autumnal glow. It is a lovely constructed haven, and clearly Margo's pride and joy. I notice that there are no steps so she moves easily in her wheelchair along the wide paths which are perfect for her. I collect the fallen apples and we have coffee and I listen to her concerns for her husband's illness as if she had no right to burden the world with her own health issues. She's a brick.

I wash my hands in the downstairs sink in the spare loo, gather my things, and give her a big hug and a fond farewell.

'Don't judge him unkindly, Will.'

'Who said I did?'

'Well, he always has to make everything difficult. He's a stubborn old mule.'

'He's got me out of a hole.'

'I just wish he would do things kind-heartedly…instead of fighting everyone.'

'That's my brother.'

Then she said something strange. 'He carries demons you know…'

'What does that mean?'

She shrugs. 'Another time, perhaps.'

'If you need to talk…'

'Not now, I'm rather tired. The nurse will be here soon. You get yourself on the road and don't…I repeat, don't…get into any more mischief.'

'My middle name,' I joke, but it's close to the truth.

*

I get a text from Isabel that Jimson is back from France and wants to see us again. I have a bad feeling about this.

I return from Dorking and head over to meet with him straight away. Isabel joins me and pours hot chocolate from a vending machine, and then she directs me to his office rather than a meeting room. I'm definitely getting twitchy…

'Come in and take a seat, the both of you.'

We do as he says, in silence.

I watch as he shifts a few papers on his desk and then sits back in his chair, his brain kicking into gear. I'm too nervous to touch my drink.

'Things have changed in the last twenty-four hours,' he begins. 'The man in custody, whom we were keen on, is not Daisy's killer. We tried for a second DNA match but failed with this. So we can discount his involvement. He has of course been arrested for a series of other crimes, including attempted rape and assault so we have a result. He'll get a lengthy custodial sentence I'm pleased to say.'

'I don't somehow think that is why you brought us in,' I respond.

He fidgets on his seat. 'The point is, we've now found other photos hidden in Romain's bedroom, this time under the floorboards.'

Isabel shoots me a look.

Jimson clears his throat. 'They are pictures of Daisy taking a shower at the farm, during the time you spent there as a family. It is obvious that she was not aware of this intrusion. Somehow, Romain cut a tiny hole in the wooden partitioning wall which allowed him a full view of her with a miniature camera.'

'He *spied* on her,' I say in astonishment.

'Yes. The hole was not easily detectable. Not something you particularly look for. The images I'm afraid are quite graphic.'

'Has he admitted to taking them?' Isabel asks.

'He denies it.'

'How come they were hidden in his room then?' she continues.

'He has no idea.'

'Bollocks,' I add.

'In his defence, he is distraught by this latest accusation and suggests they may have been planted.'

'But he has confessed to killing our daughter,' Isabel says. 'Why deny this?'

He is adamant that the only photos he has taken are those already in our possession.'

I sit forward. 'This just shows the level of obsession he had for her, but he is too ashamed to face up to his depravity.'

I'm on his case again. I hover constantly between two stools: believing in his innocence or condoning his guilty actions. It's driving me insane.

'Quite possible,' Jimson says.

'Where are the photos?' I ask.

'We have them in a safe place, and they'll be used as evidence against him which is now becoming pretty compelling. We have your man. We have also successfully matched DNA samples in the Lab from skin tissues found on the clothing worn by him and your daughter. I wanted you both to come in so I could warn you of what we have discovered before the press start to hound you. You can, of course, view the images if you wish. I don't recommend it but I want to get you both prepared so that is your prerogative. The photos will be shown in court so it is important that you know this. It will be a harrowing experience.'

'I don't want to see them,' I confess.

Isabel nods in unison.

'Things can get shitty from now on,' Jimson says.

172

I'm suddenly distracted by something on the wall behind the desk where he sits. I've seen it before but it had no previous significance. Now it hits me like a thunderbolt.

'Mr Farmer?'

I come back to earth. My head is spinning.

I manage to say, 'Did you question him about the argument with David?'

'I did. He said your brother was harassing him because of the attention he was giving Daisy. David didn't think it was right as he had seen him, that is Romain, trying to steal kisses from her earlier, and your brother saw her pushing him away. Romain insists that they were playing, and it was only because he had been eating garlic that she rejected him.'

'Why the shoving then?' I ask.

'They had had an earlier argument over who would sit where at the table, which sounds pretty minor to me. However, with drinks on the agenda, the tiff between them manifested itself during the afternoon. They ended up shoving each other.'

'And the words Romain used?' Isabel said.

'Apparently, David was being arsey and over-protective towards Daisy and in the heat of the moment Romain told him that she didn't like him, so he should back off. He's a hot-headed kid.'

Outside in the car park, I turn to Isabel and she looks frail and withdrawn.

'We'll get through this,' I say, and then repeat Jimson's phrasing, 'However, things can get shitty from now on.'

She nods feebly and I want to hug her but I keep my distance. I'm worried about something. The word *planted* keeps springing into my mind.

I suddenly say, 'How old is Jimson?'

'That's a strange question, Will.'

'Just curious…'

'I suppose he's sixty, sixty-two or thereabouts.'

'Hmm. Is he locally born?'

'Gosport, I think. Why do you need to ask?'

'Has he an Italian lineage?'

'Are you on drugs?'

'It's just that there is a framed photograph of a famous Italian football team behind his desk. An autographed version no less, which impressed me.'

I'm trying to keep things light after the heavy session we've just had to endure, and I'm not sure where my muddled thoughts are heading right now.

'So…'

'Oh, it's just the anorak side of me coming out…'

'Put me out of my misery.'

'The team's name wouldn't necessarily be significant to you, but it is to me.'

'Get on with it, yeah?'

I think of the recent photo Meg gave to me, and Luigi's endorsement in the restaurant. 'The club in question is Juventus.' I say.

'Why is that significant to you?'

I think of Meg again; the canny old bird.
'It might be nothing,' I reply, 'so forget it.'
Isabel playfully hits me on the arm.
'Talking in riddles again,' she remarks.

*

When I get back home, I immediately seek out the photos that Luigi looked at and collar the picture of the young man in the Italian football shirt. This would have been a rare sighting in England and makes the man stand out. Well, to my eyes anyway, but it still needed the prompt from my Italian friend to really get my attention. The thing is the man in the picture and Jimson have the same build, both are tall and they both kind of lean to one side as they stand. Although he was portly now and thinning on top, the resemblance between them is still uncanny. I study the image more closely. Forty years have elapsed, so you would expect big changes. I'm convinced this is Jimson. The coincidence of discovering the picture in his office was just too great to ignore and now I have established a link in the time frame. And if this was him at the fair, well, it put him right there bang in the middle of the abduction of Miriam Faulkner. Assuming he wasn't in the police force at this age (he looked around eighteen), then surely this would make him one of the many suspects rounded up to be interviewed by the cops? Was he questioned at the time? Was he eliminated from the enquiry? Did he have an alibi?

I'm paranoid. My brain is working overtime. I've said I never liked him.

Fact: It was Jimson who insisted on travelling over to France to conduct the formal investigation after Romain was first held.

Fact: Jimson got the confession from Romain.

Fact: He unearthed the photos of my daughter in the shower.

Fact: Romain denies all knowledge of taking them.

Fact: This could be a set-up.

Paranoia confirmed. The notion of things being *planted* won't erase from my brain though. Where am I going with this nonsense? And are the photos of Daisy genuine? Isabel and I declined to see them, but only on his insistence.

Observations:

1. Jimson works in our vicinity.

2. Therefore, he knows the local layout of the countryside.

3. He knew Daisy.

4. He could approach her without suspicion.

5. She would trust him.

6. I don't trust him.

To my mind, this puts him firmly in the frame of being a possible suspect in the abduction and murder of two young girls.

If I explain this theory to Isabel, she will have me immediately certified, locked up and the key thrown away. So I elect to keep it to myself. Meg might have something to say on the matter though.

Chapter 39

I'm on my way over to Meg's when my mobile goes. I pull into a lay-by and click on. It's David.

'Hi Will, I'm on my lunch break, so took the opportunity to transfer the money into your account.'

I'm mightily relieved. 'Thanks, David.'

'You should be able to access it within the hour.'

'Brilliant. I'm sorry I had to ask you for the cash.'

'Forget it, and I'm sorry I gave you a hard time.'

'When are you next seeing your consultant?'

'Smithson? Next Wednesday.'

'Do you want me to be there?'

'No, thanks. I'm just seeing him with the radiologist to discuss my options.'

'Still, it's a daunting situation, David.'

'I'll manage.'

I decide that *now* would be a good time to broach the subject of Romain.

'David, do you remember Isabel's birthday in France?'

'Of course, I do…'

'We had a BBQ and sat by the pool.'

He laughs. '…And got pissed.'

'We recorded the event on my newly acquired hand-held camera and I noticed that you and Romain were having an argy-bargy in the background that day.'

'Just fooling around, I guess. We played tennis and I whopped his arse.'

'It looked a bit more serious than that…'

'Well, he was being a right twat if I remember correctly.'

'What was it about?'

There is a distinct hesitation before he answers.

'He knocked my beer over and wouldn't get me another.'

'And that required a shoving match?'

'If I could, I would have punched him on the nose.'

'*If you could?*'

'His mum was watching and I didn't think she'd like to see her son with a bloodied nose. Besides, I'd have been arrested.'

'Did she intervene?'

'Well, she was heading our way and, as you are aware, she didn't particularly like me anyway…so I was being careful.' He laughs again.

Backtrack: This last remark referred to an incident one year when David nearly knocked Romain off his bike by accident when reversing our hire car into their drive. A minor thing but she accused him of driving recklessly. Fast forward to the BBQ and David finishes his story.

'Did you end up arguing with her?' I ask.

'No fear, I legged it, but not before giving Romain a piece of my mind...he was goading me with threats of having me ejected from the farm.'

'All a bit extreme,' I say thoroughly bemused.

'He was hot-headed and his mother was equal to him. With Nicole fast approaching he kept repeating the words: *"She doesn't like you, she doesn't like you..."*'

I'm baffled. Perhaps I had got the wrong end of the stick. David's version of the story appeared perfectly plausible.

'What's this all about, Will? Am I under interrogation?' This time he doesn't laugh.

'It's nothing.'

'He had a temper when drunk, that lad, and he was devious too.'

'I'm sure you're right.'

'Damn sure I am! That's why he's under arrest, right?'

'Right.'

'Got to go, I'm afraid.'

I click off and resume my journey. I go over our conversation and I'm confused as always. I've now had two different versions of the same incident. One of them is lying.

*

Meg says, 'Is that young Jimson?'

She studies the photo closely before continuing her observations. 'He would be about twenty-one then, I suppose...fine looking lad. See the quiff in his bryl-creamed hair? He was one of the original Ted's that gathered in town around the coffee house and caused trouble on a Saturday night.'

'How did you know him?' I ask.

'He lived on the same road as us, just a bit further down.'

'So he knew of Miriam?'

'Well, she was much younger, a mere child, but he would have been aware of her, just as she would have been aware of him. She played in our street often enough so it stands to reason they must have passed each other.'

We sit in the small garden at the rear of her downstairs flat and catch the last of the fleeting sunlight as big clouds move ominously over the sky towards us.

We drink orange juice, which I don't normally like but I'm not one for complaining at her generosity.

I try to build a picture. 'Was he trouble back then?'

'Not in our neighbourhood. But he hung about with a motorbike gang and often there would be a stand-off with the local Mods down at the beach. They all thought they owned the town and Saturday night became the customary fight night. He obviously grew out of it because now he's a big-wig in the police force.'

'Has he always worked in the area?'

'No idea. We saw less of him because they – his family –moved to the posh side of town a few years later.'

'Girlfriends?'

'Plenty! He was a bit of a glamour boy in those days…he always had a different bimbo on his arm whenever I saw him.'

'Did he have a reputation…you know, for chasing the girls, and then loving and leaving them…'

'I suppose they all did, free sex and all that.'

I longed for a cold beer but kept quiet.

'Why are you interested in this fellow Jimson?' Meg asks.

'Because he was at the fair on the day Miriam disappeared. This photo points to it.'

'There were hundreds of boys at the fair, Will. You can't just single him out.'

She's right of course. But he did have proximity and chance, and he knew Miriam. I'm also aware this is a long shot to drag his name into the equation, but he fits my profile of someone who has a strong connection to both killings, and he also holds the unique position of being able to influence events from the inside of the police force, thus deflecting unwarranted suspicion from himself.

Well, I am at the very least suspicious. I'll admit it right now, as if you hadn't already guessed. I've given you enough hints. Here's another: I'm not a fully paid-up member of his fan club. He irritates me, always looking in my direction as if I'm from the bottom of the pond. He also has an eye for Isabel. I've seen that sideways look he gives her. I'm on his case, the pervert.

He's too smart for his own good and needs pulling down a peg or two.

Chapter 40

Standing on my doorstep, Isabel has my full attention as she speaks.

'I've just found out that Frederic Petit, who we thought had disappeared, actually died two years ago, knocked down by a lorry. This incident happened three months before Daisy was murdered, so we can eliminate him from our enquiry.'

Isabel says the words calmly enough, but it is her use of an official tone which upsets me. It implies that Daisy was someone abstract, just out of view, belonging to no one…just a figure on a landscape. This was *our* daughter, our flesh and blood we are talking about. I didn't want to hear her name discussed from a subjective viewpoint. I want to scream and cry at the injustice of a life taken so young, one so precious as well; my daughter inexplicably removed from this planet. This wicked fucking cesspit of a place called Earth.

My rage boils within me like a volcano about to erupt. I can't blame Isabel for the way she delivered the message across. Perhaps it is her way of dealing with the pain, keeping it at arm's length. After all, she is on duty and has to conform to type. Me? I want to hurt someone, torture them and slowly kill them. I want to see the breath of life gradually extinguish from their lungs, I want to witness the darkness descending over their wild pleading eyes. I want to see how death slowly constricts their last vision of light to a mere pinprick …then nothingness.

Good riddance.

I'm consumed by bitterness. My vengeful spirit scares me for I have no more gumption than the next man to exact punishment if the opportunity comes. In truth, I am weak and sentimental and cowardly, and even worse than this is the acknowledgement that my estranged wife knows this too. She pities me, and I die inwardly every time this thought crosses my mind, which is about every two seconds.

So I say the first thing I can think of, which isn't very constructive.

'*How* did you say he died?'

Isabel stares down at a report sheet and says. 'Knocked over by a truck late at night. Apparently, he had been drinking heavily, as was his want, and the police report indicates that he swerved in front of the lorry and died instantly.'

We are standing facing each other like two awkward strangers. If I could, I would prefer to wither away on this very spot, such is my shame and sadness of what is lost between us.

'Thanks for letting me know,' I murmur. I hate her in uniform, it makes her hard and unyielding and steely-eyed. I suppose I begrudgingly admire her in many ways, being able to keep it all together as she does. It still fucking kills me though: I lost a wife (my fault!) as well as losing a daughter. I so much want to regain her respect and trust, but that is a much bigger ask than I'm ever entitled to hope for. We are entwined by a vortex of grief which gradually spins us away from each other in ever-widening circles.

'Thought I should give you the news first hand,' Isabel adds.

It's certainly come as a shock. This must have hit Remy and Nicole badly, losing a son in these tragic circumstances. They've had a tough time of it, having to deal with Romain's recent arrest as well, although Remy's email to me showed remarkable defiance. I'm saddened that we never got to know the news from them regarding Frederic but we had drifted apart, having stopped going over to France for some considerable time now. Time makes strangers of us all.

'Do you want to come in?' I almost choke on my words.

'No, I need to get home and out of these clothes. It's been a demanding day…'

'Please.'

'I'd rather not.'

I try to recover but repeat myself pathetically.

'Will, another time, OK?'

'I just thought…I just hoped…'

'Well, don't do any of those two things because you'll only end up being disappointed.'

'We had *something* once, Isabel.'

'And that was a long time ago, I'm sorry to say.'

She certainly knew how to raise my expectations.

'Can we at least try to start again,' I plead.

She steps back. 'I can't forget, Will, and sadly I can't forgive…and that will always come between us.'

'Is he the one *then*?' I'm not proud of myself for this cheap line of attack.

'You can't resist a dig, can you? You don't even know him, so don't try and judge the situation, eh? It's my life to live it how I want, so don't question my right to choose who I decide to be with…sort your own fucking problems out before you see fit to pour scorn in my direction. Butt out, Will.'

She turns and marches off, revving her car in indignation as she roars off and out of sight. I am shaking, trying manfully to find a crumb of comfort in her tirade of sorts. I got what I deserved: another bashing, another earful.

It wasn't what I had planned, naturally. I imagined ordering an Indian takeaway and opening a bottle of plonk, a cosy evening for two beckoning. Instead, I got an icy blast from an acid tongue and a good kicking in the bollocks. I deserved both.

*

You can't put a good man down. So later, I phone her and leave an apology on the answerphone and tell her she missed out on a cracking chicken balti and a Tesco's best merlot (on special offer). I've got thick skin and know how to win a girl over.

If at first you don't succeed…

I clear the cartons away and take a shower and settle down for a bit of telly. I check my bank balance online and hey presto the money from David is firmly in place. It certainly helps calm the anxiety of being out of work and undesirable to the opposite sex. I'm solvent and that is all that matters, the rest will fall into place within the universal scheme of things. At least I'm no longer up the creek without a paddle.

I detect a bit of heckling from one or two of you. Well, thanks for nothing. Remind me to offer support to you next time you are crawling out of the mire.

I'm not done with you yet. You may snigger at my recent downfall, but consider your own miserable lives first: how many of you manage to walk the tightrope between abject failure and mediocrity on this unforgiving and brittle world of ours without falling off? Not so easy is it? How do you measure actual success? Only one person at a time can win the gold medal. Does that make the other two runners-up feel less diminished when you put into context their colossal efforts to achieve a lifetime best? Tomorrow our roles can be reversed in a blink of an eye, so think about that when you consider my plight from now on, you smug little self-righteous shits. I'm trying my hardest, so get off my case and give me a break.

It's obvious that I'm on a short fuse, so I apologise for the outburst.

An email comes in:

So sorry, I was an arse. Another time, yes? Sometimes it's so bloody difficult to cope and so I build a wall of steel around me for protection, which means this supernova bitch should be avoided at all costs. Not your fault. You just got me on the wrong day. Oh, you should know better… I prefer King Prawn balti…my treat Friday, that is, if you want there to be a next time. Isabel.

What is this? An apology from the high princess! I'm ecstatic, bowled over in fact.

I type: *Can't think of anything better, Will. PS. Thanks for restoring my faith in human nature.*

Then I click SEND.

I told you that there are ways of reversing one's fortune.

Ye of little faith.

Chapter 41

What the hell, I take a massive gamble and book a budget flight to Carcassonne for the next morning using my newly acquired wealth. I hire a car online for two days' duration, pack a small rucksack, dig out my passport and buy a hundred quid's worth of Euros from the local post office.

I'm going to revisit the farm where Romain lived with his parents. Why am I compelled to do this, I bet you're asking?

Well, I simply want to discover the truth about this boy first hand as I don't have faith in Jimson and his motley crew. I repeatedly feel uneasy with the tidy package of guilt surrounding this boy's confession. His parents are good people and I find it hard to believe they would have brought him up without respect and honour towards Daisy. I remember him as a sweet kid (my brother overreacted with his condemnation) with a mild fixation for my daughter. Maybe he did try to push his luck and maybe he did overdo the attention but does that make him a killer? I want to find the answer to that question.

If he is guilty, so be it.

If he has been set up, I need to find out by whom.

I am fearful of what I may uncover. I am also worried by the reaction from his parents, who must be going through purgatory having just lost one elder son, albeit a rum character by all accounts.

I'll take it as I find it. I can't just sit at home and twiddle my thumbs. I check that Meg is OK and leave a text with Isabel that I'm unavailable for a couple of days. And I also suggest that we have the takeaway she promised for this Friday night. I can only hope in miracles.

I make myself busy for the rest of the day, do a bit of local landscape photography and generally distract myself from what's going to come my way from the forthcoming trip. In the evening I use up any leftovers from the sparse fridge and down a beer for comfort. Then I'm off to bed, ready for the early alarm call.

I make the city airport at five thirty bleary-eyed and a tad reluctant to carry through my *mission impossible*. I'm no Tom Cruise, but then again I don't intend to jump off roofs and zoom around on a motorbike at one hundred miles per hour. Well, at least I hope I don't!

Reality strikes home. What if I get the cold shoulder from Remy and Nicole when I suddenly turn up at their home unannounced? I guess that I'll just have to scuttle off to find a nearby hole to crawl into. Or, as an alternative, hold my hands up, admit this was a foolhardy idea and sample the delights of the locally made wine and drown my sorrows in a road side bar. I consider the options, could be worse ways to spend a few hours. Tom usually gets the girl; I'll lay a wager I pick a fight.

The flight is bumpy, but I survive. The car is ropey, but beggars can't be choosers. The sun is out, the vineyards ripe and the CD blares out Neil Young. I suddenly feel alive and energetic and eat the miles up along the D610 toward Olsanac. An hour later and I'm there, searching for the farm track which I pass several times as it is now overgrown with weeds which have hidden the nameplate on a gate. My heart thumps, and I admit that I backtrack into town to grab a beer to pluck up Dutch courage. This is going to be trickier than I imagined.

I purposely delay my return (I've got the jitters) and watch the world go by as I sit outside a street café under a brightly-coloured parasol. I'm on my third beer. I could get comfortable here. My French is passable but I'm not confident to strike up a conversation with a delightful woman on the next table sipping Cava and toying with her iPhone. I feel hopelessly inadequate and out of my depth. *What clever one-liner would Tom say to catch her attention?*

And then I freeze and forget her and any clever riposte in an instant. Remy strolls past me with bread in his hand, stops, does a double-take and stares at my face as if he has just seen a ghost. I've been rumbled. He looks bewildered. I'm just shitting myself.

'Monsieur Will…Is that really you?'

I stand and offer my hand half-heartedly.

'I've come in the hope of speaking with you, if you'll spare me the time…'

He eyes me suspiciously, takes my hand reluctantly and slowly shakes it. His palm is sticky in the heat.

I point to my half-empty glass. 'Beer?'

He sits awkwardly and I can see he is both crushed and baffled by my intrusion into what was going to be a simple shopping expedition for him.

I order two more beers, and we face each other in silence. Luckily the woman departs which leaves us by ourselves. The drink arrives and we sip quietly.

'I am sorry for Frederic,' I say. 'We had no idea until recently.'

He shrugs and murmurs something in French. I pick up that he implies that as I didn't particularly know him then I couldn't really be sorry at all. This is going to be painful.

'I'm pleased we have emailed each other.'

He nods and generously speaks my language. 'Why are you here?'

'Because I need to find out things,' I say feebly.

'And you expect us to help you do that?'

'We go back a long way, Remy.'

'Maybe too long, eh?'

'When did you last see Romain?'

'Yesterday…'

'When is he being transferred over to England?'

'Within a matter of weeks…'

'I'm sorry it has come to this, Remy.'

'I am sorry for your loss as well, we loved Daisy like the daughter we never had.'

His eyes are flat and colourless, his skin leathery from the sun. I feel desperately sad for him and his good wife.

'How is Nicole bearing up?'

He shrugs like only the French know how. 'She isn't.'

'Can I call on her?'

'What is the point, Monsieur?'

'I want to offer comfort; show I care…'

'Do you forgive our son his sins?'

I have to tread carefully here. Daisy was gone and I would despise their son if he was found responsible for her death in a court of law. The evidence is stacked up against him for sure. Forgiveness is a big *ask*. But I so want to find a way forward if I can.

'He is innocent until proven guilty,' I say. 'If I can get a grasp of the events as they happened, see for myself, get to see his perspective then, of course, a kind of closure can be achieved…for all of us. Does that make sense to you?'

'I feel your sorrow, your agony…but we need to be left alone to endure our sadness, particularly as it is so raw at the moment. Both our sons have been taken from us, and a daughter lost to you and Isabel. How much agony can we all take?'

That I couldn't answer.

'I'm here until tomorrow,' I offer.

'Where are you staying?'

I gesture with my hand, pointing along the tree-lined road: 'A B & B just down the avenue called Maison Martine.'

'I know the establishment.'

'Then that's where you'll find me.'

He shrugs and lifts himself wearily from his chair and thanks me for the beer.

'I hope you find some kind of peace,' he says and walks away grasping the bread in his hand. He takes a slow pace, one that I figured meant that he was in no hurry to get home and relay our conversation to his wife.

I shout after him, 'I hope you find it in your heart to call on me.'

Then I throw some money on the table and move off in the opposite direction, lonely and lost. I'm not hopeful that my latter words have reached him: that probably applies to all of them from the last half-hour, in fact.

*

The next morning, after a restless night, I receive a message from Madame Martine that I have an invitation to call over to Remy's farm any time after breakfast. It takes a second or two for this to sink in.

I close my bedroom door and compose myself. Then I shower, sling on some clothes and order croissants and coffee in the little garden at the rear. I am both joyous and apprehensive. In some respects, I am the enemy. How will Nicole greet me? I shudder to think but she has opened the door and that is all I can ask for. My nerve must not desert me.

I've come this far and I'm not about to turn tail, even though I'm a quivering wreck at the prospect of confronting them in their own home. I am an intruder, an inquisitor, the judge and jury. Once I was a welcomed friend, now I will be perceived as the elected executioner of their son.

I drive over and three times I bottle it. At the fourth attempt, I make it down the long rutted drive. Now, I stand before the heavy oak door with the green peeling paint and hesitate before knocking. I muster the courage and bang loudly and hold my breath for what seems like forever.

Then I hear footsteps approaching from the other side.

Chapter 42

This is a surreal moment. We sip tea on the wooden veranda and small talk about the lack of bountiful fruit on the trees this year which surround the house and the absence of insects which normally thrive on the large pond at the end of the garden. The chatter is a necessary distraction, as we are all on a knife's edge.

We discuss anything really which avoids the inevitable. But there's no real hurry. My flight is not until eight this evening. I am simply grateful (overwhelmed actually), that they see fit to have me in their home.

I then make my first blunder.

'Where is your lovely dog, Mimi?' I ask, aware that their faithful companion is not sitting with us as she usually would.

Remy shifts in his seat. 'She is gone, I'm afraid.'

'Oh?'

'There was an incident.'

'My daughter loved Mimi,' I murmur. 'What happened?'

Remy confers with his wife, shrugs, and says quietly, 'She was shot.'

I'm knocked sideways. 'Shot?'

'Yes, shot…we have no idea who did it, but she had been seen making a nuisance on the neighbouring farm, and so we suspect them, but we will never know who was responsible…it is very, what you say, upsetting for us.'

'Were the gendarme called?'

'Of course, but these things are never solved. We live with the sadness, Monsieur.'

'I'm so very, very sorry…'

I cannot begin to understand the turmoil that they are going through, having me in their midst ready and waiting to bombard them with questions and accusations that they are ill-equipped to deal with. They are simple farm folk, caught up in tragedy and deceit and betrayal, none of which is of their own making. Like me, they are broken beyond repair and suffering too.

My second blunder follows just as quickly. I simply ask how they are coping. Nicole almost drops her cup in shock and gives me both barrels with her sharp tongue, as if waiting for this very moment to vent her fury. She doesn't speak good English but I get the gist of her tirade. Tears well up in her eyes and her cheeks redden. I sit and take it, and watch Remy try to console his wife but she's on a roll. She spits out the last of her words and hurries from the room.

Remy slumps back in his chair.

I don't need an interpretation of her words.

'This was a mistake,' he says.

'What can I do to make amends?' I ask.

He shrugs. 'Probably leave us, Monsieur…'

'I understand her anger.'

'No, I'm afraid you don't.'

A further outburst reaches us from the kitchen. Her voice is still shaking.

'I'm sorry, but I don't understand what she is saying,' I mutter.

Remy stands. 'My wife wishes for you to depart. She says you have no business interfering with our lives. She has lost one son and now risks losing the other. Inviting you here was our politeness to the past. It was an error.'

I realise I have overstepped the mark by just being here. It was madness to think they would welcome me into their torment.

I retreat to the car and shake Remy's broad rough hand and take comfort from it. It is firm and I am grateful.

'I am sorry you had a wasted journey,' he says.

I lie. 'I didn't.'

'Perhaps one day, eh?'

'When the dust has settled.'

We stand awkwardly and I fumble for the ignition key of my car.

Then Remy surprises me. 'Romain is not evil, Monsieur, but misguided by love.'

Love?

I am struck by this word. It is such a powerful expression. You do not kill for love. You kill for jealousy, revenge, perhaps rejection…but not love. Love is pure and all conquering, it binds people, not destroys them. And I believe that Romain, naively, did love Daisy. They were having a baby together, and maybe that's what brought him to England. It seems preposterous that he travelled over to track her down and then take her life. It doesn't add up. I could see in his father's eyes that it didn't add up to him either.

I avoid the subject of the pregnancy, assuming Romain had not told his parents. Another shock like that would tip them over the edge. It didn't really matter in the great scheme of things anymore: there was the inescapable truth that he had confessed to Daisy's murder. That sealed his fate.

I drag some words up of my own.

'Do you believe in your son's innocence?'

'Yes, with all my heart. He is incapable of something so…what do you say in your country…so devilish.'

I take my gaze beyond his and settle on the handsome stone house which stands solidly amongst the olive trees. I try to remember the interior layout and point upwards to the gable end. 'Is that his bedroom?'

He follows my line. 'Yes.'

It's a simple thing but it sticks in my brain.

'The shower room which we used is on the other side of the house, yes?'

'Your memory is good…'

'And if I recall correctly, it is in a separate annexe, the one which we used the last time we were here after you renovated it.'

He smiled. 'It was good timing. Your tent was leaking and it rained a lot that year.'

I smile at the recollection.

'We were indebted.'

'You were friends.'

'The police found photos of Daisy in the shower which were hidden in your son's bedroom.'

He squirms and nods in resignation.

'But it occurs to me that Romain wouldn't be aware that Daisy, or any of us for that matter, was taking a shower because we were living in private quarters.'

'Monsieur?'

'He lived separately from us and his bedroom (I point again) is situated on the opposite side of the house, far enough away, so he couldn't easily spy on what we were doing. Besides, if they were in love with each other then I ask the obvious question: Why would he *need* to secretly film her?'

At this point, I am reminded that Daisy had in fact posed for candid pictures, according to Jimson, which makes this high-risk ploy a highly debatable proposition as far as Romain was concerned. The bottom line is this: he had a willing partner anyway, so why risk further trouble by doing something as foolhardy as this? I don't believe he would.

I snap out of my private cross-examination and repeat the question: 'Why would Romain *need* to secretly film Daisy?'

Remy's eyes light up.

'Monsieur, what are you saying?'

'I'm saying that this puts sufficient doubt into the case against your son.'

He puts a hand to his mouth, then mumbles, 'But he has confessed...'

I put my hand on his shoulder. 'It occurs to me that someone could be setting him up.'

'I think perhaps you need to come inside again, so we can talk further...'

I lock the car door. 'I think I should. Have you got a good bottle of cognac to help us mull things over?'

Chapter 43

Remy has a private word with his wife, who now looks at me differently as she joins me across the table. This time, there is compassion in her eyes.

We slowly raise our glasses and bring them together, not in a celebratory salute but rather in a renewed gesture of respect. The cognac, as you would expect, is excellent vintage.

We begin our conversation as anyone would, from the beginning. Over time, each of us tells our perspective of shared experiences and a picture gradually materialises, a picture of friendship, cultural divide, passion, bad jokes, disagreements and denial. Although we grew closer as the two families reunited each year, in truth, none of us wanted Romain and Daisy to form such a strong attachment and I suppose we all chose to ignore such a possibility. The lovers, just kids, hid it well. For my part, I just thought he had a schoolboy crush on our daughter. Whenever I raised the issue with her, she giggled and said he had garlic breath and the manners of a pig. I believed her.

He was an awkward lad, and tubby when we first met him but then he developed muscles and a strong jawline over time. Anyone could see he possessed the easy trait of Gaelic charm and arrogance, which girls like Daisy so easily fell for. Looking back, he played hard to get, she played hard to get. They circled each other, fighting like cats and dogs. I smile ruefully, evidently not!

Frederic was entirely different. He was the older son by ten years. A loner, he was shy and distant and we never gelled with him. In fairness, he wasn't always there during our visits. He came and went, and we never enquired as to where he vanished to.

'What did Frederic do for a living?' I ask after his name pops up.

Remy is their spokesman and does me the honour of speaking in English whenever he addresses me directly. 'He was a carpenter and a very good one at that.'

'I assume he worked for you on the farm?'

'Not always. He went where the work was, but when he came home I always had a list of jobs to do.' He smiled softly.

'Handy then to have him return.'

'Nicole missed him. He and I bounced off each other, if you know my meaning.'

I do. That's how I feel with Isabel at the moment. There's always sparks flying.

'Did he get into trouble with the gendarme?'

He huffs. 'Petty stuff. None of us are perfect.'

I can vouch for that last bit. 'Did he have a girlfriend?'

'Not that we were aware of…he was private to the extreme.'

'But damn good at his profession, yes?'

'He could turn his hand to anything. He rebuilt the annexe where you stayed and did all the plumbing and electrics.'

He could turn his hand to anything.

The words stick in my throat. 'He built the entire thing?'

'Yes, he even designed the layout.'

I'm intrigued. 'Can we have a look again?'

Remy raises his eyebrows, whispers to his wife and the two of us amble over to the building. It brings back bittersweet memories. I inspect the shower and examine the hole from which Daisy was filmed. A horrible thought suddenly occurs to me. *What if Isabel was filmed too?*

'You know, Remy, the same thought keeps coming back to me. If your son was already in a physical relationship with my daughter then why would he want to take secret snaps of her in here? I mentioned it to you earlier. It doesn't make sense.'

My dear friend drops his gaze and sighs.

I really don't want to say the name, so I wait.

'Frederic,' he offers calmly.

'Frederic,' I echo. I feel sick. It is inconceivable that Isabel would have escaped his snooping. The temptation would have been too great to resist. He had both mother and daughter in his sights. Romain protested his innocence when confronted by Jimson with the evidence. I can see why. I am beginning to believe his story, that the photos were planted in his room. But by whom?

'Was Frederic jealous of his younger brother catching the eye of a pretty girl…a girl he himself had a fascination with?'

'It seems so, Monsieur.'

'When the police arrested Romain and brought him home to search his room, do you think Frederic had already planted the photos on him before he died in order to deflect blame from himself?'

'Quite possible, but we will perhaps never know that now…'

'Was he close to Romain?'

'No. Frederic was only close to his mother.'

'We know he didn't kill Daisy, which confuses matters.'

I take a stroll around the courtyard to clear my head. When I return, Remy is slumped on a bench, a defeated man.

I sit beside him. 'Suppose Frederic didn't plant the photos.'

'Then who did?'

'Tell me, Remy. What happened to Frederic when he was killed?'

'He was hit by a truck late one night.'

'Had he been drinking? Was it a terrible accident?'

He hesitated. 'We will never really know this either. Of course, he had been drinking. But I think he was a deeply troubled person who carried great shame on his shoulders. I believe we now understand why.'

189

'I think we do…'

'It was odd, really. The coroner pronounced death by misadventure, but after the inquest, the driver, who incidentally tried to console me, said he didn't agree with the verdict. It questioned his driving ability and his job was on the line.'

Remy was bereft. I waited.

'What did he say?'

'I hated him for his conceit, but he was convinced that Frederic jumped out in front of him.'

'Suicide?'

He gripped my arm. 'This is our secret! It would break Nicole's heart to hear that pronouncement. But the driver was adamant. I live with that notion in my head every day.'

'I won't utter a word.'

'It would destroy her, I'm afraid…'

'You have my solemn promise.'

We sat for a while, the dappled sun caressing our weary faces.

I break the silence.

'You know, we'll never understand what happened with the photos, but there is another theory.'

'Eh?'

'The police searched the whole farm, I presume?'

'They turned the place upside down…'

'And that would include Frederic's room.'

'He slept in the attic whenever he graced us with his presence.'

'Then perhaps that's where the pictures were discovered.'

'Meaning?'

'Well, Jimson needed a fall-guy. A confession was one thing, hard evidence quite another.'

'What are you implying…?'

I'm desperate for another shot of cognac but press on. My mouth is as dry as the soil beneath our feet.

'Perhaps Jimson found the very thing that would make your son fall.'

Chapter 44

The flight is turbulent as we break through the patchy cloud cover over the Solent, which gleams silver white under the glare of the full moon that I can see through my window on my right hand side. The city below is bejewelled by a million lights. I am nearly home, and I quietly reflect on the crap that is beginning to pile up ahead of me in the coming days. The plane touches down fifteen minutes early, for which I was grateful. I'm not a good flyer.

I have the money, so I'm extravagant and hail a taxi and I'm back in my little palace at just after eleven. I sling my bag down, ignore the post and crawl into bed, exhausted. I sleep for England.

The ring tone from my mobile alarm nudges me awake. My bleary eyes tell me it is eleven in the morning…Twelve hours kip! That's a record, I reckon. I pad to the kitchen to put the kettle on and notice the draught hit my face and then I realise how cold the flat is. My eyes alight upon the broken window. Shit. I skim over my surroundings and quickly recognise the disruption to my personal belongings. The flat has been ransacked (Yes, I can hear the first quip from one of you: How can you tell? Ha-ha). I reach for a beer to calm my nerves. Stuff is strewn across the floor, drawers turned over.

Someone has done a number on me.

I don't have insurance, so phone a mate who agrees to pop over and fix the damage. In the meantime, I tidy up and check if anything is missing…but everything appears OK. Most of the photos are with Isabel, thankfully, and I carry the rest in my coat pocket. Is this the reason for the intrusion? I concur that this is not an ordinary break-in. I'm being targeted. It's not a good feeling.

I collect the phone from the bedroom with a degree of apprehension. Do I call the police or Isabel…? Who can I trust in this situation? I punch in Meg's numbers instead.

'Where have you been hiding out?' she asks playfully.

I relax at the sound of her voice. 'France.'

'Oh, all right for some! Have you been picking grapes?'

'Ha-ha, brains actually…'

'I've been doing some digging as well…'

'Let's meet up.'

'How about *Mia's* for afternoon tea?' she suggests. 'My treat, but you'll need to collect me.'

'Deal.' I quickly calculate how long it will take for the window to be repaired. 'How about four o'clock?'

'See you then.'

191

Meg sounded animated. She has obviously dug up some juicy titbits.

*

I take a long hot bath and then brew coffee and make toast from stale bread (can you taste the difference when it's heated through?). I have a few hours to kill so I sift through the mail, tidy the kitchen, sweep up the broken glass and do a spot of clothes washing whilst I wait for Steve, my handyman. He arrives and gets on with the job. I'm happy for him to think of it as a petty crime. I really don't want to go into details and tell him my life story.

I reflect on my trip. I'm out of pocket by about three hundred quid but it was worth it. I now have a new insight, shared by other people!

Frederic no doubt had major issues, but they were largely to do with his dysfunctional lifestyle and crippling shyness. I think he was jealous of his brother's easy going appeal and couldn't form the same rapport with someone of the opposite sex. So I reckon he spied on them instead. I hate him for such behaviour. He was weird, potentially dangerous…and if he wasn't crushed under the wheels of a truck then who knows what trouble he might have caused in the future? Perhaps he knew this and took his own life, consumed by guilt for what he had done to my family and others like it. I cannot believe my wife and daughter were the only victims. After all, the farm attracted many holidaymakers throughout the summer months. Maybe Romain knew of his compulsion. No doubt we will find out in the fullness of time. I feel desperately sad for his parents, who would have been only too aware of his low self-esteem, which Remy hinted at to me. Sometimes it is difficult to support those on a path of self-destruction. Only God can be the final judge.

Romain was the opposite of his ill-fated brother. He loved Daisy and she was pregnant by him. Whether this created a divide between them I cannot fathom. What I do know is that she never confided in me about him or her looming problem. Eventually, we would have noticed of course but perhaps she was weighing up what to do. Who knows what happened when he came over to see her. He was volatile, moody and headstrong but again…was he capable of murder? At first, I was convinced of his guilt. I even encouraged Isabel to get Jimson to pursue him. Now I'm not so sure and I'll tell you why.

A confession can be extracted out of someone by methods of bribery, extortion or bullying. It can also be bought by a trade-off. It can involve blackmail in extreme cases. It can, of course, be the truth, the whole truth and nothing but the truth. I ask myself: Which of these applied themselves to Romain's confession?

Here lies one of the many dilemmas that confront me. Meg and I maintain that there is a link between the murder of Miriam and Daisy, but so far we are struggling to find it. But it is there, hidden away. In my opinion, there are clever people covering their tracks and bamboozling us, stifling our efforts. They've even resorted to breaking and entering. But we shall prevail. I just need one big breakthrough, and I'm close to it. I can smell the fear in the air.

I repeat: Romain did not harm my daughter. I've changed my opinion. He came over to help her, stand by her side, and perhaps talk to Isabel and me. He was her protector. Did something go horribly wrong between the young lovers? Only he could give the answer to this question now, if only I could get to him. Clearly, he got caught up in something way out of his control because he remains under arrest, the main suspect. Which makes me think more of him as a scapegoat.

I'm interrupted by Steve. He's finished and I slip him thirty quid for his efforts. I'm grateful that he's running late and needs to get to another job, which means I don't have to chat about old times. I want to concentrate solely on the here and now.

So who remains if Romain is innocent? Who is out there who is free to strike again? I consider the options.

One man under consideration (the salesman), who preyed on vulnerable young girls, has already been eliminated from police enquiries. The choice narrows.

This then leaves Remy's odd wayward brother, Robert, who has a history of misdemeanours. Isabel is looking into the family background, but I am doubtful of his compliance.

This leaves the man in black, the mysterious clown without a name.

This also leaves Carl Jimson, known as the local jack-the-lad back in the swinging seventies.

Both were at the fair that day in 1973.

I have the proof.

Chapter 45

Sitting down to afternoon tea and cakes is lovely. Sharing them with Meg is lovelier still. In spite of her telling me about the new treatment she is to undergo at the hospital (which is evasive), she looks radiant in an emerald green cardigan, white silk blouse and navy blue skirt. Oh, I shouldn't forget to mention the obligatory set of pearls around her neck.

'You have a mischievous grin,' I venture.

'I've been on a date…'

I broaden my grin. 'Who's the lucky guy?'

'Harry.'

'Harry *who*?'

'Mr Levi of course.'

'Wow, you're a quick worker!'

'I need to be at my age.'

We both fall about in a fit of giggles.

'Seems we have more in common than first thought,' she adds.

We break off to dive into the array of fancy cupcakes and I top up the teapot for a second brew. This is wonderful news for Meg, and I can see the happiness radiate from her impish face.

'Spill the beans,' I say, eager for news.

'Well, here's the thing. I got chatting to Harry, who's lived in this area all his life – he's now in his late sixties – and he used to work for Felix Winters Sport and Leisure back in the early seventies. They were a Jewish firm similar to Milletts and had several big stores on the south coast.'

I wrack my brain. 'I'm vaguely familiar with the name.'

'They went bust and disappeared from the high street after thirty-odd years trading. Anyway, that isn't the story. Apparently, the firm had a staff football team that performed in one of the Havant and District leagues or something like that.'

I sip my tea, yawn and try to concentrate on this uplifting monologue, but my mind is really fixed on the burglary. This puzzled me. Who was after me? Meg saw my lack of focus and wagged a finger in my direction.

'Listen up, young man. This is important. At the time, the teenagers at the firm were very keen to impress in their…what do you call it…first strip?'

'That's the term.'

'Well, lo and behold, they chose the outfit worn by Juventus, who were the big Italian giants at the time. The so-called coach, who worked in the central warehouse, came from Turin and got a deal on the kit. He thought the kit would give them the kudos to go out and…these are Harry's words "kick arse".'

My levels of concentration heightened.

Did she just say Juventus?

'Well, according to Harry, the team, all decked out and raring to go, were useless and lost their first match 1-16. Is that possible?'

I laugh. 'It is highly possible if they were crap.'

'Harry was the goalkeeper. Anyway, they lasted just one season without winning a game and then disbanded.'

'Sounds the right decision…'

'Harry turned to tennis and went on to county level.'

I saw the sparkle of admiration in her eye. However, my patience was being tested to the extent of me tapping the tabletop which annoys her.

I persisted. 'There's a punch-line coming, I presume?'

'The left winger was a lad called Jimson, who worked at the Portsmouth branch before jacking it in and becoming a copper on the beat. Yes, they really existed in those days.'

I appreciate her dash of humour. My brain then kicks in. This story fitted in neatly with the photo of him parading the football shirt at the funfair and the autographed team picture on his office wall. I want to know more.

'Can I meet Harry?'

'I'm sure you can.'

'Assuming he socialised with Jimson all those years ago, your friend will be able to give us an insight into what kind of young tearaway he was back then. There's *something* about Jimson that doesn't add up and he's hiding it, I'm convinced of it.'

I stare at Meg, who gently raises her eyebrows.

'There's more, isn't there?' I ask.

'Harry said he lost contact with the other players over the years, which is understandable. Four of them have since died. Anyway, we were chatting about many things and I happened to mention you and how you had helped me move home. The name *Farmer* struck a chord with him.'

The suspense was killing me.

'He suddenly recalled that last year he saw Jimson in town with a familiar face from the past, the centre half from their great all-conquering team, and although he didn't approach them for a chat, he remembered the name of the other player, because he was always bossing him about and giving him stick for letting in so many goals.'

'And?'

'His name was David.'

'David?' I was slow to cotton on.

'David Farmer, your brother.'

I was too dumbstruck for an immediate response; such was my shock at this apparent sighting. It didn't seem possible. Firstly, I didn't know that David played in this particular team, and I'm equally shocked that Jimson did and was, therefore, a colleague of his. *Were they still pals after all this time?* I searched my brain for a logical answer and it dawned on me (such was my relief) that there was a plausible explanation for this connection.

'It's simple, Meg, so I have no reason to be alarmed. David would have been interviewed by Jimson as a matter of routine because of his close relationship to Daisy, and the fact that he frequently came to France with us.'

She shrugged. 'Granted, no doubt that would have happened.'

'They may not even have recognised each other.'

'That too could be true…'

I was feeling uncomfortable. 'I can detect a "but" in your voice, Meg.'

'*But,*' she emphasises, 'for the fact that Harry spotted them coming out of Whistles nightclub in Portsmouth around midnight one Saturday night.'

Fuck. '*Together?*'

'They got into a taxi.'

I can't work this one out. My mind's in a spin…

I had no way of defending the situation.

It was clear to me.

The two of them were out on the razzle, together.

They were still pals after all these years.

Chapter 46

I can't hold back. After dropping off Meg from the cake shop, I return home and phone David immediately.

'What's up, fella? Spent the money already?'

I ignored his facetious remark.

'Saw an old pal of yours the other day.'

'Oh, yes…?'

'He asked me to pass on his regards.'

'Who's that then?'

'Harry Levi.'

'Never heard of him…'

'He worked at Felix Winter's back in the seventies.'

'Christ, that's going back, Will!'

'I didn't know you worked there.'

'I had a Saturday job and sometimes worked there during the holiday break from college. That name is a blast from the past.'

I waited, then said, 'Do you remember him now?'

'I think we played football together…yes, that was it.'

'He was the goalkeeper.'

'A fucking useless goalkeeper if I recall!' He roars with laughter.

I go for the jugular. 'Do you still have your Juventus shirt?'

I keep quiet in anticipation.

'I reckon I do, somewhere in the attic.'

'Do you mix with any of the gang these days?'

'Nah, I wouldn't recognise any one of them if they walked past me in the street.'

'Great days though, I bet,' I remark, wondering at what point did my brother become a liar to his own family. I'm gutted.

He's on a roll. 'Brilliant days in fact. We may not have been a very talented bunch, but boy, did we look the part.'

He roars again.

'Anyway, Harry just wanted to say hello.'

'How did my name crop up?'

'Oh, I think he said he spotted you in town with another member of the team…but he couldn't remember his name.'

'Not me, I'm afraid. I think he was mistaken. As I said…'

'You've lost touch with everyone.'

'Exactly. How do you know Harry anyway?'

'Just through a mutual acquaintance of ours, a lady called Meg. I'd been having tea with her. She'd been harking back to the good old days with him, and your name came up.'

'I was legendary, which would explain it I suppose.'

Now it was my turn to laugh. He was not known for false modesty.

But my laughter masks nervousness. David and Jimson were not just linked by their past, they were still forged together in the present. But he didn't want to admit it to me.

I ask myself another question: What secrets bind them together?

*

Within the hour, I get a call back from David. I'm intrigued.

'I'm off to the caravan next weekend. Fancy joining me?'

I wasn't expecting this. I ask nervously, 'How long for?'

'Two days, return Sunday night.'

'Sounds great actually,' I reply confidently, but I'm all over the place.

'I fancy doing some serious walking, you know, blow the cobwebs away. I thought about a climb up Roseberry Topping.'

'We haven't done that since we were kids.'

'Exactly.'

'When are you leaving?'

'Friday night. Take a slow drive up, get a couple of pints in and get our heads down for the next day's trek. Weather looks excellent.'

'Great. Shall I come over to you?'

'Makes sense.'

'What shall I bring?'

'Good boots.'

'OK, I'll see what I can dig out.'

'Get to me around four and we can make a decent start to beat the traffic.'

I click off. For some reason, I check the online weather forecast for next week. It promises heavy rain and low-lying mists.

Is he trying to hoodwink me on this as well as his friendship with Jimson?

I start to feel queasy, and it isn't from the fry-up I've just eaten.

*

I've got the bit between my teeth.

This time I phone Isabel at the cottage.

'What's up?' she asks cagily.

My suspicions are aroused: Is there someone with her?

'Would Jimson have formally questioned my brother personally in regard to Daisy?'

'Well, your brother would have given a statement to eliminate him from our line of enquiries. I'm not sure if it would be to Jimson.'

'And that would be done down at the station?'

'Normally, yes. We request people to come down as a matter of course.'

'Hmm.'

'Is there a problem, Will?'

I hear noises in the background and a faint giggle from Isabel.

The bastard is back on the scene.

'No,' I answer sharply.

'You could have asked your brother that question.'

I was in a corner. 'I could, but he's away at present.'

'Is that it then?'

My blood pressure is rising. I wanted to tell her about the break-in but this is obviously not the right moment.

'Yeah, sorry to disturb you,' I say.

'You aren't.'

I'm incensed.

Fucking Hell, is everyone on a mission to lie to me?

I want to keep her on the phone and annoy him, the slimy wanker, that way. I'll keep him from putting his hands all over her body.

'Can I ask you a really gross question?'

'That depends on *how* gross…'

I think of the shower cubicle at the farm and my mind goes hyperactive with the idea that Jimson has possibly seen Isabel naked from the photos secretly taken there. Surely it stands to reason that the voyeur (whoever it was), wouldn't just target Daisy. Isabel was a very attractive lady. The temptation would be just too great to ignore.

'Well?' she adds impatiently.

In for a penny: 'Has Jimson ever made a pass at you?'

Silence.

Now it was my turn. 'Well?'

'Why do you feel the need to ask that?'

'I've seen the way he looks at you, especially since we parted.'

'Ask me again.'

'Has he ever made a pass at you?'

'Several, in fact.'

Then she slammed the phone down on me.

Chapter 47

I'm pissed off.

I asked for that put down from Isabel, meddling in business that wasn't my concern. Then again, I have a right to know. After all, she is still my wife and I want to protect her from the advances of a scumbag detective. I'm angry with her, I'm angrier with him. If there are naked pictures of Isabel then it is a fair assumption that he has been gawping at them. That's why he has the "hots" for her. He's obviously tried his luck. What she didn't say to me was what her response had been to his advances.

She left that bit dangling in the wind. *Bitch.*

I have to remind myself to let these things go. Move on, buddy. That's what Philip said he was going to do. I need to do the same. The problem is I still love Isabel, care for her; I want to guard her against men like Jimson. There's a whole bunch of bastards out there, and I don't want any of them messing with her. Especially, *him with the big ears and crooked teeth.*

Isabel's off limits. Some joke that is. She's with someone right now. The joke is on me. I try and distract myself from this emotional torture and find a pair of climbing boots. How sad is that? A beer helps, and then I watch celebrity Masterchef on the TV before falling asleep propped up against the lounge wall. It's only when I stir for a pee that I realise it is four in the morning. That's not so bad until I start thinking that I have a stiff neck to contend with whilst Isabel has something else much stiffer to amuse her. I crawl into bed and conclude that I've got to get a life. After all, I've been a bastard as well!

*

First light and my mouth tastes disgusting, like dog's breath.

I need a run but it's raining which makes my mind up; sod the exercise, it can wait. I glance out of the window and observe the line of bored gulls perched along the top of the roof opposite. They're not eager to do anything either. I clean my teeth and go back to bed for an extra hour of kip. What luxury. It doesn't last long. The mobile buzzes.

It's Isabel on the warpath.

'What was all that shit about last night?'

I sit up and try and clear my brain.

'David denies knowing Jimson yet they were seen out on the town together,' I splutter.

'I'm talking about the other crap you pulled on me.'

'I just don't like the way he looks at you.' I didn't dare mention my fears regarding the possibility of incriminating pictures. She would truly freak out at this. 'I'm sorry; I had no business to ask.'

'Too bloody right!'

'Has he?'

'What?'

'Well, you know…'

'Tried to get into my knickers?'

'I never said that.'

'He's my commanding officer, asshole.'

I'm suitably chastised.

'And besides, I hear on the grapevine that he has a very small dick.'

It takes a few seconds. Then we burst into a fit of laughter.

'I'm sorry,' I mumble again, aggrieved that she is still hooked up with lover boy, 'I'm just a little paranoid…'

'What's this about your brother?'

There it was again, her refusal to use his name.

I explain the related story.

'OK, they may just have bumped into each other, had a chat about old times and shared a taxi because neither could risk driving home after a drink.'

'Maybe, but David lives in Dorking. That's an expensive fare home.'

'True. I'll look into who conducted the interview with your brother and we'll go from there.'

'Sounds a plan.'

I avoid telling her about the broken window again. Nothing is missing and a neighbour has told me there have been similar incidents in the area, all drug-related. So I pass. I go on and tell her about my trip to France. She is aghast, happy and horrified at the same time. I think she is impressed with my bravery but mortified by the trickery of one of the sons on the farm. I deliberately avoid bringing Jimson into the equation at this stage. There are hot potatoes and then there are *real* hot potatoes.

It doesn't take her long to twig.

'Fuck, suppose there are pictures of me?'

'It hasn't been mentioned, Isabel, so try not to worry.' It was a poor argument and she knew it as a policewoman.

'Jimson has seen the photos.' She says.

'We don't know what's on them.'

'Christ, that's what I'm worried about, Will.'

Chapter 48

We agree to meet up at The Ship Inn tomorrow at lunchtime, after Isabel had a chance to do a bit of digging around. I knew I had spooked her with the revelation of what really happened at the farm. She is beginning to take me seriously, at long last. I am no longer considered the buffoon; at least I hope I'm not.

I phone Meg and get her to introduce me to Harry. I explain we have to keep it "light" so as not to make him feel threatened by my questions. I have nothing to fear when we hook up at the shop. He is charming and relays the story just as Meg had told me at *Mia's.* I believe in his sighting of David with Jimson. There is no hidden agenda as far as I can tell. I thank him, buy a few bits from the counter and leave them to it, managing to give Meg a quick wink of approval.

I take the Rav in for an MOT (it passes miraculously), buy a local paper and half-heartedly search for a job. My mind is on other matters. At home, I check the emails and find one from Remy thanking me for helping his wife come to terms with things a little better. All I did was stir up a hornet's nest and hate myself for intruding on their private lives. I feel inadequate, but I am thankful to receive a show of gratitude.

I eat pizza, but I'm sick of it and leave most of it on the plate. I just don't have an appetite and go for a run and it feels great, and I cover about six miles along the coastal route, catching the breeze as it whips off the surface of the high tidal water. A small yacht in full sail skips past and I wave back to the high spirited crew.

Back home, I strip and blissfully remain under the hot blast from the shower. It dulls the aches and pains screaming from my body in protest of the years slipping by. In truth, I feel ancient, beyond my sell-by date. I hate the world as it has become, and start to cry loudly, but you wouldn't know as the torrent from above drowns out my sorrow.

*

The next day I feel more optimistic and look forward to seeing Isabel, hopeful that she has something for me. But what can I realistically hope for?

I dress, put a clean shirt on, shave and head into town and get a haircut. I told you I am feeling optimistic. The shirt I choose was one Isabel bought me for my birthday many moons ago. I hope she notices. I put the Rav through a car wash, fill up with fuel (normally this would be a tenner's worth, but I have the funds remember) and slowly I make my way over to the pub on the harbour front. I'm early so I snap the local birdlife on my camera (not what you are thinking…) and occupy a vacant table on the patio to get the best view across the bay before the crowds arrive.

Isabel parks up, strolls over and she looks fab in a red cotton summer dress and white sandals. I can't ignore the sight of her toned bare arms and legs. Her brown hair is long, the sun catching the blondish highlights.

'What are you staring at?' she asks, conveying a secret knowing smile.

I half-stand, and stutter the word, 'Y-You.'

She sits opposite me and proclaims, 'Even I can scrub up well if I make the effort.'

I'd ordered her favourite, white Chablis and pour a glass for her.

'I'm impressed, but don't think this gains you any favours…'

'Isabel!'

'Sorry.'

'We're not here to score points, OK?'

'You're right. Nice shirt.'

I'm won over in an instant.

Perfect setting, perfect girl.

We order quickly. Ribeye steak for me, sea bass for her. The wine flows.

I don't want to talk about the boyfriend, Jimson, photos, the forthcoming trial, listening to Romain's testimony, the disclosure of our daughter's pregnancy, in fact any of the whole shitty scenario that's constantly thrown in our faces. I just want to talk to Isabel, stare into her eyes and remember those treasured memories we once shared so intimately. She seems to relax.

Two hours vanish in a flash.

'Crikey,' she says, 'we haven't got around to what we came here for.'

I pour coffee. 'Does it matter?'

'I…I suppose not.' Her defences are down thankfully.

I raise my hand and catch the waitress's attention for the bill.

'I'll get this,' Isabel says, fumbling in her handbag.

I touch her arm, and she doesn't withdraw it.

'You get it next time, OK?'

'Maybe there won't be a next time…'

'Maybe there will.'

Her eyes narrow. 'How come you're feeling flush?'

'I have my methods…'

'You still owe me two hundred quid.'

'Didn't think for one moment you would let me forget that.'

She stares at me, blinks and half-smiles encouragement.

I stand; drop sixty quid into the little basket on the table and say, 'Now, shall we go and visit our daughter?'

A tear suddenly forms in the corner of her eye, and I'm sure it isn't from a fleck of dust in the air.

Chapter 49

This is the stuff dreams are made of.

I don't expect you to be on the same wavelength with this, but for me it's a huge breakthrough. Isabel is, at last, coming towards me again.

I feel it in my bones.

Am I deluded? We will see with the passage of time. In the meantime, please let me wallow in my wishful world of fantasy and false hopes.

We sit at the kitchen table in Eggshell cottage, the night drawing in as the sun finally dips behind the headland. Our journey out to the cemetery was poignant in that the three of us – the four of us, actually – were together in unity. We huddled in silence and listened to the sigh of the wind as it threaded through the trees and cooled our foreheads. We cried and hugged and whispered our fears and prayed that Daisy sleeps well. It is the living, not the dead, who bear the scars now.

So here we are, *the living.*

That's what remains. It's a sobering thought and as I look at her I am determined that we will not simply shrivel up and die a slow death. Instead, we will dust ourselves down and fight the formidable odds that stand in our way. We will not be beaten. Tough talk, but really I'm crazy scared.

'I'm scared,' she says as if reading my mind.

I reach out and take her hand in mine.

'Then we'll be scared together.'

She squeezes tightly.

But I'm on a mission. 'Now, what have you got for me?' I ask.

*

She hasn't got a lot, to be honest, but I don't show my disappointment. She is too fragile, and I want to build her up, not knock her down.

I do learn one thing though.

'It was Jimson who interviewed your brother.'

'Then why does David not admit to knowing him. What has he got to hide?'

'Or lose.'

'Have you spoken to your boss about this?'

'Not yet, as it doesn't seem pertinent. After all, he is not under suspicion. I just looked up the records to satisfy your curiosity.'

I'm taken aback by her little aside. 'Is David under suspicion then?'

'Not necessarily, but we do need to question him about the argument he had with Romain and clear the matter up. It could be relevant to the case. With regard to Daisy, it was a matter of routine that he would have been interviewed.'

'It was just the implication.'

'At the time, everyone was under suspicion. Including you.'

I come out in a cold sweat just thinking about it.

'I've had a word with David about the argument,' I say, 'and his version seems innocent enough but it differs from Romain's account...so one of them is pulling the wool over our eyes, but to what end I don't know.'

'Don't worry, we'll nail him down.'

Then I change tack. 'Why don't you ever mention my brother by his name?'

'What do you mean?'

'You never call him *David*. It is always *him* or *your brother...*'

'Do I?'

'You know you do.'

The doorbell rings conveniently and she leaves the table and collects the Indian takeaway she promised, while I open a bottle of wine and grab two glasses.

I persist. 'You don't like David do you?'

'He is what he is.'

I watch as she sets the food down on the table in their silver foil containers and hands me a plate and fork. I pour the wine; she serves the grub. I don't let the inquisition drop: 'Which is?'

'He's an arse.'

'Why does he warrant such a compliment? I thought we were all close, especially on holiday.'

'He was especially an arse on holiday, always dictating what we should do, where we should go, what we should eat...blah, blah, blah.'

I'm taken aback but eat greedily as I am starving despite a big lunch.

I retort, 'Well, yes, I know he can be domineering...'

'He also made a pass at me.'

Fuck.

'*When?*'

'One Christmas, a few years back.'

'Where?'

'When we all went to stay at the house in Dorking.'

'What happened?'

'It doesn't matter; it was a long time ago.'

'It does, so tell me.'

'It was the year when Margo was first ill and confined to bed. I cooked the festive dinner and wanted to make an impression, so I did a big spread. He came into the kitchen afterwards, drunk of course, and slapped my bottom and remarked that I was the best dish on offer.'

'Did you not just laugh it off?'

'Normally I would, but he persisted with his boorish manner and tried to grope me. I pushed him off, but Daisy saw us and it didn't look good.'

'Did he apologise?'

'We never spoke of it again.'

'Did Daisy mention it?'

'I just brushed it aside and told her he was fooling around and to ignore it. I think she was only five at the time so no harm was done.'

I take a generous gulp of my wine.

'What a tosser,' I say.

'It was no big deal.'

'It clearly was, because it upset you.'

We continue to eat.

'That's not what upset me.' She replicated my action with the wine, with even more gusto. 'A year later, when we were in Bezier, he tried the same thing with a waitress that he got over-familiar with at one of our favourite restaurants. She slapped him and threatened to file a complaint to the gendarme.'

'Christ, where the hell was I when all this was going on?'

'Playing the piano rather badly.'

'At the Bebelle brasserie?'

'I thought you were too pissed to remember.'

'And at the same time he was groping a waitress…?'

'I luckily intervened and dragged him away and smoothed things over with the girl and the management.'

'Is that why we never went back there?'

'Spot on. Your brother was banned.'

'And I thought it was my rendition of *Candle in the wind* that blew it for us.'

'It probably didn't help our cause but in reality, he was a very lucky man to get away with it, especially with his professional background. It could have destroyed his reputation if she had pressed charges.'

'Did he thank you for your intervention?'

'Did he hell!'

'Jesus, I never knew any of this.'

'Well, you do now. That is why he isn't exactly flavour of the month in my book.'

I change the subject. 'I haven't told you, but David has prostate cancer.'

'Oh, that's terrible news, Will…I didn't want to trash him but I'm not going to defend him either. Is he going to get specialised treatment?'

'Yes, but it's a worry.' Then I think of him manhandling Isabel and the waitress. 'He just can't handle his booze,' I say, embarrassed and angry.

'No, but he thinks he can handle the goods, even when they've not on offer, which is a dangerous thing.'

I couldn't argue with that.

Then I am reminded of my own behaviour. I am just as guilty, except my crime is worse. Rape is rape.

Coldness suddenly descends upon us. I think Isabel has picked up on my shame because she looks away and stares at the floor.

'I'm so very, very sorry,' I lament, and want to crawl into a hole such is my disgrace of what I did to her.

Two brothers, two bastards…

Isabel picks up on my crushed expression and takes my arm.

'We weren't talking about you, Will.'

Chapter 50

I am grateful that Isabel allows me the luxury of sleeping over on the couch, as it has gone midnight and I have consumed far too much wine. The next morning I have the hangover from hell. Stories of David's escapades simply compound my misery. What a damn fool he had been…and to think he was still at it, if Harry Levi's eyesight is to be relied upon. What the hell was David doing at a nightclub at his age? I feel betrayed by my own brother, someone I look up to, and here he was trying it on with my wife, and others for that matter. No wonder Isabel detests him.

She's left early and entrusts the key with me. That's progress, I suppose. I sleep in until eleven, fold away the bed sheets and clean up the kitchen before leaving a scribbled note on the hall side-table:

Dearest Isabel,

Forgive us our sins. I cannot vouch for David but if I can, I will make it up to you…however long it takes. A bad man is a bad man, but a misguided one can be taught the right way. I hope you can teach me.

Love, Will.

I lock the door and push the key back through the letterbox. I walk to my car and hesitate. On the windscreen is a note:

Let's do it again, and soon / Me x

I clutch the note to my chest as if it the most treasured thing I possess.

*

I'm angry with David, and now he expects me to go away with him for a couple of days. What do I do…cancel or grin and bear it? And to think I trusted him. I feel like punching him square on the jaw.

Then, as if he knows I'm speaking ill of him (subconsciously) he bloody well phones me. I'm driving so I manage to pull into a lay-by.

'Change of plan, I'm afraid…'

'Oh?'

'There's been heavy rain for two days solid and the caravan is flooded, so we can't use it.'

I was sharp with him. 'Well, just call off the trip, it's no problem.'

'You OK?'

'Fine.' I'm seething.

'I need to go up and assess the damage. Luckily, the owner of the site has managed to put a temporary tarpaulin over the roof which will stop any further

208

rain leaking in. So I'm committed to travelling up to assess what needs to be done but it buggers up staying there on this occasion.'

'Whatever…'

'So I've booked us into the B & B down the road.'

Oh, fuck, fuck, fuck.

'I'll expect you at four as arranged.'

Then I have a brainstorm.

'Another change of plan. I can't make Friday, (Isabel and I pushed the Indian takeaway forward in case you are asking) so I'll come up early Saturday under my own steam, and I'll still get most of the weekend in for a hike and a few beers.'

'Suit yourself. That'll give me a chance to get over to the site and inspect the damage and try and sort it out. The place we are staying at is the Dale Croft Lodge…google it for directions.'

'OK.'

'Hopefully, we'll meet up around late lunch.'

'Perfect.'

I click off and ponder my options. It would have been easy to cancel the trip but there is a method to my madness. *Game on.*

*

I call round to Meg's with news that will upset her.

I get straight to the point. 'Thought you should hear it from me first.'

'I think I know what is coming…'

'Your old house was demolished yesterday morning.'

She sits and reflects quietly.

'That's forty-odd years of memories just wiped away,' she says.

I do what anyone would do in the circumstances. I put the kettle on.

'The bulldozers do what bulldozers do,' I comment. 'But I have to say that you are better off where you are now, Meg.'

'It's not the same, Will.'

'I know, but then you wouldn't have Harry in your life if this didn't all happen.'

She smiled. 'Or you for that matter.'

'I'm just the consolation.'

'No, Will, you're the shining star.'

That's the second time today that my spirits have been uplifted. If this carries on, my faith in human nature will be restored permanently. That doesn't sound right!

Chapter 51

It's evening; the TV is rubbish so I do a bit of packing for the trip back home to East Yorkshire. That sounds odd. This region is where I was brought up but I feel alienated from its natural charms. I wish the circumstances of my journey were better suited to nostalgia, but deep inside I feel like a failure as a returning son to the soil of my birthplace. It's a proud county, inhabited by a tough and upright people. Why then did I think I was crawling back in, keeping under the radar? Lack of self-worth, I suppose. I just don't feel I have anything to offer this noble place…which raised me in the right manner and sent me on my way to make good in this world. The least said about that the better.

My parents were decent honest folk. I owe them.

I have to keep my head held high therefore, in memory of their name.

Meg taught me how to be strong and able (some joke), and how to fight against hardship, with gravity and a belief that justice will prevail (some hope). She learnt how to deal with personal tragedy and the loss of innocence. So must I. Above all, she showed me that sometimes those closest to you are in fact those farthest away from understanding shared grief. Hence, my battles with Isabel. She had her own demons to conquer before she could consider mine, and I was too selfish to recognise this.

It would be easier to simply let the past go, fade away. But that would be wrong even though we dwell over-keenly in what went before. But it is today that matters. There has to be someone prepared to stand up and fight for the righteousness of victims. Meg has given me the strength to succeed. I am that person.

I decide to call over and see Isabel but phone beforehand (to avoid embarrassment in case *he* is loitering with intent)…I didn't want to just barge in. I explain to her what I intend to do over the next few days and ask her to conduct a search into matters which don't necessarily relate to what's on my mind. I'm even confusing myself. I'm looking for a pattern, a puzzle, a connection…the route to finding a killer. Isabel stares at me first with pity, then wonder, as I bring her on board with my mad bonkers ideas.

'Hold tight, and keep with me on this,' I implore.

'Where is this leading?'

'Just do the homework as I ask, OK?'

'I'm frightened, Will. What am I looking for?'

I jump in and kiss her on the mouth, and hold for an extra second. I release her and our eyes lock.

'A way home, Isabel, a way home.'

Then I turn and leave her standing there, bewildered.

Me? I'm frightened too, but I'm on cloud nine as the kiss still lingers on my lips.

Chapter 52

The drive up north, along the A1, is tedious and takes just over four hours. I turn off to Teesside and I arrive at the lodge for lunch, as agreed with David.

I am no longer miffed with him, just saddened by his behaviour.

He's not there. I wait, phone and then text him. No response. I order a pint of the local brew, a plate of sandwiches and a packet of cheese and onion crisps. It's decent enough weather-wise to sit outside on the patio. In the distance, the local landmark, the nipple of Roseberry Topping, protrudes into the leaden sky. Proud and erect, just like the natives. You couldn't put a Yorkshire man down if you tried. I am testament to that. Once, I would not have aspired to that notion. Now I am strong and resilient, just like the mountain in the distance.

As proof to that, within twenty minutes I'm back in the bar, nestled beside a log fire. It was colder than I thought outside on the patio!

David waltzes in an hour later and grabs a beer. I'm unfazed and ask the landlord to bring the extra sandwiches I'd ordered in anticipation of his late arrival.

'Good fella,' David says and pats me on the shoulder like a child at school. He knocks back his pint and gestures to the barman for a refill.

'What's the problem with the caravan?' I enquire.

'The seal on the blasted roof has rotted in one corner and the driving rain has forced itself in.'

'Much damage?'

'Not a disaster, but it's damp and the sofa is sodden, which is where you would have kipped down.'

'Have you fixed the roof?'

'It needs specialist glue, but I've patched it for now. Eric will keep an eye on it until someone can come out.'

'Eric?'

'The site owner.'

'I wanted to see it, for old time's sake.'

'Another weekend, eh?'

I play the game. 'Where do you keep it? I've forgotten where you said…'

'I don't recall telling you.'

'Yes, when we were with Margo, but I think you were a little worse for wear.'

'Um, perhaps.'

Another pint for him, I settle for a half.

'Well?'

'Well *what?*'

'Where do you keep it…the caravan?'
'On a site just above the ridge as you come down into Whitby.'
It was like trying to get blood out of a stone.
'Does it have a name?'
He is irritated. 'What, the bloody caravan?'
I let it drop, for now.
He is still irritated. 'Did you remember to bring your boots?'
I nod.
'We've got a big day tomorrow. It could be a dangerous climb.'
I nod again.

Chapter 53

After such a long arduous drive and a boozy lunch, I take a nap in the afternoon which hopefully will recharge my batteries. Later, I shower, dress and then decide on a stroll around the village to stretch my legs. I go into a bookshop, peruse the well-stacked shelves and buy a paperback copy of Michael Fowler's *Heart of the Demon*. I'd enjoyed another of his crime novels and decided to reacquaint myself with DS Hunter Kerr. That should while away a good few hours. I also buy a *Sun*, a can of diet coke and a packet of mints from the Newsagents next door.

I visit the local church, take a pew and say a prayer for Daisy. The solitude is comforting. I stay for half an hour, and then amble back just as more rain descends from the dark mushrooming clouds above. I detect a roll of thunder in the distance. I hurry on, ready for my evening meal at the aptly named *Farmers Arms* a few doors down from where we were staying.

I skip through the paper and start the novel. By page ten David arrives and heads for the bar, oblivious to me and orders a gin and tonic with lime. He turns, sees me and laughs.

'How long have you been sitting there?' he booms.

'Twenty minutes maybe.' My current glass is empty.

'Do you fancy the same?' he asks, raising his glass.

'Don't mind if I do.'

He brings the drinks over. We sit by a roaring log fire, stoked up by the barman. On such a wild night, this was definitely the place to be, although I would prefer my companion to be Isabel, to put it bluntly. I knew straight away that this idea of his was a mistake as I listen with fake interest his droning on about politics in general, the educational chief in particular, and the lack of school funding which hinders his plans for a new sports hall. Dreary, dreary, dreary…

I want to bring him down to earth sharply.

'Isabel said to say "hi".'

'Oh, really?'

'I told her what I was doing this weekend.'

'Are you two an item again?'

'Good grief, no.'

'But you're talking, eh?'

'We're having to, as Romain comes over next month for pre-trial.'

'That will be tough for you both, I guess.'

I state the obvious. 'Horrendous, especially listening to things that we would rather forget.'

He sips his drink and scans the headlines on the front page of the *Sun,* and remarks casually, 'Exactly. The last thing you want is for the past to be raked up again...'

I let my words slowly drop in like tiny bombs. 'Especially now that new developments have come to light.'

He stops drinking.

'Oh?'

'I'm not at liberty to say.'

'Yes, but surely you can tell me?'

'Unfortunately, you are involved and so I can't say anything that might prejudice your viewpoint.'

His face whitens. 'Involved?'

'You'll certainly be called as a witness in the trial.'

'I hadn't thought about that possibility.'

'I would now. DI Jimson will want you to testify against the lad.'

I go in search of the loo, aware that he was shifting awkwardly in his chair.

*

We have dinner, and the conversation is, as expected, rather muted. David is in his own private world, just where I wanted him. The very mention of Jimson's name makes him jittery. He could chew on things for a while. Messing with my Isabel was the last straw, even though she handled it admirably at the time. Clearing up his mess in France was also commendable, and he owed her big time. But she owes him nothing but contempt.

Let him squirm, I think. Later, we retire to the bar and things pick up a bit as the wine flows merrily. We finish on brandy and coffee and walk the few yards back to our respective rooms at the B & B, and go our separate ways upstairs. I reckon he will toss and turn all night but I'm bushed and fall asleep quickly.

I'm up early and refreshed, which is unusual for me. I peep beyond the curtains and see a heavy sky and low mist, as predicted.

I go down to the dining room and David is all togged up and raring to go, munching on a full English breakfast and looking like he doesn't have a care in the world. I join him and tuck into a similar spread, minus the black pudding.

We're set up for the day and drive over in my car to base camp, which is a car park and embark on our climb. It starts sedately enough, across a meadow and then up a rutted track which zig-zags through a wooded embankment. It's muddy and slippery, and the going is slow. Already, I'm struggling with my breath and take a break. (you wouldn't think I jogged back in Hampshire!)

'Come on, you lazy bugger!' David barks as he marches on with speed.

I curse him and follow. I've spent my whole life following him.

We hit the first outcrop of rocks and heave ourselves forward and then it gets considerably steeper as we push upwards. The rain lashes down and the mist is

215

cold on my face, but we are not alone. A group ahead of us disappears from view behind slabs of sandstone boulders. We pull into line behind their footsteps and climb steadily, gripping firmly as the rocky path narrows. In spite of the foul weather, I'm exhilarated by my efforts. I vow to get even fitter on my return south, perhaps join a gym and cut down on the beer. *Some hope.*

An hour later we reach the summit and I collapse on a makeshift stone plinth and wipe the sweat from my face. I swig from a water bottle and survey the majestic scene spread out before me. Not the best of days, but the panoramic view is awesome, to say the least. Normally, you can see fifty miles of terrain from this position. The wind makes things hazardous as I step towards the edge and peer down into the swirling abyss. I breathe in deeply and marvel at the vista.

The group start their descent. We are alone and stare in silence, as David positions himself on another platform, just above me. I then lose sight of him. My mobile goes and I jump at the intrusion.

'It's Isabel, where are you?'

I laugh, and shout above the gusting wind. 'At the summit of Roseberry Topping.'

'Must be howling a gale, you sound very faint…'

'I can just about hear you.'

'Is your brother with you?'

'Yeah.'

'We need to talk, Will. I did as you asked and I've come up with a few things that you may not like…and they…concern…your…brother.'

'You're breaking up, Isabel.'

'Hello?'

'I said…'

'Are you there, Will…?'

It was becoming impossible. Then I heard her say: 'Don't…trust…him, just get…down…from…the…mountain…'

I lose the bloody connection and click off, worrying about her last words, which were muddled. What the hell was that all about?

Suddenly, I am gripped tightly around my throat as an arm swings over my shoulder from behind and pulls tight. I am momentarily knocked sideways and I stumble towards the slippery edge. Sickness and dizziness hit me twin-fold as I try to correct my stance.

David screams his delight at scaring the shit out of me and maintains his grip.

'I wondered if you were standing a little too close for comfort and wanted to keep you from harm's way,' he says. He then deliberately levers his arm more firmly to make me gag, dragging me back in the same motion. Then he releases me.

'Are you fucking insane,' I snap, planting my feet firmly on rock and guzzling more water.

'It's easy to fall if you're not experienced with this kind of tricky landscape. I thought you were wobbling a bit too much for my liking.'

I am livid with him and know precisely what he is up to. He wants to exercise his control over me, just like he did when we were boys; always the prankster. Well, he has succeeded. My knees go weak as I steady myself.

'You never did have a head for heights, Will.'

'I'm here, aren't I?'

'Under protest, I reckon.'

'Piss off.'

'Good idea.' And with that remark, he fumbles with his jeans and urinates into a crevasse. Then he buckles up and turns to me again. 'Shall we go down before you do something silly and fall off a cliff? You should be grateful I'm here to protect you.'

Then he is gone, leaving me confused and cold. I try to make sense of Isabel's warning, but it was lost on me. Now I'm not so sure. Gradually, I negotiate the muddy path and gingerly step down, catching sight of David recklessly bounding ahead without fear. He'd hurt me with his unexpected strength, and I'd have the weal to show for it later.

I'll get him back, make no mistake.

Chapter 54

In the afternoon I keep my distance from him and, after a long soak in the bath, drive over to Great Ayton and have a sniff around the shops. Later, I stroll beside the shallow river that runs the length of the pretty village all too aware of the painful bruising around my neck.

After cooling off, I get back to the B & B in search of David but, much to my amazement, he has departed. There is a message from him at the reception:

Sorry to bugger off, needed at school urgently. Apparently, we have a major flood. What is it about water with me at the moment? See you back home…and apologies for manhandling you earlier. It was just a prank. Forgive and forget? David.

Like hell I'll forgive and forget, but it is typical of him to reduce the incident down to a "joke" on his part. He bloody well scared me, and it was a dangerous lark whichever way you viewed it. Good riddance to him. This gives me the chance to do what I set out to do in the first place.

I shut myself in my room for privacy, get a signal and punch in Isabel's number and sit back on the bed. The sun is finally out and bathes the distant hills in a golden hue. She picks up.

'Hi, Isabel.'

'What happened up there?' she asks sympathetically.

'The wind and rain played havoc with the signal and you were cut off.'

'I tried calling back…I was worried.'

'No need to have been,' I lied. 'What have you got for me?'

'Can David overhear you?'

That's a first. *David.* 'Not unless he's got telescopic ears.'

'Oh?'

'He's done a runner. According to him, he's needed back at school so I'm all alone. Fancy a trip up?'

She chortles. 'Sounds a blast with all that rain. I'll skip it if that's OK.'

'A good call.' Secretly, I wished for a different answer from her.

'Will, you're not going to like this. I've dug up some odd business on David which is hard to fathom.'

'Try me.'

'He's a little bit more than a straight-laced Head Teacher at a school in Dorking, which is what he wants us all to believe.'

I smirk. 'You mean he's an international spymaster for MI6?'

'No, but he is a seriously adept entrepreneur with fingers in many pies.'

'*Our* David?' I'm aghast.

'Shall I list his hidden assets?'

I was all ears, but nervous at the same time.

'He part owns the *Whistles* nightclub in the city for starters…'

I jump in. 'That's where he was spotted with Jimson!'

'Now you know why. He also owns a florist in Havant, a garage and an online dating agency in Southampton. They all belong under the umbrella of a holding company called Pleasure Dome Limited. He is the principle director and majority shareholder.'

'Who are the other shareholders?'

'Wait a minute…someone called E. Razzoni.'

That name strikes a cord but we move on.

'David also owns a three bedroom penthouse apartment in Harrogate.'

'Fucking hell, he's loaded.'

'He's a big time Charlie, your mister respectable brother.'

'I'm flabbergasted; he's never let on to me. Do you think Margo knows?'

'Difficult to say. He's a man of mystery.'

'I knew he was once involved with the local newsagents but this is entirely on a different planet.'

Isabel speculates. 'I reckon the place in Harrogate must be worth four hundred and fifty K at a conservative estimate.'

I could kick myself; there I was begging him for a measly few grand when he is rolling in the stuff. What a dark horse he is turning out to be.

'There's more, Will.'

There had to be, and the tone of her voice suggested a darker element to what had so far been discussed. I brace myself and crave a gin and tonic.

'Go on…'

'I looked into his background in the seventies as you asked. He was twenty-three in 1973 and, as a matter of course, he *was* interviewed by the police because, like Jimson, he was at the fair on the day when Miriam was abducted. The police file at the time revealed that he was actually brought in two times for questioning.'

'Meaning?'

'Meaning the police were taking a keen interest in him.'

'Why?'

'Because of minor discrepancies found in his alibi,' she says.

'Shit. Would that be enough to make alarm bells ring?'

Isabel goes silent on me.

'Isabel?'

'I'm here. Listen to this: Three months earlier a girl named Sylvia Smith was molested near a bus station in Cosham and described her attacker as someone who wore a black and white striped shirt.'

'The Juventus shirt…'

She concurs. 'Several lads were brought in for questioning as it was a shirt worn by a particular mob around town.'

I cut in. 'They all played football in a Sunday league for Felix Winter's at the time, which was a sport and camping store. They had several stores on the south coast, so there was plenty of willing players.'

'How do you know all this nonsense?'

'I just do. I have my informants. The team became defunct but the shirts gained legendary status. That's why they were so distinctive in the area. It became like a badge of honour to the young lads who wore them, but I'm not sure why.'

Isabel cuts in this time. 'A lesson in local history circa 1970 and onward.'

'Jimson also had one of the shirts; I have the photo to prove it.'

'His name keeps cropping up,' she reflects.

'Heed my warnings…'

'I hear you loud and clear.' She deliberates, and then says, 'When I did the research, instructed by you no less, I found the names of all eleven members of the original team which included Jimson and your brother. Actually, there was about eighteen in total. I think it's called a squad, right?'

I humour her. 'Right.'

'We digress from the bus station attack. The point is, your brother had to attend an identity parade along with other gang members, but he was not picked out by the girl. However, his name was now known to us and I have no doubt this would have triggered police suspicions when Miriam was found dead soon after.'

'But he was released without charge in relation to the Smith girl?'

'He was, but there remained a question mark against him because he didn't have an alibi for the night when the incident happened.'

'Well, surely she either identified him or she didn't?'

'There's more to it than that. The police were convinced enough that the girl was telling the truth about the attack because the shirt was a compelling argument, and so few men wore them. In fact, I suppose you could point to eighteen men in particular. But she wasn't prepared to point the finger when push came to shove. She bottled it, I reckon.'

'One of the shirts could have been borrowed or stolen.'

'True, but I don't think so. The guy in question was apparently flashy and paid no heed to getting caught, which suggests he had friends in high places.'

I'm insistent. 'Are we talking about immunity? Someone from within the force?'

'Quite possibly, or she was paid to keep quiet, which I favour.'

'Apparently, they were a cocky bunch and thought they could operate above the law, so flashing the cash seems logical. Besides, I don't think Jimson joined the force until much later, so he had no influence at that stage.'

'He might have actually,' Isabel counters. 'He had an uncle in the force who was basically instructed to take early retirement soon after the incident.'

'*Really?*'

'He's dead now, but his file referred to disciplinarian measures taken against him, but I couldn't find the specifics…it seems he was pushed into leaving.'

'That tells a story in itself.'

'We can't point any fingers, to be fair.'

'But a question mark remains, eh?'

Isabel seems uncomfortable with this and changes the subject.

'Unfortunately, in the case of Sylvia Smith, DNA sampling wasn't invented then which would have nailed the arrogant bastard responsible.'

'Could they not use that now?'

'The girl was molested, not raped, and the case was dropped. We're talking over forty years here. It wasn't a high profile case. It was buried.'

'So how did you find it?'

She enlightens me. 'From old hand-written files stored in the basement of HQ, which were gathering dust until I disturbed them. Now everything today is recorded on a national database.'

'And so David avoided a criminal record?'

'He did, but his name was kept on file.'

'And Jimson?'

'Strangely, there is no mention of his name among the group of men brought in for questioning at the time of the assault.'

'Could it have been erased?'

'Your guess is as good as mine, but I'm thinking along those lines.'

'Would that incident have come up for scrutiny when David applied to become a teacher?'

'Again, quite possibly: it would naturally have gone against him if brought before a committee doing the interview at the school level that's for sure.'

'Unless…'

Isabel takes it further. 'Unless someone-in-the-know conveniently removed the file at that time. It would be normal for a governing body to want to check up on a potential candidate and request such information.'

The suggestion was clear: my brother in later years had someone working on the inside to help deflect his involvement in the attack on the girl.

Jimson.

The two of them went back a long way. The two of them held high office (still do), and the two of them shared a keen interest in nightclubs…and girls.

'When did Jimson join the police force?'

'I reckon around 1977.'

I do the math. 'David joined the teaching profession in 1979, so he had someone on the inside to smooth his path through the interview process.'

'Are you saying they worked in partnership?'

'I'm suggesting it, Isabel.'

'To what end? It seems too far-fetched…'

I think of the girl at the bus station, I think of the abduction of Miriam, the murder of Daisy. Beyond that, I start to envisage the suffering of lots of little girls lost down the years. Forty years to be exact. The line I've been looking for is staring me in the face.

I nearly say it out loud, but Isabel intervenes as if reading my mind.

'Don't say it,' she commands.

I click off, my head spinning from all this craziness. It was a long and complicated call. *Corruption* is a word that figures large in my thoughts. What the hell is Jimson and David mixed up in?

Resting my head against the pillow, I feel the painful bruising around my neck and know precisely where my next destination is going to be. I'm itching to get there, convinced it holds the key to unlocking this whole sorry mess.

And David and his strong-armed tactics aren't around to stop me.

Chapter 55

It's not easy trying to locate a particular caravan and keep a low profile at the same time. People soon get talking.

I've driven across the Cleveland Hills on the coastal road and stopped at several holiday parks and made my enquiries but to no avail. I carry on towards Whitby and eventually find what I am looking for: Sunny Ridge Caravan and Camping Park and, lo and behold, the site had a great view of the sprawling town below and the abbey in the distance.

Before entering, I first take a diversion and park up on the harbour front, and treat myself to fish and chips and go in search of a clipboard. I have to transform myself into a convincing *Mr Jobsworth* if I'm to trick my way in and view the caravan.

An hour later, I return to Sunny Ridge and walk into the cabin marked "Reception".

A rotund woman, all heaving breasts and exposed cleavage, looks up from her desktop.

'Is Eric around?' I ask, holding my clipboard to my chest, pen in hand.

'Not sure where he is to be honest. What can I do for you?'

I pretend to read from the clipboard. 'I've come to inspect a caravan belonging to…David Farmer. I'm an insurance assessor and I understand that he has had a problem with a leaking roof.'

'He has.'

'I've come to assess the damage and make a report.'

She peers at the screen on her desk.

'Row four, site number twelve.' She catches my eye and gestures with her fingers. 'Left out of here, go to the far end, and then turn right. It's numbered on a post. Great view…'

I turn, switch back, look down at her and say, 'Thanks.' Great view as well.

I follow her instructions and I'm soon staring at an ordinary white caravan with a tarpaulin dragged over one end and tied down with makeshift guy robes attached to the ground. This is it: Number 12. It brings back memories! I poke around and try to look important, scribbling nonsense on my notepad. I attempt the door. It's locked. Not a surprise. I peer in through the windows but it's too gloomy.

I'm despondent, but what did I expect: a welcoming party?

I go back to the cabin and try my luck.

'Do you have a duplicate key?'

She sits back and her bosom spreads.

'Only Eric will let you gain access, and he's not here as I explained earlier.'

'Any idea when he'll be back?'

She checks a diary, stands up and peers out of the window and then back at me. The twin weapons of mass destruction point in my direction. I feel under threat and take a step back.

'Don't think it will be today,' she says, smiling. 'Can you come back tomorrow?'

'I might have to if I can't get inside now.'

'More than my job's worth to let you have a key.'

'You can always accompany me if security is an issue.'

'I'm not insured…health and safety, I'm afraid.'

It was me who should be worried about health and safety; I could suffocate if she got too close and personal in such a confined space. But I am tempted with the idea. *What a way to go…*

'Tell you what,' she says, pouting her ruby lips, 'let me know where you are staying tonight. I'll then get back to you when Eric lets me know when he is likely to be in. Does that suit?'

I catch her drift but I'm not aroused enough to warrant such drastic action. *Be honest, would you be?*

So I try and bamboozle her and say the first thing that springs into my head. 'I'm staying at the Holiday Inn.'

'Didn't know there was one around here,' she sniffs.

I'm snookered and distract my eyes from her enormous chest.

She suddenly looks for all the world like a girl on a mission who's suddenly had her hopes derailed by a bare-faced lie.

I can act like Tom Cruise when the need arises but I don't fool anyone, certainly not her. 'It's new,' I explain and beat a hasty retreat.

All joking aside, I'm not going to get away with this ruse of the insurance assessor once Eric is on the scene. He'll insist on identification, no doubt. I'll have to try another way to gain entry(a hefty boot should do the trick…and sooner rather than later).

I spot a man parking up. Our eyes meet. Damn.

I push my luck. 'Have you seen David lately?'

He looks me up and down. '*David*?'

'David Farmer, he has the caravan over there.' I point lazily.

Recognition flickers in his eyes. 'I know David vaguely, but I've only just arrived for a few days' break so I have no idea if he's been here or not, to be honest.'

'How often does he come?'

'Two or three times a year, I guess.'

'On his own?'

'Yeah, he's a bit of a loner, to be honest.' He then narrows his eyes. 'Who wants to know?'

I wave the clipboard and use my stern voice: 'Health and safety.'

He instantly mumbles, 'Oh, god…'

That gave me the space I needed. I retreat to my car.
He shouts in my direction: 'Any problems that we should know about?'
I give him an icy stare and reply: 'None that I can see…at the moment.'
'That's a miracle then,' he says, shaking his head in bewilderment.
I know what he means. I drive off before I'm rumbled again.

Chapter 56

I've already booked for the room at the B & B for the extra night, so I decide to stay over to get value for money, which is typical of a tight-fisted northerner like me. Waste not. I ask for a refund. No chance. I'll travel back tomorrow extra early to get a good start and beat the traffic build-up.

I stretch my legs as far as the pub next door and demolish a pint in a few seconds, then reorder. It's been a stressful day and Isabel's words are still reverberating around my brain. What is David trying to be, bloody Richard Branson? It is unreal that he should be so capitalistic and successful. I'm envious if the truth be known. I am also a little disenchanted that he has never confided in me in regard to his other ventures. I just thought he was a stick in the mud, a plodder, not a whiz kid. I'm angry too that I didn't get into the caravan, although this was a long shot if I'm honest. And what was I hoping to find anyway?

I order a chicken salad, the lunch still heavy on my stomach. My mobile bleeps. The text reads:

Girl attacked at Robin Hood's bay yesterday afternoon. Where was David around this time?

Jesus fucking hell. Is Isabel on the warpath?

Then I recall my movements during yesterday afternoon. I was in Great Ayton, alone…

I text back: *He wasn't with me.*

Bleep/receive: *Was he agitated when you eventually saw him?*

Send: *I didn't see him, but he's always bloody agitated.*

Bleep/receive: *Come home. I have something to show you.*

Come home. Come home?

This sounds wonderful.

Send: *I can come now.*

Bleep/receive: *Tomorrow night is fine, and bring a bottle of gin. You've going to need it.*

Was that a threat or a promise?

*

I get my head down on the pillow and ponder. My sleuthing skills would have to be refined somewhat if my second attempt at getting into the caravan is to be successful. I will have to plan it better and travel up again. Isabel wants me and I want her.

I digress: If David was hiding something, where better than here? Or am I just being paranoid, a bit silly? After all, he invited me up. This is my boring brother we are talking about, although, according to Isabel, his past misdemeanours and present day escapades could not be construed as staid. He's a bad boy and I'm learning more about him as each day passes.

I'm restless. Images flash into my head, snippets of conversation bounce back and forth ("A girl at Robin's Bay has been attacked…"), but mercifully my eyelids slowly close…I sleep.

I go home the next morning with my tail between my legs (clueless about the secrets of the caravan), wondering what Isabel has in store for me. I'm intrigued. If it involves my David in something underhand, I'll get in the car and come back up here without hesitation. I'll break the door down to the caravan if necessary, but at this stage, I'm right up to my neck in conspiratorial theories, with no hard facts to connect anyone directly with my daughter's murder. Romain still remains the number one suspect according to the police.

I make good progress on the road and get in at just after two in the afternoon. I unpack, put the dirty clothes into the washing machine and kick my heels for the rest of the day. What I really want to do is burst into Jimson's office and break his nose. Then I'll do the same to David. Both the bastards have tried it on with Isabel. But I'll bide my time. They won't get away with that kind of sordid behaviour. To me, the satisfaction of revenge is to do it quietly and methodically, and allow the victims to feel it gradually creeping up on them…then POW! Am I talking about myself here?

So I'll keep a low profile and let them think they have the superior position, the upper hand, whilst I manoeuvre myself like a deadly panther in strike mode, hiding in the undergrowth, undetected. At least that is the plan. I feel empowered. In the meantime, I boil a couple of eggs in a saucepan and cut the toasted bread into soldiers and dip them into the yoke: yummy. This is the perfect comfort food to prepare me for battle. *They should be scared.*

*

Isabel opens the door and ushers me in, but not before checking the deserted street which only intensifies my feeling of dread. She pulls the blinds down which really gets me worried. Luckily, I've brought the bottle of gin and a pack of tonics so we get straight into it.

'Ice and lemon?' I ask, mixing the drinks in long tumblers.

'Perfect. Have you eaten?'

'Not much,' I say.

'I'll put the oven on and heat through a chicken pasta bake…that OK with you?'

'Sounds great…' Then I hand her a drink and see just how wonderful she looks in skinny bleached jeans and a white V-neck top.

'Cheers,' she says, raising a glass.

'You look fantastic.'

'Don't push your luck…'

I'm nervous and take a gulp from my glass. I notice she has lit some candles and decorated the table with them…cosy and inviting.

She adjusts the oven dial, grabs a bag of green leaves and salad bits from the fridge and whacks everything into a mixing bowl. I stand there like an idiot and refresh the glasses (more gin this time, less tonic) and wonder what's on the agenda.

Then she says, after setting out the cutlery, 'Come with me.'

I'm led into the bedroom and now the nerves really take hold. Never in my wildest dreams did I…then I'm confronted with a sight which soon diminishes my ardour. *What the fuck is this?*

I ask: 'What the fuck is this?'

A zillion photos are spread everywhere: across the double bed, atop the dressing table and covering most of the floor. On closer inspection, I can see they are holiday snaps from our time in France. I'm puzzled by the overkill.

'Are you reminiscing over old times?' I joke.

'Kind of…'

'I assume this is what you wanted me to see?'

'Yes.'

I try to be cool. 'I'm all eyes and ears.'

'Take a long hard look, Will, and see what you come up with. I'll put the pasta dish in…you'll have about thirty minutes while it heats through.'

She leaves me to it. To be honest, I'm perplexed at first. She's playing the same game I played on her but I don't get it. I study the rows of pictures and soon conclude that they are in date order, but struggle after that. Many of the photos bring the past into sharp focus and those which feature Daisy soon bring tears to my eyes. I'm overwhelmed actually.

It's only been five minutes and she's at me already.

'Well?'

I turn and face her and she sees my anguish.

'Need another top-up?'

'Yeah, that would be good.' I give her an empty glass.

I'm lost. All I see is the same pattern that I first noticed and brought to her attention: the distance between Daisy and Romain widening as the years progressed. What am I missing?

'Here,' she says, handing me my refill.

It tastes divine, a better mix than mine. I scratch my head. I don't quite know what to say to her, for fear of making myself sound foolish. I repeat my theory, assuming it is somehow connected to this.

'Look again, with fresh eyes. It becomes more apparent if you take Romain out of the equation. Don't become blinded by just him and our daughter, which is exactly what you did first time around.'

I search again with eager eyes but shake my head.

She intervenes. 'It took me a while; then it just clicked.'

I was getting frustrated.

'Start at the beginning.' She points at a particular picture featuring Daisy. 'When was that taken?'

'I reckon when Daisy was…six?'

'Yes. Describe what you see.'

'She's sitting on David's knee eating an ice cream.'

'And this one?'

'She's having a wrestling match with David on the beach…I remember that day, it was great fun. Was it the same holiday?'

'Yes.' She points again. 'This one?'

My eyes scan down. 'That was the following year. Ah, David had her on his shoulders at the market place to help lift her above the crowds…'

She points again.

'The dinner party…Remy's birthday bash?' I volunteer. 'Daisy would have been nine.'

'What's happening?'

'Well, nothing, just a bunch of us at a gathering, drinking ourselves into oblivion. Oh, and David is cuddling Daisy with the Pettit's dog going loopy in the background.'

Isabel stretches forward and hands me another snap. I'm getting a little irritated with this game.

'The picnic beside the river,' I say. 'That was the day Daisy was glum and wouldn't talk to anyone.'

'Where is David?'

'Looking equally glum seated next to me.'

I'm handed another.

'A picnic, the following year I guess.' I laugh nervously. 'David's looking glum again, probably in need of more wine.'

Isabel isn't laughing. 'Where is Daisy?'

I shrug. 'In the background, sitting by herself. Where is this leading, Isabel?'

'Humour me.' She points again.

I grin stupidly this time, recalling the silly hats everyone wore. 'Ah, the street party! I remember it was boiling hot that day and I got sunstroke. David made a fool of himself and tried to dance with all the women, including Daisy but she got into a strop…'

'She was thirteen, Will.'

'A proper little madam if I recall.'

Unease creeps into my stomach.

'Last one.'

I stare closely and this time I'm slow with my words. 'It was the last night celebration dinner by the pool. David is sitting with Remy, both of them pissed as usual…Daisy is back-turned to us all at the far end of the table as if she doesn't want to be part of the fun.'

'See the pattern, Will? The ever increasing distance between them.'

I feel nauseous, and it's not from the booze. *I don't like him.*

'It took me a while to spot it, but then it becomes obvious the more you look further.' Isabel announces.

I stare into space, thinking about Philip and his missus doing the same thing in the pub. Then I transposed the same notion on my daughter and Romain, but the distance she was creating was not against him but against my brother, and I missed it.

'Will?'

'I get it.'

'It was staring us in the face, Will, and we fucking missed it.'

Hell.

Isabel speaks for us both. 'We failed our daughter…'

I place the photo down on the bed and pick another one up, a view on the deck of the return ferry from Calais. A passenger must have taken it because we were all in it. David one end, Daisy the other, her eyes lifeless, defeated, clinging to her mother like a tortured soul.'

'She was fourteen when that was taken, Will. One year later she was dead.'

I slump on the bed, unable to speak.

'We only wanted to see the bad in other people,' she says, 'but perhaps we should have looked closer to home. We were too eager to condemn a young boy when we should have spotted something far more sinister happening right under our noses.'

I found my voice. 'I'll kill him, Isabel, if I find he laid a finger on her.'

'He tried it on me.'

'*So help me…*'

'Daisy would have been a lot easier to handle.'

She puts her arms around me and whispers something that really cuts into me.

'The innocent is always the first to suffer in this world.'

I start to howl.

Chapter 57

We sleep together but do not make love. Instead, we hold on to each other in silent prayer, neither of us daring to close our eyes for fear of never waking up again. Perhaps that would bring blessed relief. For me, the pain is dagger-sharp and excruciating. I watch as the cold silver dawn seeps through the slats in the window shutters like a cancer seeping through a body, undetected but growing more powerful, and for the first time, I see an image of David as an affected man and realise how hideous this world has become: it has claimed us all.

If he is guilty of harming Daisy, I want him to die from his cancer.

There, I've said it in silence to myself.

But the term "Innocent until proven guilty" shoots into my head. All we have is a bunch of photos, a cryptic message and an assumption of wrong-doing. But our gut feeling is deep-rooted and intensely strong. *We just know.*

Now all we have to do is nail the bastard. And that is a promise I am determined to carry out, whatever the consequences. Our beautiful daughter deserves justice, her killer the rightful punishment.

The morning brings its own problems. Isabel and I are united but separated. There is a distance between us still. I am aware that she is accusing my brother of molesting Daisy, as the photos indicate by default. I cannot deny that she has a compelling argument and I too feel that he is at the very least accountable to us. But how I go about tackling him is a different proposition entirely. In the cold light of day, I believe we need hard evidence…not assumptions…to bring him to task. She doesn't say it, but she probably wants him dead.

You already know my thoughts on the matter.

Isabel pours coffee and I manage to eat a slice of buttered toast, but it has no taste. We just go through the motions, like a couple of robots. I don't know what to say. I'm numb, to be honest.

Isabel speaks first. 'There could be more you know.'

'More *what*?'

'Girls.'

'We don't know anything as yet, Isabel. *You* more than anyone should know that we need incriminating evidence to arrest him. We have nothing.'

'Are you trying to defend him?'

I was incensed but held check. 'You know I'm not.'

'We'll get the evidence, mark my words.'

'He's a Headmaster. It just doesn't make sense…'

'It makes perfect sense if you think about it.'

I wasn't going to argue this point; she was ready to explode with rage.

'We can't just barge in and confront him with a bunch of accusations; and he's too clever to fall into a trap, Isabel.'

'*That* I do agree with.'

'I'll go and search the caravan, do a bit of breaking and entering.'

'I'll happily turn a blind eye.'

'I can talk with Remy again…see if he is aware of anything suspicious…although I'm sure he would have said something to me.'

'He's only interested in his son, and besides, if we didn't suspect a thing then I doubt he or his wife did. It's Romain we need to break down and question and of course, we also need to speak with Margo.'

'Margo?' I didn't see that one coming.

'She can identify the times he was away at the caravan or the apartment in Harrogate. Then we can check these dates against the unsolved attacks on women in the areas he would find accessible to carry them out.'

'Do you really think he is capable of this…you're talking now about a serial stalker.'

'I'm talking about a serial killer, Will.'

I shake my head in horror.

'We can't dismiss the possibility,' she snaps.

'He's weird, he's controlling and he's a pain in the neck…'

'But…he's your brother, your own flesh and blood and this is too close to home, yes?'

I finish my coffee and gather up my jacket, standing awkwardly, not knowing whether I am coming or going.

'Margo won't be keen to play ball,' I suggest.

'We need to play it carefully, that's for sure…'

She comes to me and strokes my face, and I am grateful for that. 'This is what we do, Will. It's my profession. We track down killers so trust in me. I'll do the background checks, snoop around and check to see if anything untoward has happened at his school…you know, complaints from staff or pupils…even parents. Jimson can tackle Romain, you can talk with Margo, find out what you can and whatever you do…don't let on to your brother that he's under surveillance. Act as if nothing has happened, OK? Keep calm and continue to portray the idiot brother that he thinks you are. That way, he'll drop his guard and just maybe say something he'll later regret.'

'I don't trust Jimson.'

'He's all we've got, and remember he is my superior commanding officer. If I go above his head, I'll be dead meat for sure.'

'Watch him; he's implicated in all of this.'

'If he is, then he's right where I can keep an eye on him. I can smell a bent copper a mile away.'

'Then he should reek when you're in the same room together.'

'I'll bear that in mind, Will, but at this stage, I'm not prepared to pinch my nose and carry an air freshener around when I'm in his company.'

'*That* could give the game away.'

'Leave Jimson to me, I can handle him.'

'Ask to see the photos of Daisy, and see what reaction you get.'

'What reaction are you expecting?'

'Reluctance,' I suggest. 'He'll put you off.'

'Because my worst fears will be founded…'

'I sincerely hope not, but we need to know. All the photos would not be of our daughter, especially if she was willing to pose for him. And especially if Romain didn't take the photos as he claims.'

'It stands to reason that Jimson would have removed any pictures of me, to spare me the embarrassment in court.'

'Not his style, Isabel. Yes, some would be revealed but he would want certain pictures of you for his own private collection to gloat over.'

'Christ, Will…that's sick.'

Chapter 58

I want to see David as a matter of urgently. I want a private moment to stare deep into his eyes.

I want to see if the devil lives there and preys on the innocent, as Isabel plainly sees it. If he has blackness to his eyes then I now want to discover if he has blackness in his heart. I cannot believe this is possible, although I feared for my life recently. I have known him all my life. How well can you truly hope to understand someone? What if we have got it all wrong? Suppose there is a rational explanation for our fears…and we are pointing the finger through paranoia or vindictiveness? Is Isabel's judgement coloured by events of the past? The last thing we want is a witch hunt.

I remember being targeted myself; it was a nasty horrible experience. People stared and whispered behind my back, but never confronted me with the reason for their doubts against my character, which were ill-founded. I don't want that to happen to David if he is innocent of any wrongdoing. It will ruin his career, destroy Margo. As much as I am angry with him, I am also conscious that Isabel is driving this crusade against him. We need to tread carefully.

I have an excuse to see him. In his desire to get away from our weekend get together, he forgot his walking boots which he had left under the bed. The proprietor handed them over to me when I came to pay my bill.

Now all I had to do was return them.

Firstly, though, I want to see Meg. I had arranged for Molly to pop in and keep an eye on her while I was away, and I've had a text from my colleague explaining that Meg wasn't feeling good. In fact, she's had the doctor in.

I drive over and let myself in, courtesy of a key she entrusted me with in case of situations just like this. She's in bed, weak and white-faced. I feel guilty that I have neglected her but she smiles warmly at the sight of me.

I try to be upbeat. 'Hi pudding…fancy a cuppa?'

She nods, and I scamper off to the kitchen happy to oblige.

I return with a tray and pour the tea and sit on the edge of the bed.

'I'm dying, Will,' she whispers.

My heart sinks.

'Nonsense,' I counter.

'The doctor is trying to get me into the hospital for further observation.'

'I would take his advice, Meg. I don't like you being here alone…'

'You and Molly have been wonderful.'

'But it's not enough, is it? Suppose you got up in the middle of the night and fall over. That would be a disaster.'

She coughs. 'And how have you been coping?'

'Me? Just brilliant, everything is just hunky-dory. I'm having the best days of my life.'

'Ha-ha!'

We laugh together. I help prop her up so she can drink her tea in more comfort, and notice how thin she is becoming.

She flips my thoughts. 'You need to put some weight on; you're getting too scrawny for my liking.'

'Yes, ma'am.'

'I've had visitors, Will.'

'Oh, yeah?'

'A man and a woman.'

'What did they want?'

'It was strange, they asked about you.'

My ears prick. 'Me?'

'They wanted to know about Miriam and why you were looking into her death.'

'Who were they Meg?' I don't like the sound of this.

'People from internal affairs, or something like that.'

'The police?'

'Yes, I suppose...'

'Did they leave a card?'

'He just showed me a badge, but I didn't pay much attention. At first I thought they were from the council making sure I was settled in my new home.'

'What specifically did they ask?'

'I was exhausted and not much help, and he was agitated with me.'

'What was his name?'

'I can't remember, Will. Most of the conversation was a blur to be honest with you. I'd just had my tablets and wanted to sleep.'

'Agitated?'

'He mentioned you by name, and I thought perhaps you knew them...or even sent them over to have a chat with me. Should I not have done so?'

'That depends.' I think of Jimson and his cronies keeping tabs on me, the recent break-in, and now someone putting the fear of god up an old lady.

'I'm scared, Will.'

I caress her frail hand.

'No need to be, Meg.'

'My powers are waning, Will.'

'You just need to rest, spend a few days in the hospital, and then you'll bounce back.'

'I no longer see faces from the past, or speak with the dead...I can't even picture Miriam anymore. I think my memory is going.'

'I won't hear of such nonsense.' I top up her cup. 'If those two come back, I want you to get a nurse to call me immediately and I'll shoot over and speak to them myself, OK?'

'OK.'

'Would you recognise them again?'

'Oh, yes. He wore cheap aftershave and she had breasts the size of bazookas, so big they had a mind of their own.'

I laugh, but secretly I want to scream. Had I not encountered this very same woman just two days ago at Spring Ridge Caravan Park?

My mind is on overdrive. I imagine that everyone is on my case. Who am I to trust?

It seems to me that I've disturbed a hornet's nest, and the swarm is attacking not just me but all those who stand defiantly by my side.

Chapter 59

Sometimes you do things because they just have to be done and bugger the consequences. I'd bottled it the other day, now I am ready for the fight.

I get home, sling a sandwich together, grab a Coke and head off back to where I had just come from, the Cleveland hills. This time I am ready and armed. On the back seat of my car is a crowbar which will do the job nicely. I'm not going to ask permission to do what I have to do on this occasion. Big tits would just have to lump it if you'll forgive the pun.

The drive up is heavy going, with road works and minor accidents slowing down my progress. It takes just over five hours, so on arrival, I'm grumpy as well as thirsty, hungry and seriously on edge. I want to get the job done, quickly and without confrontation. My new motto is: *Don't mess with me.*

I pull into the car park as distant thunder rumbles in from the sea. The first drops of rainfall as the sky deepens reddish black, like a biblical scene from a Titan painting. The light in reception is on but I skip past and head for my destination, crowbar hidden discreetly under my coat.

The caravan site is in near darkness, and I curse that I will need to use a torch, which might attract attention. I'm not well suited to this sleuth lark. In spite of this, I approach boldly, check out the neighbouring caravans for signs of life (no lights on, which is a relief) and sidle up to the door. Before yanking it open I try the handle first. Miraculously, it shifts this time and I have entry. My heart is beating fast, my legs like jelly moulds. Within a second I am in, the dank air invading my nostrils. Luckily, I'm wearing brown trousers such is my trepidation.

I switch on the torch and peer around, pulling the curtains tight as I do so. I learn fast. Then the realisation dawns on me. The caravan is empty. By that I mean there is the requisite fitted sofa and bed, but all signs of human life have been removed: drawers empty, no food or milk in the fridge, bed linen gone, no knick-knacks on show. I've been rumbled.

Persons or person unknown knew of my impending visit. I bet even the fingerprints of the last occupants have been cleaned off the work surfaces if the police have a need to check my suspicions.

I'm fucked and realise I've had a wasted journey. I move toward the door and my foot inadvertently kicks something small and hard against the skirting. I shine the torch down and pinpoint the object: a floral metal hair grip. A corner of my brain engages to a pertinent remark of Meg's (*you need to find the dark object*) but I'm interrupted by a noise outside. Now I really do want to shit myself.

The door suddenly opens wide and a bigger light flashes into my face, blinding me.

A male voice booms out. 'Who's there? You'd better show yourself.'

I do, rather sheepishly, but not before bending down and lifting the item from the floor and hiding it in my pocket. The voice is still commanding.

'Who are you, and what the hell are you doing snooping around here?'

I try to shield my face from the glare. 'My name is Will Farmer, brother of David farmer...he owns this caravan.'

'This is private property.'

'I was hoping David would be here.'

'So you try and make yourself at home with a torch, eh?'

'It's not what it looks like...' I'm buggered.

'Most folks announce their arrival at reception, that is, those with nothing to hide.'

'I called the other day, for what it's worth.'

My attempt at dark humour wasn't going to get me any brownie points.

The man lowers his torch slightly as if eyeing me up and down, seeing if I was going to be trouble. Under my coat I clench on the crowbar with a sweaty hand.

'Your arrival was recorded on CCTV, and I got the call to check you out.'

'Eric?'

'That'll be me. I run this place, and I particularly dislike intruders.'

'Phone my brother, I'm sure he'll vouch for me.'

'I might just do that, or run you off site with a kick up the backside.'

'I'm not here to make trouble. I'll go quietly.' The last thing I want is to pick a fight with a deranged nutter of the first degree.

'I reckon you will, mister.'

I edge forward and drop down from the step onto the grass and see him for the first time: squat, muscular, mean. Beneath his jacket I recognise a familiar football shirt. I'm in a bad place right now. I really don't like this face-off.

'So, what were you hoping to find on your little adventure?'

I really was out of my depth and just wanted to crawl away.

'David asked me to inspect the roof...'

'Is that right?'

I've got verbal diarrhoea. 'It's not easy so for him to get up here...'

He interrupts me with a jab of the torch. 'Just two days ago you were masquerading around here as some kind of poncy insurance assessor. Well, I don't buy any of it. This is private property and you're trespassing full stop. That means I can have you forcibly removed.'

'I was asked to check the place out...'

He grins with menace. 'No, you weren't soldier boy. As you can see, the caravan has been vacated for the winter. David has been.'

'Well, my timing is rubbish then, I guess.'

'I guess.' He crowds me, his whisky breath exploding in my face. 'Now I suggest that the best course of action for you to do is fuck off, right now. Is that clear enough for you?'

I couldn't agree more. 'I can do that,' I mutter.

Backing off, I turn and make my way across the mud path, mindful that his laser eyes were burning a hole in my back.

Keep going, keep going...

I get to my Rav, grateful I'm still in one piece. As I fumble with my keys I suddenly become aware of someone standing right behind me. I fear the worst, ready for a beating. I grip the crowbar in anticipation, but surprisingly my eyes aren't met by those of Eric the Marauder, but by another of lesser persuasion. I'm mightily relieved.

It's the same man I encountered the last time I stood almost in this exact spot.

This time he is less convivial and grabs my jacket collar, causing me to reappraise my good fortune. 'Get off my patch,' he whispers in my ear, 'you're interfering with my investigation and I'm not about to let you fuck it up.'

I'm confused.

'Who are you?'

'Let's just say that at this very moment I'm your saviour, so clear off and don't come back.'

'I could call the police.'

He tightens his hold. 'I don't think you're in a position to do that, what with your amateur antics spoiling the party tonight. I think if you stick around any longer then it's you that they'll want to interview...'

'I'm not intimidated by your threats,' I say defiantly.

In the gloom, I can see Eric approaching.

The man with the cheap aftershave says, 'It's him you need to be seriously worried about.'

'What's going on here?' I demand. Then out of the corner of my eye I see Ms Big Tits hovering in the doorway at reception. Are these the two who harassed Meg? I don't get a chance to find out as the hand on my jacket collar is released, the inference being to cut loose and run for it. His words are straight to the point.

'I know who you are, Will Farmer, so listen good and listen fast. We are infiltrating a gang of dangerous criminals in this area, so if your wife needs further information on our activities then the codename "Domino" will assist her. Now piss off and leave this to the professionals.'

I'm out of here. I start the engine and spew gravel into the air as the tyres finally get a grip. I vanish like a ghost on heat.

Chapter 60

I'm only ten minutes down the road when my mobile goes, but such is the state of my frazzled mind that I put another ten miles on the clock before I pull over in a lay-by to ring back. My shirt is soaked through as I check my rear-view mirror and gingerly pick up the phone. The call was from Isabel. I dial.

'We've opened up a whole big can of worms,' I announce.

'Will, I've just been warned off my covert probing by an anonymous caller.'

'Is this connected to Jimson?'

'I really don't know, but the more I call on support further up the food chain the more I come to a dead end. This is bigger than Jimson, Will.'

'Have you ever heard of something called "Domino"?'

'No, should I?'

'It's a codename.'

'How did you come by it?'

I spurt out my little escapade.

'Do you think David is involved in this gang?'

'I do. He was seen with Jimson at the nightclub, which implicates them both.' Then I remember the hair clip in my pocket and examine it. 'The thing is, Isabel, the caravan has been hurriedly emptied. What do you think was hidden there that I wasn't supposed to find?'

'Incriminating evidence is my starter for ten.'

Perhaps I had just that in my hand.

The word *Domino* strikes into my subconscious.

'Christ, Isabel.'

'What is it?'

'The gang members…' I hesitate, catching my breath. 'David told me once that he enjoyed going down to the local pub to play dominoes with a bunch of pals from the caravan club.'

'Get home, Will. We need to regroup and discuss what the hell is going on. We've uncovered something almightily complex…too complex for our pea brains to work out.'

*

I get back at two in the morning and crawl into bed, exhausted. I am tempted to go straight to Eggshell Cottage, but think better of it. I don't want Isabel to think I am assuming that "getting home" means her place…although it is my preferred choice. Right now though a bed is all I need, and I don't require extra complications. Although my mind is a whirl of ifs and buts I manage to clock off quickly.

A hot shower five hours later does the trick of revitalizing me. Refreshed and starving, I whiz down to the local café, Sam's, and tuck into a full English breakfast and a large cappuccino. Then I reflect on my lucky escape last night. That Eric fella could have made mincemeat of me, even if I'd pulled out the crowbar. He looked fearsome and itching for a fight. Why was David apparently mixing with guys like this? And who and where was this supposed gang the undercover cop was interested in?

I'm also intrigued as to the significance of the Juventus shirt that I'm sure Eric was wearing under his jacket. Was he too part of the infamous football team in the seventies? Perhaps Harry Levi would be able to shed light on this.

Then I think of poor Meg. I need to show her the hair clip and discover if it belonged to her daughter. If it did, then what else had been stored at the caravan before being conveniently removed? Was it a secret lair for collecting and hiding victims' memento's over the years, and I was about to stumble upon it and give the game away? Was Daisy's jumper hidden there? I feel sick just thinking about it.

I need to get together with Isabel, as she suggested. She could be in danger if Jimson thinks she's getting to close to his cosy set-up. The fact is, if Jimson is associated with David, then he is also associated with Eric. And who else is part of their domino group? We need to find out before I tackle David.

I phone Isabel and ask her to meet me at Meg's in one hour. I settle my bill with Sam and drive over to Meg's, but she doesn't answer my knock. I check with Molly but she doesn't know anything. Damn. Then I make a call to the local hospital and discover that she was emitted overnight for observation. Was this a good time to burden her with my recent discovery? I have to take the chance and redirect Isabel to the hospital. This could be a crucial breakthrough.

We sit by her side, and I can tell Meg is delighted to see me with Isabel, who thankfully is not in her uniform. That could have been unsettling for Meg in her condition. She is, I hate to say it, fading fast, her breathing laboured.

We make small talk, but she isn't easily fooled.

'That's not why you came here, now is it?'

Isabel pours a glass of water for her and gently gets her to take a sip.

'I've got something to show you, Meg.'

'Will it upset me?' she asks.

'We won't know until you take a look...' Even Isabel is unaware of what I'm about to spring on this frail old woman.

I slowly reveal the item and place it in Meg's outstretched hand, and watch as she tightens her fingers and feels the object, and then she does a curious thing: she closes her eyes and smells it. I'm mesmerised, and so too is Isabel.

Gradually she opens her eyes and looks at the hair clip. I can hardly breathe given the magnitude of the occasion, and what it might mean.

She takes my hand and pulls it to her cheek.

'I've waited forty years for this moment,' she whispers.

I get the answer I'm looking for.

Meg begins to tremble, the emotional pull too vast to grasp, and I can tell she is barely coping, overcome by a tidal wave of grief. It is a precious piece of her daughter's identity being returned to her at long last. Isabel starts to cry, and then I shed a tear as well. Four decades of waiting and wishing and praying for someone to finally bring closure, that is forty summers and forty winters to endure without hope. This is one courageous mother in front of us.

Meg lifts the hair clip and asks the question I'm dreading. 'Where did you find it after all these years?'

I cannot answer her, for it stains my history, but I try.

'Too close to home, I'm afraid.'

This is a terrible admission on my part but I cannot suppress the truth, the whole truth and nothing but the truth. It is my duty to explain the failures of mankind, and so for the next fifty-odd minutes I do just that, and Meg listens without reply. I talk of the killing of innocence, the violation of the right to live and the fundamental denial from the law of the land to protect those in most need of help, whatever the cost to society. That is, informed society, structured by supposedly morally just people, the same people who have failed Meg Faulkner and her daughter, the same way that they have failed Isabel and me.

I make a secret promise to myself to rectify that situation if only I can summon up the strength and fortitude to make those guilty of their heinous crimes accountable in the eyes of God. I look at two women embracing in the union of motherhood and know in my fractured heart I dare not fall short of what is expected of me.

We are the victims.

Chapter 61

Later, in the hospital car park, Isabel stares at me long and hard. I sense what's coming.

'You know what this means, don't you? Finding that vital piece of evidence places your brother at the scene of the crime, at the heart of the matter. It points to him as the killer of Miriam Faulkner.'

The wind goes out of me, leaving me utterly deflated. I try to find an excuse for him, but my reply is unconvincing. 'Unless it was planted on him.'

Isabel is giving no quarter.

'You can believe that if you wish but I doubt the wisdom of your argument.'

I try to regain my inner strength, which I'll need if I'm to face David.

'Only one way to find out then, isn't there?' I reply boldly.

*

I once told Isabel in a note to her that I was misguided, rather than a bad person, and that I could learn from my mistakes if given a chance to redeem myself.

I'm now asking for that chance. Only she can grant it.

We go back to Eggshell cottage and make love for the first time in nearly two years. It is tender, passionate and spirited, and Isabel gives herself willingly to me, which is more than I deserve. I sense that I am slowly getting my life back again, before the *bad* thing happened. We linger in each other's naked arms, entwined in the bitter memories of the past and the cosmic mysteries of the future. We say nothing, but I can smell her skin and that is enough for me.

Our breathing is the only sound, the damage to our hearts; a forgotten thing. I seek forgiveness, and her loving embrace is proof of that.

I never want to mention or think about the rape or have it directed at me ever again from this day forward. I am home, and it makes me fulfilled to be as one with my wife once more.

Much later, I whip up an omelette as she quickly showers; seeing her pottering about naked and without condemnation of the man she grew to hate is both heart-warming and reassuring. It helps to rebuild my confidence in the passion we once shared. I adore her and crave the feel of her body in my hands...I never thought I'd experience that again. Sadly, she is now dressed, and she notes happily my disapproval of this fact.

We eat ravenously (as we did during the night), and dart glances at each other and smile nervously, like two teenagers on a first date...

But there is a monkey on our shoulders, and *it* needs to be removed, banished forever. The shadow of Daisy's death hangs over us like a spectre of terrible misfortune. We have for too long been sinking under the weight of despair, but I am determined we will cling together and rise up against all odds. We owe this to each other: it's called survival.

'How do we do this?' I ask nervously.

'What?'

'This thing called *living.*'

She cups her face in her hands, and speaks through her fingers: 'How about we just try putting *honesty* at the head of the queue.'

I like that, it resonates with how I'm feeling right now.

'I like that, Isabel, I really do…'

She smiles. 'Then that's our starting point.'

I pick up the photo which we last looked at, the one featuring us all on the ferry, and study Daisy's solemn expression. I hate what it infers. 'How do we do *this*?' I say, tapping my finger against the image of my evil brother.

She kisses me softly. 'Keep everyone guessing.'

'How?'

'By confusing them with conflicting information,' she says confidently, 'which usually works a treat in extracting guilt. It draws them out into the open, and that's where the mistakes are made.'

I joke. 'You sound like a professional.'

'My dad taught me well.'

'Tell me how it works.'

And she does, carefully and methodically. Now we have a plan. As I see it, the difficulty will be carrying it out. So far, I see my role as a hindrance, more akin to an interfering weak-willed preacher than a swashbuckling hard-line Jack Reacher type but Isabel assures me I can do the job. I just need Lee Child to write the script.

'OK, I've got it,' I announce.

She implores, 'We trust no one.'

'No one…not even Meg?'

'We don't know who's been trying to get at her, so keep quiet.'

I protest. 'Our agenda is to find Daisy's killer.'

'Will, the last thing we want is to put Meg in danger's way.'

'Someone wants us silenced.'

'And they are desperate people, determined to block off our every move in order to protect their identity.'

'Are you telling me that we can't even trust those from the police investigation?'

She shakes her head. 'Especially those from the police investigation; I'm being tagged from the inside. The bottom line is this: Who is protecting who, and why?'

Then she leans over and kisses me again, longer this time.

Now is the time.

I get back to my flat with fire in my belly. For too long I have been the doormat around here, and now the dynamics of power are shifting. I change into fresh clothes and mark out my intended territory like a prowling cat. I have things to do. There is no room for indecision, the margins of error thin. I have to think and act like a predator, just as my quarry will do if cornered with no route of escape.

I pace the room.

I worry about Meg.

I'm nervous for Isabel.

My gut twists with fear.

I hesitate.

Breathe slowly, control the flow.

This is it.

I make the damn call.

Chapter 62

The first thing that hits me is the smell of a smouldering fire in the garden, which doesn't bode well with my vivid imagination and nervous disposition.

But instead of finding the remains of old clothes belonging to the roll call of faceless victims, I see dead leaves and broken branches swept into a pile and set alight. I'm relieved, actually.

The imposing house of David, all red brick (like an institution) and handsome casement windows, sits high above the gloom of early evening, as the mists gather and swirl across the impeccable lawn and shrubbery beds. I've never liked this house, less so now. It is a Victorian gothic masterpiece of turrets and steep roofs, encased by clinging ivy walls and false grandeur: a bit like David himself. It is the sort of house Stephen King would write about.

I approach the impressive arched oak door, set within a large stone portico, and clatter the metal door knocker. The sound echoes beyond. I await a response and nervously brace myself for the confrontation which will surely follow. I'm not here for the fun of it.

I hear a sound behind me, turn and see a black crow scratching at the gravel drive, its beady eye ever watchful of any false move I make. Right at this moment I want to do a runner, but Isabel's words of encouragement keep me cemented to the spot.

The door opens noisily, like the sound of a train's screeching brakes. The crow takes the hint and buggers off, leaving me face to face with my brother.

'Margo said you were coming over…something about bringing back my walking boots? Seems a bit extreme, but come in and get warm. I've lit the first fire of the autumn now that the nights are drawing in.'

I enter slowly and hear the crackling of the hearth in the lounge.

'Margo's doing a bit of supper, so I assume you staying to eat with us?'

I nod; my mouth dry.

'Lost your tongue, Will?

'Something like that…' I drop the boots on the floor, duly returned.

'Thanks,' he says, 'you need a glass of fine burgundy.'

He slaps me heartily on the shoulder, but I can already sense his unease: his usual bravado is missing. So is mine. Whilst he pours me a drink, I poke my head into the kitchen and embrace the wheel-chaired Margo, who is rustling up a feast to die for. Christ…I want to retract that thought straight away.

'Be about half an hour…' she suggests.

I go back to the lounge and David isn't there. I hear a clattering far off and go for a wander. I find him in the conservatory, which he uses as a potting shed...a rather grand potting shed it has to be said.

'Ah, there you are.' He points half-heartily to a rickety table. 'Brought the bottle down here, so pour a glass...'

I do, a rather good measure to bolster my Dutch courage, or lack of it to be more precise. My eyes scan the rows of decaying plants, the tangled network of tomato vines, the neglected courgettes, the stacks of empty terracotta pots weighing down the bowing makeshift shelves. I quickly conclude that my brother is not naturally gifted in this department. What the hell does he do in here...except kill vegetables? The smell in the air is pungent and stifling. I glance upward. Hanging from the glass ceiling the thick interlocking cobwebs sweep down like gossamer clouds. I put my hand over my mouth and move toward the door to the garden, which is ajar. I breathe in the freshness of the early evening air.

Then I realise why we are here, in this forgotten place. We are alone, out of earshot from Margo. Although David has his back to me, he radiates bad vibes. Perhaps this wasn't such a good idea of Isabel's. Whilst I am considered his willing guest, I still feel entrapped, caught in his web. The spider turns and faces me.

'I somehow doubt you came all the way over here to return my boots.'

I take a gulp of my wine, and let him fester.

He knows though and plays the game cleverly by quickly changing the point of attack.

'I'm sorry for my silly prank the other day,' he adds.

'I lived to fight another day.'

I think he gets my message loud and clear.

I'm still here, big shot.

'It was uncalled for and rather juvenile.' He has thunder in his face but he's holding it together. 'Sorry I had to shoot off as well...work is never ending.'

'I survived.'

'More wine?'

He tops my glass up, and I'm aware he is holding a sharp pruning knife in his other hand.

'How is Isabel?'

'Fine.'

'Have you found a job?'

'No.'

The small talk was becoming stretched.

'I understand from Eric that you visited the caravan...can I ask why?'

The small talk just ended abruptly.

Chapter 63

You try to imagine what a stand-off entails, and right now I feel in a difficult position, inferior in mind and body as he looms over me with his superior intellect and viper's tongue. I try to repel his confrontational pose by holding firm and sticking my chin out but find myself involuntarily stepping back, away from his intense gaze. His aggressive tone has me cowering in a corner.

'What do you think you were doing, snooping around undercover of the dark? What were you hoping to find? Cuddly toys, a set of saucepans…for fucks sake.'

I had a plan of attack, now I am lost. His soft/hard stance has taken me by surprise. I don't care for the weapon in his hand either as he waves it in my face.

'It wasn't the first time either, was it? Debbie said you were sneaking about and asking questions on an earlier occasion. I call that prying into my affairs.'

Little does he know that Debbie big tits is not quite who he probably thinks she is…certainly not the dumb receptionist, even though she looks the part.

'Eric isn't as placid or accommodating as her, as you discovered. You were lucky he didn't split your nose in half.'

My throat's constricted, dry as parchment.

I have to say something and soon.

'The point is, Will, you're meddling into things that are beyond your scope of understanding. They shouldn't concern you. You're a small fish in a big pond, and if you're not careful you'll be fucking eaten alive. You and your interfering missus are not dealing with a bunch of feeble piranha, more like mad hungry barracuda. In other words, you two are out of your depth, swimming against the tide and the big fish are circling…Do I make myself clear?'

I had never heard him talk like this before. No way was this a stand-off. He was suitably antagonistic toward me and I was well and truly boxed in.

Say something, jerk.

He isn't finished.

'What I don't get is your obscene arrogance. You come over here and think that Margo and I are somehow answerable to your moralistic preaching on how we should behave in this perfectly pure world of yours. Well, let me tell you: this world is fucked. I don't think we have to apologise to anyone, least of all you, and we certainly don't have to be either thankful or grateful towards a society that wants us to be shiny worthy people. So, here's the thing, Will. We're not worthy, we do not want to stand on a pedestal and receive a hollow round of applause, we don't want to conform and we certainly don't want cunts like you and Isabel lecturing us on the fucking rules of life management that you both stupidly abide by as you sleepwalk through life...'

I shock myself and hear my voice. 'Why are you so *bloody* aggressive?'

I shock him too, into momentary silence.

His temper slowly subsides and he takes a pace backwards, his eyes averted to the flag-stoned floor. Somehow I have stopped the raging bull in its tracks, temporarily at least. I'm not sure how long that's going to last for.

His voice mellows. 'Shit, Will, its bad news...

He's a changed man, his alter-ego gone in the blink of an eye.

'What is?'

'This afternoon I had an appointment with the consultant at the hospital to get the results of the MRI scan...it seems my prognosis had been called wrong.'

He stares at me with watery eyes.

'What are you talking about, David?'

'The cancer has spread to my bones...'

'*Meaning?*' I knew perfectly well what it meant.

'I'm a dead man walking. There is no medical treatment that will cure me now...I just get a little borrowed time and a heavy course of chemo drugs.' Then he whispers, 'if I want it of course.'

I look beyond him toward the hallway, making sure we were still alone.

'Does Margo know?' I ask.

'No, that's why I brought you down here.'

'When are you going to tell her?'

'I'm not.'

Then I say the dreaded words, 'How long?'

'Months, maybe six if I follow the doctor's orders.'

'Christ, David.'

'He can't help me.'

One part of me is feeling terrible for his cursed predicament; the other part despises the monster hiding in him which is revealing itself tonight.

I gather my thoughts, reminding myself as to why I am here in this evil house, for that is how I now see it.

'David, I found this at the caravan.'

I extract the hair clip from my pocket.

'Hmm, I had wondered...' His voice trails off.

Slowly, my courage returns. 'What else did you have removed from the caravan?'

'All the sins of the world,' he replies defiantly.

In truth, I am petrified, my heart thumping through my chest.

'What the hell has been going on...?'

'Are you wearing a wire?'

I'm surprised by this remark, the coldness in his tone resurfacing.

'No, should I be wearing one?'

'It's the obvious ploy, having a copper for a wife.'

I unbutton my shirt and reveal just a hairy chest.

'A big mistake, if you're here for a grand confession.'

'I wasn't necessarily expecting one from you.'

'Then what are you expecting?'

'I was hoping – praying – that I was wrong about you, and that there was a rational explanation as to why you would have something like this in your possession.'

'I can make one up if that would satisfy you, Will.'

'This belonged to Miriam Faulkner, but you know that, don't you?'

'Forty years is a long time, but I remembered taking it from her as if it was yesterday. That was my first keepsake, Will.'

I feel ill and lean back against the wall, my legs giving way.

'My time is nearly up, Will. You cannot hope to save me in the eyes of the Lord.'

'Who said I wanted to save you?'

'My conscience is forever damned, this world a bloody arena for the massacre of the tortured innocents. It will be blessed relief to leave it, my thoughts no longer fixated on the next victim. So I will be free, free of my lust for human suffering, the power I crave, and free at last from the cancer that invades and destroys my body. I am pitiful, but my path is guided by my own hand…till death do us part.'

'And what of us, David?

'You are worthless,' he taunts me. His eyes glaze over.

I can't believe the words he has just uttered. My eyes blaze with hatred.

'And Daisy?' I shout. 'Was she worthless too?'

Just *Say it, say it!* I clench my fist, ready to take his teeth out.

'A confession unrequited, I'm afraid.'

'That is cowardice.'

He steps in closer, his lips quivering. Beads of sweat drip down his face.

'Did you kill my daughter?' I demand.

Without warning, he slaps me hard across the mouth.

'She defied me, and I won't tolerate disobedience…'

'Did you take this photo?' It was the one of Daisy in her bikini. I had carried with me. Now I held it up to show him.

'Yes.'

I stumble and reach out for support, knocking over a large terracotta urn which smashes on the floor. I steady myself, dizzy but all right, still reeling from his violent reaction.

'You crazy fucker,' I shout, wiping blood from my lip.

He steps in again, casting his giant shadow over me like a cloak of death. I hardly recognise him as my normally stoic brother.

'Now *that* you can call me,' he sneers in deluded triumph.

Beneath my feet, I suddenly spy a plastic bag which is half-covered by the mound of earth from the urn. I pick it up and examine it. Inside, I detect what looks like a metal comb. I shudder and spot another plastic bag and then another…out of the corner of my eye I suddenly grasp the significance of the row of similar-sized pots…they line up like winner trophies in a cabinet…which I now know is precisely what they represent. God knows what is secretly contained within each one of them…

But I do know, and a chill reverberates down my spine. I know instinctively that the horde of dubious treasures removed from the caravan is hidden here, as a reminder of dark terrible deeds.

Margo shouts from afar: 'Dinner is ready.'

We're both stopped in our tracks.

I'm not sure what to do.

'Go to her,' David orders; turning away from me. 'You won't find solace with me.'

'You can't run from this, David. The evidence is all here. I'll call the police; you can count on it. It's all over…'

He faces me again, his features distorted, his skin a deathly pallor.

I have no idea what's going on in his tortured head, but I'm in a perilous situation. I *have* to do something to make him see reason.

'It's over, David,' I repeat. Then I hold up the miniature Dictaphone that I had concealed in my pocket, the little light piercing the gloom of the greenhouse.

He simply laughs in my face.

'Over, you say?' He slowly shakes his head in resignation. 'I've known that since this afternoon.'

Chapter 64

Although rattled, I somehow compose myself and leave behind this crestfallen man as he sinks to his knees and begins to gather up his trophies from the rubble on the ground. A pitiful sight, for that is how I see him now.

In the hallway, I remember my script and phone Isabel and say my piece. The rest is up to her from this point on.

I confront Margo. How do you explain to someone that I no longer have an appetite for the food they had just cooked? Well, a darn sight easier, I can tell you, than explaining that their devoted husband is a serial killer.

But that's what I do, quietly and without hysteria, even though I'm shaking with fear and riddled with guilt, having known and not known the brother that I once loved. *Loathing* is a hard word to conjure with, but it sums up my feelings for this depraved monster.

Margo at first puts down the cutlery she holds and stares into space, seemingly in control of her emotions. Then, unexpectedly, she swings her arm out and forcibly pushes the large dish of steaming lasagne from the kitchen table onto the floor, followed by the glass of red wine which had stood beside it. A bigger mess you couldn't imagine.

Standing beside a disconsolate Margo, I feel a great sense of loss for what might have been. It is the colossal failure, this lack of faith; rather the dependency upon faith and, above all, the trust in love we all want and so rarely find that really gets to me. I am numb, deflated, worn down: utterly defeated. I can see in Margo's stricken face that she shares exactly my sentiments.

We have both been betrayed by the conceit of this man.

From somewhere the wail of a police siren fractures the air, followed by another, and then another. Blue flashing lights illuminate the gravel drive and bounce off the windows and into the room where I stand. I open the front door and quickly step aside as Jimson careers in followed by his loud and excitable colleagues. Isabel is the last to enter, quiet and controlled. She grasps my arm, and I detect a faint smile. Perhaps it's a nervous twitch. I'm just happy to see her. I hand over the Dictaphone.

There is chaos surrounding us, but this has no comparison to the chaos spinning around inside my head.

And during those minutes, which seemed like hours, Margo sits in her wheelchair, transfixed, unable to catch my eye as I kneel beside her and cradle her vacant statue-like face in my hands. Never had I seen someone age so fast. Isabel gathers a bunch of towels and lays them across the floor to halt the spread of discarded food, which was making walking over it hazardous for those in the house. The smell wasn't good either.

I could hear heavy boots trundling around the house, lots of frantic shouting, then silence. I instinctively know the *sound* of that silence, the significance, the finality. I pull away from Margo, slowly rise and nod to Isabel. She understands my meaning, leaves what she is doing and holds Margo, rocking her gently back and forth, quietly humming a lullaby as tears roll down her cheeks.

It is the end of things.

I move to the hallway, climb the stairs with a heavy heart and push my way through the bustle of men, who by now are a sombre bunch, contrite…not knowing what to do or say to me as I pass. At the head of the group, Jimson leans against a door frame, his head bowed. Then he lifts his gaze and recognises me at his side, but offers no words.

I follow his gaze into the bedroom. At first, the darkness hides its secret, but gradually my eyes adjust to the grim reality facing me. The moonlight that filters through the window, its blue hue ethereal and strangely magical, touches itself gently upon the lifeless body that dangles, by way of a cord, from one of the rafters in the ceiling.

I look up: my brother, David, hung dead.

I am pitiful, guided by my own hand…

I see it for what it is, an act of extreme cowardice, and fury boils within me.

…till death do us part.

He controlled everything, even his own wretched exit.

Once again, I feel cheated by him.

Chapter 65

In the days that follow, which are harrowing and humbling, I find courage and piety in myself and renewed faith in those around me, especially Isabel. She is the rock on which I stand.

Now you know my history. Looking back, I got so many things wrong, but my fumbling in the dark brought so many things to the surface as well, so I am grateful that you stuck with me and heard my story. It was never going to be pretty, and I'll leave you to pass judgement on my selfishness, the conceit of my ego, the manner of how I used people…how I manipulated those who became precious to me, namely Meg, dearest Meg. I trod on everyone, and I have big feet, so my clumsy footprint was felt by all and sundry and I apologise for this ungallant behaviour. But, as you know, I promised Daisy justice, and this I had to fulfil, even if it took me to my dying day. I would never have surrendered.

This I have done then, and thankfully, looking at my wife, who sits by my side, I know I have plenty of days remaining on this planet before this fateful time happens.

And what of those who helped shape these events?

I will tell you, and ask only that you pass judgement upon the individual action of each person (and their subsequent reaction), and not on how each of them became sucked into a chain of events that perhaps none of them could possibly have envisaged at the time. All of us are innocent until proven guilty. Of course, some of us are not so innocent, and this is the real crime. Evil manifests itself in the lies we want to believe. Some of us take the right road, and some of us take the wrong road.

I defy you to walk the line and always be able to recognise the difference between the two. I certainly cannot, and have taken the wrong road too many times to admit, but, hear me out, I have survived because I have learnt more about myself from taking the latter course, however painful it proved to be. To confront our weaknesses is to strengthen our resolve and find truth, fairness and dignity in the paths we ultimately choose.

I hope you remember this on your journey as well. I remind myself of these things every day. It is the distances between us that make the difference, as I have found to my cost (and now my gain). I constantly measure that chasm in every decision I make. It isn't easy but I strive to make it work.

Postscript

I will start with Romain.

What can I say that will help to undo the harm that I heaped upon his shoulders from the very beginning? I stand contrite, for here is a misunderstood young boy wrongly accused of a crime he didn't commit. I am happy to report that he was released from custody before arriving in England for trial, all charges dropped against him after his confession was deemed inadmissible in the light of my recording and the overwhelming evidence found at my brother's house. He was originally framed for Daisy's murder by the discovery of incriminating photos found in his bedroom (which seemed to seal his fate). However, these were planted by his brother, Frederic, who was being groomed to be part of an overseas criminal network selling child pornography on the internet across Europe (organised by the Juventus gang based in the UK). His motivation for helping to set-up his brother for a crime he did not commit was based largely on jealousy, and his dependency toward his boss in the paedophile ring, who challenged him to prove his commitment to the cause. It didn't take much persuasion as Romain was always considered the favoured son in the family, which Frederic resented. His tutor, it was later uncovered, was David Farmer who befriended him during numerous holiday trips to his home between around 2004 and 2011. Dim-witted, Frederic was considered easy prey to be manipulated and then drawn into serving his masters in order for the illicit underworld operation to flourish still further.

Romain was subsequently blackmailed into his confession by David, who of course held all the aces. Firstly, he was compliant in hiding the photos which he knew would be discovered by the police. Secondly, he further threatened to harm Romain's parents if he did not comply with the gang member's instructions. As a show of force, my brother arranged for the family dog to be shot dead just after the young boy's detention. He got the message. He had also unwittingly trapped himself into a confession by travelling to the home of our daughter at the time of her murder, thus putting himself at the scene of the crime.

This evidence was compelling enough to make him the only creditable suspect, especially as she was pregnant, underage and had returned home alone and alienated, without his apparent support. It was assumed at the time, wrongly of course, that he had come over to our country angry and confrontational…and perhaps fearful of being imprisoned for having sex with an under-aged minor. Sadly, Daisy never had the chance to defend his name.

The truth of the matter was that he came to give his support, admit to his wrongdoing and be the father to the child he loved. Instead, after the discovery of her body in a ditch, he went on the run, fearful of a future life behind bars. He knew that he would be implicated once the authorities found out that he was in the vicinity and, being young and hot-headed, took the wrong road and nearly paid the price for his devotion to Daisy.

I am so grateful that my meddling eventually led to his release.

When the dust finally settled, I travelled over to see him and his parents, which was a traumatic experience to say the least. But a good bottle of wine (or two) settled our nerves and we began to learn first-hand the chain of events that led to my daughter's murder. Romain long suspected that my brother had designs on her and warned him off but to no avail. One example was the shouting match which I had inadvertently recorded by the poolside. Romain confirmed that the words he used – *She doesn't like you* – did refer to Daisy, but he had to hide this during his interview with Jimson because of David's hold over him. David was obsessed with her, she fearful of him, but as it often happened, she took the blame for his irrational and inappropriate behaviour. That's why she kept his persistent stalking of her a secret from us. It is often said that the victim often shoulders the guilt. If only we had known.

Explaining his trip to England, Romain told me that he managed to confront David with the news that she was pregnant with his child and that he should back off from interfering in their future life together. Unfortunately, this just inflamed the situation further and Romain threatened to blow the lid on David's antics by telling Isabel and I. As a consequence of this, David flew into a rage, affronted by being dictated to by a mere boy and hateful that Daisy was now soiled goods. He, in turn, set out to track Daisy down and followed her home from school that fateful day. He would not accept that she was pregnant by someone else. He considered her his property.

A squabble ensued, and he struck her to the ground, hitting her head on a fence post. She remained unconscious but still breathing. Fearing she was therefore able to testify against him, he dragged her into a gulley, strangled her, removed some of her clothes to make it look like a sex attack and took her jumper before running off undetected. He had intended to place the jumper with Romain, thus implicating him in her murder and deflecting any blame from himself. David was confident he had found his ready-made scapegoat…

How do I know all this?

Because Romain had witnessed the whole thing and, much to his eternal regret, he hid during the frenzied attack; being no match against David's raging strength. He was a foreigner in a strange country, and courage deserted him. He has lived with the shame ever since. His error was to escape the murder scene and go on the run, unsure of who to turn to. I wish he had come to me. A big ask, especially as David had already manipulated the situation to place the blame squarely on his young shoulders. It was easier to run. Soon after the hanging became public knowledge, Romain retracted his 'guilt'.

Isabel and I forgive the actions of a boy.

Today, Romain is living at home in France, supported by the love of his parents, and studying commerce at the Universite de Perpignan Via Domitia in Narbonne.

It is worth mentioning at this point that Remy's wayward brother, Robert, who I wrongly highlighted as a possible suspect in the murder of my daughter was not implicated in the activities of the gang either, and nor was he approached by David on our trips to France. The impressionable Frederic was the more obvious target for recruitment to the dark side.

In spite of a lengthy custodial sentence for his involvement in car theft, Robert has the continued support of his brother, who regularly visits him during his time inside prison.

David Farmer was part of a paedophile gang, first formed in 1971, the beginnings of which mushroomed with the "introduction" of young impressionable boys attracted to playing football, most of who were unaware of the true nature of the team leader's motives, which was cleverly hidden from them at the beginning. The organisation was run by a group of criminal masterminds looking for easy converts into a world of depravity and sickness.

My brother was one such person.

Whoever was behind this secretive gang soon discovered that in David they had found a kindred spirit. Even at the age of fourteen, he had molested several girls in the surrounding area, but insufficient evidence and the unwillingness of the victims to come forward allowed him to roam free and strike again. Where this evil came from I do not know. Maybe some people are born with pure evil in their blood. I am not qualified to comment further on this, it is just an observation. What I have learnt is he was a lone predator, not a team player, and after taking the life of his first victim, Miriam Faulkner, he pursued this lust of young female flesh for the next forty years, causing havoc in the north of England in particular. Back in the seventies and even much later, police database comparisons between counties weren't sufficiently linked as it is today, with the advent on sophisticated computer networks. And so he worked under the radar, undetected.

How many victims were there? We will never know for sure. Within the terracotta pots displayed at his home, twenty-three personal items were recovered and the police today are still trying to match them to their owners. Daisy's jumper has never been found. In total, there were twelve recorded unsolved murders in the UK during this time span featuring pre-puberty girls, and hundreds of attacks reported to the police but never progressed upon, many still on file. On investigation by Interpol, the cases on two murdered girls in the south of France remain unsolved to this day. The gendarme has recently decided to reopen their files. At David's school, there were several complaints made about inappropriate behaviour by members of "staff" but these were quietly buried beneath paperwork. We need look no further, I believe, than the hand of my brother.

I wish he could have been brought to account and rotted behind bars for the rest of his miserable disgusting life. When he killed our daughter (and her unborn child), he also killed Isabel and I. There are many people like us who will vouch wholeheartedly to this admission of defeat. We live with the unbearable pain of utter loss every day of our lives. All we can do is fight it, quell it, and deny the killer his ultimate hold over us as well. Instead, we shine a torch for the memory of Daisy every day in our hearts and minds, forever.

David was undoubtedly one of the prime movers in the gang and reaped the financial rewards of his wicked endeavours. Apart from the nightclub and various business ventures, he and his gang members raked in millions from selling child porn on the internet and introducing vulnerable children as "playthings" for those rich enough to pay for their sordidness. There were plenty of takers, and the caravan site in Whitby was the venue for such activities.

I must mention the following points. David first preyed on little girls by dressing up as a respectably suited man in a clown's mask, offering an array of goodies to unsuspecting victims at the annual fairs he frequented to satisfy his murderous cravings. I still have the photo to prove his guilt, but I never look at it.

Tiny Miriam, with the use of her rampant camera actually helped track down her killer four decades later. What a clever girl she was. I wish I'd known her. In some ways, I believe I do. How Meg would have loved to have seen her murderer found guilty in the dock. It was not to be.

David was cremated in a private ceremony, attended only by his wife, Margo. I did not attend. A DNA sample (for future cross-analysis) was taken from his body before he was obliterated from this earth. Good riddance. I did not weep for him or give him a moment's thought on the day of his funeral. I never will.

The man known as Eric was arrested in Cyprus three weeks later after a tip-off from a member of the public, having recognised him from a newspaper mug shot holed up in a neighbouring villa. He protested his innocence but evidence compiled from Operation "Domino" was conclusive as to his involvement with the paedophile ring. He is currently being extradited back to England where he will stand trial for crimes against hundreds of children who were subjected to abuse and harmful sexual acts against their will. From secret files subsequently apprehended from the nightclub in Portsmouth (the nerve centre of the operation), it is believed that thousands of men worldwide will eventually be sought out and brought to justice for participating in this evil trade. The investigation is ongoing.

In all, six of the gang currently under arrest all played for the original football team nicknamed The Juve, after the famous Italian team from Turin, called Juventus. It was Eric, I later found out, who coached the team at its conception after his family moved to England from Turin and he grew up in the city of Portsmouth. He was undoubtedly the main ringleader, but not the mastermind. He or she is still at large. For my part, I avoided reading the lurid newspaper coverage at the time, wishing only to put everything behind me. Frankly, I'd had enough of being bitter and twisted.

DS Don Millington and Constable Sara Scott (Debbie) were commended for their dangerous undercover work in helping to reveal the criminal activities at

Spring Ridge Park, Whitby, East Yorkshire. Operation Domino, which was instrumental in the arrest of over ten members of the gang, is now closed, the caravan site under review, subject to further police investigation. It will not reopen in the foreseeable future, if at all.

Although formally interviewed by the police as a matter of routine, Harry Levi was never suspected of being part of the ring. He continues successfully to run his corner food shop in the locality.

All other players (those still alive), connected to the football team have been eliminated from police enquiries.

According to the information that Isabel has gathered, the six football players under arrest had past criminal records or police files held against their names. It is now known that the ringleaders originally recruited new members from travelling fairgrounds and sought their prey at the same venues because their activities were not easily detected by the authorities. Unlike today, for instance, these venues were not monitored by CCTV camera equipment, just the bobby on the beat. This fertile hunting ground, and other places like it, was considered easy pickings for recruitment and identifying victims, such as Miriam Faulkner.

DI Carl Jimson led Operation Domino, having infiltrated the gang in recent years after being seen as a trusted former colleague, having played in the football team at its conception and been regarded as "one of the lads". He offered his position of influence to enable the gang to move on to bigger things without police intervention. It was the perfect ruse and the gang bought into it. The commercial arm of the operation flourished with his key role positioned at the top table, which enabled the double-cross to work to perfection. Using his inside knowledge, Jimson was also able to identify four members of the northern police force who were secretly on the pay-roll of the Domino gang, so-called because of their monthly meetings at a local pub, playing dominoes whilst plotting their next filthy scam to bring in more cash from the punters.

DI Jimson played a dangerous game of bluff and counter bluff: the perfect smokescreen. He was seen by his fellow ringleaders as the linchpin to greater riches. It was a perfect match. However, his pivotal ability in keeping his real position under wraps, over a five-year span, enabled him and his colleagues to gather the evidence to ultimately help nail the gang, which by now had extended to associate members across Eastern Europe and into Asia.

Unfortunately, and much to my embarrassment, his undercover work was greatly jeopardised unwittingly by me and my clumsy interference. No wonder he was mad with me. I was undoing all his admirable work.

Within the past month I've learnt that DI Jimson has been awarded a citation for bravery in active service in honour of the central role he played in closing down this significant and highly dangerous criminal organisation.

I never liked him, still don't. But I admire his guts. In the seventies, he saw, as a young tearaway, first-hand what was going on as one of the founder members of the soccer team. Back then, he was considered a rascal, a womaniser, a waste of space…but the boy made good. He turned his back on a life of depravity and took the right road. In later years, he slowly regained the trust of the gang in order to secretly bust them, putting his own life in peril. It goes without saying that he corrupted himself and pushed the boundaries of legal decency to help persuade the inner circle that he was one of them. He succeeded and came back to haunt them big time, betraying their trust in him.

At a recent press conference, Jimson emphasised once again that he never came into contact with anyone outside the inner circle, and that the identity of the mastermind of the operation remains elusive to this day.

Thinking too deep never did me any good, but I have underestimated Jimson. He has balls of steel. I just wish he had not made a play for Isabel; it was a step too far. Still angry, I questioned him about the incriminating intimate photos taken in France and asked outright if he had any of my wife which he might want to tell me about. This was his chance to come clean. There were no photos, he insisted. I looked him in the eye, but he didn't blink as his gaze battered me into submission. I was the first to back away. He was a hard man and he didn't like me that was for sure. I was irksome to him. But I gave him the benefit of the doubt, anyway. Isabel is the one that has to ultimately trust him of course, working so closely with him every day. So far their professional relationship hasn't been compromised, and I rely on Isabel's judgment to keep it that way.

If I find out he has lied to me, I'll kill him. He's on probation.

What can I say about Isabel? I love her, as I have always loved her. We are taking each day at a time, which is all I can ask for. In reality, I suppose I am on probation as well. I've started well, having paid back the two hundred quid she lent me when I first lost my job. It's good to settle debts. The divorce, I am happy to announce, is a thing of the past. What of the boyfriend? He's been dumped. We are selling Eggshell Cottage and moving to Chichester, having found a barn conversation we want to do up. Miraculously, we are trying for a baby. Keep your fingers crossed, will you?

Philip is still living separately from Erica, and the last I heard he was shacked up with a twenty-one-year-old girl from Estonia. I'll say no more on that score.

Me? I thought you'd never ask. I've taken a lease on a retail premises in Chichester and converted it into a fine art gallery, something that I've always wanted to do. I'm now an entrepreneur, an art dealer, a man of substance. Don't snigger. I've found my true vocation, which I love. We sell paintings, photography, art glass and ceramics. Although it's early days, business is going well, in spite of the recession. Daisy would be proud of me. I know Isabel is.

And that, of course, brings us to Meg Faulkner, Mystic Meg to those who never really knew her.

Sadly, last month she passed away, quietly and without fuss in her hospital bed. She never had the chance to return to her new home. The night before she died, I sat with her and we chatted about politics, religion and sex. Yes, sex! She was thrilled with the news that Isabel and I were practising for a baby. She was on fine form, although exhausted from my incessant ramblings. I was a new man, and it showed in my enthusiasm for conversation.

Over the previous weeks, I had gently unravelled to her the complex web of deceit which had fatally claimed her only daughter. It was hard explaining that my brother was her killer. It was she who had at first pointed me in the right direction and identified Miriam's possible abductor: The clown. *Little did we know…*but at least the baffling crime that had haunted her all her waking life was finally solved. I just wish it had a better ending that didn't include my family. I could see in her face that she was ready to give up, slip away and re-join her daughter in a better place.

Her last gesture to me was to point to a vase of elegant white Lilly's, which was a gift from Harry, who visited her bedside every day without fail.

When I finally left, Meg was asleep, her breathing shallow. I kissed her cheek, unaware that it was the last time I would see her alive.

The next day, I got the call. I agreed to go over and collect her things and seeing the bed empty almost destroyed me. I don't mind admitting I howled; my heart punctured forever. Her death hit me big time, but she was at peace God bless her.

Have a quiet moment. This next bit takes some believing.

I picked up her bag of belongings, took the lift down from her ward on the fourth floor and reached the car park in a daze, quite forgetting where I had left my car.

A flaxen-haired nurse approached me and took my arm, explaining that Meg had been in her care and that she had endured a very bad night, tossing and turning and shouting in her sleep. Although heavily sedated she still ranted, although the nurse could not fathom her words.

I wasn't sure where this was leading but she further explained that in the morning Meg was found wandering the ward, disoriented and feeble on her feet. The nurse got her back into bed but she continued to shout my name, disrupting the entire ward. One hour later the patient was dead. In her hand was a slip of paper, which the nurse retrieved and now handed to me. I unfolded it and read aloud the words scrawled in Meg's handwriting:

The great juveniles

The nurse asked what it meant, and I wondered if it was something that Harry had mentioned to her during one of his visits. I raised my eyebrows and tucked the message into my jacket pocket. I drove home, tears rolling down my cheeks, my thoughts centred on a truly wonderful woman now departed. To be honest, my driving was so erratic I'm surprised I got back to the cottage in one piece.

Isabel was at work. I made a cup of tea, climbed the stairs and pulled the curtains tight to shut out the harsh cold light. Winter was upon us. Then I crawled into bed but I couldn't sleep easily. There were too many images swirling around my head. I thought it was about to explode. What did the words mean? David occupied my thoughts. He certainly wasn't a *great* man. But he did radiate that perception. People foolishly looked up to him. I was conned too.

But although the words on the piece of paper haunted me, I finally surrendered and slept from exhaustion.

One week later we buried Meg, and at the funeral service, I was heartened to see so many well-wishers gather to give her a fitting send off. I was proud to read a eulogy, which championed her fighting spirit and dogged determination in the face of adversity. I wanted her to be proud of me, and I hoped my speech showed how very proud I was of her. Meg was a true friend.

Isabel and I walked from the church hand in hand, nodding to strangers as if we knew them. And I suppose we did really. We were all here to be united in our love for a special person who had a gift to reach out and communicate to people that their troubles could be shared. She certainly did that for me and it made me a better person. Now we need to move on with our lives.

Today, the sun shines and it is a good, good feeling.

Every year I will watch the daisies come alive on our lawn and think of my precious daughter and know that she will not be alone. Meg will be there, standing beside her, gently squeezing her hand. Then she will be smiling at me and I will take great comfort from this image.

I know the *line* from Miriam to Daisy is finally wiped clean of evil intent.

And I firmly believe that it is Meg, from beyond the grave, who guides me on the right road – the line – to my salvation.

PS. Isabel is pregnant.

Epilogue

I've already said that some things take some believing.

It's a strange alchemy as to how the past comes back to bite you: is it a fluke of circumstance, a random throw of the dice or is it somehow mysteriously designed that way in the great scheme of things?

I first hear it on the radio in my car. It catches my attention so I turn the volume up. The newsreader reports on a riot breaking out in a high-security prison, the inmates led by the ringleader identified as Eric Razzoni, sentenced of child abuse at Portsmouth crown court the previous year.

It's that name again.

My ears prick because the very mention of him also brings into sharp focus the suffering my wife and I endured during that most harrowing of times. I thought we had put it all behind us. Isabel is doing well and is now at home, just less than four weeks from giving birth to our second child (assuming the dates of conception are correct). I am truly excited by this prospect, but I hear the news item and this puts a dampener on everything.

His name has bugged me ever since I first came into contact with it all those months ago when Isabel revealed the identity of the shareholders of Pleasure Dome Limited: David Farmer and Eric Razzoni. I search my brain again…his surname means *something* to me, but what?

Perhaps it isn't important. I'll mention it to Isabel but I don't want to alarm her unnecessarily at this stage of the pregnancy. I return to the extended broadcast: apparently, there has been an attempted jailbreak according to the prison spokesman who first reveals the information to the reporter at the scene.

I pull over into a lay-by and gather my thoughts. I'm still baffled by the cryptic note from Meg, all these months later. The legal case against the gang members was proven, the sentencing perfectly harsh as you would expect in crimes of this magnitude. We could all now get on with our lives surely. So what was she still trying to tell me? Clearly, she was deeply troubled in her sleep as the nurse had testified. Had she been visited once again through her subconscious portal, even though she had told me that her powers were on the wane? I believe so. Why else would she rant and call my name repeatedly and cause such an outcry on the ward?

Jimson holds the key; I am convinced of it. He too has moved on and we hadn't had contact for over three months now. Isabel and I never talk about him, but I know he is still basking in the glory of his achievements. Let him have his fifteen minutes in the sun, but I want to ask him a question which for some reason or another I hadn't asked before. Now was a good time.

I phone on my mobile and manage, via the switchboard, to get his attention. Funny how my name somehow still manages to alert certain people in authority…

He's cagey with me. 'How's it going?'

'Pretty good,' I answer.

No small talk from him. 'What can I do for you?'

'Does the word "juvenile" mean anything to you?'

'This is a good game,' he observes with his usual dry wit. 'In its true meaning, I would suggest childish or infantile behaviour I guess…which sums up my view of your activities in the not too distant past.'

I'm stumped, as usual; another dead end.

'Why do you ask?'

I feel foolish and at odds with myself. I always carry the note with me, and I unfold it. It is pretty tatty by now, the writing faded, but it was my connection to Meg. She was trying to reach me, but I fear I am missing the point every time I look at it. Then it dawns on me. I've always used my interpretation of the message instead of reporting the exact words, which is precisely what she wanted from me. *What an idiot I've been.*

I try again.

'How about, "The great juveniles".'

A nervous cackle. Him not me.

I nudge him forward. 'What does it mean?'

'Blimey, I haven't heard that expression in over forty years…'

I wait, suppressing my excitement.

I lose patience. 'And?'

'When the football team was first formed, it consisted of mainly young lads out for a good time…you know, booze and birds and a good kick around the pitch. We didn't take the game seriously, except for Eric, our founder coach. He wanted us decked out in serious kit, and as you know, he chose the Juventus strip which paid homage to his birth town, silly tosser. Anyway, we were pretty crap in the league and got well beat week in, week out and the kit became an embarrassment to us, and a thing of merriment with opposing teams. Basically, they took the piss out of us and we soon disbanded. Later, of course, the shirts signified something else far more sinister; they became the badge of honour among a bunch of weirdos. Sorry, but I have to include your brother in that category.'

I won't rise to the bait. 'Is there an end to this tale?'

'Can't you see the connection?'

'Only with the use of J-U-V-E as the common link between the two words that we've been discussing,' I offer.

'Exactly right, Einstein,' he scoffs.

I wanted more. 'So?'

'We were always larking about, and Eric's sister, who also worked for the firm of Felix Winter's, referred to us as the *juvenile bunch* because of the crazy pranks we pulled. Well, the nickname kinda stuck with everyone…but we somewhat enhanced it in order to inflate our ego's still further.'

'Rather inappropriate when you consider the child abuse charges later brought against the members.'

'You could say that, but even in later years we still used the term.'

'What was the name of Eric's sister?'

'Can't remember to be honest…'

'Can you find out?'

'I can always ask Eric.'

I don't care for his humour.

'Have you seen the news?' I ask.

'Just getting an update now, as we speak,' he says. 'It appears that the riot is getting out of hand… Perhaps I won't be asking him after all. It'll come to me. Pretty little thing she was.'

Something was nagging at me.

I persist with my questioning.

'When you were "on the job" so to speak with David, did you always meet at the nightclub in town?

'Yeah, it's where he kept his private office on the top floor. This was the nerve centre for all the operations.'

'Did you ever visit him at home?'

'Never, that was out of bounds.'

'So when you busted the house on the night he hung himself, that was the first time you had been there, is that right?'

'Correct. Hey, why all the questions?' He laughs nervously. 'I'm the ruddy detective around here, mate.'

Mate? I don't think so.

'So, even though you were supposedly great buddies, he'd never invited you over for a drink, for instance?'

'I told you, no. It was a rule we had in the gang. We never visited anyone's house in the UK. It was always at the nightclub or at the caravan park, except on one occasion when we all partied at the villa in Cyprus.'

'The one Eric was arrested at?'

'A fabulous place…'

'Who owned it?'

'I always assumed he did. He had the readies to afford it.'

'I assume it's now for sale?'

'Questions, questions! It's a bank repossession I think.'

'Does it have a name?'

'Christ, I can't…wait a sec, Mimosis Villa, that's it. What's all this about?'

'You said yourself at the time of the arrests that you got the soldiers but not the colonel.'

'And you think that this "reference" to something which was started by a chance remark all those years ago has a bearing on who masterminded the paedophile ring.'

'I do.'

'And who gave you this pearl of wisdom?'

'A woman from the grave,' I announce.

He laughs again, but there's an edge to it. 'Now I know you're one fucked-up, washed-up has-been who has nothing better to do than lie awake at night conversing with the dead. You seriously need to get a life. I warned Isabel about you.'

'Charming.'

'You are welcome, pal. Now, do you mind if I get on with the more serious work which needs my immediate attention?'

'I'm grateful for your help, actually.'

'I don't somehow think so.'

Then he clicks off.

I was pissed off, none the wiser…actually.

He's really got under my skin with his insults.

Two minutes later, the mobile rings.

'Jimson again, your worst nightmare,' he taunts me.

'We can't keep on meeting like this, people will talk.'

'You're not my type, too feminine, no balls.'

I'm incensed and want to scream: *Wanker! fuck-face! Shithead! Just piss off…*

I somehow keep calm despite how I really feel, as Isabel had taught me. *Confuse the enemy.* 'What do you want?'

'It's not what I want; it's something that you want.'

'Oh?'

'Her name was Margherita.'

I was on a different planet at this stage. '*Who…*?'

He sighs. 'The girl in accounts who gave us our kick-ass name, idiot.'

He was still laughing in the background as he clicked off for a second time.

I wasn't amused by his incessant mocking, but he was helping me see the bigger picture. Fool him.

*

I get home in a hurry, switch on my laptop and make Isabel a cup of tea while it boots up.

'Haven't seen you this excited since Pompey won the FA Cup,' she smirks.

'Which one? Nineteen thirty-nine or two thousand and eight?'

'Sometimes you look old enough to have been at the first one.'

'Very funny. Do you want to help me or are you intent on carrying on with the insults?'

She sat beside me at the table. 'What are we looking for?'

266

I touch her bump. 'You OK?'

'I'm good.'

'I need you to do a background search on someone.'

'It'll be quicker if I plug into the database at work. Give me the name and I'll ring in now.'

I scribble it down, but it didn't register with her.

'Is it important?'

'Very,' I say.

She moves away to get the phone.

I google *Cyprus real estate* and type into the email box a request asking for a portfolio of properties on the island for sale through repossession. I'm redirected to another page. There are thousands of them, which surprises me. I type in "Mimosis Villa". Bingo! Up it comes. I scan the interior photos and search for an enquiry email window, which I find at the bottom of the page. I play a game and add to the box that I am in the market to buy a property and make a list of my special requirements. I then press SEND.

I grab my mobile, make a call and get a 3 pm appointment in the afternoon to view a commercial property in the city, which again surprises me by the speed I'm working at and the results I'm getting. Usually, everything goes at a snail's pace.

I put a suit and tie on and shout, 'See you later!'

Isabel appears. 'Bloody hell, boy, are you off to see the bank manager?'

'Something like that,' I say. 'Listen, keep an eye on my emails and ring me if I get a response from Cyprus in the next couple of hours, OK?'

'Are you in for dinner later?'

'Doubtful.'

'Are you going to tell me what this is all about?'

'No...'

'Are you seeing another woman?' Then she bursts into a fit of giggles.

I see the joke but I'm not smiling.

'I could be, but it's not what you think.'

'They all say that, buster.'

She kisses me. 'Do I need to tell you to be careful?'

I don't respond to this. 'Have you put the feelers out as I asked?'

She salutes and yells, 'Yes, sir.'

I return the kiss.

'Remember...' I say, pointing to the laptop.

She salutes me again, and repeats my instruction, '...Keep checking the emails.'

*

I reach the city centre in forty-five minutes, park up and walk the final block. A man greets me and we enter the four-storey building, me following him, him following his clipboard.

It's an impressive place, no expense spared: Whistles Night Club & Bar.

'Thinking of the same line of business?' the man asks.

'Could be,' I reply cautiously.

'Well, the licence is renewable, so that's one obstacle removed.'

I nod. Then I realise I've left my phone in the car, which annoys me. I'm distracted by this for a moment, knowing Isabel may need to contact me.

We start in the basement and view the funky nightclub. Then we progress upwards. The ground floor houses the main bar, the first floor an upmarket restaurant. I'm only interested in the top floor, but I feign curiosity so as not to arouse suspicion. We take the swanky lift up and, after fumbling with a set of keys, we enter into a series of interlocking offices, via a three-step ascent. I hold my breath for a second when I stop to imagine what went on here. This was the devil's lair.

I feel light-headed but keep my cool.

Appearing to be business-like, I ask a few relevant questions...business rates, electricity costs, tenant's rights blah, blah, blah. I must admit, I sound pretty good for a novice.

'Does it fit with your requirements, Mr Jackson?'

I play the game with my false name, but I still haven't found what I am looking for.

I linger by a door. 'What's in here?'

He checks his clipboard. 'Storage.'

'Can we see?'

He turns the handle: it isn't locked. I follow and switch on the light and settle my eyes on the surroundings. A few empty cabinets, a stack of spare chairs, a Dyson, shelves containing plates and glasses, all that you would expect to find really. At first, I am disappointed, but then it gets interesting: there is something else in the room which makes me momentarily jump. I have to look twice to make sure the wooden structure tucked away in the corner was exactly what I thought it was. My heart pumps, the air in my lungs held captive for a few seconds. *Fuck.*

'Everything OK, sir?'

'Yes, fine thanks.'

'Have we seen enough?' he asks, checking his watch.

'Absolutely,' I say, recovering my senses.

We take the lift down.

'Will we be hearing from you in the morning?'

I shake his hand. 'You most certainly will.'

He smiles in triumph.

I turn away, my pace quickening with every stride.

*

Meg, I love you, you cunning old devil.

Just when I thought I had reached a cul-de-sac, you find a way to prod me into action. I am just a little slow on the uptake, that's all. But I get there in the end.

Back at the car, I check my text messages: nothing. I scroll last-dialled numbers: zilch in the last forty minutes. Come on Isabel, I'm not impressed!

I'm ready to back my hunch though so I phone Jimson. I'm informed he is not available to take my call.

'Make him available,' I answer tersely.

Two minutes later he calls back.

I explain, bullet-like, what I have unearthed.

'You'd better be bloody sure of this,' he snaps.

'I am.' I fail to mention that Isabel has not had the decency to confirm my suspicions, but that is a minor detail. Having said that, what is she playing at?

'How long will it take you to get there?' Jimson asks.

I check my watch. 'About an hour…'

'We'll have back-up in position by five, but first, you'll need to come in to get fixed-up if we want this recorded.'

'I need an hour alone, maybe less.'

'I'll give you thirty minutes, tops. Then we're coming in.'

'Jimson?'

'Yeah?'

'I won't be armed.'

'I should bloody well hope not.'

I click off and start the engine, and realise that this will be the longest drive of my life.

*

Thirty-eight miles to travel; a lifetime to get there…

This is it, the defining moment. I'm sorry that I haven't kept you in the loop, but I figure I need to do this by myself. As I explained at the beginning, judge me at the end. Stay in my slipstream.

Eventually, I pull into the drive, switch off the engine, get out and compose myself. I check my outstretched hand: it is trembling. I approach the door and not once but twice stop in my tracks, unsure of myself. The next step is a big step. I breathe in and breathe out slowly. Then I take that step and knock heavily on the door.

There is no going back.

It is a long wait, as I would expect. Then she opens the door.

'Hello, Margo.'

Her smile is thin. 'Hello, Will.'

'Can I come in?'

'I wouldn't expect you to stand out there after coming all this way.'

'Thank you.' I enter and follow her wheelchair along the hallway which I notice is stacked with cardboard boxes. In the kitchen she turns toward me and stares coldly at my face. Coffee is not on the agenda.

'Are you planning on moving?' I ask.

'I've sold the house, yes.'

'Going far?'

'Abroad. I've bought a plot of land in Turkey and I'm having a purpose built bungalow constructed just for my needs, especially for when I get older and therefore more infirmed. I have to plan for my future alone.'

I don't buy into the sob story.

'I assume the bungalow, depending on the cash you get for this place will be considerably larger than a prison cell, eh?'

There isn't a flicker behind her eyes.

'Naturally, I would have to say yes to that assumption. Is that where you envisage I'll end up, Will?'

'I reckon it is, Margo.'

'And that's why you came here wearing your triumphant grin, to tell me that.'

'There is no pleasure in doing this, Margo...or should I say *Margherita*?'

'That's a name I haven't used for years, Will. How did you find out?'

'Let's just say the dead never rest, in spite of your best efforts to silence them.'

Her face is suddenly drawn and waxy. 'What happens now, my dearest Will?'

'You confess, and then you go to prison for a very long time, just like the hundreds of children who you consigned to a prison of a different darker kind...and how they suffered for it. I think that is a fair exchange.'

'To be blunt, I've never put great store in the fairness of this world...'

'So you took advantage and used it for your own perverted and seedy gains. Is that an accurate assessment of the millions you stashed away from the misery of others?'

'Hmm, you do stand mightily high on your gold encrusted pedestal, don't you, Will? I seem to remember you asking for my help on more than one occasion, and I gave it willingly...have you conveniently forgotten that moot point?'

'No, I haven't, but that was before I eventually realised that you were the mastermind, the driving force, together with your crazy brother, behind the rise and rise of Pleasure Dome Limited, your sleazy secret sex empire.'

'You flatter me; I'm intrigued to learn how you found that out.'

I circle her, scanning the garden in the hope of spotting Jimson's reinforcements lying in wait. It unnerved me to see no one out there. Then I confront her again, more closely this time, so close that my breath warms her face. I want her to squirm, to feel uncomfortable, threatened even, just like her many defenceless victims were subjected to.

I begin, my eyes affixed to hers.

'Several factors came into play *and* I have to say, you nearly got away with it. I knew for instance that David was not capable of running the whole show, that he was a big player but not the main player. What do they say: *Behind every great man…*'

She was still bullish. 'I didn't think that you, out of everyone, possessed the capability to look beyond David and identify me. I offer my heartfelt congratulations.'

She was far too cool for my liking, *the cold-hearted bitch.*

I play for time.

'Little things added up,' I say.

Where the fuck was that phone call from Isabel?

'And I'm sure you're going to relish telling me every single one.'

She was teasing me, adding to my discomfort.

I pull a chair up to get close and personal. I want her to feel trapped and isolated, but I was the one sweating.

My mobile rings. *Thank Christ.*

I snap it open and listen.

Isabel drops a clanger, 'Since when did we have the money to buy a holiday home in Cyprus?'

Not now, Isabel.

'We don't,' I answer, 'and this isn't the moment to cross-examine me. Do you have what I want?'

I listen dispassionately, keeping my poker face as blank as possible. The call goes on for ages, the information stacking up. I have everything I want.

I end the call without saying a thing, knowing that Isabel will be pissed off by my rudeness. She'll get over it.

I hold court once again, my quarry beginning to squirm.

'Razzoni, now that's a name to conjure with. I first heard of it many months ago, and it didn't register with me at the time. Then I heard it again on the radio this morning, and it triggered something in my head. That's your maiden name, and Eric is your brother. Isabel ran a check on you. You were born to an Italian father and a German mother; hence your original names were Margherita and Erich. You moved to England when you were toddlers, your father a chef by trade. He opened his first restaurant in Portsmouth, now closed. As you grew up, it was not long before you were called Margo and Eric in order to fit in, and the names stuck. I bet your father was abusive to you both. Correct?'

Margo hesitated and then said, 'Correct.'

'He raped you both, correct?'

She nodded.

I was getting to her at long last.

'With your encouragement, Eric killed him and you provided an alibi. How am I doing so far?'

'I'm not contradicting you.'

271

'Eric got away with it but the two of you were by then damaged goods... and as you got older you two siblings, through the empathy of silent sufferance, became partners in crime. *Do unto those...*'

'We were a formidable team. I miss him...'

'I bet you do; especially now that the money has dried up.'

'I manage with what I have...'

'How old are you, Margo?'

'A lady never reveals her age.'

'Three or four years older than David, I estimate. In the early seventies that puts you around twenty-seven. I reckon you would have been a real catch, and David, who worked in the same firm as you, was an easy target, especially as you found out that he had a history with youngish girls. He even got into trouble at school, but it was hushed up. So you had found another kindred spirit on your doorstep, a natural-born leader.'

'Not quite, but I loved him.'

'Spare me. You loved what he was capable of...'

'We saw a way to make big money, and recruitment was our first aim, but David was a loose cannon and couldn't be relied upon. He was difficult to contain, his appetite uncontrollable. I warned him, but he was never a team player. Eric was my leader.'

'I don't recognise this same man from my upbringing as a younger brother. He was good to me.'

'He hid his compulsion well. He was extremely disciplined when he needed to be. In later years, he confessed to me, blaming his urges on his father's behaviour and a rejection from a prom girl he idolised at school.'

I wasn't ready for that insult directed at my father.

'My dad?' I screamed. The anger surfaced in me. 'Don't even go there...'

'It's true, Will. He abused David when he was eleven.'

I am bereft and confused. 'I don't believe that story.'

'It was as he told it.'

'Then he was a liar.' It was just a scapegoat, accused by David to illustrate wrongly his evil manner from childhood.

'He was many things...'

'He murdered Miriam Faulkner.'

'That he did.'

'Why did he choose her?'

'He knew of the family from hanging out with the gang on her street. I suppose he made a connection and later spotted her at the fair.'

I am suddenly reminded that Jimson lived on her street.

I almost pushed my face into her face. 'He killed an innocent little girl, Margo!'

'A major blunder, I grant you. We forced him to go to ground for a while, to let the heat die down. That was never part of our plan, the killing of a child.'

'You wanted the children alive.'

She didn't flinch.

'David was a liability,' I suggest.

'He was also my husband.'

'And so, out of misguided duty, you protected him for over forty years, Margo. Loyalty knows no bounds.'

'You could say that…'

'My God, you were a bunch of evil bastards.' David's last words haunted me.

'You could say that as well.'

I'm numb to the bone from her callous disregard for human dignity.

'And so you formed the football team, and recruited through it, gaining the trust of younger boys who you could easily manipulate. The football shirt became your emblem, your membership calling card. It signified what you had become, similar to that of a Nazi uniform.'

'We wore it with pride.'

I could so easily have slapped her hard, but I held firm.

'And it was you who nicknamed them: *The juveniles.*'

'It seemed to fit, and they liked the play on words. I think it was David who added the word *great.*'

'Hardly befitting,' I comment. 'And so you kept it over the years, as a bit of fun, to mock all those that you slowly tortured and buggered. How noble of you to have your own motto.'

Margo was defiant. 'Is *that* all you have?'

I was far from finished.

'David owned a PC, but it was clean when the police confiscated it. I wonder why.' I look beyond her to a desk in the corner. 'I notice that you possess an Apple, which is what was used at the nightclub and the campsite. The police didn't think to check your laptop, because it was David who was under suspicion. You portrayed the little lost wife to perfection. Why would anyone suspect you in this sordid enterprise?'

She twitches.

'You were very clever, Margo. You weren't grieving for David in the kitchen on the night he took his own life…you were grieving for his sacrifice. It was a great acting accomplishment on your part.'

I point to the laptop. 'I wonder what the police will make of that because they're bound to want to have a peek now, wouldn't you think?'

'You can't tie me into the nightclub operation.'

'Can't I? I've just come from there and had a good sniff around. It's surprising what you might find. For instance, there is a purpose-built ramp in the storeroom, designed specifically for your wheelchair to get up the steps to the main offices. And let's not forget the villa in Cyprus, which I've just discovered was also purpose-built for someone with a disability. Your brother had no need for such facilities, nor did your husband. I wonder who did.'

She resembles a rabbit caught in the glare of headlights.

'I have money, Will. And you know the killer of your daughter.'

'Stuff your dirty cash.'

'You got justice for Daisy; you don't need to come for me.'

'David cheated me, by hanging himself so I don't call that justice.' I bristle, annoyed that she thought I could be so easily bought. 'I want every last one of you to be punished, to suffer just like Isabel and I have suffered.'

'David didn't mean to kill her; he just lost control of the situation.'

'Yeah, and tried to stitch someone else up and make it look like a sex attack gone wrong. You would both have Romain rot in jail for your crime.'

'In answer to the first bit, it couldn't have been anything else, actually. Your brother was impotent, Will.'

'Are you telling me that's where his frustrations stemmed from…he couldn't get an erection?'

'In later years, that's exactly right. His rage knew no bounds, Will.'

'He made Daisy's life intolerable, and I was unable to protect her…'

'Her death haunted him, believe me.'

'I don't, and my heart bleeds for you both.'

I stand, weary, and move to retrieve the laptop.

'Your power trip is over, Margo.'

I notice the French windows are ajar, and there is movement behind the shifting curtains. Then a familiar voice reaches me.

'I'll take that.'

I look over.

Jimson fills the gap and comments, 'I think we've heard all we need to hear.'

I'm relieved to see reinforcements at last, but I don't like the peculiar expression on his face.

'Where is the back-up?' I ask nervously, trying to look beyond him.

'No need for that, Will.'

'So it's just you then, yeah?'

'*Just* me…'

'Thinking about it, I'm not a bit surprised…'

He stands his ground.

'I'd advise you to leave quietly and go home, and forget that this little cosy get-together ever happened.'

I open my shirt collar and reveal the wire attachment.

He laughs, which grates on me.

'You didn't honestly expect me to make that operational, now did you?'

Suddenly I'm the one feeling trapped.

'I'll go to the press,' I say, my chest tightening.

'No you won't, and I'll tell you precisely why you're going to keep your big mouth shut.'

I watch in horror as he holds up a microfilm spool.

'You wouldn't want these being flashed about now, would you?'

I'm shafted, knowing he had compromising photos of Isabel.

'I always knew you had them,' I say.

'Just covering my back, pal.'

'You and David had everything planned so tightly, making sure that nothing would come back to haunt either of you.'

'Your brother was weak. I was only interested in looking after number one. He was an accident waiting to happen. Margo would concur with that.'

'I always suspected you were a bent cop…'

'Plenty of them around, I'm afraid,' he sneered.

'You knew how to play hardball; I'll give you that.'

'A modern twist, eh? I fooled everyone: I had to infiltrate my own gang in order to gain control of the investigation, which was not only gathering pace despite the "blocks" I put in its way but it was also curtailing our operations and damaging our revenues. I had to play good cop, bad cop, good cop… Some fucking achievement, yeah?'

'The term criminal psychopath sounds better suited to you.'

'Yeah, right, but I'll just stick to *genius* if that's OK.'

'Except you were being squeezed upon,' I comment. 'Ironically, by your own fucking interfering department…headed by yours truly.'

'Tricky to say the least, but I maintained control even when the heat was on from upstairs. We had too much to lose as most of us were coming up for retirement and we didn't want anyone jeopardising our fat pensions which we had worked so darn hard for. The idea when the squeeze came was to scale back and move our entire operation to Cyprus where we had friends in high places. We would have immunity there.'

'Clever,' I mutter.

'It would have been but David was the problem, attracting abnormal interest from tossers like you who had the bit between their teeth. As a result of David's indiscretions – and let's face it, he was attracting a lot of attention from our department downtown – the Domino team was set up under my jurisdiction to monitor the bigger picture…and what a picture it was! Your arse of a brother was jeopardising our livelihood on the dark net with his insatiable appetite, and that couldn't continue. You will be relieved to know that he did not have sex with the victims. His thrill was the kill. He was a control freak, and no semen was found on or near the corpses. They were deliberately disrobed to make it appear as a sexual attack by him. It worked and he bamboozled the police with their enquiries.' He roared heartily. 'Your intervention did us a favour when he topped himself, God rest his soul, the big cunt. Sorry, Margo…but his days were numbered.'

I glance in her direction. Not a flicker of regret passes over her steely face.

My mind rewinds to the time I stayed in this very house, when David and Margo and I watched the TV reporting of the girl attacked in Harrogate, and David saw fit to switch it off in a hurry…and then there was the occasion when Isabel texted me with the news that another girl had been molested near Robin Hood's Bay…both these crimes had the mark of my brother's sickening involvement. He had an apartment in Harrogate; he was in the locality of the second attack, having separated himself from me.

Christ, I despair at what I'm bearing witness to.

Jimson wasn't finished. 'Would you fucking believe it, huh? Our tidy little business operation suddenly came under threat, my position in both camps open to exposure. That would have spelt disaster. As you can imagine, I was caught between the devil and the deep blue sea. Lucky, I was at the helm to steer the good ship home.'

'That's why you had my flat turned over.'

'You'd become a thorn in our side so we were just covering our backs.'

I had nothing further to say, Jimson had said it all.

Although I stood my ground, my body was ready to collapse into a heap; such was the gradual breakdown of my reserves of fortitude. I was done for.

Jimson wasn't giving up.

'Now, take my advice and get the fuck out of here; and that can be the end of the matter.' He holds up the film.

I nod weakly.

'You shouldn't mess with the wrong people,' Margo says, turning in my direction. 'It's taken you way out of your comfort zone. It also takes a big man to admit defeat. Walk away, Will. Think of Isabel and the baby and get on with the rest of your miserable lives.'

For once I don't protest. Instead, I retreat dutifully, tail between my legs (not for the first time), and climb into my Rav, watched by Jimson standing guard at the door. He has a smug grin on his face. If I'm honest with you, I'm just happy to get out of there in one piece.

He thinks he has me in his pocket but I live to fight another day.

With speed, I drive over to the police headquarters, where Isabel waits in the car park. I look at her long and hard and grasp her hand as we walk towards the main entrance in silence. This has been one hell of a day. We smile, a smile of commitment, and then I safely hand over my Dictaphone again and leave her to do her job. At the end of the day, she knows a microfilm spool is a small price to pay if ever used against our evidence, which is compelling enough! My wife (doesn't it sound good to say this) won't fail me…that I know for sure.

Later, we sit by our daughter's graveside and say a small prayer.

That same night we anxiously switch on the TV and specifically *News at Ten*, and catch the headlines. It is the first item up:

"Following on from a major tip-off, which involves the smashing of a multi-million-pound paedophile ring that stretches from Britain right across to Eastern Europe, a senior police officer on the south coast was tonight arrested at his home shortly before eight o'clock, suspected of being one of the main ringleaders of the criminal operation. He has not been named at this stage. Three further prominent officers from the Yorkshire constabulary have also been brought in for questioning. In the last hour, it has been confirmed that an unidentified woman in the Hampshire area has also been apprehended in connection with this latest round of arrests. An updated report to follow shortly as the magnitude of the story unfolds. Also in the news tonight…"

We sit quietly and think of Daisy: our beautiful never-to-be-forgotten daughter. She will live on in our hearts forever. Then I caress Isabel's huge belly and feel a kick. It's a mighty big one.

*

Two weeks later, our beautiful, gorgeous daughter is born. We name her Rose Meg. Mother is in good health, the baby perfect! Naturally, I am somewhat biased as you can imagine. Luckily Rose has Isabel's stunning good looks, but, oh dear… my unfortunate nose.

OK, not so perfect. Isabel giggles at this, I frown. Rose simply gurgles. Life always has the habit of throwing a curveball. I'm used to it by now. Don't mock. It's how it is. *This* is just another cross to bear, I guess.

And so we end, my story complete. Think of Meg (I often do), and I truly hope you find the right road to travel on your difficult journey in time.

Oh, nearly forgot. One piece of advice to all you male followers out there: get a PSA reading from your doctor in relation to prostate cancer. I did and I'm clear.

Be cool. Sometimes there is more than one happy ending. You just have to find it. I have Isabel and Rose Meg as proof of that.

I appreciate you being there for me.

I'll do the same for you if the need arises.

The End